Martyn Whittock was ⟨…⟩ a degree in Politics ⟨…⟩ graduating he taught history in Dorset and in Buckinghamshire, and has since become Head of Humanities at a Wiltshire school. He has published a number of scholarly articles and is the author of three textbooks, *The Origins of England, AD 410–600*, *The Roman Empire* and *The Reformation*. He is also co-author of *The Crusades* and *The Era of the Second World War* and author of *The Pastons and Medieval England*. He has acted as an historical consultant to both the National Trust and BBC Radio. Martyn Whittock is in his early thirties and lives in Bradford-on-Avon with his wife and daughter, within the ten-mile radius in which his family has lived for over five hundred years.

Also by Martyn Whittock

The Dice in Flight
The Moon in the Morning

A Stallion at Sunrise

Martyn Whittock

HEADLINE

Copyright © 1993 Martyn Whittock

The right of Martyn Whittock to be identified as the author of the Work has been asserted by him in accordance with the Copyright, Designs and Patents Act 1988.

First published in 1993
by HEADLINE BOOK PUBLISHING

First published in paperback in 1994
by HEADLINE BOOK PUBLISHING

10 9 8 7 6 5 4 3 2 1

All rights reserved. No part of this publication may be reproduced, stored in a retrieval system, or transmitted, in any form or by any means without the prior written permission of the publisher, nor be otherwise circulated in any form of binding or cover other than that in which it is published and without a similar condition being imposed on the subsequent purchaser.

All characters in this publication are fictitious and any resemblance to real persons, living or dead, is purely coincidental.

ISBN 0 7472 4247 X

Printed and bound in Great Britain by
HarperCollins Manufacturing, Glasgow

HEADLINE BOOK PUBLISHING
A division of Hodder Headline PLC
Headline House
79 Great Titchfield Street
London W1P 7FN

To my dear friends, my mother and father –
who always give without thought for their own convenience –
in thanks for their generous love.

Author's Note

A Stallion at Sunrise is inspired by two of the most valuable commodities of the thirteenth century: heiresses and warhorses. Both commanded high prices and were the subject of ruthless dealing. Both were counters to be deployed and manipulated by dominant men.

It is shocking for the modern person to discover the quite open manner in which wealthy girls and widows (as well as boy heirs) were traded. Sources from the period are full of examples of heiresses and widows bought and sold to the advantage of their feudal overlords. This was a very popular way of raising money for medieval kings who were always on the lookout for ways to increase the cash at their disposal, or reward a loyal follower at minimal cost to the crown.

A document dating from 1185, with the title *The Roll of Ladies, Boys and Girls*, lists wealthy heirs and heiresses at the disposal of the crown, along with their lands and what they were worth. Joanna de Cantelo may be fictitious but she stands for countless landed women who were bought and sold regardless of personal feelings. In addition, it was accepted practice that any minor placed in the care of their lord until they came of age would have their estates milked to exhaustion by their 'protector'.

As well as heiresses, warhorses were prestige commodities commanding fabulous prices. They were a cross between modern sports cars and state-of-the-art battletanks. Far from being the carthorses of popular imagination (and a lot of fiction), they were fierce and highly strung animals, carefully bred for their monumental strength, stamina, courage and ferocity – the product of breeding and intriguing as fierce as any modern search for a record-breaking car, or a super-weapon. The horse in this story is based on the real-life dapple-grey warhorse of Hugh IX de Lusignan which was seized by King John in 1202 and held as a hostage long after its owner had been released.

I am grateful to a number of people who have helped me in the research connected with this book. Linda Poulsen of the County Museum, Dorchester, offered advice regarding the Blackmoor Vale area of the county. The Dorset County Reference Library, Dorchester, provided information regarding medieval Dorset. Alan Hunt and Ian Hewitt from the Archaeology Department at the University of Bournemouth's 'Woolcombe Deserted Medieval Settlement Project' provided the inspiration for the deserted hamlet in this novel, which I have relocated in the north of Dorset.

In addition, I must thank all my friends who assisted with advice and suggestions concerning horse behaviour, most notably Fiona Jane Holland, Natasha Wills, Rowena Crook, and Martin and Pat Williams who shared in an enjoyable evening choosing the title! As always, my wife Christine spent many hours assisting both in field research – helped by my daughter Hannah – and in the discussion of ideas and checking the text itself.

With regard to the horses in the story, R. H. C. Davis' *The Medieval Warhorse* (London, 1989) must be without equal as a study of the breeding of warhorses.

Last but not least I must thank all my family, for their constant interest, encouragement, advice and support. They, I hope, know how important they are to me and the extent of my gratitude to them.

Horsingham, Temple Buckland and the deserted hamlet are places of fiction. However, anyone who takes time to explore north Dorset between the headwaters of the river Cerne and Bulbarrow will soon find the tiny, isolated villages and hamlets which inspired them. The names are fictitious, the land is not; it is the enduring continuity, the thread, which links us to those who knew it and loved it before us.

Martyn Whittock
Bradford-on-Avon
St Agnes' Eve.

Chapter 1

The limewashed buildings about the Cathedral of the Holy Cross seemed to shift and re-form in the hovering heat; as if their very substance was being dissolved and reconstituted by the melding power of the sun. The great drum-like tower of the Court of the Chain floated above an incandescent haze of violet. Beyond it the inner harbour was a mass of trembling masts and breezeless sails. The citadel of Acre, capital of the Kingdom of Jerusalem, in the Year of Our Lord 1202.

Richard de Lacey stood in the shade of the portico and watched the progress of a lightly built galley, as it slid into the inner harbour. With swift oar strokes it slipped out of sight behind the heavy merchant ships and the harbour craft ferrying goods to the quayside. There flowed the commercial lifeblood which made this enclave of Christian power possible; which carried men and goods from Europe to Outremer, this land beyond the sea.

Sighing with impatience, he turned and looked back at the gateway into the private quarters of the Grand Master. He had been waiting a long time and he was restless; still no call beckoned him to enter. The way was barred by two brown-robed sergeants of the Knights Templar. The scarlet cross on the left breast of each crusader's mantle was drained of blood in the glaring heat. As one shifted the weight of his shield, the sun scattered drops of liquid silver across the mail of the hauberk beneath the folds of cloth.

Richard knew full well why he was being kept waiting. On the other side of the whitewashed corridor the escort party of the Byzantine Ambassador stood in the angle of shade. The lightly armed commander of the turcopoles watched Richard out of the corner of one almond-shaped eye. Beyond this there was no communication between the two men. It had been this way for a full hour; an hour of baking silence, whilst de Lacey and his escort bore the heat with little grace. Only his Arab groom tolerated the hot inactivity without irritation. Unlike him, Richard and his squire sought out the deepest recesses of shade to drink the tepid coolness which had retreated there.

At last there was a movement in the deep shadows of the doorway. The Templars straightened up and the turcopoles snapped from their torpor. Without a sideways glance the ambassador of the second Rome was out and away. He did not even glance at those who waited after him for an audience.

All there was to show for Richard's wait was the lingering scent of incense and perfume. He pulled a face at his squire and Mark de Dinan grinned back. But before either could comment they had been summoned. Leaving the escort behind, the two men passed through the sweeping archway. Behind them the mountains of Lebanon continued their own sun-soaked vigil.

William de Chartres, the Grand Master of the Poor Knights of Christ and of the Temple of Solomon, was standing in a room of startling contrasts. Through tall, thin windows light fell in sheets of furnace white. Between the windows the melting shade gathered nervously like ice before the sun. Finely fluted columns of pale stone divided the room. The walls were richly decorated with fine tapestries and mosaics fit for the palace of a caliph.

The leader of the Templars was delicately picking pips from the cupped half of a pomegranate. White-robed servants carried sherbet and ice-cooled wine to the low tables amongst the deep floor cushions. Nearby another man, with greying hair, stood sipping wine. Like de Chartres he wore a white Cistercian mantle marked on the breast by the distinctive cross of his order. Richard recognised him as the marshal: the man responsible for the military activities of the Templar knights.

At fifty-eight the Templar Grand Master was thirty years senior to the handsome blond knight who stood determinedly mustering his reserves of patience and whose restless energy seemed to crackle in the confines of the room. Unmoved, the Grand Master continued his slow action. His word was law within the order and his power was absolute. It was not his way to quicken his movements to match the passions of the young.

At last he was satisfied that he had made his point. He motioned for Richard to take a seat. The teenage de Dinan kept back, out of the circle of passion and of power.

'I trust you have not been waiting long?' The voice of the Grand Master betrayed not a hint of an apology. He spoke, of course, in precisely formed French, the language of nobility and the lingua franca of the east. 'You will take some wine.' It was almost an order, not the words of a concerned host.

Richard nodded. 'Thank you, my lord.'

As he took the cup from the servant, Richard's blue-grey eyes never once left the face of his superior. Only as he lifted the dish did his movements appear awkward, as if he had to force his right hand to raise the light bowl of silver gilt. As Richard sipped the cool drink, de Chartres cast a glance at his silent companion. The marshal nodded; he had seen and understood.

'I will come to the point.' The Grand Master spoke as if it was he who had been kept waiting. 'We have made the necessary arrangements as agreed at our last meeting.' He swallowed a morsel of the soft pink flesh of the pomegranate. 'I trust you have completed your own arrangements.'

Richard raised one hand. A ruby set in gold flashed in a shaft of sunlight. Mark de Dinan quickly stepped forward, handing over a wad of vellum. Then he stepped back out of the focus of decision. Neither of the Templars spared him so much as a glance.

Richard carefully unfolded the sheets of smooth sheepskin. He tried hard not to let his excitement show in his movements. He could feel the eyes of the Grand Master appraising him and consciously ignored the silent inquisition. So much depended on this final interview. He had built so many hopes upon it; a structure of dreams, a glittering edifice of hopes. It all hung in the balance and he could feel the pulse beating in his head.

The young knight handed the sheets across the low polished table. Unhurriedly the Grand Master ran his finger down the list. He paused and Richard swallowed hard: an error, or a problem? Instead his leader reached for one of the Famagusta oranges heaped in a polished cedar dish. Richard unconsciously ran a hand over his gingering moustache and close-cut beard.

The Grand Master rested a ringed finger on a line in the document. '*Dextrarii*?'

'There are ten great mothers of warhorses, my lord. Hot-blooded Arabs, the type the infidel call *al faras*. Their pedigree is known for twelve generations. They are the finest and strongest mares in the Kingdom of Jerusalem. As you know, the infidel pride themselves in their stallions but trace the bloodline through their mares . . .'

The Grand Master made no reply. His finger dropped a line. '*Palefridi*?'

'And ten palfreys too. There are no better riding horses either; graceful and strong. But the destriers are the main issue. These others will bring money to back my plans. It is with the warhorses that all rests.'

'Quite so. And you have made arrangements for covering these mares in France and in England?'

Richard nodded. This was it, the crux of the matter. 'There are fine stallions on my family's estates in Normandy and in England. But the search is . . .'

'For better yet.' The interruption threw him for a moment and before he could recover another sharp comment made him pause. 'And it is for this that you require the backing of the Order?'

'Yes, my lord.'

'How long have you been a companion brother of the Order?'

'Five years, my lord.' They were duelling now. Richard could sense the change in the tone. 'By God's grace I shall take my vows once the matter of the great horses has been set in motion . . .'

'The great horses. Yes, you have devoted much effort to this cause.'

Aware that the comment could be a challenge, Richard replied warily. 'It is a cause that will free Jerusalem, my lord.'

'Alone?' The tone was a little mocking and came from the silent grey-haired watcher. It was his first contribution and it was not friendly. 'This alone will return the Holy Places to the True Church and break the power of the infidel Saracens?'

Richard's jaw tightened as he stifled the rising sharp retort. Even so the passion was clear in his reply. 'Jerusalem is lost.' The words were bitter and the pain showed on his face. 'Jerusalem is lost and the holiest places in Christendom are denied to the faithful. Christ knows that our only waking thought should be the recovery of it.'

The marshal threw back his head. 'Do not lecture me, young man. No one has fought longer in the cause than I. It is whether you have anything to offer that cause which concerns us. Is it possible that this plan of yours can do anything to free Jerusalem?'

'Not alone but as a part.' When the marshal still looked unconvinced, Richard added, 'You know full well, my lord, the power of these horses. How they can shatter the lines of the enemy; how they can rend and tear with their teeth. No one can withstand them. And what we have bred so far is as nothing compared to what is to come.

'We shall raise horses to rival those in the Revelation. Horses which will be death and famine and war all in one to the enemies of God. And in time, on such horses, the forces of Christendom will triumph and Jerusalem will be ours again. It is not an idle dream.

'Even as we speak, knights for the new crusade are gathering throughout western Christendom. By this autumn there will be thousands converging on Venice, awaiting transport to the east. And when they have succeeded in crushing the power of the enemy and retaking Jerusalem it will be held by Christendom for evermore.'

Richard paused, imagining the Venetian galleys and transports conveying the might of western chivalry to the Holy Land. 'When it has been retaken, no one will wrest Jerusalem from our hands again.' His jaw was set hard; it was as if by will alone that the city could be freed. 'But it will demand the best we can offer to hold it from being violated again. Our guard must never weaken. It will be by God and our knights that it will be held. And by the great horses . . .'

The Grand Master had watched the unfolding drama as the passion rose in Richard's voice. Now he intervened as he handed back the sheets of vellum.

'I have written to the Provincial Master of the Paris Temple to have money and supplies ready for you in Normandy. And to the Provincial Master in England to accommodate you at our manor of Temple Buckland, as you requested.'

Richard exhaled his pent-up breath. He wanted to laugh out loud. The duel was over and the outcome had already been decided. He had won before he entered the room. They had been playing with him – testing him.

'You will not regret this, my lord.'

'I know.'

The confirmation almost dared Richard to fail. But nothing could spoil this moment, not even the cold reply. Then the Grand Master added:

'I shall watch your mission carefully. I shall expect you to keep the English Provincial Chapter informed of your progress.'

He clapped his hands and a servant brought in a heavily sealed document. De Chartres took it and weighed it in his hands. His steady eyes never shifted from those of Richard.

'Before you sail you will receive three hundred gold bizants to cover the cost of your journey and the purchase of horses in Normandy. On your arrival in England the Grand Commander will meet any costs for the purchase of stud stallions . . .'

'My lord . . .' Richard was stunned. Even in his wildest dreams he had never dared to hope . . .

The Grand Master waved aside the gratitude. 'I have here letters to John of England, who is campaigning in Normandy. It explains your mission and touches on other matters relating to loans from the Order to the English Crown.' He smiled a rare smile at the obvious pressure being put upon the English King. 'Guard this letter well.'

De Lacey took the wad of vellum. Glancing down he recognised the Templar seal of two knights upon a single horse. It was hard to believe it was all really happening.

'Now you may leave us. You will no doubt have many preparations to make.'

The interview was over. With a bow Richard left, preceded by his awed squire. When he was gone and the door shut the Grand Master smiled at his companion.

'The likeness is uncanny, don't you think? Have you ever seen one who so closely resembles the Lionheart?'

The marshal shook his head. 'Never. And I knew Richard of England as well as any man in Outremer.'

'Surely not as well as the most Christian sovereign the King of France?'

The marshal snorted indignantly. 'I could hardly compete in that matter, my lord. I but fought beside Richard, I did not sleep with him!'

The Grand Master laughed. There was clearly intimacy between these two men. The easy companionship of those who have known each other a very long time. 'Nevertheless, I take your point! You knew him and you see him in this young man.'

'The looks are quite the same. And there is something about the eyes, but Richard was colder; there was less of this one's passion. Still, the resemblance is striking. My informants tell me that amongst his own men he is known as "*Malik Rik*".'

The other man laughed. 'The name of King Richard in the heathen tongue! But what did you make of our Richard de Lacey. Our *Malik Rik*?'

'He is a man driven. You saw that. This dream consumes him, it is his life but it eats him up.'

'Jerusalem has eaten up more than one man.' De Chartres was thoughtful. In the century since the founding of his order it had been rare for a Grand Master to die in his bed. He too carried death about him like an aura. 'It is a dream worth dying for . . .'

'No one knows that more than I. But you asked me what kind of man he is.'

De Chartres nodded. 'And you know why it drives him this way.'

The marshal nodded at the rhetorical question. 'It is the wound, that Saracen bolt that tore his shoulder apart. He will never couch a lance again, or raise his sword above his head.'

'Quite so.' The Grand Master sighed. 'Richard de Lacey may have the heart of a lion but he can no longer hope to regain the Holy Places through his sword.'

'That is a burden to crush a man like him. The horses help him carry it.'

'It is all that remains to him.'

The marshal thought for a moment. 'I am puzzled.' The Grand Master raised an eyebrow. 'About why you have sent a *confrère* knight on such a mission. Why not one fully in the Order? One who has taken his vows of total obedience?'

De Chartres was thoughtful for a moment. 'It is a delicate time to be "horse-trading" in Normandy and England.' He poured himself another glass of wine. 'If you take my meaning aright?'

The marshal smiled, a cut in the tanned parchment of his face. 'Go on . . .'

'Those two Christian sovereigns, the Kings of England and France, are at each other's throats again.' He sipped his wine. 'You know well enough that Philip of France has used every opportunity to encroach on John's rights in Normandy. There is little love lost between them and if he can loosen John's hold on the duchy he will do so.'

'I heard at the end of last year that the barons of Poitou had appealed to the French King to arbitrate in their quarrel with John . . .'

'And that John has ignored the summons to appear in person in Paris, to answer for his actions?' William de Chartres' eyes held the satisfied glow of one who hears news shortly after it has happened. 'For while he may be King in England, he is but duke in Normandy, and the French King is his overlord there.'

'That I had not heard . . .'

'It happened barely two months ago.' De Chartres acknowledged the smile of his friend. 'You should know how soon my informants bring news to me. And so the French have sentenced him to the loss of all his lands in France and even now are besieging his Norman border castles.

'It seems that Philip of France has decided to bestow the lands on John's nephew, the Duke of Brittany. They are his if he can take them from his uncle.

'There is open warfare in Normandy. John on one side and the rebel barons on the other. Not to mention the King of France and the Breton duke, and those who hate John include the counts of Lusignan . . .'

At last the marshal understood. 'And that's little wonder, since John stole Hugh de Lusignan's fiancée from under his very nose and married her himself . . .'

'And this same Hugh is nephew of our own Amalric de Lusignan, King of Jerusalem.'

'A very delicate situation indeed. For whoever negotiates with John does so with the enemy of Paris and Jerusalem.'

William nodded slowly. 'Quite so, and that comes on top of the disapproval we have shown of Amalric's truce with the Saracens. It would be less than prudent to side with his nephew's enemy at the same time. It would not suit our purposes to sacrifice our relationship with him.'

'Whereas Richard de Lacey is a free agent?'

'What I did not tell de Lacey was that whilst he has our blessing we will take no responsibility whatsoever for his errors of judgement. If he fails, he will do so alone.'

'I understand. Yes . . . "horse-trading" indeed.'

For all their friendship William de Chartres doubted whether he really understood. It was no easy thing to throw a knight like Richard de Lacey to the wolves. No easy thing at all. But then it was no easy thing to be Grand Master of the Order and to carry the burden of the defence of Christendom. Such responsibilities did not come without cost and sacrifice, even the potential sacrifice of a knight of the purest honour.

It was tragic how one bitter loss could beget another. He could not count the number of his order who had died to defend the Holy City, only to see it lost once more. Now perhaps another was to be added to that list of lives laid down. As the marshal watched him, he crossed to the balcony. Cup in hand he looked down towards the sparkling water of the harbour. Suddenly he felt very sad. He had the clear premonition that he would never meet Richard de Lacey again.

'Do you think that he is aware that it was our very order which advised King Richard Lionheart *not* to retake Jerusalem?' The marshal asked the question suddenly.

'I should not think so.' The Grand Master seemed uneasy as he replied. 'It is not common knowledge that the goal to which we openly strive is, in fact, one we secretly think cannot be held and has little strategic value. Few who do not have to live here – survive here – year in, year out, would understand that.' He looked very solemn as he said it; very old.

'I do not think that Richard de Lacey would understand,' the marshal replied, but his superior seemed lost in thought.

'*Hierosolyma est perdita.*' The words escaped the Grand Master's thoughts and slipped like a confession through his lips.

His companion frowned. 'I'm sorry, my lord?'

William de Chartres did not turn. Instead he said very quietly: 'Jerusalem is lost . . . Jerusalem is lost . . .'

Joanna de Cantelo tossed back her long red hair. The colour of dying coals, it cascaded about her shoulders like a mantle of fire. She breathed in the fresh sea air with its hint of salt and fish, and smiled. It had been months since she had been to Melcombe Regis and she was pleased to be back. Pleased to experience the exotic sights and sounds but pleased most of all to see the fine horses that her father had shipped in through the little Dorset port.

Even as she watched him, Gilbert de Cantelo was directing the head groom's inspection of the mares landed from the horse transport, or *tarida*. The vessel lay moored up against the solid quay posts facing the deep-water channel of the Back Water.

Another horse was swung up from the stalls which were placed at right angles to the ship's beam. Despite the sacking over its head, the horse whinnied in terror as its weight pressed down on to the canvas sling cradling its belly.

The head groom shouted at the winch-men, 'Mind yourselves, or I shall have your ears off.' He cursed roundly as one quayside worker lost his footing for an instant. 'That horse is worth more than you and your family put together, so mind, you clumsy oaf.'

The workers sweated and spat but held their tongues. One of them glanced at the elegant girl who was watching the proceedings but was careful not to be seen gawping. That too would have been more than his life was worth!

At sixteen years old, Joanna was more of a woman than a girl and yet her maiden's flowing hair proclaimed that no man had yet taken possession of this valuable heiress. All about the quayside, male eyes noticed her in the way that they always did.

She was used to it and had come to expect it. With her tall figure, high cheekbones and neat, precise chin she was always turning men's heads. But her proud green eyes were more than a match for any tongue-tied household knight and the serving men watched her with something like awe. The admiring eyes averted themselves when the baron's daughter looked at them in her clear and confident manner.

'What do you think, Jo?' Gilbert pointed to the mares stamping restlessly on the quayside. 'A good addition to our brood herd?'

He knew that he indulged her too much, but as his only surviving child and with his wife in her grave it was an understandable fault. He told himself that it would have to end some day. A husband would expect more docility, but he dismissed that until another day. Today she could do anything she pleased and what pleased her most were the horses.

'Tell me what you think.' He was proud of her judgement; proud that she knew as much about the horses as his best grooms; proud of the way that she could trace a bloodline in the turn of a horse's head, in the line of its neck, or the curve of its back. 'Tell me what you think of them.'

Joanna stepped lightly towards the nearest Spanish mare. It was a fine light bay, with delicate black points. Even though it was the first out of the transport it was still frightened and skittish. She was careful to approach it from the side, avoiding the blind spot directly in front of it, which would have added to its nervousness. Even so, it shied a little.

'She is a nappy one, Piers.' She spoke in the English of the serving men. 'A proud one.'

The silver-haired head groom nodded. 'Hot-blooded and no error, my lady.' He turned his head, revealing the stump of an ear lost to a warhorse's savage bite. 'As you'd expect from an Arab.'

There was a familiarity between them which bridged the chasm of class, a bridge built from respect and even love. Piers tightened the twitch on the mare's upper lip and the nervous horse calmed down a little. The quayside workers watched with ill-concealed interest as the young woman ran a slim white hand down the soft mane and crest. She rested her hand on the withers and the horse shivered beneath her touch.

'The eyes are large and bright,' she said to her father, in French. 'There is no meanness of spirit in her. And her head is elegant too.' Very carefully she stroked her hand back along the horse, feeling the tensed loins and croup. 'A fine sweeping back will give a good ride and there is strength in her hindquarters – no slope to the croup.'

'So you think I have done well to buy her, then?' Gilbert smiled slightly. He knew full well the value of this horse, as he did the accuracy of his daughter's examination.

Joanna nodded. 'Her coat shines like it has been polished, and there's not a trace of scurf on the skin.'

She slowly put her face near that of the mare. With great care she raised the lip to reveal the salmon-pink gums beneath. The same warm colour lay about the eyes and nostrils.

'She is in peak condition. You have bought well, Father.'

Gilbert took her arm. 'I know.' They smiled at one another, a self-congratulatory smile. 'I have done very well indeed.' They both smiled again, for he was not discussing the quality of his horses this time.

As Piers supervised the movement of the horses away from the Back Water he could not help but smile too. His own wife had acted as wet nurse to the infant Joanna, and in a secret compartment of his heart he harboured a little claim to fatherly feeling. Not that he would ever admit to it. Piers was a proud man but he knew his station. There were things best kept secret in a man's own thoughts.

Still, he was as proud of her as the baron was, and with good reason. Most of what she knew about the horses she had learned from him, and of that too he was justifiably proud.

'Come on, Stephen,' he called to his son. The twenty-year-old Stephen grinned back. 'And pay attention to that mare, boy. Or you'll get a kick where it hurts!'

The admonition was more play than criticism. Blond and bearded, stocky and strong, Stephen Pierson was more than a match for the nappiest of horses, even ones cooped up in a transport for the long journey north from the King's dukedom of Aquitaine.

Piers watched the boy as he firmly calmed the hot-blooded mare. There was something indescribable about that ability to touch a horse and cool its blood, something born of confidence and gentleness. Stephen had it and so did Joanna – despite their difference in rank. Soaking up the hot morning sun and enjoying the scent of hops floating across the harbour from the Weymouth breweries about Hopehuse Cove, Piers had to admit that he was a truly happy man.

While Piers and the serving men prepared the horses, Joanna and her father retired to the town house that he rented from the Winchester monks. It lay back from the quay and was separated from the tumbling wooden tenements by the wealthier burghal plots which were held by the lords of the manors of Radipole and Broadway. Unlike the houses of these other lords, the one occupied by Gilbert and his retainers was built over an expensive stone undercroft. It was elevated above its neighbours in more than just structure.

It was noon and time for the main meal of the day. Gilbert had ridden south the previous day accompanied by his household knights and grooms and, of course, by his red-haired daughter. As he sat down to eat the talk was of the war in Normandy.

'Is it true, Father,' Joanna questioned as a servant laid a trencher of fresh fish before her, 'that the King has turned the tables on his enemies at last?'

Gilbert broke open a flat cake of bread. 'That is what the word is all over the town. It seems John's enemies were so intent on besieging his mother at Mirabeau that he caught them napping.'

He chewed on the warm, fresh bread. 'It seems that John made a forced march from the castle at Le Mans and caught the lot of them. Including the Lusignan lords who were in arms against him and his nephew the Duke of Brittany. The rumour is it happened at the beginning of the month. Some say the first day of August.'

'King Richard would have been proud of him, Father.'

Gilbert grunted. He had fought with Richard in the Holy Land and knew both brothers. 'Perhaps – but then Richard was always hard to please.'

As they talked, the household knights hovered about the table. The young sons of Gilbert's knightly tenants, they vied with each other to display the rules of etiquette that they had learned as part of their knightly education in the baron's household. More than one looked anxiously at Joanna. She gave no sign that she was even aware of them, whilst she was, of course, cognisant of their every self-conscious gesture.

Immediately behind Joanna stood her personal lady attendant, Matilda. Only a year younger than her mistress, she wore a plain linen wimple held firm across her forehead by a brightly stitched head band. From within the frame of light material dark eyes watched her mistress' every mood and small white hands held the finger bowl for Joanna to wash after each course.

As she placed the bowl before her mistress a secret smile passed between them. Of all the serving women, Tilly was the closest to Joanna and accompanied her everywhere, just as Gilbert never travelled without his household knights.

The noontime meal over, it was time to begin the journey northwards to Gilbert's head manor, situated south-east of Sherborne. The new horses had been bridled and were loosely strung out on a line. Piers was holding the reins of his lord's roan palfrey. Stephen held those of Joanna's white jennet.

He helped her up as she slung her leg about the shaped pommel of the side-saddle. As he adjusted her stirrup she smoothed out the creases in her green wool gown where it flowed away from her narrow waist belt. The sun flashed on a gold brooch which fastened the gown together below her throat. The knotted trailing sleeves hung down on either side of her saddle. She and Stephen grinned at one another like brother and sister.

On his more spirited riding horse Gilbert watched as the lower retainers manoeuvred their broad-chested West Country cobs. The hairy little ponies stood in stark contrast to the tall, sleek riding horses of their social superiors. It was a mark of favour that Piers and his son rode jennets. The other retainers veiled their envy behind the expressionless faces crafted over a lifetime of fuedal service.

From the port the road ran eastward between the Back Water, formed by the estuary of the river Wey, and the sea-scoured 'mixon' – the sandy beach used by the town as its rubbish dump. After about half a mile the road turned north and began to climb away from the sea. To the west lay the reed-fringed lagoon of Radipole Lake; to the east the marshland of Lodmoor.

In the fields beside the dusty road the villeins were carrying in the harvest. The August sun shone on backs bent over sweeping sickles. At the edges of the track poppies and corn marigolds splashed the dusty grass with livid strokes of red and gold.

Ahead lay the green wall of the Ridgeway. The road cut steeply up it – a chalky scar. At the foot the horses were rested and allowed a brief drink from a clear spring. A little refreshed, they began slowly to climb the daunting slope.

Piers and Stephen stopped their own mounts at short intervals to check on the progress of the newly landed mares. Twice they caused the party to stop. It had been a day of trauma for the horses without further distressing them. They were allowed a few minutes' rest while cropping at the verge grass.

Gilbert and Joanna rode ahead, content to leave the care of the mares to their trusted grooms. Behind the two rode the knight escort, lance pennants fluttering in a slight breeze. Shields were slung on guige straps over their shoulders; open-faced, flat-topped helmets revealed alert features.

At last they crested the Ridgeway. Behind them the light silvered the water of the bay and the island of Portland rose like a fist above the sea haze. Before them the land fell away slightly and then recovered to form a slightly sloping plateau down as far as Dorchester, four miles away.

Joanna reined back her mount a little and motioned for Tilly to ride up beside her. Until that point the servant had placed herself at a discreet distance behind. 'How is Stephen today?' Joanna asked. 'Is he well?' The question was simple enough and yet seemed to have a considerable effect on the maid. Matilda blushed and glanced down at her reins.

'He is well, my lady. You saw how he handled the horses on the quayside.' Her embarrassment could not hide the quiet pride in her voice. 'He has such a way with them . . .' She blushed deeper as she realised the revealing nature of her comment.

Joanna smiled openly. Tilly's affection for the groom was very obvious. So was her shyness in the presence of the young man. 'When I next go into Sherborne you must both ride with me.'

'If that is what you wish, my lady.' Tilly seemed anxious to deny her feelings at all costs and she spoke as if the decision had nothing to do with her own pleasures. However the look of gratitude on her face belied the neutral acceptance in her voice. Her eyes were bright at the prospect.

It gave Joanna pleasure to show a kindness to a servant of whom she was very fond. For a moment she wondered what Stephen would think of her matchmaking, or for that matter Tilly's father. As a tenant of the baron – holding a small manor worth half a knight's fee at the foot of the downs – he undoubtedly had a more advantageous match in mind for his daughter than the son of the baron's head groom.

'How is your father, Tilly?'

Joanna knew already, because her father held few secrets from her, but she asked because it was better to ride and talk even when the conversation uncovered little that was not previously known.

'He is well, my lady.' Tilly pushed a loop of black hair back below her wimple. 'I briefly saw him at Lammas when he came to speak with your father about the King's war. He has gone to Normandy with the King as one of your father's contribution of knights.' She sounded excited at the thought of her father's tiny role in the great issues of the day.

'My father has told me that he has sent half of those knights he is bound to supply to the King, and the rest he has paid scutage for.' Joanna was uncommonly knowledgeable about these things. 'In truth it seems that the war against the King of France is likely to be so long that it will quite exhaust the forty days' service owed him from each knight. I think that he is happier with the payment of money to hire those who will fight as long as he wishes.'

For some time now Gilbert had elected to supply an ample quantity of silver pennies instead of the full quota of knights he owed the King, in return for the manors that he held from the Crown. He himself had not fought since he had accompanied Richard 'Lionheart' on crusade over a decade ago.

Tilly frowned. 'I have heard terrible things about some of those hired for the wars. There was a fishmonger at Melcombe talking about tales he had heard.' She paused to recall the gossip. 'He said that many were Brabançons who feared neither man nor God. He said they flocked to the wars for rape and pillage.' She crossed herself at the thought of the atrocities which the fishmonger had taken perverse delight in recounting. 'I thank Our Lady that we shall not see the likes of them here . . .'

Joanna reached out and touched her maid's wrist. 'You've no need to fear in my father's house. And besides, the King would never let such as those into his own kingdom. He will only use them against his enemies in France.' She nodded to underscore her confidence on this point of strategy. 'King Richard even hired Saracens to fight for him in Normandy but you don't think you shall come upon any here, do you?' Tilly shook her head. 'Then fret not, for you'll not meet any of the others either!'

Riding a little ahead, Gilbert smiled to himself. He could catch just a drift of the conversation and could hear his own voice in the words of his daughter.

Seeking to guide the talk back to more pleasant matters Joanna asked: 'And what of your mother?'

'She too is well.'

The answer was formal and without elaboration. Matilda's

mother had died giving birth to her sixth child after Tilly and her father had of course remarried. There was clearly little affection between Tilly and her teenage stepmother.

It was with some relief that Joanna noted the strangely sculptured hill which reared up from the left side of the road. The ancient hillfort rose in vast tiers of banks and ditches against the cloudless afternoon sky.

'See, 'tis Maiden Castle.' She pointed with her riding crop. 'It sprawls like a green dragon across the plain, don't you think?'

Tilly brightened at the new topic of conversation. 'I also heard at Melcombe how a man ploughing last spring found a pot full of Roman silver . . . up inside that place . . . And he used it to run away with the wife of the reeve of his manor. She a free woman and him a villein too.

'The lord of the manor has hunted for him high and low, what with the silver being his by rights and the man not being free to leave the manor without permission, let alone steal another man's wife.'

That was the best thing about Tilly, Joanna thought to herself: despite her shyness she always seemed to hear the best gossip.

They spent the night at Dorchester where Gilbert owned a town house complete with paddocks, gardens and stables. It lay in the northern quarter of the town between the castle and the little Jewry; in the parish of St Peter's.

As Joanna was assisted down from her mount by her father, she noticed that Stephen was offering the same service to Matilda. The maid was scarlet and so, to her surprise, was the young groom. Joanna hid a smile and resolved to ride to Sherborne as soon as she was able.

The next morning, with the horses rested, they completed their journey. As was their norm they rose shortly after dawn, breakfasted and then set out. Crossing the clear gravel ford of the river Frome, they slowly climbed up on to the downs. Soon the meadows about Dorchester were left behind. The road, running north, followed a high ridge of land between the valleys of the Cerne and the Piddle.

The sky was cloudless and a thrush-egg blue. On the right-hand side the undulating downland fell away until it merged with the morning haze. From the broad, rounded valley on the left, the bells of the abbey at Cerne pealed for the morning service of terce.

At last they reached the northern rim of the high land. Far below, nestled at the edge of the vale, was the church and manor of Temple Buckland. It lay in a shallow bowl of land pushed up against the downs. A dry valley ran up from the vale to the edge of the chalk, like the tapering handle of a skillet.

At a walk the riders descended the 'handle'. Beyond in the vale lay Horsingham. It could not yet be seen but it was there. They had come home.

Richard de Lacey was alone in the silent chapel. A light burned before the altar; he could smell the aroma of the pure beeswax. All else was dark and the gilded statues in their niches were reduced to charcoal shades, gazing down on him with hooded eyes. He was alone – utterly and totally alone.

The double abbey of Fontevrault was the mausoleum of the Plantagenet rulers of Anjou and Normandy; of Aquitaine and England. It was the spiritual heart of the great empire which John was even that very day defending against his enemies. Richard and his party had stopped there on their long ride north-eastward from La Rochelle. It was in the burial place of kings that Richard de Lacey kept vigil.

He had knelt for hours before the side altar and his knees were stiff with cold. The cool of the night had eaten into him. He felt chilled to his core and still he did not stir from his vigil. He had framed his prayers until words had failed him and the agony alone remained. Then that too was gone and all that was left him was the suffocating ache of despair and desperation.

He gritted his teeth as he rose. For a moment he steadied himself against the wall with his right hand. The movement mocked him as he felt the dull ache rise from deep within his back and shoulder. In fury he clenched his fist and raised it to strike the wall. Even that expression of pent-up feeling brought no relief to him, for he could barely raise the fist above his head. Even his anger brought him face to face with his disability.

With his back to the wall, he sank once more to the floor. For long minutes he sat there in the shadows. His breath was shallow and fast as if he had been running. 'Holy Mother of God . . .' he muttered with his eyes fixed on the dark ceiling. 'Will this mock me for the rest of my life?' He shook his head urgently.

The church seemed peculiarly dark. There were no solid pillars and squat arches to provide security and secrecy. Instead, the nave was without aisles and possessed only the slenderest of columns and tall windows, beneath the Aquitaine domes. By day the columns looked like sand in sunlight and the church was ablaze with light. By night there were just huge empty spaces for the dark shadows to fill.

Richard once more thought aloud. As if to persuade himself he laid out the framework of his plans. It was a ritual which he went through every night, his private exorcism of the ghosts which haunted him. No one else was aware of it, for it was his own private agony. In the guest rooms of the abbey Mark de Dinan and the other retainers were sound asleep. They would not hear the silent litany which the knight repeated to himself.

'For a start it may yet heal . . .' He tried to ignore the pain. 'And if it does not . . .' He paused to allow the enormity of that possibility to sink in. 'And if it does not, then I can still play my part. Without me the great horses will take years to have effect. No one else pursues them more than I.' Richard considered the enormity of his responsibility. 'But with my work they will come: greater, fiercer, more terrifying than ever. They will come and Jerusalem will be ours again . . .'

Despite the practice of this ritual he still could not banish the disappointment in his voice. For he knew that he was but half a knight. No minstrel would sing of him the way that they did of the Lionheart.

All that was over, his chivalry was shattered. He could no longer couch a lance and could barely raise a sword. The disappointment was intense, for it had disrobed him of all that noble vestment which his knighting had bestowed upon him. He felt naked, as if his manhood had been stripped from him.

Shaking his head, he got up. The night was well spent and soon there would be activity in the church. He had better get back to his bed. One more time he paused before the burial place of King Richard and his father, Henry II. The stone effigies of both were new, even though Henry had been dead for thirteen years. Each lay on a draped bier and was painted in lifelike hues. The night, though, turned all their colours to shades of grey.

They had been commissioned by Eleanor, Henry's widow. The woman who had fomented revolts against him and who had conspired with his own sons. The woman whom he had imprisoned and yet who had outlived her gaoler and now held Aquitaine for John, as once she had for her favourite son – Richard.

'Well, my lord. You knew enough disappointments, didn't you?' The realisation that he was not alone in his anguish gave him some consolation. 'Was there a son who did not conspire against you?'

'And you, my lord.' He ran a finger along Richard's painted cheek. 'You too knew the kiss of a crossbow . . .'

The bolt that had struck Richard at the siege of Chalus-Chabrol had been his death wound. It was a legendary blow: the lightly armoured king making sport of a siege and applauding the man-at-arms who dared to fire at him from the walls. Then leaping aside too slowly; still laughing as the stunning impact drove him to the ground. Then days of agony; the festering wound; the warrior dead. A moment of futility marked down and seized by ever-watchful death.

'Enough of this.' Richard had heard the first tolling of the bell for matins. 'Enough of this.' He strode from the church. If he did not conquer this darkness he would go mad. The first hurrying monk started as he strode past him in the opposite direction.

Mark was asleep in the huge bed they shared. Exhausted, Richard lay down beside him. The sleep which finally came was shallow and gave little rest. When finally he awoke, the sun was pouring into the guest dormitory and he was still very tired. Despite his exhaustion, it was time to move on. From Fontevrault the road struck north to Le Mans. In the countryside autumn was now clearly marked in the leaves of the trees. Gold amidst the green pointed a gilded finger towards winter and death. It was Thursday, 17 October – the eve of the feast of St Luke.

Not that Richard was openly morbid. By day he was more determined, more energetic than any of his sergeants, or his squire. It was only in the sleep-robbed dark that he was a prisoner of his thoughts. By day he wore his worries out in activity and ambition. In fact many found his very presence exhausting, as if he possessed the energy of three men.

Richard rode in the company of his squire, twelve lightly armoured men-at-arms – his sergeants – and a Saracen mercenary who acted as groom to the hot-blooded horses. He had been personally selected by Richard from the expert grooms employed by the horse breeder who had supplied the precious Arab mares. He was a man of few words but with deep expressive eyes which revealed the active mind behind the curtain of silence. It had taken a bag of silver to make his master part with him and a good supply of the precious metal to keep the groom in his new employment. From the way he handled the horses, Richard concluded it was money well spent.

As well as the Arab brood mares other beasts stirred the dust on the road. Every other sergeant had the reins of a hairy little packhorse looped about his heavy limewood pommel. The two lead packhorses carried Richard's baggage, spare weapons and spare hauberk of mail; the other sweated under the baggage of the rest of the party.

Mark de Dinan, mounted like Richard on a well-bred riding horse, led the pair of ill-tempered destriers which Richard rode into battle. Mark's palfrey was noticeably nervous of the two warhorses and bore the teeth marks of at least one of them to justify his nervousness.

'Le Mans was worse than I had imagined.' Mark grimaced at the thought. 'Not that I ever liked the place much . . . .'

'Apparently John burned it this summer,' Richard replied, remembering the wrecked houses with their fire-blackened spars. 'Though it will rise from the ashes, have no doubt about that. These places always do.'

He had seen enough burned towns. It was the way of a world at war. Always the destruction of peasant messuages and the burghal tenements of merchants and artisans in order to strike at the prosperity of those who, behind their castle walls, were spared the slaughter which came upon the common and middling folk.

'John has stamped his authority hereabouts and there is no doubt about it.' Mark recalled the signs of destruction across northern Poitou as they had travelled to Fontevrault. 'The rebel barons will not be troubling the southern manors of Normandy and Anjou this winter.'

'Licking their wounds more like.' Richard smiled grimly. 'And doing their best to see that the King of France will make it well worth their while if they are to start the same trouble next spring. I daresay there will be those who will make their peace with John and wait for a better opportunity to break their oaths of fealty – when it promises a better and more reliable return for their treachery.' There was no disguising the disapproval in his voice.

'No doubt when the time comes they will claim the excuse that their first allegiance is to the King of France. And John has him as overlord for his French lands, as they do.' Mark pondered the incongruity of the King of England's position in France. 'Though by St Peter, he's an overmighty subject for the taste of the court in Paris.'

Richard nodded. There was no doubt about it, and the thought was disconcerting. Perhaps a time would arise when every lord in John's French lands would have to make that very choice of allegiance. It was a disturbing thought, for Richard was not alone in holding manors on both sides of the narrow English Channel.

'I would not worry about that today, Mark.' Richard refocused his attention on more positive themes. 'John has taught the rebels a lesson they'll not forget in a hurry. I think his Norman lands are safe enough.'

He twisted in his saddle and looked back over Mark and the ill-tempered destriers. Between them and the sergeants the Arab mares were strung out on a long leading rein.

He smiled to see their blond manes stirred by the breeze; their rich, deep, dark eyes; their shining chestnut flanks. They were enough for him to worry about. What did he care about the treachery of princes? How could they bear comparison with the mission that was his?

Already he had visited one of his smaller manors in the vicinity of Fontevrault and left five of the palfreys in the hands of the steward who had care of his demesne there. Their offspring would be sold in due course and tall stallions purchased. It was height and strength that Richard desired. The other five palfreys were destined for his manor east of Falaise, in Normandy. Here too they would be put to stud and their offspring sold to further finance his venture.

Richard did not tire his horses and at most the pace speeded to a gentle trot. There was no hurry and the October sunshine was mild and pleasant. They covered thirty miles a day and it was three days' ride from Fontevrault before the party – skirting the western border of Touraine – crossed the county of Maine and entered the southern border lands of Normandy.

The King's road from Sees to the fortress town of Falaise divided ten miles south of the town. Richard led his party to the east. The road here, narrower and less well travelled, wound down amongst the wooded hills about the headwaters of the river Vie. It was a land of lush vegetation; of well-watered meadows still yellow with drifts of buttercups, a green and yellow parchment punctuated with apple trees.

'It's hot,' Mark complained as he ran a finger about the neck of his mail hauberk. 'I wish the breeze had not dropped.' He looked at Richard, who nodded. Both were wearing mail beneath their long, split surcoats. The possibility of warfare seemed to have receded but neither was prepared to disarm totally.

The road sank deeper as it twisted about the hillsides. Here and there a thin finger of smoke betrayed the presence of a farmstead deep in the valley. In the roadside grasses dense rosettes of pearlwort trailed whorls of pale petals amongst the aftermath of the summer's grass-mowing.

Richard called forward his groom. 'When we arrive at the manor I want you to look at the leg of the mare with the white star on her forehead. She's picked up a scratch somehow.' The groom nodded.

'I had seen it, my lord,' the groom replied softly. 'I cleaned it with water at the abbey and used a salve to cool the swelling.' Like Richard he was always thinking of the horses.

'Well done, Umar.' Richard was pleased at the groom's attentiveness. 'I know they are safe in your hands, for . . .'

The sound of steel on steel was a profanity in this peaceful landscape. It struck discordant echoes from another world and cut off Richard's words to the groom. The startled palfreys stamped and snorted, tossed their heads and shook irritated manes.

The noise of conflict came from beyond a turn in the road, where it curled about the foot of a wooded knoll. It was disembodied violence and more disturbing for the lack of visual contact with the source of the noise. The Saracen groom looked back at his precious charges and his questioning eyes turned towards Richard. Those sergeants unencumbered by packhorses tugged at the reins of their mounts. Forced up and on to the verge, they passed the mares and converged on Richard.

'My lord?' the leading sergeant asked as he pulled his helmet close down on his head. 'Shall I ride forward and see . . .'

'No!' Richard was motioning to Mark to bring forward his shield. 'Not yet – but get ready.'

Mark had dismounted and handed his reins to a still-mounted man-at-arms. He was pulling at the shield which hung from the lead packhorse. He was impatient and even the dull little pony started as his hurried fingers tugged on leather straps.

A sergeant made as if to dismount to assist him, but Mark's red-faced glare froze him back up into his saddle. No sergeant was going to help him arm his knight. At last he pulled the shield free and, as he ripped off the sacking covering, a rearing red lion on a gold field snarled at him.

Mark raised the shield to Richard, who pulled it to him so that it covered his side from shoulder to knee. Next he freed the helm with its heavy face-guard. Richard leaned towards him and Mark fumbled with the straps. Already Richard had pulled the heavy coif of mail up from his shoulders to cover his head. There was no time for dismounting and putting on the padded arming cap.

Richard heard the familiar muffled sound of his own breathing as the helmet pressed the mail of the coif into the top of his head. Through the eye slits the world was suddenly restricted to a narrow field of claustrophobic dimensions.

He seized his reins once more and the snorting palfrey pulled up its head. It was uneasy at the activity and unused to the shield pulled tight against its flank. There was no time to transfer to one of the destriers.

'Guard the mares.' Richard gave the muffled command to Umar, before turning away. 'Guard them with your life . . .'

Mark had remounted as Richard urged his palfrey forward in a flurry of dust. The sergeants drove their horses forward, jabbing prick spurs into their mounts. Beyond the bend the road fell away steeply, then levelled out. It crossed a broad and shallow stream where willows bent their backs across the rutted track.

On the far side of the ford a small battle was taking place. A churning, terrified circle of lightly armed horsemen was surrounded by a mob of cheaply clad men-at-arms wearing patched knee-length gambesons and wielding spears and bills. One at least carried a crossbow.

As Richard careered towards the ford, the crossbowman ran forward, took hurried aim, and fired. The knight heard the whine of the bolt past his head. Behind him one of his sergeants took the shot full in the chest. He plunged from his horse which slipped and fell heavily.

Frantically, the crossbowman bent down in a desperate effort to span the bow again. Richard's horse stumbled but did not fall. The man was shoving his foot into the stirrup of the bow and fumbling with the hook about his own waist. Desperate fingers trembled as they caught hold of the bowstring. The hook engaged.

Richard jammed in his spurs regardless of the wild, foam-flecked neighing of his mount. The crossbowman stood up, spanning the bow in an arc of killing tension, as with his free hand he shoved another bolt home.

At that moment he looked up. His eyes snapped open, wide with terror. The great sword-of-war sliced through the crown of his kettle helmet, the look disintegrated and the man was broken and tossed beneath the hooves of Richard's palfrey.

Agony seared Richard's vision. He rolled in the saddle as his arm swung free and pain lanced across his shoulder. Mark seized the bridle of Richard's horse and pulled it up in a confusion of hooves and water, while Richard fell forward against the pommel of his saddle. Winded, he gasped as his helmet pressed close on his face.

Mark had dismounted and was steadying both horses with difficulty. He was joined by two of the mounted men-at-arms, while the others pursued the gang of French soldiers who had fled away up the track. The three caught Richard as he fell from the saddle. He was almost doubled up as he clutched at his arm and shoulder with his left hand.

Mark held him as he sank down, half in the stream. The water soaked the white surcoat which covered his mail. The young squire pulled on the leather straps and freed the confining helmet which fell with a loud splash into the stream bed. The sergeant swept off his own helmet and filled it with sweet, cold water. Mark held it to Richard's face and the knight drank hungrily, then he sank back against the grassy bank, cursing silently.

When Richard looked up, his vision was still swimming. Before him stood an elderly stranger wearing a fine-spun woollen riding cloak. Deep, intelligent black eyes looked out from under a fringe of black hair glossed with silver threads.

'I owe you my life, my lord. Though it seems it has cost you.' There was genuine concern as well as gratitude in the watching eyes. 'We could never have defended ourselves against those curs. Cutthroats in the pay of the enemies of the King.'

Richard ran a hand over his face. The water cleared his thinking and ran down his well-trimmed beard and moustache. However, before he could speak the stranger anticipated his question.

'Forgive me, my lord. I am travelling under the protection of the warrant of the King of England. But for you I would be a dead man.' He smiled wryly before he volunteered the next piece of information. 'My name is Aaron – Aaron of Dorchester. Sometimes I am known simply as Aaron the Jew . . .'

Chapter 2

'It's good horse country this. That is why my lord has made Horsingham his chief manor.' Ranulf Dapifer turned his long, clean-shaven face to where the pastures spread away towards the steep, rising edge of the downland. 'It was held by the Abbot of Milton before the Conquest, actually.'

As steward to Gilbert de Cantelo, Ranulf was familiar with every aspect of the manor and its history. He liked nothing better than to outline the attractions of the manor to strangers. He felt it was due to his good stewardship that it had prospered as well as it had done. At thirty, he had spent a third of his adult life in the service of Gilbert and was well aware of his privileged position within the hierarchy of the baronial household.

His listener smiled. Like the steward he did not have a beard but instead a long moustache drooped at the corners of his mouth. Despite a similarity in age – he was but five years senior to the speaker – there was little else similar about them. Unlike the tall, slim steward he was short and stocky. However, it was a build which spoke volumes about physical strength rather than corpulence and sloth.

The listener was, however, used to the ways of clerks. Living within the household of the Bishop of Salisbury it would be difficult to be otherwise. He let the steward speak uninterrupted.

'The meadowland is the secret to the success of the manor, you understand.' Ranulf gently rubbed his hands together as he spoke. 'It is very extensive indeed. My lord Gilbert holds more in lordship here than in most of his other manors put together. The grass is very sweet and gives us abundant fodder for the winter months. Almost all lies within the demesne land held directly by my lord and stewarded by me.

'There is a tenant who holds two hides over there, in return for knight service.' With one well-manicured finger the steward indicated towards the south-east. 'But most of the knights that Gilbert owes in fealty to the King are subtenants elsewhere.' Ranulf smiled. 'And of course there is abundant timber here, being on the edge of the Royal Forest of Blackmore. The King has granted us the right to pasture the horses on this side of the forest. It is a fine manor.'

Falkes de Mauleon knew one or two things about a good stud farm. As the bishop's marshal, or 'carry-axe', he was not only his trusted personal manager but responsible for the smooth running of the episcopal stables.

He was well aware of the reputation of the manor which Gilbert held from the King. And so was the bishop, who knew a thing or two about horse flesh as well. It was no coincidence that the bishop regularly paid good silver pennies to have his marcs covered at Horsingham.

'And was that the baron's daughter that I saw this morning in the fields?'

Ranulf frowned. 'It is possible,' he replied warily. It was clear that Falkes had touched on a slightly sensitive point. 'It is possible . . .'

'I doubt there can be another woman like the one I saw as we rode in.' The marshal patted his powerful barrel body. 'With hair like a fox . . .'

'That was my lord's daughter . . .'

Falkes sensed the steward's urge to change the subject and kept on tenaciously. 'A most beautiful young woman indeed. But I was surprised to see her out in the pastures with the horses. Only her and a blond lad, a little older than her I would say . . .'

'Quite so, quite so.' Dapifer was clearly not happy with the direction that the conversation was taking. 'The lady Joanna takes a very great interest in the horses. It is an interest which her father indulges . . .'

As soon as he had said it he wished that he had chosen another word or phrase. He had given away too much concerning his own opinions. The smile at the edges of de Mauleon's mouth said it all.

'But I am sure that you will take more wine with me as we discuss next spring's arrangements for covering the bishop's mares.' Dapifer motioned towards the manor house. 'We can talk over the wine. I am sure that you will find it congenial.

'My master will be back at the manor for the noontime dinner. His business in Sherborne kept him at the castle last night but he will return today and will no doubt wish to speak with you.' Ranulf looked meaningfully towards the substantial hall of the manor, across the courtyard. 'But first some wine . . . It's warm for this late in the year.'

'An excellent suggestion,' Falkes said with a grin. He was an experienced campaigner and knew when he had someone on the run. No need to rub it in. 'A very good suggestion indeed.'

Ranulf Dapifer motioned for the bishop's marshal to go ahead of him. As the steward turned to follow, he glanced towards the pasture dotted with clumps of golden oak trees. He saw a figure amongst the grazing horses. A figure with red hair talking with a blond-haired boy. He frowned as he turned towards the manor house.

Joanna and Stephen Pierson were studying a mare with great interest. The great swelling belly shone as the still-bright sunshine caught the taut chestnut. She was cropping the last of the fading autumn grass.

'She's foaling late.' Stephen's eyes sparkled as he considered his own statement. 'It's never good to have them this late in the year. The best of the grass is long gone and you know that, fine as the hay is, it's best for the dam to have the summer grass behind her milk . . .' He threw a quick sideways glance at his mistress. 'And she's a bit young too. I'd prefer them to drop their first foal at five years. She will barely be three come All Saints' Day . . .'

Joanna smiled. She knew full well how Stephen's father had counselled against the covering of this particular filly in the December of the previous year. He had given his judgement to Gilbert and been firmly, if kindly, overruled. The sire of the foal about to be born had not been available earlier in the year.

Gilbert had paid well to have the stallion brought over to Horsingham from the royal stud at Gillingham. It was probably only the fact that the royal grooms had likewise counselled against a covering of their own mares so late in the year that had made it possible for Gilbert to get access to the stallion at all.

'She will be fine, Stephen.' It amused her to hear him use the personal pronoun when in fact he was reiterating the words of his father. She also knew he was teasing her. He was the only man who did so. 'She is a good, strong filly and the hay crop has been abundant this year. Besides . . .' she grinned at the arch in the young groom's eyebrow, 'there will be few other foals born this autumn and so it will get more attention than if it had been born with the others in the summer.'

She spoke in the English of the servants and retainers, as she always did with him. She was, of course, fluent both in English and the socially more exalted French of her father's chamber.

Stephen sighed; there were times when it was just like listening to Gilbert when his daughter spoke. And there was no gainsaying either of them when they had made up their minds.

Even with his peculiar closeness to the baron's daughter he had to recognise that there were limits to what he could achieve. She was a young woman who knew her own mind. More than that, she was used to getting thoughts translated into reality. After all, she was Gilbert de Cantelo's daughter and he was merely the head groom's son. He could never quite forget that. He doubted that she had cause to think on it.

'When is she due, would you say?'

Stephen ran a hand along the mare's flank. She turned and nuzzled his shoulder. The snuffling nibble of his woollen tunic revealed the trust between horse and man. Gently and slowly, Stephen stroked the underbelly from the brisket backwards. The mare butted her head against him. Enough was enough.

'Easy . . . easy . . .' Stephen removed his hand and patted the white blaze which ran in a broad band down the middle of the chestnut face. 'Not ready for a midwife yet, eh?'

Joanna too stroked the intelligent face and brushed away the last few flies as they buzzed about the great deep eyes. 'Before the end of the week?' she queried.

Stephen nodded. 'Her teats are well waxed up. I think it will be in the next day or so.' He paused to think. 'It might be tomorrow, or perhaps Saturday.'

'If she lasts until Sunday and it's a filly we shall call it Faith . . .' Stephen nodded, accepting the wisdom of the suggestion. 'For Sunday, 6 October is St Faith's day. I think that my father will agree . . .'

Stephen nodded again. He was sure of it. There was little that the baron did to restrict her freedom. Of all the inhabitants of the manor she was the most unfettered; free to come and go as she chose. Free to be whatever she wanted.

Whatever Joanna willed to do she could. Whether it was the expected duties of running the household, in the place of her dead mother, or the less expected duties of wandering the cobbled stables, or lunging the half-broken colts, she seemed free to indulge her interests. And despite all her freedom she was refreshingly unspoiled. It was as if the free air that she breathed was so abundant that it had never occurred to her to deny it to another. For, as confident and certain to be obeyed as she was, she was also without malice.

Stephen loved her – and sometimes even carefully teased her – as if she were one of his own sisters, but he envied her a little too. It amused him to think that he actually envied a woman. But that was what Joanna de Cantelo could do – she could turn the world upside down, if she wanted to.

As the two strolled back towards the manor house they were met by Tilly, Joanna's maid. She came to greet them with the news that the steward was entertaining the bishop's marshal in the great hall.

Joanna smoothed down the fine wool of her gown and adjusted the embroidered fillet which ran like a sparkling stream through the red river of her hair.

'We must go, Tilly, and see that he is properly entertained. After all, I am mistress of the household!'

'Aye, my lady.' The maid blushed as she half glanced at the young groom. He smiled back, no longer as ebullient as before.

★ ★ ★

Richard de Lacey lay face down on a broad goose-feather mattress. In one corner of the room a mutton-fat candle burned with the usual greasy flame. The room was smoky and a thin veil of grey hung about the wooden rafters of the chamber. A tapestry hung on one wall and the figures on it moved slightly in the flickering light.

'Easy, Mark, or you'll make me wish the rogue had killed me.' Richard laughed but it was edged with pain. 'Or are you trying to finish the job for him?'

Mark de Dinan ignored his knight's strained jokes. Richard's humour was worse when he was trying to be funny than when it came naturally. He had never been a very good patient, even when he had first sustained the wound. He was too active to take enforced rest, and when he was hurting, his efforts to exude *bonhomie* were a bit too much. It was as if he just could not lie still and be quiet for a bit.

The teenage squire, assisted by two of the sergeants, had removed the heavy knee-length hauberk of mail. It lay, carefully folded, in one corner of the chamber, beside the white linen surcoat with its snarling lion. Beside this martial pile lay Richard's mail leg protectors and, perched on the mail chausses, a pair of fine gilt spurs.

Richard raised his head whilst Mark pulled at the laces which held together the neck of the aketon. The squire tugged at the long quilted garment which was worn under the mail. With difficulty both the knight's arms were freed from the rag-padded linen.

Falling forward on to the mattress, Richard was naked to the waist. Very carefully Mark wiped the reddened shoulder with a cool damp cloth. A bucket of cold well-water stood on the stout planks of the floor.

All about the inner edge of Richard's shoulder blade, directly below the line of the neck, the skin was twisted and puckered with scars. They crisscrossed in angry red seams.

'It was a bad time for such a wound as this . . .'

Richard grunted. Now it hurt too much even for him to joke.

His teeth were clamped firmly together as Mark applied water to the old wound.

'The planets were in Gemini. The Greek physician was loath to cut out the head of the bolt, knowing it best to avoid incisions in the shoulders and arms until the ascendancy of Cancer . . .' Mark dipped the cloth in the bucket again. 'But there was no delaying the work. The heat had already caused the wound to smell.' He laid the cold flannel over the scars. 'So he cut it out . . .'

Richard grimaced as he recalled the blade slicing into the monstrously inflamed wound. It was as real now as when it had happened. It could still make sweat break out on his forehead to think of the knife. Now he had wrenched and torn the wound once again. Inwardly he cursed with despair and the disappointment was a bitter twist in his stomach. A turmoil which gave the lie to his stoicism and surface humour.

The man whom Richard had saved at the ford leaned over the wound. 'And the bolt drove the mail deep into the flesh?' There was no need to answer the question. All about the scar the skin was pitted where the riveted links had burst apart and been driven into the shoulder by the force of the impact of the crossbow bolt. 'A cruel wound indeed.'

Mark took a pot of ointment from the Saracen groom, who stood silently beside the bed. He dipped his fingers in the pot and began to massage the ointment into the shoulder.

It was lucky that the skirmish with the French raiders had taken place so close to Richard's manor, amidst the lush pastures of eastern Calvados. It had been relatively easy to transport the wounded knight to his own hall and chamber, rather than rely on the hospitality afforded by some neighbouring lord.

'The ointment is?'

Without glancing at the questioner, Mark replied: 'Distilled parsley leaves and feverfew in goose grease . . .'

The Jewish merchant touched a little of the ointment and sniffed at it with the steady purpose of one who knows what he is about. It was this air of knowledge which had won him the information offered by de Dinan.

As Mark watched the Jew he shrugged. He would take advice

from anyone if it would heal his master. Even from a Jew and a Saracen. Even from enemies of the faith. He loved his knight that much.

He looked from one to the other of the aliens who shared the room with his master and himself. Yet it troubled him a little, for, despite all the sights he had seen in the east, he could never fully trust the exotic and the strange. But his master accepted it, and if it was good enough for Richard de Lacey then it had to be good enough for Mark de Dinan. Yet whether others would be so open-minded was difficult to say. The thought made him frown.

'There is mutton fat in it too?'

Mark nodded in answer to the question. 'He makes it up to the prescription given by a physician at Fontevrault.' The squire flicked a glance towards the Muslim attendant. 'The goose grease is stiffened with mutton fat and beeswax.'

'Yes . . . the Saracens have a great reputation for skill in the healing arts. I have heard much of the work of their physicians in Spain and in Sicily . . .'

'Well this one looks after the horses and mixes the ointments. That's all . . .'

A low laugh reminded them of the patient before them. Richard pulled himself up once more. 'As you see, Mark does not fully approve of my Saracen groom . . .'

Mark flushed. Any word of criticism from Richard was a rebuke to him. 'It is not that, my lord . . .'

Richard leaned on one elbow. 'It's all right, Mark.' He grinned at his squire's blush. 'As you can see I am by no means fussy about the company that I keep.' He looked at the groom, with his deep, dark eyes, tanned complexion and wavy black hair. 'Am I, Umar ibn Mamun?' The groom, who spoke passing French, simply bowed slightly. Richard gave a half-smile as he looked back at Aaron of Dorchester.

The Jew smiled. 'With a Saracen and a Jew together in one room there are many who would doubt whether you will ever recover. What with so many demons in attendance.'

Mark pursed his lips but Richard nodded. 'And perhaps they are right . . .' His eyes narrowed. 'What do you say to that,

Aaron of Dorchester? For I am bound to the deliverance of the Holy Places from all the enemies of Holy Church.'

The taut note in his voice and the edge of passion would have been recognised by the Grand Master in the room of sunshine and shadows in Acre.

It was clearly a point which had occurred to the Jew. 'The Saracen does your bidding and is your servant for silver. He will not stand between you and your goal. And I . . .'

He gave the practised smile of a survivor. 'I am the loyal servant of the Christian King of England. Besides, there is more Jewish money than Christian funding the crusaders who travel this autumn.' He coughed. 'And more than that, we have freely loaned John much of what he needs to fight his enemies in France.'

'So I should not fear your presence here today?' Richard did not look particularly concerned. The brittle edge had gone from his voice. 'You will not bewitch me?'

'No, my lord. There is no one here who would stand between you and your goal . . .'

Richard had been in the Kingdom of Jerusalem long enough to accommodate the presence of the alien and the unfamiliar. The enemies of the faith whom he fought were only those who stood against providence. And to them he would be the angel of death. But, like the Lionheart before him, he was able to accept the existence of aliens who had come to terms with the inevitability of the victory of Christendom.

'I wonder if all would agree with that?' Richard raised a quizzical brow.

'Not all, my lord.'

Richard thought that it was true. He glanced at his squire's taut mouth. 'I can well believe that . . .'

He motioned to Mark to bring him his linen shirt. Wincing, he pulled it on. Swinging his feet about, he sat on the edge of the bed as the squire pulled the aketon down over his knight's strong thighs. Richard stood up, his nakedness half covered by the edge of the shirt.

One of the packs had been brought in from the hairy little cobs.

It had been opened in a corner of the chamber and from it Mark lifted a precisely folded garment. Laying it out on the mattress he opened up the folds, smoothing out the worst of the creases. It was a long, mustard-coloured tunic made from Italian cloth. From the high collar to the wide border of the hem it was luxuriously embroidered with fleurs-de-lis. A tunic fit for a knight.

Richard pulled on his hose and then, assisted by his squire, dropped the tunic over his head. He sat as Mark put boots on his feet. All the while Richard talked as he was robed.

'What brings you to Normandy under the King's protection?'

Aaron ran a thumb against a bent forefinger. 'Money.' When Richard did not respond, he continued: 'In England my cousin is one of the Justices of the Jews. He is appointed by the King to arrange the taxes paid by the Jews of England to the Crown.

'As you will know, my people live under the protection of the Crown.' He paused but if there was any sense of irony it did not show on his finely sculpted features. 'And as such we pay tallage to the Crown alone and to no other lord.'

Richard smoothed back his blond hair, ruffled by the pulling on of the tunic. 'A right which the King exercises freely.'

Without comment, the Jew nodded in a knowing manner. It was common knowledge that King John extorted huge sums of money from the Jews living in his lands, with cynical regularity.

Richard continued: 'But that does not explain why you are in Normandy. What business of the Exchequer of the Jews would bring you here?'

Aaron's eyes glittered as if somewhere behind the crafted exterior there were emotions all the more real for their imprisonment. 'The matter of raising tallages for the crown is not as smoothly organised in Normandy and Anjou as it was in the days of the King's late father. And yet – what with the war – John needs the money delivered more swiftly than ever. It was once very well organised, but . . .'

'But not as well as you could do it!'

' . . .but twelve years ago the Jewish organiser was visiting the community at York. He was a most wise and learned man. A true and gentle rabbi and well versed in Talmudic studies. Also a trader in fine cloths from the east . . .'

Richard looked away to where the candle flame was sinking low. 'I understand . . .'

The destruction of the Jews of York, by an inflamed mob, was well known. The news of it had spread across the realm, so great had been the killing.

Aaron did not hesitate and his voice betrayed no emotion. 'He died on the night of 16 March 1190. Along with one hundred and fifty of the Jews of York.' The date was as crisp and clear as any mortgage repayment date in one of Aaron's ledgers. 'In the language of my people it is remembered as *Shabbat Ha-Gadol*. I do not know precisely whether he was actually murdered, or committed suicide rather than fall into the hands of . . .'

'The mob . . .' Richard suggested quietly.

Mark frowned. It was common knowledge that the Jews of London, Stamford and York had been plotting against King Richard's expedition to liberate Jerusalem. Why else would they have confessed their crimes when seized by the outraged citizens of those cities?

He loved de Lacey but was beginning to feel puzzled. Was it really possible that his master felt some sympathy for these people? The thought was staggering and Mark dismissed it at once.

Aaron shrugged. 'He died. And with him ended the efficient collection of tallages. It has been less well organised since, and the King's need is great. I am here under the Crown's protection to improve the efficiency of the collections. The King demands it is delivered more promptly and it is my duty to see that things improve.'

Mark turned away slightly. Try as he might to imitate his lord, the usurious obsessions of these people disgusted him. They thought of nothing but money, and that exacted from good Christian souls.

'It is very important that we pay our tallage to the last penny owed. It is the right of the King to exact it and vitally important that we pay it completely – and quickly. Or else . . .'

Richard shifted his gaze from the dying candle flame. For a few moments he stared at the stranger whose life he had saved. Aaron did not blink. At last Richard glanced away.

'I think I understand . . .'

Mark de Dinan was fiddling with another candle and thinking, *Which is more than I bloody well do*. Then he was called from his task by Richard's request for more wine.

Umar ibn Mamun, the other alien, listened to the strange conversation with a hint of a look which indicated that, unlike Richard's squire, *he* understood very well indeed. He stepped forward to replace the candle that was burning into a puddle of wax. It was close to Richard and at once Mark intervened. Before Umar's fingers could snuff out the faltering wick, Mark was there.

His back was to Richard, who consequently could not see the look which was directed at Umar, but the Arab saw it clearly. For a moment he gazed intently at the animosity in the eyes of the young squire, then, without a word, he backed away. Satisfied, Mark replaced the candle for his knight.

Richard took a goblet of Poitevin wine from the tray offered by his youthful squire. It was a good St Jean d'Angely which his butler had selected from amongst the hooped casks in the stone-floored coolness of the buttery.

'When I am recovered, in a day or two, I intend to ride to Caen, by way of the horse fair of Guibray, below the castle at Falaise. You are welcome to ride with us, under my protection.'

Aaron sipped at his own wine. 'Thank you. I shall be very pleased to do so. And I am in your debt.'

Ranulf Dapifer was tense. Whenever his master gave a feast it reflected on him. The butler and pantler thought it was their responsibility but they were wrong. The success of the venture was in his hands and they merely played their part. He alone saw the picture as a whole and choreographed the entire magnificent display.

In this case the display was in honour of Hubert de Burgh, Earl of Kent, chamberlain to the King and overseer of the hereditary doorkeepers of the King's chamber and the keepers of the royal whores.

He was also sheriff of Somerset and Dorset, a man charged with making sure that every baronial household paid its dues in fines, reliefs and loans to the Crown. A man of power indeed and on his way to hold the royal fortress of Falaise against the King's enemies. Before October gave way to November, he would be in Normandy with the King himself.

Retainers were rolling a cloth-wrapped 'Wilton weight' of cheese out of the flag-floored store. It was cool here in the stone-arched undercroft. Above, in the great hall, servants were spreading clean straw and laying out trestles and benches.

Ranulf turned to cast a critical eye on the efforts of the cheese-carriers before he returned his attention to the pantler. Despite the cool of the undercroft, the object of his attention was perspiring freely.

'This time you will not stint on the chopped dittany and violet leaves in the *omelette aux fines herbes*.' The pantler made as if to reply but his protest was cut off. 'Nor will you use wine dregs in the bread sauces served with the roast heron.

'If it smells like vinegar, use it for the lower tables and the servants. I don't want a sniff of it on the high table – do you understand?'

The pantler reddened. 'It was the butler who . . .'

'Quite. But you went along with it and it won't happen again. It'll be only the Poitevin wines and the unfermented verjuice used in the sauces . . .'

Ranulf waved the pantler away to take out his anger on the cooks and scullions, then he summoned the butler who, with set jaw, took the instructions with ill-disguised resentment. 'Top table will have the Gascon wines and the Moselle. The wines from the vineyards at Durweston are too thin and hard on the palate. So serve the English wine to the squires and pages. The Weymouth beers and ales can go to the grooms and the scullions can finish off the wine that's turning to vinegar. Is that clear?'

The butler looked triumphant. 'My lady Joanna gave me instructions this morning. She said to give beer and ale to the scullions too – as it is a celebration . . .' He looked very pleased with himself.

Ranulf was tight-lipped. 'Then do as your mistress instructed and be off with you. My master will not want to eat later than noon, so you had better hurry.'

As the butler went off with a grin, the steward clucked with annoyance. The lady Joanna was free to do whatever she wanted. But it was a good job that *he* stuck to his post and did not indulge any whim which came his way. A good job *he* was single-minded in his service to the household.

Not everyone could afford to be indulged in the way the baron's daughter was. Jealousy soured his thoughts, for it was not fair that she was so free. No good would come of Gilbert's laxness with her.

No girl should have the freedom that she had. It was not prudent and it was not right. No husband would stand for such a thing. Joanna should long ago have restricted her interests to the house and the solar. He thought of his own wife, Emma. A dutiful spouse who upheld his rank with her own careful conduct. A sincere and meek woman and, most important of all, a quiet one.

In the same way that her attendants knew the discipline of their stations, Joanna should know hers. Ranulf brushed back his tonsured chestnut hair, the mark of his station; that of a learned clerk in minor orders and steward of the baronial household. It was neatly and precisely cut; disciplined and in its place, like him. There was no room for exceptions. Things should be as they were planned to be and meant to be. In this same way he ordered his own life. If only all the world were as structured and in its proper place. Ranulf Dapifer shook his head sadly, knowing that it was not.

Across the yard, in the cobbled stable, Stephen and Piers were talking hurriedly with one of the other grooms. The chestnut three-year-old was standing in a heap of clean straw. She was restless. At intervals she pawed the ground and a sweat had broken out on her neck and flanks. Every few moments a violent contraction shook her body.

By the time Joanna arrived, the horse was lying down and in obvious distress. The great dark eyes were dilated and the grunts and groans which issued from the foam-flecked mouth indicated that something was going wrong.

'She should have foaled by now.' Joanna leaned forward over Stephen and Piers, who were crouched by the mare's tail. 'What's wrong?'

The silver-haired head groom barely looked up. 'It may be a breech.' He stared intently at the raised tail of the mare. There was a lot of blood and water soaking the straw, but no sign of the coming foal. 'She's taking too long . . .'

'It's not good, my lady.' Stephen stood up and stretched his cramped limbs. 'The waters burst some time ago. It should be out now as easy as that . . .' He passed one palm swiftly over the other. 'Most don't even need us.'

Joanna had watched the birth of many prized horses and knew the truth of Stephen's words. It was usually so easy. Many mares foaled at night as if they actually wanted to avoid the interference of a human midwife. Not so this filly.

'Let me see.'

Piers made way, glancing at his son as he did so. Stephen pulled a wry face and his father acknowledged the look with a nod. He knew better than to try to come between the lord's daughter and her horses.

Joanna knelt down in the straw. She was wearing the deep-necked green overgown that she had worn to Melcombe in the summer. The long sleeves, with their fashionable knots, trailed in the soiled straw.

'My lady . . .' Piers could see the dirt on the cloth. He could also see the baron's face when he surveyed it. 'It might be best . . .'

Joanna half turned, her face set in concentration. 'What is it, Piers?'

'It will soon be time for dinner, my lady. I am afraid that this stable is not suitable for your . . .' He paused, trying to frame his thoughts correctly. 'It's filthy . . .'

'So? This horse may die. What is the more important – this

valuable mare and her foal, or a little dirt on my dress?'

'As you wish, my lady.' Piers gave up his attempt. 'As you wish.'

He wanted to add that her father kept trained grooms to avoid the necessity of his only daughter grovelling in the dirty straw of a foaling stable, but thought better of it. He understood better than anyone Joanna's feelings about the horses. He scratched at an itch behind the stump of his ear as he considered how he had helped instil them in her. He just hoped that the baron would understand. He had a sneaking suspicion about who would get the blame if he did not.

Piers looked across at his son. The boy – usually full of high-spirited good humour – was staring thoughtfully down at the kneeling woman. Was he, like her, concerned at the fate of the mare? Or was he considering her father's reaction to the dark stains that were even now spreading across the fine weave of her dress?

'Console her, Stephen. She's very frightened.' Joanna had pushed her head up under the mare's tail. 'The legs of the foal are stuck somewhere. I can feel them out of line.' She glanced back at her childhood friend. 'Go on, Stephen. It's no good just standing there!'

Resigned to the inevitable, Stephen knelt down beside the mare and stroked her sweat-matted mane. He crooned to her in a lilting accent the way his mother had to Joanna when she was a child. Piers too now accepted there was no way back. He reached for a wooden tub of goose grease and crouched down beside the baron's redhead daughter.

'I'll apply the grease, my lady. You feel for the little hooves. See if you can guide them out.' He patted the heaving point of the mare's buttock. 'She will help you as best she can. But it's guidance the foal needs. Guidance and a lot of grease.' He leaned forward and set to work, Joanna beside him.

Meanwhile, in the wood-panelled solar, Gilbert was in conversation with the sheriff. The room was sparsely furnished with a heavy locked chest in one corner, a trestle table beside the unshuttered window and two carved oak benches. The sleeping mattresses used by Gilbert, his pages and chamber knights were stacked by the door. On the wall a hanging carpet, of Middle Eastern design, was evidence that once Gilbert had 'taken the cross' himself.

Hubert de Burgh was studying the masterpiece carefully. 'A very fine work.' He ran a scarred finger across the threads. 'Well executed. You were with King Richard in the Holy Land.' He turned a heavy-jowled face towards his host. The cheeks beneath the dark beard were pitted from a long-past disease.

Gilbert signalled to one of the hovering household knights to bring wine from the discreet butler who stood in the corner. Hubert held out his silver goblet and it was instantly refilled.

'I took the cross in '90. The year after Richard did.'

His tall, slightly stooping frame straightened at the thought. It had been twelve long years ago. Before his hair had thinned and faded from the intensity of his daughter's shade, before grey had dusted his beard, like ash on old coals.

'And you fought with the Lionheart at the battle of Arsuf. A great day for Christendom.'

'That it was, by God's grace. I can still feel the heat on my back. Can still see the dunes beside the sea and the Saracens pouring from the forest beside the coast road.' He murmured as it flooded back. 'There was some sword-play that afternoon, I can tell you. And at the end of the day the field of battle was ours . . .'

'But the Holy City untaken from the infidel.'

The comment was matter-of-fact but in its own way brutal. Gilbert looked carefully at his guest. Was he seeking to make some kind of point? It was possible. Anything was possible these days. A man had to be very careful.

'That is a sadness which is with me still. I saw it as Richard did, but we could not take it back.' He took another sip from his goblet; the wine had a fine bouquet. It seemed far removed from the dusty road to Jerusalem. 'Do you know what he did? He covered his face with his shield. Said that if he could not free it, then he was not fit to see it. He was quite a man was Richard.'

Gilbert placed his goblet on the trestle. What he did not add was that Richard had returned from the Holy Land because his brother John had conspired against him in his absence. But de Burgh knew that and must know what was in Gilbert's mind for, after all, de Burgh was the King's chamberlain and John's man. Gilbert smiled carefully, for there were things best left unsaid.

'You have a fine manor here, Gilbert. Everyone knows of the richness of the grazing and the excellent horses you breed. The King himself delights in your success and in the loyalty you show him.'

Gilbert did not take his eyes from those of the sheriff. 'I am the loyal servant of my liege lord the King.'

'I know.' Hubert smiled a thin smile. 'Yet there are those who are less than eager in his service.'

'The barons of Poitou and the French King have learned to their cost that God protects the rightness of the King's rule in his French lands.' Gilbert phrased his words carefully. 'And the King's nephew, the Duke of Brittany, has paid a heavy price for his treason against his uncle.'

'But even here, in this realm, there are those whose loyalty is less than it should be.'

De Cantelo made no reply. It was less than a year since this very sheriff had humbled the proud Lovells of nearby Castle Cary. Now no baron was safe from forced loans as proof of his loyalty to the Crown. Gilbert knew he was more closely hemmed in than ever he was at Arsuf, between the forest and the sea.

'You may convey to John that my house holds its honour dear and its loyalty to his person no less dearly. What I hold is from him and all I have is his to call upon . . .'

Hubert de Burgh smiled again. 'I know, Gilbert. I know.' The sheriff coughed. 'And after you, your daughter will be as loyal, even though her sex will not permit her to fulfil the same knight service as you.'

It was difficult to tell whether this was a statement, or a question. Gilbert pondered its implications with a slight sense of unease. 'Of course. She loves the King as much as I do.' He tried hard to penetrate behind de Burgh's words.

Hubert yawned. His teeth were large and very white. Gilbert

noticed that one, in line with his moustache, was strangely pointed, like that of a wolf. The analogy troubled him.

It was long past time that Joanna was betrothed, he admitted to himself. There had been tentative alliances and it was only a twelvemonth since a nine-year-old well-born fiancé had been carried off by the white fever. Now it was time to act and not to tarry any longer. Now was not the time for an heiress to stand alone. Perhaps he had played out her childhood for too long. Sixteen years made her a woman; she was no longer a child. The thought saddened him.

Something about de Burgh's interest disturbed him. Things were unsettled in the realm. Gilbert de Cantelo looked out of the window to where the sun played over his manor house and his beloved horses. They were his to hold and protect – for her, his beloved daughter.

'I have not yet had the honour of meeting the lady Joanna today. She was but a slip of a girl when last I saw her. Now she must be almost a woman grown. I hear that she is very beautiful.'

Gilbert too was beginning to wonder where his daughter was. Out in the adjoining first-floor hall the dinner was almost ready. Soon it would be time to settle at the top table with the sheriff and his retinue. Joanna should have been there.

'I must pass a message to my steward, if you will excuse me a moment.' De Burgh nodded with practised geniality at Gilbert's request.

Out in the high vaulted hall Ranulf Dapifer was hovering. Gilbert summoned him and spoke briefly. The tonsured steward frowned and replied cautiously. He spoke quietly and only Gilbert caught his words. The effect was immediate. The baron's face creased with a frown and he shook his head.

Matilda was passing on her way to Joanna's chamber. As she came close to the baron and the steward she caught a few words of their conversation. Only her eyes registered a flicker of alarm, for she knew where Joanna was and how filthy the stables were. Otherwise her face was perfectly composed as she left the hall with quickened step.

Gilbert spent a little time watching his busy servants, then he turned back towards the solar where the sheriff was waiting. Before the door he paused as if he had changed his mind. He strode back down the hall and out past the scurrying servants.

He hurried down the external stone stairway and past the open doors to the undercroft storerooms. For a moment he paused, looking across the courtyard. Anxious and puzzled retainers hovered about, unsure of how to react to his sudden unattended presence.

In the stable Piers and Joanna were pulling on the shoulders of a struggling foal. Only its head was as yet unrevealed. 'Easy,' Piers counselled. 'It'll come if we pull at the next contraction.' He dipped his fingers in the goose grease and eased them around the shoulders of the foal.

With a united pull the foal was out. It lay exhausted on the straw, almost in Joanna's lap. Stephen let out his breath in a noisy sigh.

'Well done. Well done.'

Whether he was congratulating the mare, the foal, or Piers and Joanna, it was hard to tell. As he leaned against the mare to look, the baby shook its head and shivered violently.

'It'll be on its feet in no time.' Piers was suddenly aware of how high the sun was. 'Your father will be wondering where you are, my lady.'

Joanna stood up and surveyed the wreckage of her dress. 'Don't forget, Stephen – if the foal has not suckled by nightfall, you'll need to milk the dam and . . .'

Stephen grinned rebelliously. 'Thank you, my lady, I'd not have thought of that on my own!'

Joanna laughed at herself. Who was she to tell them? Then she was aware of the shadow at the doorway. She turned in surprise.

'The mare is fine, Tilly. We thought that we might lose her *and* the foal. But now both will be all right . . .'

She stopped as she saw that her maid had been running and had a scarlet velvet gown draped over one arm. Before she could say anything, Tilly hurried forward and whispered in her ear.

A look of concern crossed Joanna's face. For a moment she hesitated as she considered the news which her maid had brought.

Then, the concentration giving birth to action, she turned to the two men.

'I am changing.' When their faces registered total lack of understanding she added, as if it was the usual routine, 'I am going to change into a new gown. And I will be doing it here.' She had a way of commanding circumstances and making the most ridiculous ideas sound like perfect decorum. 'Watch the door for me. I have no intention of putting on a display for the stable boys.'

Piers regained a little of his composure. 'But my lady, surely you cannot . . .' His words began to melt away. 'Not here. Not . . .' Stephen was grinning.

'I most certainly shall. And right now. So out of here, the both of you. I'm relying on you two to guard my honour. And to keep quiet about this . . .'

Only in the last sentence did her confidence waver a little. It was as if the statement was a request. A request to trusted friends and conspirators. Piers nodded. He gave his laughing son a shove and propelled him out of the stable door into the yard.

'Now hurry, Tilly; if you are right I have little time to accomplish this. For if Father wants me in the solar already I shall never have time to change at the hall . . .'

The two young women ducked to one side of the nearest wooden partition. Behind them the mare leaned forward and licked at the damp and shining body of her shivering foal.

When Gilbert arrived he found his two best grooms occupying the doorway into the stable in a most suspicious manner. He knew exactly what was going on. He knew the foal was due and could see the blood on their hose and tunics. Frowning, he ordered them to explain themselves. A sound of scurrying from within made him forgo his interrogation. Instead he ordered them aside.

When Gilbert stepped through the door the first sight which met him was that of his daughter. She was standing quite composed and was watching an unsteady foal attempt to stand. She was wearing a bright-red gown. The expanse of expensive cloth was quite untouched by dirt or stain.

Before he could speak, she turned. 'Oh, Father, it is a colt. I knew that you would be so pleased. I am so glad you have come. I could not wait to tell you.' She stepped lightly to him and kissed him on the cheek. She was all smiles.

'The sheriff is waiting . . .' He was clearly nonplussed and looking at Tilly in the most suspicious manner. She bowed meekly at his gaze.

Joanna raised a hand to her mouth. 'Oh, Father, I am sorry. But as you can see I am quite ready. Shall I come with you now?'

Gilbert looked as if he wanted to say something, and the corner of his mouth twitched. Instead he allowed himself a slight smile. 'I think that would be best, Joanna.' He beckoned to her to take his arm. 'And after dinner we must talk about this new addition to the manor. And . . .' the words betrayed his curiosity, ' . . .and about whatever happened to the green dress you were wearing when you left the hall this morning.'

Joanna took his arm and answered half his question. 'The foal is fine, Father.'

'I am sure that it is, my sweeting.'

Gilbert had the look of one who was more interested in the second of the two questions. He also had the look of a man who had dismissed the disquiet raised by de Burgh's comments, at least for the present. He walked across the yard arm in arm with his beloved daughter. As they passed the steward, neither noticed the creases in Dapifer's frowning brow.

Behind them, Stephen and Matilda were standing by the doorway of the stable. Both seemed quite unaware that they were standing so close that their hands were lightly touching. Then Tilly glanced down, suffused pink, pulled up her gown and ran after her mistress.

In the winter of 1202 King John wore his crown and celebrated Christmas at Caen, the fortress of the 'Conqueror' and first city of the dukedom of Normandy. It was a season of little goodwill. The summer campaigning had not closed with the King's seizure of Tours and Angers in late September. Neither had there been the traditional 'harvest truce'. Instead, the fighting – which it had seemed for a moment might have been stopped by John's dramatic victory at Mirabeau – had dragged on into the winter.

Within the high walls of the castle, great braziers burnt in the halls and chambers. But it was a mild and wet December. The fires burnt as much to dry robes as to heat the stone-walled rooms.

All excursions ended in mud and soaking clothing; it seemed to have rained for weeks. Even the sparrows chirped in an irritated manner from the eves of the painted towers of the donjon and were reluctant to venture forth into the drift of grey rain.

It was the fast day on the eve of St Thomas' day; Friday, 20 December. In the bedchamber of the King all was activity. Around a great tub of hot – and now increasingly greasy – water hovered the King's ewerer. Beyond him were the other chamber officials of the royal household – the King's tailor, the King's bed carrier and the King's butler. Looking on, from before the locked royal treasure chest, were the ever-alert court chamberlain and the chamberlain of the Winchester treasury.

Every simple task was the jealously guarded responsibility of a member of the nobility, all of whom waited for the slightest gesture of the royal hand, or nod of the royal head.

Reclining in his bath with eyes shut, and seemingly unaware of the host about him, was a man of below average height, with a well-built frame drifting towards excess. A close-clipped beard and wavy dark hair, cut below the ears, framed a face that was dark in complexion.

John, by the grace of God, King of England, Lord of Ireland, Duke of Normandy and Aquitaine, Count of Anjou and Mortain, opened his eyes. Like his complexion they were dark; like the set of his face they were slightly mocking.

'Come.'

The chamber knights sprang forward. As the King rose naked from his bath, one draped a thick woollen robe about him. Jewelled rings were slipped on to outstretched fingers. A goblet, worked from white silver, was instantly brought to the summoning palm.

The king drank deeply of the wine. Without a word he handed the goblet back to the retiring butler and took the wand of gold offered by another pair of obedient hands.

'So – what do we know about him?' John stepped from the tub and was instantly fitted with a pair of soft ankle boots. 'And what do the Christian brothers of the Temple mean by this embassy of his?' The King held up the letter with the seal of the two Poor Knights. The seal was broken.

The King's chamberlain, Hubert de Burgh, who had ridden north from his fortress of Falaise to join the court for the twelve-day feast, took the refilled goblet of wine from the approaching butler and handed it to the King himself.

'It seems he is an honest and loyal knight . . .'

'As honest and loyal as my barons of Poitou who rebelled against me?' The renowned Angevin temper was stirring. 'As honest and loyal as my seneschal of Anjou and Maine who has conspired against me this autumn . . .' The narrow, mocking eyes were alight with fury. ' . . .Or the loyal servant who now holds Tours against me and bargains with me as if I were a common whore?'

The chamberlain let the moment of fury pass. Only a fool would contradict John in such a mood. But his emotions were mercurial. The anger would pass; the restless energy would turn aside and focus on something else.

A timid retainer picked up the wet gown which had slipped to the floor. Others stepped smartly forward with the clothes of the day. John sat on the edge of his bath while his richly patterned purple hose were drawn up his legs.

He raised his arms as first a pure linen shirt and then a calf-length surcoat of white, embroidered with gold and silver thread, were lowered over his head. He rose to his feet and a beautifully stitched belt of fine leather was drawn about his waist; all the time his eyes never left de Burgh. But the fire of fury was burning lower.

'There is nothing to connect him with any of those who have committed treason, sire. He holds manors in Normandy, Anjou and in England. He is neither great nor small, but his manors have paid scutage for all that is owed this past year, though he himself was in the Holy Land.'

'Ahh . . . a companion no doubt of my dearly lamented brother?'

'He took the cross after your brother returned from Jerusalem.'

John smiled. 'No doubt while Richard was the guest of the Emperor.'

There was a note of triumph in the King's voice, as if his brother's imprisonment on his way home from the east was something to be set in the scales against his glorious reputation.

'What manner of man is he, then?'

'By all reports a chivalrous one whose courage is remarked upon. But he has been injured. He will not fight again as once he did. Now he pursues the selection and breeding of warhorses. It is his mission . . .'

John smiled. 'A man with a mission. Well, well . . . That will be a new experience at my court, where I am surrounded by timeservers and traitors. I must meet this man with a mission. Bring him to me. Bring him to me now.'

Richard was waiting in an antechamber. From an open window he could see down on to the crowded burghal tenements and messuages of the town. Smoke rose, drifting up through the dripping thatch of countless crowded timber-framed houses. Somewhere down there his prize mares were stabled under the protection of Umar and the sergeants.

Before he had left them he had discussed the mares' feed and bedding with the Saracen. He had come to rely on him and, despite his own considerable knowledge of horses, he respected the Arab's quietly spoken opinions. Richard looked across the roofs to where his hopes were even now resting in their stalls.

Mark de Dinan leaned against the wall beside him and followed his gaze. It seemed months since the fight at the ford in the hot dry days of October. Now, he mused, it was hard to believe that there had ever been cloudless skies. He glanced at his knight, thinking that Richard had not healed as swiftly as he had hoped.

It had been well into November before they had escorted the Jew to the safety of the square grey castle of Falaise, set up on its rocky crag. There in the shadow of the donjon they had passed the merchant moneylender into the safekeeping of the little garrison which was awaiting the arrival of its new constable from

England. Then it had been on to Caen to await the arrival of the King.

'I've never seen the King.' Mark tried to keep the excitement from his voice. 'What is he like?'

'Wears a crown. They all do.'

Mark was not put off by the tease. 'No, my lord. Not what does he look like, but what is he like?'

Richard smiled at his companion's curiosity. It was at times like this that he realised how young the squire truly was. Or was it just that he felt older nowadays?

The city was full of rumours from the east. Of inadequate numbers of crusaders travelling to Venice. Of the very future of the crusade being in jeopardy. There was even talk that the money-grubbing Venetians were using crusader knights to fight their own private war against the King of Hungary before they would transport them to their destination. Whether they were true or not, there was a sourness in the rumours.

Richard shrugged off the grey thoughts. He would not let the shadows spoil things now. He focused his mind on the horses and the importance of his mission. Soon now John would hear of it. The letter from the Grand Master in Acre would be the key forward. The King's favour would be so important.

'The King, my lord?' Mark looked at him, seeming a little confused.

Richard dismissed his contemplations. 'The King? He's got more mistresses than you've met women. He has a temper and a tongue that would blister paint. He is ruthless and angry – but clever.' He laughed to see Mark's concentration. 'More than that, he can be grasping and generous, astute and reckless, determined and irresolute . . .'

'But that sounds more like two men than one.'

'That's John. Enough character to make a contradicting army. And they say you never know which one you'll meet. It perhaps explains why not all like him and why many fear him. He is also permanently short of money.'

Mark glanced about with concern. He wished he had not asked the question now. It was too typical of his master to speak his mind and Mark had heard that the court could be dangerous.

Richard noticed the look. 'Have no fear. There are none can hear us here. And when I am with him I shall be as careful as a rutting hedgehog.' Over his squire's head he saw the approach of Hubert de Burgh. 'Hush now. Here comes a hedgehog on heat . . .'

De Burgh beckoned with a ring-laden finger and led Richard along a corridor, the cold stones of which were covered with tapestries. They passed through an open door into a room abuzz with activity.

Richard knew immediately who John was, though he had never seen him before. The movement in the room revolved about him. He was the pivot, the one fixed position, the hub of the room. Besides which, no one else wore cloth to compare with his.

The King was eating a boiled egg. A clutch more lay shelled on a silver dish. Richard had heard of the King's passion for them.

'The Grand Master of the Templars recommends you to me.' Before Richard could speak he added: 'And informs me that your aim is the breeding of bigger and better horses. It is a noble aim. There are no finer horses than those on my own stud farms. Do you not agree?'

'That is quite so, my lord. But it is bigger and fiercer yet that we must have, horses which will take a man better armoured than ever. Horses that will carry armour themselves and shrug off arrows and the jab of spears . . .'

John reached for another egg. 'That would be a horse indeed.' His narrow eyes bored into Richard's. 'And how do you mean to find such horses?' He bit into the yielding white.

'I have ten magnificent Arab mares. Each has been chosen for its height and strength; for its hot blood and its great intelligence.' The passion was obvious in his voice. 'I seek stallions to match them. And then of their offspring, to mate only the greatest and discard the rest.' The restless energy was abroad once more.

De Burgh glanced at the King, who smiled pleasantly at Richard. 'You may find there is great expense in this work.'

'I have dedicated the best of my manors to this. I do not lavish wealth on myself.' The King raised a disbelieving eyebrow. 'And the Templars have a financial interest in this also. For they too desire the security of Christendom.'

'Ahh yes. The Grand Master says you have his "approval".' The monarch let the word drift away. 'Though you are not a Templar yet. That is most unusual. Do you not think so?'

De Lacey considered the question. 'I hope that it is a measure of his confidence in me.'

'Yes,' John agreed, but his eyes were cold, 'perhaps that is what it is.' He rubbed an emerald which shone from his ring. 'And with whom will you trade horses in Normandy?'

Richard saw the danger. 'Only with those who are loyal to your majesty.'

'Good, good . . .' The dark eyes narrowed again. 'For the Templars have many manors granted by my perfidious enemy the King of France. And is not the uncle of Hugh de Lusignan – whom I have seized for his treasons – is not this very uncle King of Jerusalem?'

Richard felt the ground quake beneath his feet. 'The Knights of the Temple do not take sides in the disputes of kings.' John looked unimpressed. 'And besides, as you have rightly pointed out, I am not actually a Templar.'

There was silence. Then the King laughed. He laughed and laughed. His chamber attendants took the cue and joined in with him. 'Well answered, knight. A man with a mission but also with a quick tongue. I like it. And more than that, you saved my fine milch cow – the Jew of Dorchester.' John laughed sharply. 'I'll not have another milking that fine herd or slaughtering them without my permission. You have done me a good service in rescuing him . . .'

John beckoned to Richard to approach him. 'You have my best wishes. I want to hear of the progress of your mission.' Richard had hoped for more than best wishes but said nothing. 'When I have crushed this treason in Normandy, attend on me again.' The King took another bite out of his egg. 'Hubert . . .'

The chamberlain beckoned to Richard to follow and led him from the room.

Half to himself John murmured, 'Well, well, a man with a mission. I shall watch this one.'

★ ★ ★

William Catface had a small face with a snub nose and big eyes. With an agile frame and a light step he had been called 'catface' since he was a child. The matter was quite simple – he really did look like a cat. If ever a feline transmuted itself into human form, it would have resembled William.

His peculiar nickname had become so well established that everyone now used it. It could even be found in the manor court roll. Immortalised by Latin and ink – and by the minuscule hand of Ranulf Dapifer – he was raised up above the anonymous mass of the ubiquitous villein Williams who also appeared in the rolls.

They were fined for numberless misdemeanours, were taxed and chastised and then vanished back into oblivion. Not so William of the big eyes and the light step, for he had achieved more than they. He had become an individual – even in Ranulf Dapifer's eyes. He was William Catface. The irony was that his poor home was the most rodent-infested hovel on the manor.

This morning he had tired of broth made from dried peas and lentils, had grown sick of mouldy bread smeared with the sour scrapings of bacon fat and lard. It was three days after Christmas – Holy Innocents' Day – and William had resolved to eat something fresher and altogether more exciting. He had risen early in his dilapidated, smoky one-roomed cottage, where he, his wife and children shared the same bed. He had thrown off the threadbare blanket, picked straw out of his ears, killed the first flea of the day and then slipped out into the misty half-light.

It had taken about half an hour to climb by narrow paths up on to the downs. All was silent except for the singing of thrushes and the whirring call of wrens in the tangled bushes. The grey veil held back the dawn light.

In a narrow combe, deep-set with brambles, he kept his two dogs. Not ones with their feet mutilated according to forest law but ones which could chase a deer with fleet movements and fill his belly with something better than pease pottage.

Together with his dogs, he hunted out into the rolling plateau, between the many stands of trees; in a land silent and still, except for the breeze rubbing its unseen way through the downland grasses. The bleating of distant sheep, from the Glastonbury Abbey sheepruns, seemed to come from somewhere far away.

He had been out of luck this morning. With daylight well up and the mist clearing, he had turned back towards the edge of the downs above Horsingham.

The thudding of hooves sent him scurrying for cover into a clump of badly coppiced hazel. The horseman was riding hard, clods and grass flying up behind him. There was something familiar about him.

William half stood up to get a better look. No one was more curious, and it was as he stood up that he let go of the scruff of one dog's neck. In an instant it was out.

'Bloody 'ell . . .'

Horse's hooves and dog collided in a chaos of limbs. The horse pitched forward. It drove chest first into the ground. Flailing hooves were crushed beneath the weight of its own body. The rider was flung away like a straw doll.

William was frozen – half crouched, half rising. The dog, unharmed, jogged back, its pink tongue lolling from its open mouth. The horse, however, rolled in agony and could not rise on its broken legs.

At last the poacher moved forward and approached the motionless rider. Dew had soaked the heavy riding cloak and William had a sick feeling as he bent down, for the cloak was very good quality indeed.

He turned the man over. His head lolled in a fluid way and at an unnatural angle. It was obvious from the twist of the neck and the staring eyes that the man was quite dead.

'Bloody 'ell . . .' William knelt down in the wet grass. He turned to the dog which panted beside him. 'You damned cur, just look an' see what you've been an' done . . .' The dog seemed unaware of the catastrophe which it had caused. William punched it savagely and it snarled and leapt away. ''Tis only Gilbert.' He spat with futile anger at what he had done. ''Tis only Gilbert de bloody Cantelo . . .'

Chapter 3

The week after Christmas, Umar, the Saracen groom of Richard de Lacey, was out on the streets of Caen. He knew better than to go alone, even though the Normans had seen Saracen mercenaries operating in the duchy under the authority of the late King Richard.

It was one thing to show grudging respect for a body of armed soldiers living under the protection of the Crown; quite another thing to extend that to a solitary alien. Umar was all too well aware of the hostile stares that he attracted. He had no intention of being lynched by a Norman mob and went in the company of two of Richard's sergeants.

His job this early morning was to purchase a good quantity of bran from the marketplace in order to make a warm mash to accompany the hay and hard feed of the horses. The presence of the veritable army of retainers accompanying the King had driven prices through the roof and made a scarcity of such necessities.

'Down through this way,' one of the sergeants muttered tersely. 'It's a short cut back.'

The men-at-arms were disgruntled at having been hauled from their beds to accompany the Saracen. They found little amusement in tramping the grey streets of the city under an overcast late December sky. They were keen to get back to their dice and the inevitable women who were attracted to the vicinity of bored men with money in their pockets.

The short cut led under the great tree of scaffolding clinging to the two west towers of L'Abbaye-aux-hommes. From within, the bell was tolling for prime and soon the plainchant of the monks would be floating through the damp air.

After a while the short cut dropped down through alleyways with overflowing central gutters and under the creaking signs of cheap craftsmen; tenements whose once whitewashed mud and stud walls were now green with age and mould.

Near the quay the sergeants stopped to purchase food from a street vendor. Umar scorned the slices of pork on trenchers of bread dripping with thick garlic sauce. The sergeants ignored him as they gossiped and spat out the more rancid bits of meat.

'What was that?' Umar turned to one of his reluctant protectors. 'You heard it, no?' His French was a little slow, but clear enough, despite his accent.

The man was irritated at having his snack disturbed. 'Heard what?' It was only the fact that the infidel was held in some favour by de Lacey that stopped him from cuffing the groom for an unwelcome interruption. 'Heard what? Get on with yer bran and leave us in peace!' The other soldier sniggered.

'There it is.' Umar was angry. 'You heard it that time!'

The sergeant cocked his ears but waved an angry hand at the Saracen. 'It's nothing to do with us. Just eat or be silent. We've enough work of our own.'

Umar was not to be so easily dismissed. He had heard it and he recognised it. He threw down his bag of bran and ran along the quay. His boots splashed in the puddles amongst the pitted metalling of the road. He had heard that sound before – the sound of a horse lost in the bloodlust of battle.

The chewing sergeant spat out his mouthful of bread and meat. 'The soddin' heathen,' he exploded in fury. 'What the hell is he up to?'

'We'd better go after the fool,' his companion replied, irritation clear in his voice. 'If he's killed, Malik Rik will have our hides off our backs.' Leaving behind them an open-mouthed trader they set off after the groom.

Umar ran between the leaning wooden warehouses and the vessels tied up at the quay. The noise was getting louder; there was no mistaking it now. He turned a corner and there it was. One man was sprawled on the cobbles. There was blood mingling with the muddy rain water. He lay still. Another man was on his knees, his hands crossed over his face to shield him from the death which reared above him.

'Help me, for God's sake . . .' the man was screaming. 'For God's sake, get it off me.'

No one moved amongst the crowd pressed back against the warehouse timbers. No one went to his aid as each looked to his own safety. A stallion had broken loose. But no mere horse; rather an angel of death in equine form. One of Richard's horses of the Apocalypse had burst through the veil between this world and the next and had become destruction and terror to all who stood in its way.

As Umar watched in fascination and horror, the great hooves struck and the kneeling man was flung backwards. Drops of blood flew from an open wound. Somehow the beast had snapped the standing martingale which had run from the girth, under the mighty breast, and so to the noseband. Freed from the restraining hold of the martingale, the stallion could throw its head wherever it wanted. And it wanted to kill.

It plunged forward. Lips drawn up, its great yellow teeth were bared as it lunged for the crawling man. The ears were laid back and the nostrils pits of blood. Teeth closed upon the back of the man's neck, where it met his shoulders. Umar could hear the crunch as the mighty jaws snapped shut on the man. The scream when it came was a howling gale of terror and pain.

The horse shook the man like a dog breaking the back of a rabbit. Arms flailing, the man was lifted up. He screamed and shouted, his words incoherent in his agony and his fear. The furious horse released its hold and kicked out again, smashing the man's crumpled body. It had been trained to kill, that was clear, and it was dedicated to its task when roused.

Umar ran forward. He snatched a spear from a gawping man-at-arms. 'Oh, oh, oh,' he shouted at the top of his voice. 'Back, back, back.' The horse shied at the unexpected interruption.

Umar ran directly at the stallion and the sudden movement immediately before its nose startled it. The broken leather strap swinging from the cavesson like a whip, the snorting horse leapt backwards and almost fell. One of the watchers made as if to seize the loose leading rein but was smashed against stout timbers by a swing of the massive head.

Umar seized the opportunity to take hold of the blood-sodden padded gambeson of the fallen foot soldier. The man was semi-conscious and clutched at Umar's knees. He was sobbing and vomiting.

Then Richard de Lacey's groom looked up. He could feel the blood drain from his own face at what he saw. The stallion had shaken off the attempt to secure it and was throwing itself towards *him*. All he could see were the great teeth and the dilated pupils as the horse charged.

There was only one thing to do. Even if he could have outrun the stallion, the terrified man was clutching at his feet. He shoved the ash shaft into the face of the oncoming horse. It must pull away, it had to – they always did. His hands and arms were trembling uncontrollably as he clutched the spear.

However, *this* stallion came on with madness blazing in its eyes. Umar thought he was about to die. Words unintelligible to the gawping men-at-arms tumbled from his dry lips. The confession of faith was said as the hooves struck sparks before his eyes.

'*Allahu akbar, Ashhadu alla ilaha illa . . .*'

At the last moment the charging beast pulled away and collided with a warehouse wall. It stumbled and men – emboldened by Umar's raw courage – were on it. Hands clutched the trailing rope, the matted mane, even the broken martingale.

Try as it might the horse could not break free. A man swinging on either side of the bridle, the savage head was at last brought low. After the loss of one man's fingers, the upper lip was seized and twisted with a short length of rope. Stupefied by the twitch the stallion ceased its frenetic efforts to break loose. The battle was over. Already the dead man was being dragged away and mates of the man-at-arms were disentangling the wounded soldier from Umar's legs.

Only now could Umar begin to take in what lay around him. He fought the stabbing pain in his chest as he drank in the cold air like new wine. He was surrounded by foot soldiers, a motley crowd in knee-length padded cloth gambesons and battered kettle hats. Here and there, one more elevated than the rest sported a thigh-length mail hauberk, or a shorter, waist-length, haubergeon. Most were cradling crossbows, though a few held spears.

He realised that they were Brabançons – the feared mercenaries of the king. Clearly they were escorting the stallion to the transport tied at the quayside. Umar shook his head to clear his thoughts.

A handsome yet disturbing face was before him. The chin, square beneath a recently trimmed blond beard, was set arrogantly at him. A long pale scar ran the length of the left jawbone. The hair was fashionably cut below the ears and as white as salt. But the eyes . . . Umar could not break the grip of the eyes. They held him until all he saw were those two pale-blue orbs as cold as a winter sky at dawn. There was interrogation but little gratitude in those eyes.

Then hands were upon Umar, the sergeants were pulling him away to safety. Their irritation was gone, replaced by fear. Umar could almost smell it. They were frightened of the man with the freezing eyes. Trembling, they were excusing themselves and Umar, as if he had inconvenienced the mercenaries instead of having saved a life.

The whole episode was unreal. As if in a dream Umar allowed himself to be drawn away but the details were so vivid. He saw that the man wore mail which, unlike that of even his most exalted companions, was not spotted with rust. He carried a sword too and his gambeson was whole and clean. A kettle helmet hung at his waist.

But more important was the horse. Trembling, it was being led towards the ship, and it was huge – at least eighteen hands tall at the withers. It was dapple grey and terrifyingly beautiful. All this Umar memorised for his master. For he knew that the horse was what Richard de Lacey was seeking; indeed it was what de Lacey's life was built upon.

Joanna de Cantelo sat in one corner of the solar, a small sewing box, with ivory inlay, on the trestle table beside her. It had not been opened and beside it lay the needlework – laid ready but quite untouched.

Tilly was with her, but today there was no chatter about the plans to visit Sherborne; no shy references to Stephen Pierson or news about the maid's father with the King in Normandy; no gossip about the son of the manor's woodward, who had felled the reeve in a drunken brawl. All news, plans and gossip had been eclipsed.

A steady rain fell against the shutters on the windows. It was only a couple of hours after noon on this January day, but the light was already fading away. It had turned a little colder since Christmas but there had been no frost; no silver coverlet cast down over the trees and meadows, or laid across the face of the sleeping hills which looked down on Horsingham.

Instead, the colder weather had come accompanied by low cloud and rain. For days on end the horizon was shut down by a wall of grey. The scarp of the downs was only a shadow and the world reduced to the soaking manor and its steaming horses. It seemed appropriate, for it was as if the world were enveloped in a great sadness, a cosmic mourning of endless tears.

It was quite unlike Joanna to brood this way, but nothing like the death of her father had touched her before. She sat and listened to Ranulf Dapifer and part of her was convinced that at any moment she would awake from this whole dreadful dream.

'The coroners will report to the shire court about the circumstances surrounding your father's tragic death.' He made sure she was listening to him. He had never seen her this way before – so subdued. 'It is expected that you will attend the court to hear their findings . . .'

Joanna nodded. 'I will attend . . . It is my duty and I shall be there.'

In the week following the discovery of her father dead and the horse mortally injured, the knights elected as coroners by the shire court had ridden to the manor. She knew them, of course, for they were country knights as her father had been. As one of the lesser barons, he almost had more in common with them than with the greater tenants-in-chief who held vast tracts of land from the King.

Their grief had been as real as her own. So it was with particular diligence that they carried out their unpaid duty of investigating this sudden death. Now the results of their enquiries would be published before the full shire court where representatives from all the local hundred-courts met before the sheriff and the itinerant judges of the King.

Ranulf coughed slightly. It was an irritating cold he had picked up in the damp weather, for no amount of rain came between the steward and his duty. 'There is no doubt that your father's death was an accident.' He held his hands together as if in prayer. 'The juries empanelled from the four neighbouring manors found no malice in the death. Though only Our Lady knows why the horse stumbled . . .'

'It has paid the price for its fall. As dearly as my father paid.'

There was no vindictiveness in her voice, only a grim acceptance. She knew full well that Piers had cut the throat of the broken stallion and put an end to its misery.

Ranulf continued: 'It will take little time to present the matter at the court. The King's judges are more interested in accusations of felony brought forward from the hundred-courts and in hanging rogues caught in the act and held over by the sheriff.' He shuffled pieces of paper. 'It is the custom regarding the price of the horse which . . .'

'Which killed my father.' Joanna nodded. 'Thank you, Ranulf, I had almost forgotten the deodand. I shall have Piers estimate the worth of the horse . . .'

Her voice stopped. Ranulf looked up with surprise. Her throat was working convulsively and her eyes were brimming. She reddened at his stare but could not finish her sentence. She did not trust herself to speak. At any moment she expected the sobs to break forth in a torrent.

Tilly watched her and shared her agony but could do nothing for her. At last Ranulf broke the silence and ended the need for further conversation.

'I took the liberty of estimating the cost of the offering to the church, my lady.' He glanced down at his slip of vellum. 'It seems that the price of the horse was ten pounds.' He frowned. 'It seems high for even your father's palfrey but the stock was very good. It was an excellent riding horse.'

Joanna nodded, composed at last. 'Ten pounds . . . how many silver pennies is that?'

Ranulf paused. 'Two thousand, four hundred, my lady.'

Now there *was* a note of bitterness in her voice. 'Then that is the price of our gift to the church. The worth of the horse that killed him. The price of my father's life . . .'

Ranulf Dapifer made no reply. It embarrassed him when she allowed her emotions to show in this way. But this much he granted her – the death of her father seemed to have brought her down to earth at last. He had hardly seen her amongst the horses since Gilbert's death. She had spent most of her time about the hall ordering the business of the funeral.

It was tragic but it seemed that only such a sorrow could bring her to an acceptance of her true place. Her free flying had been constrained. Ranulf was sad for her but could not help but feel that it was all for the best. After all, no one was free to do anything that they pleased. Acceptance of one's station was part of the order of things. He had long accepted his and now it was time for her to accept hers. Gilbert living had never been able to supply the lesson of duty as well as Gilbert dead.

Ranulf felt strangely more comfortable in her presence now. It was as if a ghost which had haunted his thinking had been exorcised at last. Listening to the rain against the shutters, he would have been hard put to name that which had once so troubled him. But name it or not, since the death of Gilbert de Cantelo the jealousy that the steward had felt for Joanna had declined dramatically.

'There is one other matter, my lady . . .'

'If it is the matter of the bequest, then I have made up my mind.' Joanna was composed again but still brittle. 'I shall make over the sum, requesting that prayers be said for my father's soul daily and to celebrate mass on the anniversary of his death.' There was a distant look in her green eyes and it was as if she was suddenly alone. 'It seems right to settle the endowment on St Mary's, in Sherborne. He loved the abbey and was a good friend of the church there, as well as the one here on the manor. It is as you would have wanted . . .'

Ranulf caught the word 'you' and frowned. 'I think that your decision is a wise one, my lady. But it is of another matter that I would speak with you.'

Joanna nodded. 'Go on.'

Ranulf pursed his lips. His brown eyes narrowed as he considered the subject. 'It is of the matter of your wardship, my lady . . .'

'You have heard more than I have?' The girl's tone was sharp and questioning. 'If so then I will know now.'

Ranulf noted the emotion in her voice and chose his words carefully. 'I know no more than you, my lady,' he lied. 'But it seems right that we should prepare ourselves. The sheriff is back from France, though for how long I do not know. It is clear that now he is back he will settle the matter of your wardship.'

'I had heard that he was at Falaise.' Joanna was surprised. With the King in Normandy and the sheriff across the Channel too she had hoped that she could avoid thinking about the inevitable. 'When did he return?'

'I heard in Sherborne that he landed at Southampton last week. It seems likely that he will organise the wardship while he is here.'

'I should not be a ward, I am sixteen and no heiress should be taken as a ward of the King beyond her fourteenth year.'

The steward noted a flash of the old Joanna. Lines creased his forehead. 'There is little doubt that the King will place you as his ward, my lady.' A tiny note of triumph played about the edges of his voice. 'For in such troubled times it is not likely that he will allow the lands of your father to lie for long in a woman's hands . . .'

Joanna reddened and Ranulf continued quickly as if to absolve himself from any blame in the matter. 'My late lord – your father – must have advised you of the way in which these matters are handled. No land owing knights to the King can remain out of the hands of a man . . .'

'I can pay scutage as well as my father did.' The argument was rehearsed as if she had been expecting such a conversation. 'What does it matter whether the pennies come from my hand or that of a man?'

Ranulf paled. He could hear her using the same argument before the sheriff, perhaps even higher . . . The thought troubled him. Not that it would do her any good. There was nothing that a woman could do and she must see that. What concerned him was the trouble that such futile resistance might cause. He had no wish for trouble in this matter. It would disrupt the smooth passage of the baron's manors into royal wardship.

'It is the way of things.' He relaxed in the presence of the argument, for custom subsumed individual resistance. 'By rights the King may – and will – take the estates of your father into wardship and you will be in his gift.'

'The gift of the King . . .' The words were pitched low. It was as if once more she spoke to another. 'The gift of the King . . .'

'Aye, my lady. You are in his gift – to give in marriage to whom he chooses.' Ranulf bit on the impulse to add that in the present financial climate there would be many who would seek her by offering good silver to the outstretched royal hand. 'It is the custom for all heiresses to be in the gift of their lord.'

Joanna looked directly at him. It was as if she had only just heard what he had said. It was as if her words had been merely rhetorical and she was shocked by his reply.

'I am well aware of that, Ranulf. As you say – it is the custom. The custom for high and low.'

'Yes, my lady.' The steward looked relieved. 'For high and for low.'

Joanna stood up. She looked at the grief-stricken face of her maid. There was nothing that Tilly could do for her. No amount of loyalty could overcome the great force which was sweeping away her life. One fall on the downs and the familiar had been swept away as if it had never been. Joanna's eyes met those of Tilly. If there was a mirror held up to her pain then she was gazing into it.

'I shall remain here until the matter is settled.'

Ranulf nodded. It had been the custom for Gilbert to spend the autumn at Horsingham, the spring on his manor in Gloucestershire and then return, via his estate on the Somerset-Wiltshire border, to his Dorset manor in time to survey the results of the summer foaling. It had been a routine which with some variation was as reliable as the cycle of the year. Gilbert had only broken it the previous summer to personally supervise the arrival of the mares at Melcombe.

'I think that you are wise, my lady. With this manor being the chief estate it is appropriate that the sheriff of this shire will have responsibility for the whole matter. To remain here until it is settled is prudent.'

It gave him a surprising sense of wellbeing to stand in quiet judgement on her actions. He was also relieved to hear the passion die down out of her voice. He had no time for passion.

On Friday, 1 February 1203, Richard de Lacey sailed from the port of Honfleur. Safely harnessed and slung in the hold of the stout little ship were his precious mares. To port the tall, deeply indented cliffs rose above the pebble beaches. It was a slow day's sail along the Norman coast in the face of changeable winds.

Standing in the forecastle of the vessel, Richard wiped a tear from his eyes. The wind was making it hard to see. Mark leaned on the rail beside him and was also peering into the distance. He was feeling sick and was already beginning to hate the journey. Though even torture would never have made him divulge his weakness to his knight.

'Umar was right, the horse sounds like a prince amongst stallions.' He looked to where the Saracen sat beside the entrance to the hold, where the precious mares were. Richard was smiling despite the cold and the spray. 'What a shame I could not have seen it myself.'

Mark nodded in agreement, although it went against the grain to give credit to the Saracen. 'Is it what we are seeking?'

Richard grinned. 'It most certainly is.' Ever since Umar had returned with his report, de Lacey had been tireless in his quest for the great horse. 'All who have seen it remark on its size, strength and ferocity. It seems to have spirit like few other warhorses, and I've seen a few . . .' He chuckled. 'I heard only today – before we left Honfleur – that the creature is called Soloriens. A fitting name for such a proud beast – Sunrise!' It was a fitting name too for the stallion of the rebel baron Hugh de Lusignan, who had risen in arms against King John.

Mark was happy to see Richard so pleased. Consequently he was loath to put a fly into the ointment. Nevertheless there was a matter which intrigued him.

'But if the King has taken it as a hostage, how will we ever gain the use of it?' De Dinan was sure that Richard had thought of something.

Richard saw the look in the eyes of his squire. He had not yet worked out how he was going to manage the matter but was not going to say so. Instead he said, 'Hugh de Lusignan must be an angry man indeed.' And so avoided the issue. 'It must have been bad enough to have been seized himself at Mirabeau, but to know that John has taken his prize warhorse for stud! That adds insult to the injury all right.'

Mark was thinking hard. The concentration was fairly obvious and Richard grimaced. 'It looks painful, Mark. What particular thought is causing you such grief? Out with it before it gives you a seizure.'

Mark sighed. 'Hugh is nephew of the King of Jerusalem and John's enemy.'

'Very good!' Richard was always amused at Mark's step-by-step thinking. 'That's why he tried to grab John's mother at Mirabeau. Though personally I'd as soon steal kisses from a cockatrice.'

Mark was not diverted from the progress of his thoughts. 'But the King of Jerusalem is very important to the Templars. And now John has seized his nephew. He cannot be best pleased with this.'

Richard could begin to see the way that the conversation was going and he was not thrilled by it. He made as if to interrupt his squire, but then thought better of it. Mark did not notice as he continued his deliberations.

'So that leaves us trying to persuade John to let us use the horse, which he has seized from Hugh, which must anger Amalric of Jerusalem, whom no Templar would wish to annoy . . .'

Mark looked pleased that he had managed to say it all at once. Richard was a little less overjoyed. Instead he steeled himself for the inevitable question. 'Yeees . . .?' he said slowly. 'Go on . . .'

'How are we going to do it without upsetting either John, or the Grand Master, or even both of them?'

The question was so profound that it was only weakened in its impact by the fact that Mark was clearly unaware of the tremendous impact of his point. He looked at Richard, expecting him to knock down the obstacle with a simple statement of genius.

Instead Richard just laughed. He pointed to the horizon. 'Do you see that stack there? You can see why it's called the "Dog's Tooth", can't you?'

Only then did the realisation finally dawn on Mark that they really were facing a very difficult enterprise indeed. One so difficult that Richard himself had not yet got any idea how to accomplish it.

Following Richard's pointing finger, Mark had to agree that it did indeed look like a dog's tooth, or better still that of a wolf. He had a niggling feeling that that was all too appropriate. For he sensed that they were being tethered out for the wolves. It was not a very pretty prospect.

The conversation was over and without further comment the two men watched the wind drive the waves. When darkness fell they retired for the night with few words between them. Richard slept badly in the narrow cabin that he shared with his squire and the other passengers of knightly rank.

The thought of the horse, Soloriens, was like a beacon. Whenever the bitter thoughts and fears swept over him, he held it up, the light blazed and the darkness fled. When Umar had told him of it he knew that it was what he was seeking. He had never seen the groom so impressed with a horse, and Umar was not a man given to unstinted praise.

Richard wrapped the blanket more closely about him, for the cabin was cold and damp. He pondered on the question raised by

Mark. It was the blot on the page of vellum, the little cloud on a summer horizon. He could not ignore it and knew it was too important to disregard.

It would be no easy thing to get access to such a stallion at the best of times. And these were not the best of times. Mark's straightforward question had laid that out all too clearly. Now was just the time when putting a foot wrong had become a very common game. Those now languishing in the dungeons at Falaise knew that well enough.

As he pondered, Richard reflected ironically that at that very moment the stallion's owner was probably lying awake thinking of it too. What would he say if he knew how badly Richard wanted to get hold of it? Richard laughed softly. And what would John say? What would the Grand Master say? And Amalric – in his fortress at Acre? Richard did not laugh any more. It had ceased to be funny. He would have to be very careful indeed.

With the dawn the wind veered until it was at their backs. The sail filled and the vessel drove along the eastern side of the Cherbourg peninsula. The change in the wind promised a favourable speed for the Channel crossing once they headed out into the open sea.

The horses were restless but safe in their hammocks. Richard supervised Umar as he distributed the hay brought on board for the purpose of feeding the animals on the short crossing. When that was done there was a light noontime repast of cold salted meat and damp bread. Then there was little to do but watch the dark sea as it flowed past the confident thrust of the little hull.

'There's a ship over there keeping pace with us . . .' Mark de Dinan pointed to starboard. 'She's been there a while now.'

Richard paused from eating the last crust of his flat loaf. Mark was right: sure enough, they seemed to have picked up a companion. Like them it dipped and rose in the choppy sea. He pondered the other vessel for a few moments before he replied.

'Someone to keep us company. You had better spew on the other side this afternoon, Mark.' Richard indicated the port beam. 'I doubt that they'll want to witness your supper being fed to the fish.'

Mark gave a pained and rueful look. Until Richard had mentioned it, he had forgotten his nausea. Now he was once more aware of the slowly rising sickness in his stomach and throat. Without opening his mouth to reply he made his way across the shifting deck timbers.

Richard finished his bread, noticing that the other ship was still with them. If anything, it was closer – a lot closer. De Lacey could make out the men in the bulky castles fore and aft. Other men were active about the ropes below the square sail, which was flapping and cracking from the single, central mast.

'Rather different from the ships off Acre aren't they?' Richard remarked casually to his returning, pale-faced squire. 'There they always seemed so much lighter somehow, for all that they carried two masts . . .'

'And the sails like a pennant, not like these great heavy square things.' Mark peered at their neighbour. 'They are very close now, aren't they?'

Richard had stood up. He was frowning. Around him sailors were staring too. Something was wrong. Their ship's master called something across the rapidly closing distance. There was no reply, and the gap between the two cogs was lessening by the minute.

'Get my sword, Mark.'

The squire was leaning over the rail watching the vessel on its converging path. He did not immediately catch the drift of Richard's words. Then he suddenly turned; surprise was written on his features.

'Now, Mark.' Richard's voice was low but already there was a note of concealed tension. 'And be quick.' De Dinan was gone to the cramped cabin.

Around the deck hatches sailors were running to and fro grabbing staves and bills. There was no doubt about it now. It was clear what was going on.

'French pirates, Mark.' De Dinan was fumbling with the belt about Richard's waist. 'No doubt they wish to make John pay for the French ships seized by the Cinque Ports last autumn. And we are clearly the goose they intend to pluck today.'

Richard was grim as he looked to where Umar was clambering up from the restless horses. There was too much at stake for it all to be destroyed now. His life rested on it. He would not stand by and watch it snatched away.

'Forget it.' Richard pushed away the belt and the heavy scabbard. 'The blade, Mark. Just the blade.'

The sea was thrown up between the vessels. The hulls struck and parted. There was no time to wear the sword; only to wield it. Richard was not in armour. He had been expecting a simple sea crossing, not a war. His mail shield and helmet lay carefully packed in the cabin, away from the salt water.

Mark raised the great blade in its buckskin scabbard and Richard threw back his heavy riding cloak. As the ships struck again he seized the silk-bound grip with both hands. The dull sun caught the edge of the blade as he drew it forth. As he turned he saw that the first rope had snaked across from the French vessel. Its iron grapple caught and held. Others flew and bit into planks and railings. The two vessels were flung together in a grinding of hulls. There was no shaking off the Frenchmen's violent embrace.

A ladder was swung across the gap. Eager, howling figures rose from the pirate ship's decks and scrambled across it. A crossbowman on Richard's vessel fired from the aft castle and the singing bolt struck a Frenchman from the bridge. He plunged screaming between the splintering hulls.

As Richard leaned out over the rail he saw that the sailor had been reduced to a scarlet stain on the rending planks. A surge of water and even that was gone. But there was no time to think, for already the pirates were aboard.

A vicious battle was taking place between the deck hatches and the rails. Spears jabbed into the intruders. Bolts and arrows whined across the deck. The Norman sailors were struggling to push the invaders back over the side. One of the intruders, then another, evaded the axes and punched and dodged through.

Richard swung the sword with both hands and one of the ducking pirates fell; his body cloven from skull to chest. Richard was dragged down with him, fighting to free the blade and slipping on the bloody planking. His back was on fire and his hands were numb. With tingling arms he struggled to extricate the sword but his fingers refused to work.

Agony stitched across the side of his neck. He collapsed to his knees, with his head swimming and lights dancing before his eyes. Mark made for Richard, knowing exactly what had happened. As the squire lunged forward, his boots slipped on the wet planks of the deck. He fell headlong, striking his forehead against the rail. Richard was unaided, for the sergeants were separated from the knight and the stunned squire by a grappling knot of seamen.

Richard looked up to see a spear point thrust at his forehead. The hatred was carved on the face behind the violent action. He tried to avoid the blow but his movements were sluggish and slow. He willed himself to jump away but his body would not respond. As in a nightmare he faced his own death and was impotent to escape it.

A heavy booted leg flew across his field of vision. The spear blade sheered across his shoulder as the boot struck it. The attacker – his full weight behind the blow – was thrown totally off balance. He crashed past Richard and sprawled on the deck. As he raised his head, Umar brought an axe down on him.

Through the daze of his pain Richard felt hands about him pulling him clear of the murderous mêlée. Falling back against the raised edge of a deck hatch, he tried to make sense of the screaming and shouting which seemed to make rational thought impossible.

As Umar stood beside him, axe in hand, the French pirates were forced back off the deck. Several fell as they struggled to regain the safety of their own ship. The grappling ropes were severed and the two ships fell apart with an exhausted sigh of aching timbers.

The Norman sailors, cheering at the defeat of their enemy, leaned over the side, the close proximity of their own destruction only serving to fuel the energy behind their shouted triumphant obscenities.

Mark de Dinan came to on the bloodied deck. His head ached from his fall, but worse was the humiliation at the sight of another, standing – weapon in hand – at the defence of his knight.

That the other was the Saracen did nothing to diminish the shame and anger that seethed in the squire's heart.

As Richard – recovering somewhat – praised the quick actions of the Muslim groom, Mark busied himself retrieving the fallen sword and wiping it clean; anything to put off facing de Lacey. When at last it could be delayed no longer he approached his knight with the weapon.

There was no rebuke; only a good-natured question about the squire's own injury. 'How is it then? It seems that we two did so much injury to ourselves that we have no need of any enemies.' Richard rubbed at his still-swimming eyes. 'Fetch a flagon of wine from the forecastle. And we shall drink to a victory won in spite of us!'

For Mark, the kindness and humour stung more than vinegar on a wound; more than the cauterising iron on a severed limb. It would have been easier to have faced condemnation than sympathy. As he turned away there burnt hatred in his heart for the Saracen groom, Umar ibn Mamun.

William Catface squatted by the fire burning on its plinth of baked clay and heat-crazed stones. The smoke hung about the cramped little room as if it had forgotten the way to the thin patches in the thatch which allowed smoke out and rain in. In his hands he held a long arrow shaft of ash wood.

'They'll hang 'ee for sure, Will. God's my judge an' they'll have 'ee swingen like a sack of flour. Yer moond in yer 'ead to go so regular like . . .'

Will ignored his wife. Instead he raised the arrow to examine its fine barbed head. It had cost him a quarter of a well-clipped penny and he was proud of it. And so he should be, he reckoned, what with it taking half a day's wages, and that paid for carrying muck from the stock pens to the downland wheat fields of his wealthier neighbours.

'You'll listen to I, when they putsa rope round yer neck.' She stirred the pot of thin porridge which hung over the fire. 'Then 'twill be too late for 'ee. Lot of good 'ul come of listening then.' With an old, blunt knife she scraped shavings from a rancid block of dirty pig's fat. It was the sole difference in ingredients between this supper meal and the morning's breakfast. 'Then 'ee'll listen, but 'twill do 'ee no good at all . . .'

Catface looked with a pained expression at his wife. 'If yer smiled yer face 'ud crack . . .' Then before she could scold him he added: 'Pass that glue . . .'

Reluctantly she handed over the crude little bowl which was warming by the hearth. From behind her came the lowing of one of their two cows – separated from them by the thickness of a wattle partition. In another corner their two little children slept on the piled straw of the bed. Part of a single patched blanket covered their filthy nakedness.

William scratched at the stirring of a flea, more persistent than the others within his woollen tunic. Holding the arrow firmly he raised the last of the four flights of feathers from the crushed straw of the floor. With great concentration he dipped it into the glue, then carefully slotted it into a narrow slit cut into the arrow shaft.

He wiped the excess glue on to his clothes and then reached for a length of tarred twine which lay near his feet. As he twisted the twine about the shaft to secure the flight, he talked, without once looking at his wife.

'Just listen. None about 'ere knows our business. God, with the racket the bleedun dog put up when I cut out his claws all the village must 'ave 'eard it. None will accuse us of 'avin' a dog that ain't bin lawed as it should be.'

He laughed. 'An' 'ee well knows every dog in Blackmoor 'as 'is front claws dug out, by the King's orders. So that the poor deer – Lady Mary bless the poor beasts – will not 'ave dogs chasin' 'em to death.' He dropped his voice. 'And no one knows about the other dogs I keeps, so quit yer panickin', woman.

'And besides, yer eats the meat as freely as I does, so don't 'ee get pretty about it now. Venison 'twill bide us through the winter and, God knows, there's nuthin' else will do that . . .'

She would have liked to have contradicted him but she knew he told the truth. They were the poorest cottar family on the Horsingham manor. They had a mean little three-acre plot – for which they paid sixpence a year and still owed weekly unpaid service on the lord's land, as well as unpaid carrying for the steward. They only survived because they sold their muscles to their wealthier villein neighbours at times of heavy work. And because William poached the sacrosanct deer and game of the King.

As if he read her thoughts, Catface added: 'An' for the soddin' spit of land I cut out of the King's forest – which was worth bugger all to 'is majesty – I'll 'ave to pay a twelvepence fine at the forest court and a penny a year rent . . .' He frowned at the wilful hatred of the high and mighty and at the bad luck of being born William Catface.

Rising to his feet, he picked up his bow and arrows. He opened the ill-fitting door a crack. The darkness outside was silent and total.

'For God's sake, take care, Will . . . If they do get 'ee . . .'

Catface grinned. 'They gotta catch I first . . .' Then he slipped out into the night.

As he trudged off through the dark he reflected on his wife's words. He knew in his heart that as desperate as their circumstances were, this was not the only reason for his poaching; at bottom he enjoyed it. Nothing gave him as much satisfaction as killing the King's deer. Not that he had anything against the deer. It was just the thought that he – William Catface – was supping on the venison meant for the Crown. It was something to set in the balance against the little misfortunes which life delighted in pouring into William Catface's lap in an unending stream.

On a bad day he would grin while he was heaving dung for a pittance, or tending the heavy clods which passed for soil in his trifling plot of land. He knew how the secret joke annoyed his wealthier neighbours. After all, they must be thinking, what did he have to smile at? That thought only made him grin all the more.

Only one thing did pain him, though, and he could not shrug it off. Gilbert de Cantelo had not been a bad lord. They were all bastards, of course; just rich bastards. But William had had nothing personal against Gilbert. As rich bastards went, Gilbert was tolerable. Consequently it was a matter of some disquiet to Catface that the lord had been killed by one of *his* dogs. For who knew who would replace him?

'Not the girl . . .' William muttered to himself. 'Nice body too . . .' He rued the short-sightedness of a world where the quality of a woman's body was not taken into account when choosing a lord. 'Now the bloody place will be in the King's hands . . .'

The thought worried Catface, for that might spell out a lot of trouble. And if anyone ever discovered it was his doing . . . The consequences did not bear thinking about. Even the thought of killing the King's deer did not quite blot out the speculation of what big people with blunt minds and sharp implements might do to the tenderer parts of William Catface's body if the truth ever got out. He reflected on this as he picked his way along the narrow track which led eastward, into the royal forest of Blackmoor Vale.

The manor of Horsingham lay on the western edge of the Blackmoor Vale. Even in the depths of February its undulating pastures were like the swell on a breeze-brushed sea. And to the south lay the tree-darkened ridge of the north Dorset downs.

But it was not south that Joanna rode on the Thursday morning of the feast of St Valentine; it was north-west. Beyond the manor complex, within its stockade and moat, the road led down towards the meadows and marshes about Sherborne, and it was to Sherborne that Joanna was riding. The journey to the royal castle lay on the route to the meeting of the shire court at Ilchester, over the Somerset border. Joanna had no intention of allowing the decision of the coroners and the resulting judgement regarding her status to take place unopposed.

She had bade a tense farewell to the loyal but tight-lipped Ranulf Dapifer and headed north. The steward was certain that she would only cause herself further grief by resisting the inevitable. When at last he had realised that she was deaf to his entreaties he had asked that he might at least accompany her. This request she had turned down. The manor was unsettled enough following the death of Gilbert. Joanna charged her steward with bringing the running of the estate back into line by the time she returned.

'Will the sheriff be at the castle, my lady?'

Tilly rode with her mistress and four of Gilbert's household knights as escort. A little to the rear, Stephen Pierson led a well-laden packhorse. It was the journey to Sherborne which Joanna had promised her maid the previous summer. Only the circumstances were beyond anything in her wildest nightmares of the year before.

Joanna nodded. 'Ranulf assures me that he arrived in Sherborne this week. He has been raising more money for the King's war since he landed in Southampton last month. Now he is on his way to attend the shire court.'

'How long will we stay there, my lady?'

Joanna smiled. 'Long enough to explore the market a little.' Tilly looked pleased at the prospect of a return to more normal days. 'Perhaps three days. I will see the sheriff tomorrow, and the day after we will ride on towards Ilchester.' A little of her former, lighter spirit returned. 'This afternoon we can see what the silversmiths are selling in Cheap Street. I promised you a silver ring last year, did I not?'

'Yes, my lady, but . . .'

'There are no buts about it. What I promised I will do. I have been too full of my own troubles. We shall find one this afternoon, then you can show it off to whoever you wish to.'

The slight tease brought a flush to Tilly's face. She glanced backwards involuntarily to where Stephen was riding, and Joanna laughed. Then the moment of humour – rare enough these days – passed like a sudden breeze.

Before noon they rode down the highway which crossed the marshy valley of the river Yeo, by St Andrew's mill, and entered the southern suburbs of the abbey town. Gilbert had kept a town house in Sherbourne; it lay on the northern end of Cheap Street with its garden plot backing on to the wall of the abbey grounds.

After the midday meal – prepared by the servants, who had been alerted to the arrival of their mistress – Joanna took Tilly on the long-promised exploration of the shops of the silversmith's guild, on the western side of the marketplace; just above the great eastern gate into the abbey precincts.

Joanna was dressed warmly. An over-tunic of dark green and a fur-trimmed cap of brown velvet kept out the worst of the damp weather. Her long red hair was tied up and she wore a white wimple, close-fitting about her face, appropriate for a woman in mourning who was no longer a girl.

She and Tilly soon found a fine silver ring. The maid was very pleased and casually held it out to Stephen in an unspoken display which the groom could hardly ignore.

Joanna had determined to hear the end of parish mass at the Church of All Hallows, attached to the western end of the great abbey. As she went inside to pray, her escort waited in the porch of the church. After a little while, he summoned up the courage to address Matilda.

'It's a beautiful ring.' Stephen was unusually formal. 'It looks well on you.' Tilly glanced at her hand and smiled.

'Thank you, Stephen.'

Her tone was soft. And although the reply was short it ended on a note which seemed to say: 'You may say more if you wish.' She lifted her petite hands and the silver twist was clear on one slim, white finger. Her dark eyes glanced at him shyly.

Stephen's throat was very dry, and when he spoke there was little in his voice of the usual confident laughter. Indeed there seemed nothing to show that he was the young man who dared to gently tease the baron's daughter.

'It is a fine ring.' He paused as he found himself repeating himself. 'Very fine . . .'

'Yes. You said so.'

Her shyness was melting a little. It outthawed his and put him at a disadvantage. He coughed to clear his throat but was really seizing on time to clear his mind.

'It would look pretty on anyone . . .'

She did not let him finish. 'Why, Stephen, whatever should a lady make of that?'

It stung him into speaking swiftly. 'I meant . . . I meant that it would look pretty on anyone but it looks beautiful on you!' His face deepened to a hot red. He nodded his blond head and his muscular body shook with the vigour of it. 'Everything looks beautiful on you. Because you are . . .'

At that moment Joanna reappeared and Stephen jumped back as if a lash had landed on his back. Joanna glanced at Tilly, who smiled a little too quickly and then glanced away. It was all a little obvious but Joanna stifled a comment. After all, she could hardly approve of this flirting between her maid and the groom who – whilst almost a brother to her – was still only a groom. Nevertheless the thought lifted her out of her sorrow and seemed to summon memories of better times.

They turned away from the church porch, with its carved stones and gazing angels, and Joanna almost collided with a man crossing the courtyard. He was taller than Stephen and a few years older. His colouring was not unlike that of the groom but he was slimmer and his face was tanned. His whole carriage was altogether different, though, for it exuded the unspoken assumptions and confidences of another world – Joanna's world.

He turned to apologise and Joanna could see that he held himself stiffly as if in pain. He was richly dressed; a well-embroidered cloak fell from his shoulders to his thighs, and as it fell open at his throat she saw he wore a fashionable, knee-length green tunic of soft wool velvet. Its hem was dagged and hung in long, sword-shaped pleats. Joanna approved; though she knew it was the height of fashion, she had not seen many men wearing the style.

Yet this man seemed to be no dandy. He wore the clothes quite casually, as if unaware of his own good taste. Joanna frowned slightly as he apologised, and his hands – calfskin gloved – released her arm, which he had taken to stop her falling as a result of the collision.

'My apologies. It was all my fault.'

The voice was strong and cultured and the Norman-French without a provincial accent. But it was distant, as if he was thinking of something else. As he turned, Joanna could not help but admit how good-looking he was. She was perhaps more conscious of it because he seemed so unaware of her.

She was used to men looking at her. The admiring glances were not so much encouraged as assumed. It was simply how things were. She accepted it and was not made insufferable by it. Why should she be? – only the insecure gobble up compliments. A steady diet had always been fed to Joanna and she had grown used to the fare without developing any inclination to gorge on it.

This man, though, quite ignored her. It was as if he had not really taken her in at all. Only his squire looked back with the expected curiosity. Joanna stood and watched them until the two men left the abbey precinct by the east gate. A dark-skinned servant was waiting there, the like of whom Joanna had never seen before. Then they were lost in the crowd of traders in the market of Sherborne Bow.

'My lady?' Tilly touched Joanna's arm. 'Are you all right?'

Joanna nodded. 'Of course.' She was still looking towards the east gate. 'I am fine, thank you.' But there was a challenged look in her bright-green eyes.

Chapter 4

A full morning moon still held court, although with the advancing of the hour the eastern sky was lightening. Away at a respectful distance was her attendant knight star; watching with silent sorrow the fading silver of her daily waning.

William Catface stood at the head of the rounded valley. Below him the trees and grazings of the Blackmoor Vale stretched away into darkness. In frequent places the shadow thinned where innumerable pastures and assarts had eaten into the fast-retreating woodland.

There was less there than when William had been a child. And – if the human neighbours of the King's deer continued their relentless encroachments – there would be fewer trees still when he died. It gave him a curious pleasure to ponder on these trespasses on the King's land. For, fine the miscreants as the King's verderers regularly did, the royal officers could not halt the pressure of population within and about the vale. The little people cut their perch patches and their tiny acres from the wood and, though they paid their fines, the wood did not return when once it had been cut.

It had been a fairly productive night. Over one shoulder the poacher carried the limp bodies of four rabbits taken from the warrens at the foot of the downs. Yet he was not fully satisfied. He had startled a two-year-old buck in the thin, grey dawn, recognising the distinctive pricket antlers in the early-morning light.

A fast loosed shot from his knarled yew bow had taken the deer in the shoulder. To William's chagrin the buck had not fallen. Instead it had sprung away into the shadows taking his precious arrow with it.

'Soddit.' William looked again at the sharp little hoof prints in the patch of soil exposed by the winter rain. 'Soddit – buggers off as bright as a penny.' He peered towards the lip of the ridge. He had never pushed this far east and south from Horsingham. As a creature of habit he was unsettled by the alien feel of this foreign territory.

When it came to the downs and vale about the manor there was no man better able to point to the best place to tickle trout in the clear streams flowing out of the chalk hills, or to find the glades where the stags clashed antlers in the autumn, and the thickets where the hinds dropped their fawns in the spring. He knew all the paths which ran between the great open wheat fields of the Glastonbury Abbey tenants, on the edge of the high chalk. And beyond that there was the landscape of wood pasture grazed by the great flocks of the monastic sheep and those from the Templar grange at Temple Buckland. Catface knew it all very well, but now he was in a strange land and it made him restless.

Yet he could not turn back just yet; the arrow had cost him too much. 'Damned bloody buck'll run a'way to Milton . . .' He spat with annoyance. His wife would scold him when he came home. He spat again.

From the vale below, the downs looked like a solid green wall. Close up they were less precisely formed. Where they fell into the flatness of the vale they were broken by rounded valleys and combes which divided the profile into a less tidy collection of hills and wooded folds. Following the buck's trail, Catface crossed the whaleback between two such wooded inroads into the downland plateau. To the south-east the cold grey mist was breaking before a thin breeze which rustled the dark branches on the bushes about him.

Soon it would be full light. Already the trees on a further swell of the plateau were silhouetted against a veil of palest misty lilac. Light brought people and people brought trouble: shepherds and ploughmen; hunters and travellers. And all of them intent on turning William Catface in to the law. Or so it seemed to him.

William did not like people very much. In his opinion this was fully justified. After all, he had met a fair few and each meeting reinforced the prejudices of the last one. People were invariably the prelude to trouble. He hesitated, then he thought of his two children fighting over their breakfast of thin porridge. The thought prompted him to go just a little further before he turned back towards home. And so it was that William Catface pushed through a copse of beech and hazel and stumbled on the hamlet.

It was not much of a place, just two cottages with green thatch. One of them was larger than the other – a longhouse boasting a byre attached. Someone had begun to cobble a corner of the yard and then given up. The footings of another cottage occupied the third side of the roughly square yard. Piles of grass-grown white, grey and black nodules demonstrated that there had once been a plan to raise a low flint wall as a foundation for the cob construction of the cottage.

The fourth side was open; beyond it a track ran away between the overshadowing shoulders of the hills. Trees crowded it and rose in untidy tiers up the side of the slopes. A little spring broke out at the foot of the slope and followed the track in a bubbling course – the only sound in the valley.

'Well now, Will me lad. What 'as I found 'ere then?'

He unslung his bow and fitted an arrow. He acted without thinking, and after he had done it, glanced down at the barbed head almost in surprise. He smiled but felt uneasy. There was something menacing about the silent place. A feeling of desolation and death hung about the yard in the last long shadows of night.

William knew that deserted bothies and buildings could be the abodes of nameless things, yet he pressed on, for he was eaten up with curiosity. It pricked him like a spur and overcame his natural fear. A cat so curious . . .

'Go easy, Will me lad. Don't want to disturb anyone . . .'

There was no one to disturb. The door to the larger cottage was half open and grass grew in the doorway. Cautiously he pushed at it. It moved reluctantly on perished leather hinges. It was clear that no one had disturbed it for a long time.

Inside it was quite dark. To his right William could smell the heaped straw of the animal byre. Even after long desertion the stench of animal waste hung about the longhouse as it always did in his own smaller cottage. Straight ahead was the facing doorway, lost in shadows.

With one hand he felt along the smooth cob wall on his left which separated the living space from the cattle stall. It was wet with the condensation of the night. On his palms it was sticky – like blood. He shivered as he groped for the doorway.

When he found it, he entered though the opening and found himself in a room much larger than his own. He could not see but rather could sense the space opening out around him. Crouching and feeling he identified a long-cold hearth in the centre and a drain which ran back the way he had come to the soakaway situated outside the door.

To his astonishment there was a tiny chamber which occupied the end of the human area. Such a luxury of privacy was experienced by only the better-off villeins and freemen in Horsingham. Like the cobbles in the yard and the good strong wall it indicated that the owner of the silent settlement was richer than William would ever be. But where was he?

A scuffle in the corner made William leap about. The bow string was against his chest, the arrow ready. The unmoving shadows menaced him – then a rat darted across the floor to its hole at the foot of the cob wall.

'Bloody hell . . .' William's heart was pounding and he could feel the cold sweat on his brow and cheeks. 'Bloody hell,' he swore again to the watching dark.

At last his breathing returned to normal. It shook him to be afraid, for it was not in his nature. It was the place which did it. Where were the owners? What nameless force had driven them out?

Outside once more, in the cold air, he sat down on the unfinished low wall. He felt better now, for it was getting light. He also felt better because a plan had come to mind despite the fear that the place engendered.

For here was a perfect hiding place. A lonely shelter to escape to if ever he was pursued in the southern woods of the vale. A place to hide incriminating evidence. Even a place to hang up poached deer and return another night to cut it up. Fear was giving way to planning, as it usually did with him. He could see that the hamlet had possibilities.

In one corner of the yard a rick had been built and thatched. It sagged out of shape as the result of winter wind, but was well made and would survive another couple of winters. William inspected it, pushing his arm shoulder-deep into the wet and clinging bundles of hay. That which he withdrew was still dry and sweet despite the state of the outside of the rick. Someone had dried it well in the field and it would last a long time yet. From the state of the rick as a whole it had probably been made the previous year, or possibly the summer before that.

'Someone left 'ee a while,' William mused to the silent rick. 'An' mayhap'll leave 'ee a time more yet . . .' He pondered on the thought, for it boded well for his plans.

Before he left the hamlet he picked up a sharp flint. With one sharp edge he scratched a crude cat's face on the wall of the largest house as a simple statement of ownership. The place was his – whoever had built it – and he was going to use it.

The day was a faint band of pink above the dove grey of the furthest hills when William scrambled up from the secret valley. Looking back, he could no longer see the hamlet behind its screen of trees. Well pleased with himself, he sauntered home. He was so satisfied he did not even think about the arrow lost in the shoulder of the runaway deer.

The same morning that Catface found the deserted hamlet, Hubert de Burgh woke early in his private chamber in Sherborne Castle. Since he had returned from France he had had a lot on his mind. His sleep had become somewhat restless. Things had not gone as well at Falaise and Caen as he might have wished. The war had dragged on over the winter. And now the initiative of the previous summer seemed to have been lost. There was a slight unease dogging his thoughts as he sat on the cold seat of his garderobe.

Outside in his chamber his household knights, squires and pages were preparing his clothes, and he could hear a page being scolded for some minute breach of etiquette. But it was not the draught blowing about the garderobe which disturbed him. No – it was something deeper.

The holding of Normandy was going to take more than the startling victory at Mirabeau. For a moment he pondered on the magnificent destrier which he had seen being loaded at Caen and the prisoners languishing in the dungeons at Falaise. He sighed, for since the summer John seemed to have lost something of his resolve. And who could blame him?

Heaven knew that there was little love lost between far too many of the Norman lords and their Angevin duke. And the ruthlessness of John's brother, Richard, had thrown away hearts as well as silver pennies. The French King was as wily as a nest of adders: he knew that all John's resources were stretched to their limits in order to defend the mighty empire which his father and brother had built, and which they had also weakened by their costly wars and the granting away of Crown lands.

Hubert brooded on the cost of it all. As the King's chamberlain it rested on him to force as much as possible out of the reluctant baronage: taxes and tallages from manors and boroughs on what remained of royal land; fines paid for offences real or imaginary; reliefs paid to enter into inherited lands; 'gracious loans' extracted with the maximum pressure and fear; wardships and heiresses exploited to the full . . .

'Wine . . .'

And now the Count of Flanders – a crucial ally – had decided to join the Fourth Crusade wintering on the Adriatic. Just when the peace talks with the French King were floundering. It was not a good start to the new campaigning season.

'Where is that wine?' The irritability in Hubert's voice mirrored the concerns which preoccupied him. A panting page drew back the curtain and a squire knelt with a brimming goblet. 'What time is the lady Joanna de Cantelo arriving?'

He sipped his wine thoughtfully as the squire hurried away. At least this was an issue which was clear-cut and without complications. The thought gave him more pleasure as he imbibed. A better subject to dwell upon than the news from Normandy. A few moments later the squire returned with the information he had requested.

'If she's coming that early, I had better be ready,' Hubert muttered to no one in particular. Then in a louder voice he called: 'My robe . . .'

Standing up suddenly, he handed the cup to his startled page and walked naked back into his chamber where a brazier was burning. As he was dressed, a succession of his household clerks brought him letters to sign and advised him as to the business of the day. His mind, though, was not on the details of the size of the loan extorted from the Jews of Bristol, or the outstanding scutage owed by this, or that, knight of the shire. Instead it was Joanna that he was thinking about.

Even when he went to hear mass in the first-floor castle chapel, only half his mind attended to the chaplain. As he sat before the niched statues of SS Michael and Probus, Horsingham was closer to his thoughts. And even as he considered it, the lady Joanna was mounting her horse in the courtyard of the house on Cheap Street and about to ride to the castle.

The castle of Sherborne stood to the east of the town, separated from it by spreading marsh and wet pasture. This seat of the royal government of Somerset and Dorset had been originally built by the Bishop of Salisbury and lost to the Crown by its builders' disloyalty to Stephen during the terrible years of civil war which had racked the West Country sixty-four years earlier.

It was said that Bishop Roger had died of fury at the news of the loss of his castle. Be that as it may, another simmering fury was this very morning riding to the King's castle. Joanna had slept little the night before. She had been thinking of what Ranulf had said and as she did so the weight of her grief was lifted by the force of her indignation. It was in a determined mood that she crossed the causeway linking the castle to the town and entered the squalid little settlement of Castleton pressed up towards the north-west angle of the castle's steep, dry moat.

She reined in her palfrey before the south-west gatehouse. 'Well, here it is then, Matilda.' The formality reinforced her own mood. 'Do you think he means to shut me away in there?'

'Heaven forbid, my lady . . .' Tilly looked alarmed. 'He would not do such a thing.' She looked up at the whitewashed ashlar blocks of Ham Hill stone. 'He would never do such a thing to you. For he knew your father . . . And, besides, you are a baron's daughter.'

'The lady sister of the Duke of Brittany is held at Corfe, Tilly. She has done nothing wrong save being related to her rebel brother. They say that John will never free her . . .' She grimaced as she faced the high walls.

'Be careful you do not speak so when the sheriff is about.' Tilly was alarmed. Like Dapifer she knew how outspoken Joanna could be. But unlike the steward she feared for her mistress rather than for the inconvenience such words might cause. 'Please take care,' she said impulsively. Then, seeking to bring something positive out of the situation, she murmured, 'Though I am sure that the sheriff means you no harm. He was your father's friend.'

Joanna thought about that for a moment. 'Yes,' was all she finally said.

It did not seem much of a comment when compared to either the warning, or the hope, offered by Tilly. Whatever Joanna felt about the matter touched on by her maid, she was obviously keeping it to herself. That at least acted as a contrast to her earlier outspokenness.

Listening to the exchange, Stephen Pierson frowned. It was clear that things were not right but he did not quite follow all of the complexities involved. He was better off with horses. When all was said and done they were less tortuous than people. He looked at mistress and maid and wished that they could just go back to Horsingham.

The hooves of their mounts echoed as they crossed the plank bridge and entered the enclosing maw of the gatehouse. They were expected, and the watchful men-at-arms led them through into the open ward within the walls. Joanna and Tilly dismounted and one of the sergeants took their bridles. The rest of the party remained mounted as Joanna had earlier instructed them.

'The sheriff is expecting me,' she said confidently, and, before any of the men-at-arms could reply, she walked towards the towering central keep.

Caught out by her confidence a sergeant jogged after her, knowing that the sheriff would scarcely approve of the loss of initiative to a woman. Recovering the lead he took the two women in through the door to the great hall. Fresh rushes were strewn on the floor and scurrying retainers were about their business. Some stood and watched as the little procession crossed the hall, but Joanna ignored them.

Then they were out into the weak sunshine once more. Surrounded by high walls, a little arcaded courtyard lay like an island in the heart of the complex of buildings. Two well-dressed women were walking there and buttery servants were rolling barrels out of the low door of the east range, but of the sheriff there was still no sign.

Joanna stopped for a moment and glanced up at the rearing walls. Was this how a prisoner would feel? Her stomach tightened. How easy it had been to give full rein to her indignation within the familiar hall of her father's house on Cheap Street, or even as she had ridden here. Now, as she went to beard the lion in his den, she began to feel a little afraid.

It was a new emotion to her and one with which she was ill-equipped to cope. It disconcerted her, for it questioned all of the confidence that had been instilled in her since she was a child.

Tilly stood beside her; the maid's eyes were abrim with concern. 'Is there anything wrong, my lady?'

Joanna shook her head. 'Nothing,' she lied with a dip into her reserves of courage. 'I was just thinking . . .'

Tilly touched her arm. The compassion breathed life back into Joanna's indignation. Who were they to reduce her to such a state? To make her feel as she did? What would her father have said to see her so downcast? The thought made her bring her chin up in defiance.

Tilly noticed the movement and read the emotion. She wondered if her touch had been misplaced. She feared for her mistress if she entered into open conflict with Hubert de Burgh.

Inside the buildings once more, a spiral stair led up to the first-floor chapel and a long gallery. It was in the gallery that the sheriff was waiting. Two chairs stood beside a wooden chest. Behind the chest a trestle table carried two goblets and a fine silver wine jug. On the walls tapestries covered the nakedness of the stones, and the air still carried the waxy smell of the candles and tapers of the night before. Joanna was acutely aware of all of this as she walked into the room.

Hubert looked up from a sheet of creamy vellum laid out on the table. At his elbow hovered the ever-attentive pages, while two clerks were pointing something out in the document. He smiled slightly at the sight of his visitor. It was the formal veneer of a man who had learned survival at the court. There was no particular warmth in his eyes as his face smiled. Joanna saw the dichotomy of emotions and her lips tightened.

'I am so sorry to hear about your father.' Hubert came forward and kissed her. 'News reached me in France.' When his guest looked surprised he added: 'The King may be fighting in Normandy but he never forgets his loyal friends in England.'

'Thank you.' Joanna chose her words carefully. 'He is more than gracious to me, to be moved by my father's death.'

'Of course, of course . . .' De Burgh bade her be seated. 'The King thinks only of your interests.'

He nodded to the attendant, who poured wine and passed a goblet to Joanna. She found it hard to believe that the King lost any sleep worrying about her interests but wisely said nothing.

De Burgh sipped at his Gascon wine. 'I trust that you approve. Only the best is claimed in taxes by the King. One cask of fine wine from behind the mast of every ship carrying it from Aquitaine and Gascony. It is an excellent vintage . . .'

Joanna nodded as she lowered the goblet from her lips. It was excellent but she was barely aware of its full body and smooth flavour. She was watching the sheriff, who was watching her.

Hubert did not hurry to speak again. Instead he lowered his heavy-jowled, dark-bearded face as he studied her. They were right, he thought, she is beautiful. The spotless veil and the barbette about her head and throat only accentuated the well-formed upturn of her chin and the ivory skin of her cheeks. And the eyes were greener than he had imagined.

'More wine?' She shook her head. 'I think I shall,' he said with the air of practised informality which matched his smile. One was as much a veneer as the other. 'You're sure?' When she shook her head he smiled again.

Joanna's long gown was cut close to her body and the sheriff took in the curve of her breasts and the line of her thighs beneath the gold-embroidered cloth. It was clear that she was a woman, not a child. Why ever had Gilbert not betrothed her by now?

He took another sip of wine. John would approve, for he had a voracious appetite for women. If ever this one crossed his path he would soon enjoy the naked softness of that ivory skin. Hubert felt a familiar stirring as for a brief moment he thought of Joanna naked. Yes, a man would give a lot to enjoy her in bed with him.

He shook his head; enough of such pleasant fantasies. For a moment he thought of his wife below in the arcaded court. More importantly, he thought of the intentions laid out so clearly in the letter sealed by John at Caen and lying folded beside him.

'It is the wish of the King that you be protected as his ward.' He watched the words hit home. 'You understand that this is the custom?'

He only added the obvious appendix because he saw something like surprise in the green eyes opposite him. No – it was not surprise; it was something else. He opened his mouth to speak again but the young woman got there first.

'I am sixteen,' Joanna said quietly. 'I am two years beyond wardship age.'

Hubert coughed into his goblet. 'What?' She was challenging him and the astonishment was apparent on his face. He almost laughed. 'The King has commanded that you be taken into wardship. There is no question of whether he is right, or wrong; it is his command.' There was now a hardness in his voice. Here was the wolf which Gilbert had seen.

Joanna shifted in her wooden chair. 'You were a friend of my father's. Surely you could . . .'

'I am the loyal servant of the King, as your late father was. There is no appeal in this matter.'

It gave him a curious pleasure to argue with her. A woman of spirit was entertaining; like those whores who dared to speak in a way a man's wife would never do. The women who stood outside the rules and norms; who faced a man with brazen audacity and then delivered the pleasure that his money demanded of them. It gave him pleasure to face Joanna because he was totally confident of mastering her. There was sport but no threat in her words. She might think that she was different but she was not. There was no withstanding the royal will.

Her defiance was something John would want to hear about, though. He had an eye for a woman who was different, and in the end they all did as they were told: noblewomen with more indignation than decorum, or one of the royal whores.

'I am capable of running my father's manors. I know them all by heart, and his servants and clerks will run them as efficiently under me as under him.'

Hubert was beginning to tire of this. Enough was enough, and Joanna's insistence was starting to lose its appeal. 'The matter is decided.' He gestured with a gold-ringed hand to the letter on the table. 'The King has written to me from Normandy.' Here was the triumph – the mastering of her. 'You will remain on your father's manor of Horsingham until the King makes arrangement for your lodging in his household, or in mine. It will not be long in the deciding.

'And in the meantime my household officials have been dispatched to Horsingham, this very morning, to take preparations for the wardship and control of the manor . . .'

'You are seizing my manor?' Joanna rose to her feet. It was happening while they talked. Even as she stood before him, Horsingham was slipping from her grasp. She was appalled. 'You are taking it from me?'

De Burgh did not stir from his chair. 'It is not yours so long as it is in wardship. It is for the King and his officials to decide how it shall be run. You and your inheritance lie under the protection of the King. And you are in the gift of the King. So do not speak like a fool, Joanna. You know how things lie.'

The final sentence was crushing and there was no longer even the pretence of a smile. Joanna flushed with an anger which could find no outlet. There was nothing that she could say. At last she found a few words, tucked away behind her inexpressible indignation.

'Then you will do nothing for me?'

'I have done everything there is to do.' He looked away as if about to terminate the conversation. 'I shall return to the King after the meeting of the shire court. When you return to your manor you will find that all is in place. There is nothing to concern yourself with. All is in hand.'

He looked at the young heiress with the fine manor and the splendid horses. Oh, everything was in place all right. There were plans for Horsingham, plans which Joanna could scarcely begin to imagine and which concerned her not at all.

Joanna looked at Tilly as if seeking inspiration in this moment of defeat. The maid's pale face offered no defence against what was happening to her mistress; her white hands were clasped together, wringing out the agony.

'You have betrayed me.'

De Burgh looked up and a red hue rose in his pitted cheeks. No one spoke to him this way. He stood up and rose above her. The very action calmed his rising anger. He could crush her if he wished to. She was only a woman and the realisation of his own total power stayed his hand.

Tilly stepped towards her mistress, horrified at what she had just heard. For a moment she almost imagined that the sheriff might have Joanna confined. For who could stop him?

The same thought had obviously occurred to Joanna too. 'I am sorry,' she said, without a trace of remorse but with her anger at least muzzled. 'You cannot imagine what this means to me.'

Hubert had no experience at empathising with the lot of a woman and no intention of starting now. Nevertheless the suggestion satisfied him. She had stepped back. They always did. Despite this he could not let the matter be ignored.

'You will never speak to me in that way again, my lady de Cantelo. Had you been a man who questioned my honour I would have killed you.' His raised eyebrows dared her to contradict him. She said nothing. 'So go now. I shall see you at the shire court at Ilchester.'

He drained his goblet while Joanna curtsied stiffly and turned for the door. Only then did she realise that her humiliation had been observed by the sheriff's clerks and the sergeant. There was no hint of understanding in their mocking eyes. For a moment she almost wept, so great had been her defeat. Then – as if the men did not exist – she raised her chin and walked out of the gallery.

Behind her Hubert signalled for another cup of wine. He was thinking of the details laid out in the letter from John. Horsingham would never be the same after the wardship was finished. The King had need of good meadow land for his horses. But he had more than this planned for Joanna's manor. Gilbert had died at just the right time.

De Burgh read the letter once more. He smiled to see the last sentence. The King clearly had plans for Joanna, as well as for the manor. The sheriff sighed with not a little envy. Despite her total lack of manners, the girl had a body worth bedding. But John had thought of that, of course.

Hubert glanced at the letter once again. It was no surprise, for she was now in the gift of the King. His to give, or sell to whom he chose. And the King had chosen. It was a choice which said a lot about John. Hubert smiled a savage smile. If Joanna had resented the loss of her manor, how much more would she resent the King's choice of the man who would have the pleasure of deflowering her?

'Here's to the lucky bastard,' de Burgh murmured to himself as he raised his goblet.

The watching clerks exchanged knowing looks, but when Hubert glanced at them they were wearing the emotionless masks of their station again. For they too had learned the meaning of power and of survival.

Richard de Lacey stood in the meadow grass with his head lowered as he caught his breath. The blow had driven it from his body and his head swam. Painfully he flexed the muscles in his arms; they were knots of agony. They had not ceased to ache so since the clash with the French pirates.

'Again, Mark,' he said in a voice pitched low. Then, as if ashamed of the pain in his tone, he forced a laugh. 'We'll see if I can do better this time.'

De Dinan did not look convinced, despite the clear instruction given by Richard. It was unlike him to be slow in serving his lord. His whole life – first as page within the de Lacey household, and then as squire to the eldest son – had instilled in him discipline and the etiquette of obedience. One day when he was knighted, the same unswerving loyalty would be his to command and to expect. Yet now he hesitated.

Richard drew himself upright again and was looking at him, expecting him to act. Still Mark delayed. The squire could not bear to begin the whole painful episode once more. It was terrible to see Richard in such pain and weakness.

A short distance away, in the shade of a pollarded oak, the Saracen, Umar, was checking one of the horse's hooves. With a sharp knife he was working out a stone from the delicate tissues about the frog of the foot.

He was talking softly to the mare in Arabic but he was watching Richard. Mark hated him for that. He hated this heathen who was witness to the humiliation of *his* knight. Eyes abrim with venom darted at the alien groom; sharp with the edge of contempt and resentment.

'Mark . . .' Richard was puzzled at his squire's slow movements. 'It will soon be dinner. Set it up again.'

Mark fiddled with the ropes of the quintain. He had rigged it up on Richard's instructions. A tall gallows of a thing with two outstretched arms, and hanging from the tip of each outstretched limb a heavy sack of earth. With a sick feeling, Mark took one of the sacks in both hands and propelled it at de Lacey. Richard met it with a two-handed blow of his great sword. The assaulted sack was hurled backward by the blow. Its counterweight was flung round anticlockwise towards the knight.

Mark could see the muscles tightening in Richard's neck as he fought to control arms solid and heavy with pain. The earth sack swooped as de Lacey twisted his wrists, bringing the sword blade about to face the awkward arc of the swinging dead weight.

Once more he was too slow. As the blade rose, the sack struck him on the side of the head. The solid weight threw him off his feet. The sword fell from numb fingers and the blade drove into the soft earth of the pasture. Richard fell heavily, the lights leaping before his eyes in a dazzling constellation of earthbound stars. His fingers clawed into the earth and he felt the damp grass pressed against his face.

Umar the Saracen put down his knife and stepped forward. A withering glance from de Dinan froze off his automatic offer of assistance. Mark knew that Richard would not wish to be helped. This madness was something that he insisted on going through alone.

It was that which so distressed Mark. That he was cut off from the man he so admired when he most needed him. That and a curious disquiet that his knight should so publicly display his weakness for the ridicule of the world.

Alone, Richard pushed himself up to a kneeling position. The blood thundered in his ears. Once more he was on the dusty road from Acre to the Jordan, along the road that followed the Wadi Halazun. The arrows were flying. A horse was neighing wildly and a man was screaming as if his life was being torn from him. But it was *his* voice screaming as the shaft of the bolt sliced through surcoat, hauberk, muscle and bone.

Then his hands – pressed against his face – brought the damp smell of grass and soil to replace the vision of dust and blood. Slowly his head cleared; he was breathing deeply and drinking in the aroma of the earth. It steadied his mind.

'My lord.' Mark could stand it no longer. He was at Richard's shoulder. 'My lord, it is enough. Surely it is enough. The bishop's marshal will soon be here. It is over?' The voice was almost pleading, and very young.

The tone of Mark's voice, like the soft scent of the earth, drove back the vision of the ambush in the wadi.

'Yes, Mark. It is enough . . .'

Richard reached for his sword. It stood before him, the hilt uppermost; blade driven into the ground, the tapering quillons making a cross. He stared, for it was with such a weapon held in such a way that he had sworn to liberate Jerusalem when he had 'taken the cross'. When he had made the solemn promise that he was now unable to fulfil.

He reached out and touched the incised letters on the broad blade: *Homo Dei* – Man of God. The despair welled within him and he desperately tried to hide it.

'Yes, it is over. It is finished. Let us be about dinner, for I've worked up an appetite as well as a headache.' Richard forced a weary smile.

Relieved, the squire pulled the sword from the earth. As he did so, Richard's eyes once more fell on the letters. He clenched a fist and the movement brought jarring pain across his back and shoulders.

'It is finished,' he said softly. He bit at his lower lip as he turned away from the promise that his weakness had caused him to dishonour. 'It is finished . . .'

Together knight and squire trudged back towards the manor complex with its hall, byres and outhouses. Behind them Umar watched with fascination. He had never seen such a complex web of pain and passion as that which bound de Lacey. The hatred which emanated from the squire he was used to. That he could cope with. But the repressed energy and the charged force which swept beneath the surface of the knight . . . That was another thing; quite another thing. It intrigued him but he watched it from afar. His loyalty was bought for silver.

He had no love to be racked by watching the knight burn up in the fire of his own frustration. Unlike the squire, whose love was all too evident, as was his shame and his puzzlement as the unwilling realisation dawned that something terrible was consuming the object of his loyalty.

Then the horse beside him was pushing into his shoulder and wuffling through its nose. Umar recognised the sound of trusting contentment and pocketed his hoof-pick. He ran his fingers through the creamy mane and stroked the fine sandy neck.

'They are all the same, my love,' he whispered in Arabic to the mare. 'All the Franks are alike in their madnesses and their passions. Malik Rik eats himself up . . .' The horse blew through its nose again. Umar smiled. 'But don't you worry, my lovely. You are an Arab too. And we can understand one another . . .' The horse tossed its head a little. 'Which is more than they can. For they do not even understand themselves . . .' He patted the mare. 'For you see, when they are not busy killing others, they are busy killing themselves.'

Unlike Mark de Dinan, Umar could read the dark hollows which threw shadows across the eyes of de Lacey when he lowered his guard. Perhaps it was because *he* was not blinded by devotion. Umar ibn Mamun watched as Richard and Mark were lost to view. Between him and them the twin arms of the quintain stood like a gallows; a thing of suffering and of pain. The sacks hung like victims on a gibbet. It seemed appropriate somehow.

In the nearest manor building, knight and squire were unaware of Umar's shrewd appraisal. 'What do we know about the bishop's marshal?' Richard sipped a cup of cool wine as he asked the question.

Mark glanced up from tidying up the sword, a rag stained with dirt in his hand, his face concentrated. This was a familiar feature of Richard's conversation – to clarify what he knew by setting it before Mark as a question. Mark found it a little disconcerting. It was as if he was being examined as to the extent to which he had remembered the counsels shared with his knight. With anyone else but Richard it would have seemed inquisitorial, but de Lacey never treated Mark in that way. Perhaps that was why the squire loved him, even though he did not understand him.

'He fought with King Richard on crusade and in Normandy. Rumour has it that he commanded a troop of the King's mercenary Saracens in the wars against the French king.'

Mark looked to see if Richard was in agreement – he was. Satisfied, he continued: 'He holds a number of small manors in England. Two from the Bishop of Salisbury; sergeantry fiefs in return for which he acts as marshal for the bishop's household.

'But he also has a manor on the borders of Normandy and helped organise the recruitment of mercenaries for John, paid for by last year's scutage taxes.

'He is said to be shrewd and a man who guards his opinion. A good fighter too but not one who turns to violence unnecessarily. A clever man to be watched – no fool. And he knows his horses.'

Richard smiled. 'Yes . . . that interests me the most. As the bishop's man he has access to some of the finest horses in the south-west of England.'

Richard sighed as he considered the information which Mark had retold him. As the squire well knew it was all familiar to the knight. But to hear it laid out before him helped Richard to consider it anew. Falkes de Mauleon could become a very important part of his plans. For no one with control of so many fine horses could be ignored by a man as driven as Richard de Lacey.

Ever since he had set up his base at the Templar convent of Temple Buckland he had been on the lookout for men like de Mauleon. Now at last he was coming at Richard's invitation, stopping at the manor on his way back to the bishop's cramped cathedral at Old Sarum, in Wiltshire.

Outside in the hall the lay brothers of the order were preparing the midday meal. Richard could hear them talking through the wooden panels of the solar. 'He will be here soon,' he said softly. 'I think I shall stretch my legs in the courtyard. A little walk will work up an appetite after a morning's sloth.'

If the truth were to be known, Richard's body was aching from his exertions and it was easier to stand than to sit. The careless reference to the morning's exercise made Mark wince. He would rather forget the humiliation inflicted by the quintain. Clearly Richard refused to let it be buried. It made Mark fear that they would be out there again before much longer. And for what? De Dinan could see no point in it. When would Richard admit that his fighting days were over for good? Mark wished he had an answer to the questions buzzing in his head.

Outside in the hall the handful of Templar knights were gathering for the Friday fish meal. They were led by the conventual preceptor – the aged and scarred leader of this tiny outpost of the Knights Templar. The soldier monks had broken off from the day's routine of prayer, mixed with the running of the manor. Each wore the familiar white hooded mantle and tonsure of the order. The less exalted sergeants, in their brown habits, were also assembling.

The Templar knights exchanged greetings with de Lacey. For a few moments he stopped to discuss with them the guest who, even now, must be approaching. They had seen the letter and seal of the English provincial master and knew that de Lacey travelled with the blessing of the Grand Master in Acre.

At the weekly chapter meeting of the order the preceptor had instructed them to do all they could to assist the visiting knight within the bounds of the daily round of worship and administration. As a result they treated him with careful respect, even though he was not yet a sworn brother of the Order.

The few pleasantries over, Richard waited for the marshal in the sunshine. It was cool but not cold. It was only late February, but the winter had been its usual mix of mild and damp, and now spring seemed to have arrived early.

The wild daffodils were splashes of gold in the still-leafless woods, which gathered in the folds of the hills south of the convent. Lambs were already rejoicing as they skipped and jumped in the downland pastures above the manor. All was new life, so why did Richard feel as if he was dying? As if he was wasting away with some vile canker that ate at his inner being. He forced himself to look at the sun's rays on the thatch of the barns. It was a beautiful day and somehow he had to break the hold of this depression.

A thrush was singing its heart out in the nearby copse but all he could think about was the humiliation at the quintain. The words on his sword mocked him amongst these soldier monks whose martial energy seemed only to emphasise his own impotence.

There were hoof beats in the yard. Richard shook out his thoughts. He forced himself to smile and to enjoy the day. No one was interested in his foolishness, and now here was an opportunity to get things moving with the bishop's man. There was no need for depression, or gloom.

As at Fontevrault he drove his despair beneath the surface of his smile. Falkes de Mauleon was here and there were things to be accomplished. The brothers at Temple Buckland took their meals in silence. There were only five of them in this convent and a similar number of sergeants and lay workers. An extra trestle table had had to be added to their usual arrangement to accommodate their honoured guests.

On separate tables – lower down the hall – the sergeants and the retainers of de Mauleon and de Lacey ate their meals under the same discipline. All the while they ate, one of the white-robed Templar knights read aloud from the Scriptures.

After the meal, as the lay brothers packed away and the Templars returned to the routine of the sacred office, Richard and Falkes retired to the little first-floor solar.

Both men had eaten well, as the next day was the fast preceding the feast of St Matthias. And so it was with some relief that they settled against the dark panels of the solar and sipped at their wine.

'It's a small community this,' Richard explained to his guest as Mark waited on them. 'They administer the land of the manor and send the bulk of its revenues to the provincial treasury, from where it goes to support the work of the Order in the Holy Land.'

Falkes nodded. 'We deal with a number of Templar convents as well as with the soldier-monks of the hospitallers.'

His narrow eyes watched Richard's every move. His relaxed slouch hid a powerful body always alert. He recognised something of the same coiled tension in the knight opposite him. But there was something brittle about it; something explosive, as if the urbane exterior hid a fire almost out of control. The thought intrigued de Mauleon.

'As you know well, this is fine pasturing country. But I'm not interested in the sheep on the downs. I'll leave that to the Glastonbury monks and the brothers here. It's horses that I am interested in. And not any horses.' Richard's eyes sparked. 'Only the best and the strongest. And I know that you are a man who has the same heart.'

Falkes gave a slight nod of the head.

'I know how fine the bishop's horses are,' Richard continued. 'What I seek is a moulding of strong, heavy, cold-blooded beasts with the finest Arab hot-blooded mares . . . I know that you have high horses proud and strong . . .'

'And what is in it for the bishop?' The question was carefully put but it made Richard pause. 'As you say, the bishop has many fine horses. Strong, feather-legged work horses and proud riding horses and stallions for the hunt. What does he stand to gain from your quest?'

'You are thinking that the bishop will need a good reason if you are to do business with the Templars?' De Mauleon merely smiled and nodded. 'Because there is little love lost between him and the order . . .'

'I did not say that.'

'No,' said Richard as he put down his wine. 'But 'tis common knowledge that the Templars' right to have their own churches and cemeteries and their freedom from episcopal excommunication sits uneasily with the bishops . . .'

'I merely care for the lord bishop's horses . . .' Falkes gave a gesture of self-effacing modesty. It made no impact on de Lacey.

'I know better than that. And I have an offer to make. Firstly I will pay at least as well as anyone else for the right to have my mares covered by the tallest and strongest of the bishop's cold-blood hunter crossbreeds. I shall match the best price you can command anywhere else – penny for penny.

'And more: I shall grant to the bishop one in every three of the foals produced by my Arab mares from such a covering.'

There was no hiding the effect of the offer on de Mauleon. He was interested. 'I shall speak of this with the bishop. You understand that I cannot agree to such an arrangement without first consulting with him?' Richard nodded. 'But I am sure that he will view such a generous offer with great favour..'

'There is much in it to our mutual advantage.' Richard's words were carefully chosen but he could not disguise the excitement in his voice.

Falkes' grey eyes registered something like a passing smile. 'Perhaps you would show me your Arabs before I go on this afternoon?' He had already done his research and knew the quality of the horses of this passionate young knight. Nevertheless Falkes de Mauleon never overplayed his hand. 'I shall have to describe them to the bishop.'

'Of course.' Richard forgot the full meal and the cool wine. 'Let us go now. There is no time like the present.' It was as if he felt that the mere sight of the magnificent beasts would seduce de Mauleon to his plans. 'Unless you wish for more . . .'

'No, I have enjoyed the wine but it is enough.' The grey eyes smiled again. And then the smile was gone.

Outside in the spring sunshine Umar was talking to the visiting grooms who had accompanied the bishop's marshal. At a nod from Richard he left off his conversation and accompanied his master to the pastures. Falkes gave the Saracen a quick appraisal but there was no hostility in the look, only the same measuring observation with which he had studied Richard.

The mares came to the fence, whickering softly at the approach of familiar faces and scent. Richard stroked one white-blazed face. The mare blew through her nose with contentment. Umar fondled the mane of the mare he had groomed that morning.

'They are fine.'

Richard glanced at his guest; the approval was clear though the words were few. Even this detached observer of men could not disguise his reaction to the horses. The realisation satisfied de Lacey: it was as he had hoped and as it had to be if he was to succeed.

'Now – more wine?'

De Mauleon shook his head. 'I fear that I must decline such a kind offer. I must ride on if I am to reach my destination before dark.'

'Where are you riding to this afternoon?'

The question was innocent enough but a veil dropped across the narrow eyes. 'To one of the manors north of here, and then on to Old Sarum.' Whether all would be accomplished in one day was not clear. And Falkes clearly had no intention of elaborating.

Richard did not notice the change in look. He was too busy patting the horse. 'It is a pity, for we could have talked longer. But I understand.'

Falkes turned from the pasture. There was something else on

his mind, but that was utterly shielded from de Lacey. Two things in fact; two things which were now inextricably linked. One of them was a young woman with hair the colour of a sea at sunset, and the other . . . well that was so secret that Falkes had not yet decided what to do about it. Either way, there was nothing in either issue to share with this knight, so Falkes kept his counsel on both.

When Falkes and his companions had saddled up and bade their farewells, Umar approached his master. He was waylaid by Mark. There was a sprinkling of acid in Mark's voice.

'What do you want?'

'My lord should hear what I have discovered . . .'

Mark sneered. 'What you have discovered?' He imitated Umar's accent. 'And what have you discovered then?' His tone was challenging.

Umar's face showed no reaction. 'It is for my master . . .'

'You bloody heathen. If I ask you a question then you will give me an answer.' Mark had not forgiven the Saracen for seeing Richard's humiliation during the morning. 'I'll decide whether it is worth wasting his time with . . .'

'Mark, what is it?' Richard had emerged from the stables, hearing a raised voice in the yard. 'Is there a problem?' He saw Umar. 'What is it?'

Mark glared at the groom, daring him to be so bold. Umar dared. 'My lord, I spoke with the grooms of the knight who visited you. They were careful but I know what they were speaking about . . .'

'Riddles!' Mark regretted it as soon as he had said it. Richard silenced him with a glance.

'Go on . . .'

'There is a horse that they are seeking. It is not here yet – but it is coming. It is coming somewhere close to here. They let it slip to me and then sought to cover it up. It was clear that I should not have heard of it at all . . .'

'Soloriens!'

Umar nodded. He knew the significance of what he had heard. More importantly he knew what Richard longed to hear. 'I think so, my lord. The way they spoke of it, it could be no other. I am sure that it is the stallion that I saw. No other could excite such secrecy and yet such admiration. There were both these feelings in their words. And fear too . . .'

At that moment Mark de Dinan knew that he hated Umar more than anyone else he had ever met. He was unable to explain his loathing, but it ran deep, into a dark pit of bitterness.

Richard's face was alight, his blue eyes sparkled. It was as if the news threw off the wound and the pain. He turned to Mark, quite forgetting his earlier rebuke. 'This is it, Mark. The horse that we are looking for. And providence has brought us together. It is the hand of God.'

He flexed the muscles of his stiff arm. It had to be true. Only this stallion could blot out the despair that the episode at the quintain had once more thrown in his face. Only this mission could ransom him from defeat. It had to, for there was no other way for him. It had to be enough.

'Well done, Umar. You have done very well indeed. Has he not done well, Mark?' The words were out and Richard did not stop to see their effect. His mind was already far away.

Mark nodded stiffly. 'Very well.' The hint of praise was drawn from him like a tooth. And in his heart he knew that he must kill Umar ibn Mamun.

Ranulf Dapifer studied the ledgers before him. They recorded the numbers of cattle which had survived the winter in the stockpens and whose lowing carried even to his accounts room in the stone-built undercroft. He called one of his assistants and bade him make a note for the next manorial court. The meadows would now be in defence until the summer, and all beasts found on the precious source of next winter's hay would be subject to fines.

He looked once more at the rolls of vellum, but his mind was not on his work. He put down his quill and a thin drop of ink hung precariously from the nib and then fell in a black ball to the floor rushes. It was unlike the steward to be idle. Idleness had no place within his ordered world, but that world was changing.

'Fetch me some wine.'

The assistant scurried off about his task. Ranulf wanted to be alone; his thoughts felt all the more private for the lack of onlookers. It was hard to believe that two months had elapsed since the death of Gilbert de Cantelo. Already the sheriff's men had been all over the manor and the lady Joanna hardly back from the shire court in Ilchester. Normally such an intrusion, such an invasion of outsiders into his domain, would have outraged the steward. But it had curiously excited him. In fact he had never felt so excited in his whole life. That too was new; he was not a man given to bursts of excitement.

'Your wine, sir.'

Ranulf took it without a word, sipping it for a moment. 'Go and get yourself something to eat . . .'

The young assistant looked at him without comprehension. They had worked, as was routine, since before dawn, with the usual break for cold meats and morning mass at nine. It was still some time until the noon dinner and Ranulf never relaxed the work schedule. Suddenly realising his luck, the young man bobbed his thanks and was gone. Ranulf was glad to be alone again.

'It could be . . .' he murmured to himself. 'It could just be . . .' There was a rare light behind his usually sombre brown eyes.

A world of possibilities had suddenly opened up before him. He would never have willed Gilbert's death, but now that the tragedy had happened . . . He drank a little more of the wine. It was from possibilities like this that greatness occurred. For a man content with his station that was a strange thought, but perhaps he had never been content – only resigned. And even that only through force of habit.

For years he had expected little better than this post in the household of a minor baron who lived on the fringes of power and might. Until now . . . until now. Now all that had changed. Now the King was his master – well, the King's sheriff, but that was close enough. He, Ranulf Dapifer, was a steward of the King. The thought gave rise to that little twist of excitement again, for if he was careful he might be noticed. Everything depended on being noticed.

'God knows,' he whispered quietly, 'I deserve to be, after all the work I have done.'

Nearby, in the manor chapel, Joanna de Cantelo was praying before her father's tomb as she did every day. Only that morning Dapifer's wife had shed a tear for the 'poor young thing'. But in Ranulf's opinion, his wife – like Joanna – had little grasp of the realities of the world. For Ranulf knew that more than death had come out of that tumble on the downs. It had given him a chance, and he was not going to let it pass him by. No one was going to stand in his way. No one and nothing.

Chapter 5

Gilbert de Cantelo had long desired to improve and enlarge the little church which served both the manor at Horsingham and the hamlets around it. When he had inherited the manor from his father, the church had consisted only of the low nave, a tiny chancel and a squat stone tower. All had been built within two generations of the deaths of the last of the old landholders – those who had fought with Harold at Hastings.

This Norman church had enveloped and destroyed the little Saxon place of worship, but still – a century after its building – Gilbert had desired something better. After all, the manor had continued to prosper – despite the troubled times – and, though many others had died, he had returned safely from crusade. It had seemed only proper to record his gratitude to God in stone and mortar.

Two years before the collision with William Catface's dog, the masons and carpenters had arrived from Sherborne along with the carts of Ham Hill stone and flint rubble. Their ladders and wooden scaffolds still hung to the south side of the new tower; the work incomplete when Gilbert had gone in person to give thanks to his maker.

Joanna knelt before the candles on the side altar. To her right a tomb of freshly cut stone held the mortal remains of her father. It was too soon to top it with an effigy, but already the stonemasons in Sherborne had been paid and even now were working on the carving of mail and shield and on reproducing the once-living face in the smooth, cold stone.

Joanna prayed here every day, for it gave her a curious comfort to be near him, even though a chasm separated them. Sometimes she felt as if she heard the distant echo of his voice, but the gulf was too wide and she could not hear his words. In truth she knew it was just her heart's imagination.

She was no stranger to death. Who could be? Her own mother had died; people in the manor were injured and died; servants died of fever, in childbirth; children died before they even had names. Villagers whose faces she scarcely knew were carried to the fenced-off graveyard, sewn into their winding sheets. And once – as the spades had cut into the wet soil – she had glimpsed the shining bones of the dead of a previous generation, all jumbled up in the sacred earth. There was no denying death and yet never had it touched her like this.

'Oh, Father . . .' What could she say to sum up her grief? 'I miss you so very much . . . I love you . . .'

Then she was silent, she had said it all. She still loved him and mere death could not stop that. She had loved him the morning that he took his horse up on to the misty downland. She had loved him as she prepared for his return. She had loved him when, unbeknown to her, he was already dead. Then she had discovered that she had lost him – but love had not ceased. How could it? It had never relied on his continuous presence, only on the quality of the relationship they had built.

That quality remained; like the good work of the masons of another generation. It did not cease with their passing; indeed, its survival was mute testimony to the quality of their work. Her father was gone from her presence but she still loved him. She would always love him.

The nave was empty – just four walls and the new flagstones that Gilbert had purchased. All silent this Saturday morning of St David's Day. The March sunshine fell through the windows into the deserted nave. Joanna was alone, except for Tilly, her constant companion.

'I miss him so. It gets worse instead of better, time is bringing no healing . . .'

Matilda nodded. 'I know, my lady. He was a fine lord and a good father.'

Joanna wanted to shout out 'Not just good but the best', but she controlled the urge within her. Already she felt a secret shame that she had confessed her weakness to her maid. In the past they had shared everything but it had caused no problems then. In those days there was nothing like this in Joanna's life to be shared. The only hint of sorrow came from Tilly, when she turned from chatter and gossip and confessed how much she missed her dead mother and loathed her father's new wife. Joanna's role had been to listen and console. That had been easy.

It was easy to share when there was no cost. But to share when it revealed vulnerability – that was a new experience to Joanna. She was a stranger to it and it disturbed her; it shook the very foundations of her life, for she had never felt such feelings before. A tide of helplessness was lapping about her. She kicked at it – sometimes in anger and increasingly in distress – but it did no good. She might as well kick at the sea.

'My lady . . .?'

Joanna realised that she had been dreaming again. That too was a new phenomenon. She frequently found her thoughts drifting off these days. Sometimes the daydreams were focused on a past event and she would catch herself scrutinising her memory for every last detail. At other times they were a sombre reassessing of her present situation, all the more bleak for the fact that the hours of examination seemed to open up no new way forward.

It was disconcerting to discover these new things about herself. Emotions and habits of mind that she had never been aware of before. Her father's death and all that had ensued from it seemed to have opened a Pandora's box of new and distressing experiences.

She shook her head – close-wimpled in white linen – and squeezed the slim white hand which Tilly offered her. 'It's nothing. I just have a lot on my mind, you understand.' There was a movement at the door. Both young women looked up to see Stephen Pierson.

'Lady Joanna, there is a visitor to see you.'

'Not another of the sheriff's officials?' Annoyance rose in her voice. She was sick of their interference in her affairs. 'What does he want this time?'

Stephen frowned. He was not at all at home with the new Joanna. He had felt far more at ease with the confident young lady who was without fear. This new and less predictable woman made him wary. He no longer felt free to laugh and tease her; he found himself more formal with her.

'It is the bishop's marshal, Falkes de Mauleon. He requests to speak with you.' Stephen glanced at Tilly who offered him a careful smile. 'I left him at the hall, not being sure if you were still here. The steward has offered him wine.'

Joanna was surprised. 'I had not expected him again so soon.'

She was puzzled. The marshal had visited the manor only a few days earlier. She had missed him as she was out riding. It had been a week ago yesterday. Never before had he been so regular a visitor.

'I wonder why he is here?' She roused herself. 'I must go and see.'

As Joanna left the church, Tilly followed behind a little more slowly than usual. She brushed past Stephen although there was quite enough room to avoid him.

'I've hardly seen you these past few days,' Stephen said suddenly. Matilda looked up – half surprised at his forwardness and forgetting her own. 'Are you well?'

It was hardly true that they had not seen one another, but Joanna had gone only rarely to the stables and so the two had hardly spoken alone since Sherborne.

'My lady keeps more to the solar and the church than the stables at the moment. Are you well, Stephen?' Her dark eyes smiled at him with a mixture of shyness and desire. He seemed not to notice the look.

'It's not right.' Stephen shook his blond head.

Tilly frowned. 'What isn't right?' She had hoped for a look which at least mirrored her own feelings. When it was not forthcoming she felt rather obvious and foolish. 'What's not right?' she asked, a little sharp note in her voice.

'The way things are here. The sheriff's men about the manor and . . . and . . .' He rubbed his beard with a clenched fist. 'The way that the Lady Joanna is. She's not as she used to be.'

'You can hardly be surprised at that.' Tilly lifted her pretty little button nose. 'After what she has been through . . .'

'No, I'm not surprised.' Stephen was, however, surprised at the defensive note in the maid's voice. He had not meant to be critical – or had he? He tried to regain the initiative. 'But it's not right. That's all I'm saying, and I don't like it.' He sounded less confident than usual, as if he too was unfamiliar with the ground that he was crossing.

'Tilly.' Joanna's voice came from the churchyard.

'I must go – I am keeping my lady waiting.'

Stephen wanted to stop her, to catch her with one strong arm and draw her back; to apologise for having offended her. But instead he let her go. For the life of him he could not think what he had said to annoy her. It was as if nothing was as it used to be. The groom swore under his breath, at the events and at the incomprehensible nature of women.

Outside in the sunlight Tilly found she was spared from apologising for keeping her mistress waiting, for Joanna was no longer alone. The marshal had not waited in the hall. Instead he had come to find her himself. Matilda waited at a discreet distance, silently assessing the good-looking visitor. The only other witness to the meeting was a roughly dressed man standing waist-deep in a new grave. He threw a wide-eyed look in the direction of the man and woman who stood near the pile of fresh earth that he had turned up. As Tilly waited for her mistress she could not but notice just how much like a cat's the grave-digger's face was. The resemblance really was quite striking.

Falkes ignored both maid and grave-digger. He had caught sight of Joanna from the manor house and come immediately to intercept her. He kissed her hand and for a moment held it. She felt the edge of his black moustache against her fingers. His grip was strong – like every part of the man. Joanna saw the power held within his stocky body and carefully controlled face. There was something appealingly handsome about him, though his face was weathered and a little heavy. As she looked into the narrow grey eyes, she sensed a balanced masculinity which went deeper than simply physical proportions; a man totally controlled and relaxed with himself. It rose from a self-assurance that was as striking as it was understated.

'I hope you are well, Lady Joanna.'

Joanna was surprised, though complimented, that he had taken the trouble to meet her at the church when Dapifer had made wine available. 'I am well. Have you come to confirm the covering of the bishop's mares?' Joanna felt this was hardly necessary since all had been arranged already by the ever-efficient Ranulf Dapifer. Even the previous week's visit had not been necessary but more of a social call to offer condolences on her father's death. 'Ranulf has kept me fully informed regarding the arrangements with the bishop.'

Falkes nodded. 'It will soon be their time, and as I was passing . . . I fear you were not here last week . . .' Despite his usual reserve, he had the look of one who was thinking more than he was saying. 'I have heard that you are now a ward of the King. No doubt the sheriff is treating you well.'

Joanna had not expected concern from one who had merely come to finalise business arrangements. 'The sheriff treats me well though I have seen little of him . . .' She found herself unexpectedly tongue-tied and put it down to her surprise at the man's question.

'He has returned to France and the King.'

The bishop's marshal seemed well informed. And his narrow grey eyes remained fixed on her, never leaving her for a moment. Joanna was no stranger to men but was not sure how to reply to this one. She was no longer sure what he had come to see her about. It was almost as if he too was not quite sure.

Seeking to make up for this deficiency in the conversation she asked: 'Have you ridden far today?'

'Along the edge of the vale from Sturminster. There was some delay in my journey as the King's foresters were destroying a number of cottages some way to the east of here. I stopped to watch . . .'

'Why ever were they doing such a thing?' Joanna was happier now the conversation seemed to flow more.

'Ahh,' Falkes replied, 'it seems they found a two-year-old buck that had bled to death from an arrow wound. The inquest on the deer had not turned up anyone as a culprit for the crime, so they were destroying the two cottages nearest to the discovery of the body . . .'

A strangled cough interrupted him. The marshal and Joanna looked to where the grave-digger was shovelling as if his life depended on it. Falkes shook his head; it was as if the man had reacted to what had just been said. Realising that the workman might have a smattering of Norman-French, Falkes lowered his voice and turned away as he finished his comments.

'It was the usual business: women crying, men cursing and the King's men holding them back with spears.' He shrugged. 'From there we rode on here – on our way to Sherborne.'

He offered her his arm and Tilly came up smartly as chaperone. Falkes smiled slightly as he recognised the meaning behind the movement. Joanna took his arm. She felt the hardness of his muscles through the padded leather riding jerkin. The grey eyes were fixed on her once more and she smiled slightly. Together they walked back to the manor, with Tilly following closely. Behind them the grave-digger was hacking away at the soil as if he was digging a tomb for half the population of the West Country.

All the way Falkes politely questioned Joanna about her horses and about the running of the manor, about how she was managing since her father's death. To each answer she gave him, he nodded slightly and gave away nothing more by way of comment. It was as if the entire conversation was conducted with the absolute economy of effort and words and at no point could Joanna discover exactly why he had called at the manor. It was all a little strange.

On the downs above Temple Buckland the villeins were sowing spring wheat on the curving strips of the arable fields. It was Tuesday, 18 March, just over two weeks since St David's Day. Richard de Lacey pulled his horse on to the verge to allow a team of peasants to drive their docile little oxen back towards the manor – the morning's ploughing completed. He hoped to be in

Dorchester before the end of the afternoon and was pleased when the last of the ox-team had passed. Pulling on his reins he guided his mount back on to the rutted ridgeway track. Behind him, Mark, Umar and two of the brown-cloaked Templar sergeants did likewise. One carried a lance and its red cross pennant fluttered in the spring breeze.

'How long will we stay in the town, my lord.' Mark drew up alongside him and they cantered abreast.

'Just the two nights, I think. We should be back the day after tomorrow – before vespers.'

'Do you think that we will hear any news of the great horse?' Mark was eager to talk of their quest. 'There must be someone who knows about it.'

Richard nodded vigorously and his riding cloak rustled on his shoulders. 'I think that we should hear news of it there. It is a busy town and people come from miles about to the market. Besides, the King's fortified house is there too. Someone there may be persuaded to speak of the horse.'

'I hope so.' Mark glanced back at Umar, who rode a little distance behind. 'I'm sure it was not just idle gossip.' His eyes narrowed as he looked at the impassive tanned face behind him.

Richard slapped the pommel of his saddle. 'It was no idle tale, believe me. That stallion was brought here for a purpose, and no doubt the bishop's marshal heard of it.' He paused as he recalled the powerful face and disciplined eyes of de Mauleon. 'And he is a shrewd one, by Our Lady. He knows something and his men let it slip. But we shall discover the whole of it . . . have no doubt.'

Mark had no doubt. Richard had not returned to the humiliation of the quintain. Instead he seemed to be more positive and less obsessed with recovering his fitness. Mark was happy about that; even if he hated the man who had brought the news which had produced the improvement. As long as Richard was confident, then so was his squire, for if Richard said they would do it then they would. De Dinan glanced once more at the Saracen groom. And they would not need that alien heathen's help either. He could stop in his place and they would do it alone. Indeed there was only one irritant in Mark's mind – only one piece of grit in the oyster – and that was that Richard had ordered the groom to accompany them at all.

The road was the same one that Joanna and her father had ridden the previous summer; the high open road which crossed the watershed of the rivers Piddle and Cerne. From the patches of woodland beside the road sweet violets flashed dark-blue eyes at the passing travellers. On the rolling downs beyond, the great flocks of sheep spread out amidst the scattered trees.

'They seem numberless.' Mark shaded his eyes as he looked at the distant sheep. 'There must be hundreds.'

Richard nodded in agreement. 'And all walked down from the sheep runs about Damerham. They must be exhausted after the journey. It has to be all of forty miles . . .'

'And are all run from the abbey at Glastonbury?'

'The majority, but not all. The Templar brothers also oversee the shepherding of many hundreds too. In this high, wild country the sheep far outnumber the people.'

Richard was right, for the road was deserted. They met no other travellers until after eight miles the road dropped down to Charminster and the flood plain of the river Frome. Before they left the downs behind they stopped to eat a light meal. Compared to the usual noontime repast it was a slight dinner of flat bread and hard white cheese washed down with a flagon of white wine.

It was early afternoon when they reached Dorchester itself. They approached it over the Friary Mill ford and entered through the minor gate to the east of the castle. They were heading for a well-built house which stood in the shadow of the castle; in an arm of Holy Trinity parish and in the northern quarter of the town. Unlike its fellows, this house was constructed from stone, at least on the ground floor. There were no windows in the wall and those in the timber-built first floor were shuttered. A narrow gateway opened on to the muddy street and it too was locked tight.

Richard motioned to Mark, who dismounted. With one leather-gloved fist he hammered on the door. There was no reply and he looked at Richard, who indicated that he should try again. After the second hammering there was at last the sound of movement inside. A bolt slid back, and then another. They moved on well-oiled frames and without a rattle. It was more the swish of a snake through grass; a creature secretive and wary. The door opened an inch or two, and a pair of dark eyes looked out.

'Who calls?' The voice was careful and tense.

Before Mark could announce them, Richard leaned forward in the saddle. 'Tell Aaron of Dorchester that it is the knight who met him at the ford in Normandy.'

At this cryptic message the doorkeeper hesitated for a moment, then the door closed, the bolts sliding home once more. 'Damn cheek.' Mark was outraged. 'Who does he think he is to keep you waiting outside? We could get this door down . . .'

'That's enough, Mark.' Richard seemed untroubled at the welcome. 'It is a big enough door to break your shoulder.' And when he saw that his squire was not amused, he added less compromisingly: 'And all the Jews of England are serfs of the Crown. There are those in the royal garrison here who would soon put a stop to your housebreaking.'

Mark felt annoyed with himself at speaking the way that he had. He had only meant to show outrage at the way his knight was being treated, yet he seemed to have got it wrong. He hated the Jew, Aaron, for making him blunder. He looked away from Richard to where Umar was still sitting on his horse. There was no expression in the Saracen's eyes but he made the mistake of looking at de Dinan. The bastard is mocking me, Mark thought bitterly. If Richard were not here I would teach that black heathen a lesson he would not forget in a hurry. Only then did Umar read the murder in the squire's face and glance away. By then it was too late, for the damage had been done.

The serpent bolts hissed again and the door was fully opened. A big man in his mid-twenties stood before them. He was dark-complexioned with curly black hair. He was swathed in a thick cloak, but from the way he held himself, Richard guessed that he was armed.

'My master bids you enter.'

Richard dismounted and ordered his other companions to do

so. Mark was already on foot. They led their horses in through the passageway and beyond to a wide courtyard. It was a translation from one world to another. From a central garden a willow cast its elegant arms down about its slim trunk. Fragrant herb bushes rose from warm-coloured terracotta pots, and the walls which faced the courtyard were painted in geometric patterns of cobalt and vermilion.

Richard laughed with surprise and joy at the bright welcome of the place. Mark just turned and turned, taking in the colours with astonishment. The two Templars peered at the exotic surroundings with ill-disguised unease. Only Umar was unmoved.

'It is like a house in Acre, or in Tripoli.'

Mark was right and Richard nodded. 'Quite so, it is a world within a world. And who would ever know of its existence, with the entrance shut so tight against the curious?'

The doorkeeper seemed used to the surprise of Gentiles on entering the house of Aaron the Jew. He waited patiently until the astonishment had gone from their faces, then he gestured to Richard and Mark to follow him. From the courtyard a passageway of chequered stones led into a suite of rooms. Wine was laid on a table, and a bowl of pastel-coloured sweetmeats. Wooden benches, finely carved, stood beside the table; Aaron himself came to meet him.

'Welcome to my poor house.' He bowed before them. 'I had not expected such an honoured guest. If I had known of your coming I would have been ready to welcome you . . .'

'Instead of keeping my master waiting in the street.'

Richard shut Mark off with a swift hand movement. He resolved to speak with his squire after the interview was over.

'I apologise for that,' Aaron continued. 'It is a . . .' He paused to consider his words. ' . . .a precaution. I am sure you understand. If I had known it was you, it would never have happened.' Ever the practised diplomat, the merchant clapped his hands and a servant poured the wine. 'Please be seated.'

Richard took a seat and Mark stood beside him. Aaron waited until the knight was comfortable and then sat himself. 'Are you well, Richard de Lacey? And have you recovered from your injury? An injury gained saving my worthless life from the hands of the King of France's men!'

Richard laughed softly but painfully. 'That injury was mending, but . . .' Then he thought better of it and said instead: 'But it is another matter which brings me to you. I need news and there is none better to provide it for me than you. I know that great and small pass through your doors. And the world's news comes with it. If I need news, Aaron of Dorchester will have heard of it.'

The grey-flecked head nodded at the compliment. 'My poor house is honoured by many guests. Guests from afar and near.'

And most of them good Christian souls paying you interest, you usurious parasite, Mark thought bitterly.

'I need information.' Richard took one of the sweetmeats; it was fragrant and soft. 'Firstly about a horse . . .'

'Ah, yes, you seek the great horses. I remember.'

'There is a horse,' Richard continued. 'And not just *any* horse. It is a stallion without peer. A noble beast worth a king's ransom.' He paused to reflect upon the accuracy of his description. 'Indeed it is a hostage of sorts, for it is the warhorse of Hugh de Lusignan . . .'

'The baron who rose in revolt against King John and who was captured last summer at Mirabeau.'

'The very same. It is his horse and John has shipped it to England; my groom saw it. We have heard tales about it but always incomplete. We want to know where it is . . .' He could not hide the urgency in his voice. 'You may have heard of it. Have you?'

'Your groom saw it? The Saracen who has the winning way with horses . . .' When Richard looked surprised Aaron added: 'I am no expert with the beasts but I can spot a man who has the gift. And that one can talk to them and they understand. I saw him and I do not forget easily.'

Richard nodded in agreement. 'That is why he is my man. No other can match his skill with the hot-blooded Arabs. And as you say, he talks and they understand. It is a gift.'

He smiled, for Aaron's words praised his own judgement too. Also it was refreshing to hear someone who adopted a view as pragmatic as his own with regard to the Arab groom. Perhaps it was to be expected from another kind of alien. Richard smiled, for, unlike Mark de Dinan, he felt a reluctant warmth for the wary Jewish merchant. It battled with so much within him but prevailed. Mark could see it and was not pleased.

Aaron was thoughtful. 'It is a dapple-grey?' Richard nodded. 'And as high as a house and eats men?'

'You've heard about the same horse all right.' Richard sounded relieved that his hope had not been in vain. 'What else have you heard?'

'One moment.' Aaron left the room for a few moments. When he returned there was a hint of a smile on his face. 'The King has it on his stud farm at Gillingham.'

Richard laughed. 'How do you know? Can you be sure?'

Aaron raised an open palm. The forefinger was missing. 'High and low come here. I hear more news than they whisper in the ears of their whores and much more than they'd ever whisper to their wives! Believe me – this is so. The horse is at Gillingham.'

Richard looked in triumph at Mark, who was staring with a curious intensity at the Jew. But before Richard could say a thing, the Jew spoke again.

'But the stallion will not stay there. It is going to a manor held by the King in wardship. One which has only recently come into his hands. I know the baron who once held it, for I loaned him money against the sale of some horses. He was rebuilding the church at the manor.

'It seems he died in some kind of accident after the Christmas feast. He only had a girl child and so she and the manor have passed into the gift of the King. It is to that manor that the horse is to go. You know how it is with manors held in wardship?'

'Very well indeed. There will be little of worth left there by the time the King has finished with it. It is the tradition – to despoil the manor of a ward. Then return what is left to the ward when he comes of age – or in this case when she is married off. But what of the horse?' Richard was not interested in the commonplace treatment of wards. 'The horse is what matters . . . When will it go there?'

'That I do not know, but I will try to find out. I owe you my life and this is a small enough thing to do for you.'

Richard was clearly satisfied. 'And what of the world?'

'The crusade?' Aaron seemed quietly confident that he had anticipated Richard's request.

'Yes – that first.' Richard took another of the sweets. 'These are very good . . .' He gestured towards Mark. 'Mark and I are staying at the Templar convent north of the downs. They are providing me with every assistance, but news is often old when it reaches us.

'The last I heard was that too few knights had arrived in Venice to pay the cost of the transportation to the east.'

Aaron drank a little wine. 'My porter said that you came in the company of the Templars . . .' He mused a little as if recalling a story. 'I met a man a month ago who was in France with the King. He too had Templar connections, but that is not the nub of the matter. While he was in France he met a merchant from Pisa who was travelling to Flanders in the cloth trade.'

He lifted one long finger and the attendant refilled his cup. 'It seems,' he continued, 'that the Venetians have demanded that the payment should be in kind. The payment they demanded was that those who have taken the cross should seize the city of Zara on the Adriatic, which the Venetians covet from the King of Hungary . . .'

'But that is a Christian city!' Richard was appalled. 'They will never agree to do it.' He was adamant. 'It is unthinkable that those who have taken the cross should sell themselves – like Brabançon mercenaries . . . like whores . . .'

'They have done it.'

Richard looked up as if stung. 'What?'

'It seems that the deed is done. The man I met said that he was told that the city was taken from the Hungarians and given to the Venetians last November – some four months ago.'

De Lacey's pleasure collapsed about him as he heard the terrible news; he shook his head as if he had heard wrongly, as if his hearing had failed him. It was only at that moment that he truly realised how many of his dreams had travelled, like a ghost, with the crusading armies; unseen but there beside them. Now those dreams lay in fragments, soiled and spurned.

'But they have sworn to free Jerusalem. To free the Holy City, not sell themselves to the Venetians . . .'

Aaron turned black eyes on his troubled guest. 'I fear there is worse to come, my friend . . .'

Richard looked up and the pain was carved on his face. 'Worse? What could be worse?'

'It is only a rumour and one I cannot as yet confirm. I heard it this very week from one of my own people – a man returning to Bristol, from Aquitaine. It seems that the Venetians have not yet been paid in full. There is talk that they have demanded assistance against the emperor in Constantinople . . .'

'He is a Christian, though – God forgive him – not a pure servant of our Holy Father in Rome. But even if he is a Greek he is still a believer . . .'

Aaron wisely made no comment, merely adding, 'It seems that regardless of that he is a rival of the Venetians for the trade of the east. They would prefer to see him humbled, and this is perhaps their chance . . .'

'But this is a holy crusade, not a pack of dogs fighting over a joint of meat.' The passion in Richard's voice was clear. 'By God, I would not have thought even the worst whoreson would have so degraded his sacred oath to fight the heathen.' He paused and then added, as if talking to himself: 'I cannot believe it. It cannot be true . . .'

The cause was everything. It was his hope, his reason; all that stood in the gap left by his broken knighthood. It was sacred and absolute and now seemed set to be polluted and stained as he watched, helpless to stop it. He closed his fist about his goblet with such savage anger that the cup trembled, splashing its contents on to the table. There it lay like a pool of blood, sinking into the wood.

In April the weather was hot and sunny. It was like summer already and the horses stood in the shade of the trees which dotted the pasture and brushed off the pestering flies with great sweeps of their feathery tails. Amidst the cornfields on the downs the children bent their little backs to pick out intruding weeds. Then, as the sun sank behind the ridge, they walked wearily home, the limp stems of corn cockle and thistles stuck in their patched tunics.

Matilda had left Joanna talking with Ranulf Dapifer. The taciturn steward was showing the accounts roll to his insistent mistress. It was as if the loss of the manor to the King had made Joanna more determined than ever to know every small detail of accounts and organisation. It was as if the mere knowledge stamped her ownership on the manor.

Dapifer was too polite to say anything but it seemed to Tilly that he felt the matter had little to do with Joanna any more. Nevertheless he had little choice but to go over the details with the insistent redhead. Tilly's unconscious glances through the undercroft door towards the evening sunshine had finally been rewarded. Joanna had dismissed her and for once she had deserted her post.

She walked away from the hall, across the dusty yard to the cobbled stables. Stephen was finishing the stable tasks for the day. A great roan stallion stood contentedly in its stall. Stephen was cleaning off the dried mud from the horse's coat with a well-worn dandy-brush. Tilly opened her mouth to speak but checked herself. Instead she leaned against the chewed wood of the stall post and watched him at work.

He was singing softly. She could not hear the words but the tune rose and fell like a distant breeze. The horse nuzzled him and he crooned into its long ear. The worst caked dirt removed, he began the laborious task of brushing the glossy coat in regular circling sweeps. Tilly held her breath, afraid that he might hear her. She had never watched him for so long before. Even now she felt strangely guilty. At intervals she glanced over her shoulder, afraid that her vigil might be observed. But no – the stable was silent and no one came.

She felt curiously excited to be so near him and yet unseen, as if she had gained admittance to a secret place of intimacy, as if the observation brought him somehow closer. He had rolled up the sleeves of his tunic and Tilly could see his muscles flowing with the rhythmic movement of the brush. In the half-light, his arms seemed almost chestnut with their weathered tan. There was something so masculine about the brownness of his arms. She thought of her own white limbs and thrilled at the thought of his sun-painted strength. She was fascinated by his arms.

The little hairs on his forearms were golden, like summer haze over a lake. The wrists were strong and the shoulders powerful. As she leaned forward she could see freckles where his neck met the collar of his tunic. The woollen cloth was frayed and the loose thread ends rose from the weave like the first wispy heads of corn in early spring. All this she noticed as if for the first time. And all the time she felt the guilt of looking at a man this way, and him only a groom – herself the daughter of a knight. Her father would have been angry and his new young wife appalled. But despite the sense of guilt – or perhaps because of it – she remained. Her heart beat so loudly she thought that he must hear it.

She knew it was wrong but imagined what it would be like to feel those arms around her. She dismissed the thought but it lingered like a hound thrust away from the table. Then it slunk back. This time she did not shove it off. She knew it was wrong – a wicked sin – but she wondered what it would be like to kiss him. To feel his mouth over hers and run her fingers through his blond beard. She had never kissed a man in passion and she was a virgin. She looked, with an ache in her heart, at the groom.

Then he glanced round and she jumped; so did he. 'Tilly . . . I mean, my lady,' he corrected himself, 'I did not know you were there . . .'

Matilda was scarlet. 'I was just . . . because . . .' All her usual composure deserted her. 'I was only . . . Lady Joanna bade me pick flowers for her room. In the woods below the downs . . .'

Then she picked up her skirts – clutching the folds with slim pale fingers – and ran away, out of the stable and into the radiant evening sunlight. She was red-faced but laughing as she ran across the yard. She was without shame and could not control herself.

At the edge of the yard she stopped and looked back; Stephen had followed her. Was that what she had wanted? Was that why the words about the flowers had leapt from her lips? When Joanna had said no such thing. She felt suddenly excited – more than she had ever felt before. She threw away her cautious thoughts and turned and scampered away. Her dress rose and her slim white ankles flashed.

She ran across the meadow and the horses there scattered before her. She ducked beneath the trees that fringed the trackway up on to the downs, and only then did she turn again. Stephen had begun to cross the meadow and her heart pounded at the sight. She ran on into the woods. The green-budded branches snapped against her arm but she was unaware. All she felt and heard was her own laughter.

Halfway across the meadow Stephen Pierson stopped. He had been startled by her presence and by her words. It was as if a sweet madness had filled the stable. It was only as he saw the horses returning to their grazing that he remembered his duty. He had yet to rub and polish the great roan, and the wheat straw needed banking up against the wall, for the horse to sleep on. He hesitated, then stopped. He looked at the green fringe of the woods, then back to the manor complex of hall, byres and outbuildings. He wanted to go after her but what about the horses? What about the evening's tasks? He frowned at the choice. He could not understand what had come over Tilly. It excited yet puzzled him.

Back in the yard someone was calling his name. One last time he looked at the woods; his face was creased with intense concentration. Then, slowly, he retraced his steps to the manor. It was all very well for Tilly to act so free. It was not so easy for him, there were more constraints on him. And he was not yet able to abandon the habits of a lifetime. As the young girl pushed further into the trees, she did so on her own.

It was some time before Tilly realised that she was alone. At first she leaned against one of the trees to catch her breath, which came in quick and excited gasps. Her wimple had come loose and she pulled at the trailing linen with one quick hand. She shook out the folds of her bobbed black hair. A blackbird was singing in the undergrowth and the woods were a lace pattern of shadows and mellow golden sunlight. She finally regained her breath and listened. There were no hurrying footsteps, no cries of her name.

At first she felt puzzled, then guilty at her wantonness, and then angry at her humiliation. Without a doubt, she was alone; he had not followed her. She crushed the wimple in one little white hand and threw it to the ground. It landed in a clump of nettles and cow parsley.

'Damn you, Stephen,' she murmured. And then, when she reflected on her own rank and the way in which she had acted, she said it with more bitterness. 'Damn you, Stephen Pierson . . . damn you.'

The sense of outrage burned almost as fiercely as her sense of shame, one fuelling the other. She sat down against a tree and tried to collect her thoughts. What was she to do? How could she ever go back to the manor? And yet she could not stay here much longer, for the tired sun had almost sunk behind the line of hills; the shadows were deepening in the tangled trees and bushes. The light was redder than before, and fading.

She heard a noise and started; it sounded like voices. They were close at hand and a little below her. Separated from her by the bushes was the sunken road which led up on to the downs. Nervously she pushed aside the branches. Her humiliation was temporarily forgotten as she squeezed through the undergrowth, ignoring the pulls on her dress. She was always curious; that was how she came to know the gossip on the manor before anyone else. Now her curiosity gripped her and pulled her towards the source of the noise.

The voices grew closer. Who could be approaching the manor at this time of day? The voices were masculine and confident and there was no attempt to hide their approach. That at least argued for the travellers being law-abiding folk. Below her, the track twisted and so she could only see a few yards. Then, as she held her breath, they rounded the bend. Her stomach tightened with excitement and fear. The gang of men who came into view were soldiers. Through the filigree of branches she saw mail and crossbows, kettle hats slung nonchalantly from spear points. Some of the men were singing.

A great horse was in their midst, a vast creature, a dapple grey now deeper dappled in the shadows of the wood. It was taller than any horse she had ever seen. She leaned forward to get a better look. The proud beast was harnessed in a way that she had never seen before. A heavy sheepskin cavesson cut the animal's vision and forced its head down, a tightly fitted martingale stopped the horse from raising its head higher, and the bondage was completed by a dropped noseband which was fitted below the snaffle bit and held the mouth shut. The creature was in chains. As well as the usual groom holding the reins in his right hand, a soldier on the other side also held a trailing rope. It was as if the animal was a captive; a prince held hostage. The other soldiers spread out around it as if shielding it.

Tilly leaned against a branch and it broke. She flailed wildly but failed to get a grip and fell. Head over heels she tumbled, striking her head as the branches whipped against her. Everything whirled about her and then with a jarring blow she landed in the rutted road.

Many hands pulled her up. Voices were raised, at first in alarm and then in amusement and derision. Tilly fought to make sense of the movement amidst the shadows. An arm gripped her about the waist and crushed the cry of protest from her. She was lifted and thrown from one soldier to another, like a hare tossed between hounds. Each one made the most of fumbling her as she was manhandled. All she could see was a kaleidoscope of leering eyes and bearded mouths laughing, and the hands were all over her.

Then the movement stopped and she found herself crushed against an unyielding body clad in cold mail and leather. A vice of a grip held her arms and pressed her into the leather jerkin and the links of the hauberk. The shouting had stopped and the silence was terrifying. Only the horse was snorting with alarm and being backed off up the track.

Matilda tossed her wayward fringe out of her face and looked up into two bright-blue eyes that seemed devoid of feeling, like glittering cold marbles. They frightened her but also stirred something strange within her. She was disturbed by the feelings and she struggled to be free.

The vice-like hands held her and she was quite unable to break their hold. She was too frightened to speak and when she opened her mouth to scream no sound would come. The hard and handsome young face stared down at her. A long scar ran along the jaw beneath the closely trimmed beard, which was as blond as snow. She felt her body melded into his own; he was the rock and she the sea. He was unyielding and she flowed about him. She was pressed to him; her legs parted and his thigh thrust between them against her. She struggled but it was no use.

Then he let her go and she fell. For a moment she was too stunned to think, then she leapt to her feet and ran. She ran as fast as she could, her legs pale as she pulled up her skirts, and her breath came hard and fast. She ran back to the manor with tears streaming down her face and her heart bursting. Behind her she could hear their laughter and the snorting of the mighty stallion.

It was Hokeday 1203 – the second Tuesday after Easter – and this year the day before the feast of St George. It was five weeks since Richard de Lacey had had his troubling interview with the Jew, Aaron of Dorchester. Once more the young knight had taken the high road across the open downs to the town beyond the meadows of the Frome. This time it was with one thing in mind: he had to know when the horse Soloriens was to go from Gillingham to Horsingham. The old Jew had promised to find out without either the King's men or the occupants at Horsingham learning of Richard's interest.

Whilst Richard took wine with Aaron, he sent Mark and Umar to collect new harness and a saddle which he had ordered from a leather-worker in the parish of All Saints. Due to the smells associated with leather tanning and working, the workshop was situated well down High East Street and up against the town's wall by Durngate, almost out of the town altogether. Here most of the offensive odours could waft away and pollute the residents of the royal manor of Fordington instead of the good burghers of the town.

Mark was determined that the Saracen groom should do the worst of the carrying and had ordered him from his horse to shoulder the wooden frame of the new saddle. As Mark paid over the silver pennies which Richard had entrusted to him, he became aware of the hostile mutterings of the leather-worker's apprentices. His irritation was soothed when he realised that it was directed against the dark-skinned groom; Richard had warned him to keep the Saracen safe from the hostile attentions of the town's citizens. De Dinan smiled grimly to himself; perhaps the eve of St George's Day was not a good time for the heathen to be seen about the streets of the town.

A crowd was gathering in the narrow alleyway outside. The overhanging wooden jetties of the surrounding buildings made it shadowy even in the early evening sunlight. To the south the buildings gave way to fields and gardens within the walls but the way back to de Lacey lay through the alleyway with its onlookers.

'Ther'll be trouble, I'm fearin.' The leather-worker pocketed his money and nodded towards the crowd. 'Best be off with 'im and get away frum 'ere.' He did not want trouble outside his workshop.

Mark nodded, and leaving the shop, he remounted his horse. It was obvious how the hostile stares were focused on Umar. The thought pleased the squire, who almost smiled. 'Don't dally,' he said sharply to Umar. 'Your master will not want to be kept waiting at the house of the Jew.'

It secretly pleased him to think that, despite Richard's lack of animosity towards Aaron, the knight was well enough aware of community opinion not to spend too much time there. Mark motioned to Umar. 'Keep quickly after me.' He glanced at the crowd as if that was reason enough for the Saracen to hurry. 'Let's go then.' His tone was brusque.

He pulled up the bridle of the groom's horse and led the two palfreys away at a slow walk. The crowd parted to let him through and then closed behind him. There were mutters and someone jostled Umar's arm; he shrugged and ignored the hatred. He kept his eyes fixed on the flicking tail of de Dinan's mount. It was strange but it seemed to be drawing away from him. Umar quickened his step but it was hard to go much faster, burdened as he was.

Mark could have made for High East Street, the east–west thoroughfare through the town. Instead he chose to turn his horse's head towards a more circuitous route up Durngate Street. As he did so, he noted that the mob was increasing in size. With a slight pressure of his knees Mark urged his mount forward and drew away from the overladen groom.

It was hard to tell who struck the first blow, but once struck there were others, and spitting and howling. The hate for the alien overflowed in a dark tide. Umar shielded his face with the raised cantle of the saddle, but a stone caught his forehead and he reeled. Another anonymous hand – made hero by the presence of the mob – threw another stone. Umar looked wildly for de Dinan but could see only the encircling faces of hate.

Further up Durngate Street Mark turned his mount to watch the riot. A smile of satisfaction played across his mouth and conker-brown eyes. Umar was almost lost now beneath the kicking mob. The rising gradient of the lane gave Mark a fine view of the Saracen's destruction. It also gave him a fine view of the bottom of the lane up which they had come. As a result he saw Richard before anyone else did.

'Damn!'

Clearly de Lacey had grown tired of waiting and had come looking for his servants in the company of the Templar sergeants. Mark could see the red cross on the brown breast of each soldier's mantle. As he had crossed the end of the lane Richard could not help but notice the riot. He had turned and was spurring his horse now, cantering up the lane.

'You lucky bastard,' Mark muttered, looking to where Umar was surrounded. 'You lucky bastard . . .'

De Dinan jabbed his heels into his palfrey's flanks and led the two horses into the mob at a rising gallop. The crowd scattered at his presence. Cries of alarm indicated that others had seen the approach of the other riders too. The mob had no stomach for violence against those who could fight back, and it broke up and fled.

'Thank God you were with him.' Richard was lifting the saddle off the semiconscious Umar. 'If you had not been here they may well have killed him.'

Mark had dismounted to kneel beside his knight. 'It was nothing, my lord. You ordered me to protect him. I only did as I was bidden . . .'

The horse chestnuts were in bloom, their great pale candles of blossom lighting up the tree's dark tower. From the woods the gentle breeze brought the aroma of wild garlic. In the pastures the horses lifted their heads to savour the fresh morning air, still dew-damp. As usual, Joanna and the household had been up since just after dawn. After three hours' checking through the manor court rolls she had breakfasted lightly at nine off the usual wine, cold meats and bread. Then she had returned to Dapifer's accounting room in the shadowy undercroft.

It was nearly noon and the main meal of the day when she finished dictating a letter to her steward. Tilly sat quietly in one corner as Joanna paced about the flag-floored room. Ranulf stood before a tall writing desk and was following her instructions, tight-lipped.

'. . .and furthermore, my lord sheriff, I beg . . .' She pursed her lips at the word. '. . .I beg your gracious attention in removing the common soldiery who have been billeted on this my manor.'

Ranulf hesitated and his pen hung in mid-air. He glanced at the young woman, who threw him a sharp look. 'Who have been billeted on this *my* manor,' she said with renewed emphasis. 'For they fear neither God nor man, treat my servants with nothing short of contempt and myself as if I am of little account.

'I doubt that it would please my lord the King to learn that they have no more respect for his loyal subjects residing in his realm of England than they do for rebels and traitors in Normandy and France . . .'

Dapifer's long face creased at the words but he wrote as he was bidden. The beginnings of a frown signalled his disapproval of Joanna's outrage. He thought of his own quiet wife supervising the kitchen servants in the way that he had taught her. In his opinion, Joanna de Cantelo could do a lot worse than learn from the women of the manor – those who, for all their different ranks, kept a discipline appropriate to their station. The very word discipline seemed alien to the young woman before him and he knew that the lack of acquaintance would bring only trouble.

Unmindful of Dapifer, Tilly was following Joanna's every move, as if every gesture and word was holy writ, her gaze intense and pale. It was as if the words were being wrung from her mistress rather than issuing freely forth.

Joanna stopped her perambulations in front of the steward and closed her dictation. 'I await your reply to my loyal request and beg your aid in righting this injustice which has been done to myself who am in your care as a ward of our lord the King.

'Written this day, Thursday, the fifteenth day of May, following the feast of St Matthias in the Year of Our Lord 1203, in the manor of Horsingham, county of Dorset.' Joanna narrowed her green eyes at Dapifer. 'Read it back to me, Ranulf, if you please.'

She leaned against the cool stone wall as the steward did as he was told. Her fine high-boned cheeks were flushed with the passion of her letter; she breathed slowly through delicate nostrils still slightly flared in anger. Tilly watched her and could not help but think how much she looked every inch like a human embodiment of the hot-blooded, proud horses that she loved so much. She was beautiful and yet it was a proud loveliness; a noble and sensuous beauty all the more poignant for its present captivity. It was as if one of the manor's finest hot-blooded mares had been laden down with chains of gross iron. As she thought of her mistress' captivity, she could not avoid thinking of the agents of that imprisonment. And most of all she could not help but consider Savaric de Breaute, the mercenary commander.

She could still feel the strength of his grip as he held her on the woodland track. She shivered as, in imagination, she felt herself once more pressed against him, his mailed thigh thrust between her struggling legs. She bit her lip; how she hated him, how she hated his arrogance, how she despised his lack of respect for her mistress and the way he looked at them both. She thought of him often; he invaded her thoughts. That disturbed her too and she hated him for it as well. It was a feeling so intense it shocked her and shook her.

As if reading her thoughts Joanna asked: 'Where is that brute who commands them? Where is he today?'

Tilly jumped and went red. 'I do not know, my lady. I think he has left the manor.'

It was nothing new. In the three weeks since their first arrival, the mercenary leader had been off the manor more than on it. It seemed that he had other work to do and Horsingham was merely part of a grander design. The great horse too had only recently returned. It was as if Horsingham had become the focus of some play in which its residents were assigned side roles only; not for them a view of the whole script, and yet the sense of drama gripped them with a fever.

'He acts as if this manor was his own.' Joanna tossed back her head in anger. 'I had thought we had experienced all possible humiliations until this. And what is worse is that while he has been here he has scarcely deigned to answer one of my questions, or explain himself adequately. He treats us all with utter contempt.'

She pushed a wisp of red hair back within her wimple with an irritated hand. 'He has no grasp of his station or mine.'

When he had not dismissed her questions he had looked at her as if she was a mere camp follower. No man had ever looked at her that way with those sharp and forward eyes. Cold eyes which seemed to stare through her rank . . . and her clothes. Her fists clenched involuntarily, for nothing in her experience had prepared her for a man like the handsome mercenary Savaric de Breaute. As she thought of him she dismissed the word 'handsome' as too good for him. It was ruthless arrogance which best described him and she hated him for it. No man had ever treated her with such lack of respect.

As she considered it she suddenly thought of one another. A knight who had looked at her and through her, the day before she had visited the sheriff in Sherborne. That had never happened before either, and all of this since Christmas. Both her honour and her pride felt slighted by these twists of behaviour.

'Anyway, Tilly, we have the butler and pantler to speak to.' Before she left she gave final instructions to the steward. 'See to it that the letter is sealed, Ranulf, and taken to the castle in Sherborne.'

'Yes, my lady,' he said as he reached for the pot of powdered pumice and scattered it over the wet ink. 'I will do as you command.'

When she had left the room, Ranulf folded the sheet of parchment carefully. Picking up a horn-handled knife he proceeded to cut the letter up. When he had finished he pushed the fragments inside his tunic. He had no intention whatsoever of allowing such a troublesome document to reach Hubert de Burgh. Joanna would never know; she would assume that the sheriff had ignored her plea.

Ignorant of Dapifer's actions, Joanna spent the remaining time before dinner about the hall. After the meal she sent Tilly to fetch a glove she had left in the church. A short search turned up the missing article near the stone font. Leaving the church, Matilda almost ran into the wiry little cat-faced man whom she had seen digging graves.

'Beggin' yer pardon, my lady, but I've a message for yer. Said 'e was a friend who 'ad summit of yers.' William Catface thought for a moment. 'Said yer'd recognise 'im when yer seen 'im. Said to find 'im out beyond the meadow . . .' William had a fair idea of what was going on but it was none of his business. Besides, the message-carrying had earned him half a silver penny, and that was all he was truly interested in.

Matilda felt a flutter of fear within her, and a twist of something else which she hardly recognised. Had Stephen Pierson found the article of clothing and with it found his courage at last? The thought sent her heart and mind racing like twinned greyhounds. She knew that she should tell Joanna; she knew that it was beneath her to receive such a message from a lowly creature like the cat-faced man and could not understand why Stephen had selected him. She knew that the cat-faced man was watching her and she should have told him to be off. But she did none of these things. Instead, in both shame and excitement, she left the manor and crossed the pasture. At each step she expected to be apprehended by someone who would accuse her, but, of course, no voice called her back, except for the one vainly calling in her mind, and that one she stifled.

At the edge of the field she pushed along the narrow path now overshadowed with leaves. She went a long way into the woods and the manor was left behind her. A footfall came from behind and she turned, a shadow falling between her and the filtered sun. She looked at the ground and when she at last raised fluttering eyes saw that Savaric de Breaute was standing on the edge of the grass-grown path. She gasped with surprise and fear, but the lithe greyhounds were up and running again and the way back to the manor was blocked by the man who had once seized her on the roadside. In his hand he held the wimple she had lost that evening.

'It's yours.'

He held it out to her but when she reached for it his grasp imprisoned her hand. She cried out but there was no force behind the sound to alert a passer-by, for the cry was smothered by her fear and her excitement and by the mercenary captain's mouth.

Chapter 6

William Catface crouched in the darkest patch of shadows; away on his left the glade was a fretwork of moonlight. He pulled out the leather flask which he carried in a battered, patched scrip which hung from his shoulder. Levering out the greasy bung he sipped on the cool, sour buttermilk. It was better than wine on such nocturnal outgoings, as he needed to keep his wits about him.

He reckoned that he was about five miles from Horsingham and it would take him at least an hour to get home. He looked again at the deer sprawled at his feet and shook his head. Better make that two hours or more – the deer was heavier than he had imagined, or was he just unfit? He pondered, then shrugged and took another swig from his bottle before stuffing it back into his satchel.

'Come on, me 'andsome, you'm a long way from home yet . . .'

He hitched up the awkward weight of the deer; it was all lolling head and limp legs. What with his bow and quiver it was not an easy task to walk at all. Through a gap in the trees he saw the long crescent of the moon. If he did not get a move on it would be dawn. He spat and moved off along the familiar track. Within the next hour he stopped three times. The last time he even lay down for a few minutes. It was a bad move, but his body ached. Lying amidst the woodland grasses and bluebells he breathed in the cool, damp air of the night. All about him the moist breeze was fragrant with the scent of wild garlic. He savoured it and realised just how hungry he was. It reminded him of the bubbling cooking pot over the hearth at home.

'You'm gettin' too bleedin' old for this lark, Willy me lad,' he chided himself. 'You'm in the woods more'n a singing thrush, or that bloody gapmouth . . .' He listened for a moment to the rising and falling pitch of the nightjar's song.

Since the soldiers had come to the manor he had been working hard. He knew the main chance when he saw it and soldiers always had more money than sense; these lazy sods were no different, he mused contentedly. There was always a penny or two to be made around soldiers – fetching and carrying for them; doing things they should do themselves. But on top of the labour service he owed to the manor, and his poaching, he was wearing himself out.

'Ne'r mind, make hay while sun's a shinin'. 'Tis a long time rainin',' he consoled himself. 'An' they lazy buggers'll pay to wipe clean their very . . .'

Then he sat bolt upright. There was a noise, somewhere distant but it was a noise. No fox or badger made it, it was the sound of someone stumbling. Catface had fallen over in the dark often enough to recognise someone else doing it. He grabbed his bow and scrambled to his feet.

In this part of the vale the woodland thinned into a patchwork of glades, assarts and deeper, darker undergrowth. It was a good place to find deer feeding. It was also a bad place to run into the King's verderers. Catface silently cursed himself for relaxing; they had probably been following him for some time. It had been a mistake to try and carry the whole deer home. It was too heavy and took too long, with too much noise. Catface cursed himself bitterly; now he was going to pay for his stupidity.

A movement some way to his right made him freeze. For endless moments he screwed up his eyes, staring into the impenetrable dark. Beads of sweat stood on his forehead and were cold against his skin. Then a badger lumbered off into the night, while Catface swore silently and pressed on. After about half a mile he stopped again. There it was – the pad of footsteps on the damp earth, and more ahead of him too. They were all about him. The dead deer's antler caught on a branch and shook the leaves. The soft noises stopped and he knew *they* were listening. He looked sideways into the dead eyes of the buck.

'Well done,' he hissed. 'From that there noise they'll 'ave 'eard us from Sherborne to Gillingham . . .' He shifted the weight on his shoulder. 'An' whose side be you on anyway? After I killed you so politely like . . .' The deer made no reply, but someone else did. There was a voice in the dark, followed by a whistle.

'Bloody cocky now . . .'

It was clear to William that the verderers were out in numbers – maybe even with one of the King's foresters – and what was more they were sure of their quarry. He had no illusions about the whistle; it meant 'close in – we've got him'.

'We'll see about this, my pretties . . .' He unslung his bow. 'Now where are you comin' from?' Notching an arrow he stared to left and right.

Another whistle was followed by movement to the left. Then there was movement behind him. He rose on the balls of his feet, ready. Another whistle came, and closer now; movement rustled the trees. Bushes were pushed aside, for they were not even trying to hide any more. Then the cat in William Catface decided that discretion was the better part of valour. Just before they tied the knot about him he fired at the shadows. There was a sharp cry. He leapt over his deer – abandoning it – and ran madly into the dark.

Colliding with a verderer he almost fell. The other man was sent reeling and William rolled and ran again, into the deepest shadows with bedlam all about: voices shouting and someone squealing like a stuck pig. Catface ran and zigzagged, fell, rolled and ran again. Thank God they've not got dogs, he thought; his own he had left behind this trip, distempered and feverish. Even when the noises faded, he kept on running, home to his verminous little hovel.

By the time he reached the squalid little hut he was all in. But one thing he resolved as he knelt and retched into his vegetable patch: never again would he carry a deer such a distance. Next time he shot one so far out in the vale he would take it to the deserted hamlet, to the silent settlement in the wooded fold of the downs.

★ ★ ★

Joanna had attended mass in the little manor chapel along with the household. It was a hot morning although it was only eight of the clock – Wednesday, 11 June, the feast of St Barnabas. As she had watched the chaplain elevate the host before the altar she had prayed for herself and the manor; she had prayed fervently for divine assistance, for things were going from bad to worse.

Outside in the churchyard a small flock of greenfinches flitted amidst the ancient yews, but she did not notice them as she walked out into the sunshine, for her mind was full of the manor. The neighing from the nearby pastures, though, did make her pause. She looked to where the horses were grazing. One of the new stallions was asserting his dominance over the uncertain mares; he dropped his head and drove about them as she watched. Normally she would have enjoyed the scene but now she just frowned.

There were more horses at the manor than she had ever seen. Since the arrival of the soldiers, more and more had been brought to Horsingham, more than the manor could ever support. Now Joanna was determined to have it out once and for all with the mercenary leader.

'Please come with me, Matilda, I wish to speak to de Breaute.' Tilly looked up startled and then quickly nodded. Behind her Joanna's entourage seemed nonplussed at the sudden movement of the lady of the manor.

Ranulf Dapifer noticed that Joanna was moving away towards the stables. 'My lady, would you have me come with you?' She shook her head but he accompanied her just the same, dismissing his wife and the servants to their duties about the manor house. There was a worried look in his eyes.

The soldiers were dicing in the shadows, their weapons lying on the cobbles. Battered mail hauberks hung from scarecrow-like frames, the rust spattering the once silver rings. The soldiers were half asleep, leather wine jugs cradled on their laps. They looked up with interest at the approach of the grand lady and her maid and steward; a diversion was always welcome.

One of them raised his wine flask to Joanna in a movement of open disrespect, and when she ignored him crowed, 'Not up to yer standards, yer ladyship?' He swigged and the wine ran down his unshaven face. 'Sure yer won't 'ave any?' His French was heavily and coarsely accented and Joanna followed his words with difficulty. The cheap red wine smelt thick and rancid with an aroma of pitch – a soldier's drink. 'Best wine we get, innit, lads?'

The others sniggered and one – behind Joanna's back – made a vulgar gesture. The others roared with laughter, viewing the two young women with professional interest. On campaign with the King they would have raped the two of them as soon as they had arrived at the manor, but this was the King's realm and Savaric would have skinned them alive if they had laid a hand on either – yet.

'Where is de Breaute?'

Joanna stared hard at the man who had offered her the drink. She felt a new sensation – fear. She had never felt the aura of her authority to be so thin before; indeed, she suddenly wondered if she had any left at all.

With more bravado than confidence she asked again, 'Where is he?' And before the soldier could reply facetiously she added: 'I saw him at breakfast in the hall and I know he has not left the manor. Where is he?'

As the man made to reply another voice was heard. It was smooth and deep, and though the Norman-French was accented, the pronunciation was not uncouth like that of the men-at-arms. Yet there was a cruel edge to the voice, a supercilious note as if the speaker never ceased to enjoy a savage joke at the expense of his companions.

'My lady, I had no idea that you were visiting this morning, else I would have dressed.' Savaric leant against the door frame of the stable. His tunic was unbuttoned and a mass of golden hair pushed forth from his tanned and muscular chest.

Joanna could not deny the handsome turn of his face, but it was a handsomeness made savage by every glance of his eyes. Suddenly she hated his strong, hard looks. A turmoil of emotions rose in her and she wanted to strike him on his confident face. The urge shocked her and she mastered the rush of emotion with difficulty and horror.

Savaric seemed to notice the race of passion in her eyes and gave a smile which brought the feelings rushing to Joanna's cheeks in a flurry of red. 'My men are not used to ladies of quality. You must excuse their lack of manners.' He looked casually at the soldier who had spoken to Joanna. 'There's a lot of horse shit to shovel in the other byre. Get a spade . . .'

The man laughed. Then he saw the cast of Savaric's eyes and frowned. He looked at his comrades for some solidarity but they all contrived to be looking somewhere else.

'Thanks, mates . . .' he muttered viciously.

'Did you say something?' Savaric's voice was as warm as a glacier.

The soldier paled. 'I said . . .' He licked his lips. 'I said . . . where is the shovel?'

Savaric smiled a thin, freezing smile. 'You'll find one. A man of your intelligence and initiative. Or if not – you can use your hands.' The other soldiers sniggered. Their own fear of Savaric was the cause of the lack of solidarity. The soldier got up stiffly and walked away. 'Now, my lady, will you please come in. I apologise for the smell . . .'

Joanna sniffed. 'I know horses very well, sir. It is not their smell which pollutes this manor.' Savaric made no reply but his eyes glittered with something like pleasure at the display of his power and her hatred.

It took Joanna a few moments to adjust to the dim interior of the stable after the bright sunshine of the yard. After a few moments she realised that they were not alone. Two of Savaric's men were also there. One of them was with one of the manor's four-year-old fillies, the other held a stallion by a leading rope. Joanna immediately recognised the horses, and her indignation rose and overcame her fear of the cold blue eyes watching her.

'Who gave permission for this covering?' She could feel the emotion trembling in her voice. 'These are my horses. Why was I not consulted?'

She knew that her grooms had quickly grown frightened of these brutal intruders and did their bidding with confused and lowered heads. They did not know where authority lay any more and were wary of the King's writ on the manor, but she would have hoped that Stephen, or Piers, might have told her about this.

The two men-at-arms glanced at Savaric. As if he had not heard Joanna he motioned to them to carry on. At his command the soldier leading the stallion took it into the filly's stall. The stallion snorted through its nose with excitement at the scent of the filly, its sexual arousal clear from the enormity of its erection.

Joanna looked at Savaric with pale astonishment. Nothing had prepared her for being ignored in such a way before social inferiors. 'Both the filly and the teaser stallion are mine. I demand that you explain yourself . . .'

In the stall the excited stallion was straining at the rope; it bit at the neck of the filly and began to rear up. The filly snorted too and it was with some effort that the soldier – now assisted by his companion – managed to haul back the male horse.

'So she's ready.' Savaric looked at Joanna as if there had been no questioning of his authority. 'As she's not bitten or kicked the teaser I'm sure that you will agree she's as keen as he is.' He gestured to the two soldiers. 'Get it out of here and let's have the real one.' The mercenary leader leaned against one of the wooden partitions. 'You will soon see a horse that shows that teaser up for the nag that it is . . .'

Joanna had already guessed. 'The stallion you brought with you?' Savaric nodded. 'But you have ignored all of my questions and I demand that you answer them. Why have I not been consulted as I should have been?'

'Because my orders are from the King.' Savaric raised his eyebrows as the shaft drove home. 'I do not have to explain myself to anyone but him – saving the sheriff. This manor is in wardship . . .' A slight smile touched his lips.

'And is that why you are destroying it?'

Savaric refused to be provoked. 'I trust you can explain that accusation, my lady.' His eyes flicked towards Tilly, who looked down. 'It is a serious charge.'

Ranulf stepped forward. 'What the lady Joanna means . . .'

'Thank you, Ranulf,' she interrupted him, 'I can explain

myself.' Her green eyes were flashing like emeralds in sunlight. Once more she wanted to strike the square jaw.

'I merely meant, my lady . . .'

She ignored his apology. 'Sir, you know as well as I that a manor can only sustain so many horses. No matter how rich it is, its resources are not limitless. This is a fine manor. God was kind to it and my father husbanded it well, but it simply cannot sustain the number of horses that you have brought here.

'Since you arrived you have scarcely been a full day on the manor. And your work is now plain to see. You are bringing here horses from miles about. If it rains, the pasture will be poached with so many hooves. And before the summer ends it will all be overgrazed.'

The anger had faded from her voice. Now there was pain – pain for her beloved manor. 'A year or two like this and all the pastures will be horse-sick; bare earth and rank weeds where good grass once was, and the earth infested with worms.' She ran a hand along her neat chin, brushing off a fly which had settled on her ivory skin.

'My orders, as I have said, are from the King himself.' Savaric seemed unmoved by her plea. 'I am not required to explain myself to you, but I shall say this much. It is His Majesty's pleasure that this manor should be grazed by the best of his fillies and stallions from Gillingham and southern Somerset. It is my duty to see that this is done and to see that the manor is guarded in the meantime from all harm.'

'From all harm?' There was despair in Joanna's voice. 'Who else could harm it as you are doing? You will destroy my inheritance. You are the harm yourself!'

Dapifer closed his eyes for a moment. All the while Tilly was watching the face of Savaric. She had lifted her submissive eyes and could not take them from his face. There was hatred and something strangely alien in her stare. Savaric saw it and another smile passed across his lips and was gone. Tilly blushed crimson and looked away.

Joanna missed this because at that moment there was a commotion at the door. The sun was blotted out as four men led in the giant horse, Soloriens. It was blinkered and bridled like a prisoner; even so it tossed its great grey-dappled neck and pulled at the straining leather of the martingale. Its nostrils flared at the smell of the in-season filly. It lunged forward and only with difficulty was it held back. It turned its head and Joanna caught a glimpse of proud dark eyes. Pity rose like a spring within her at the imprisonment of such a noble beast.

Savaric laughed. 'See how keen he is. He can't wait to get on top of her.' Joanna knew he was trying to embarrass her and ignored him. 'And by St Peter's chains I'll wager she's as eager to have it plunged inside her.'

De Breaute bent and picked up a riding crop. He leant and lightly tapped the huge swollen organ of the stallion. 'Enough there for three women. What would you say, my lady? Is there not enough there for a whole gaggle of whores to delight themselves with?'

The stallion almost reared at the unseen touch and strained at the ropes. Its yellow teeth showed wickedly as it fought to open its mouth.

'On with it, lads. Her ladyship is waiting for a good hard mounting.' Savaric's words were shockingly incongruous when set against the smooth, deep voice. 'I mean of course the filly in the stall.' He looked at Joanna with brazen insolence; he was enjoying his domination of her.

'You will regret your wickedness, sir.' Joanna could think of little else to say; no one had ever dared speak so in her presence before, let alone to her. The sexual heat in the stable and in Savaric's words was so intense she felt faint. A pulse beat in her temples, a throbbing of outrage and of fear. 'There are those who will not stand idly by and see a lady so downtrodden.'

But with the household knights summoned to join the King in France and Dapifer her only aid, she could think of no one who would carry her favour on his lance point. She picked up the edge of her skirt and turned her face sharply from her tormentor.

Tilly glanced to where the great stallion was rearing over the filly, pawing the air as it mounted her. It thrust and neighed as it pushed deep inside her, its whole body shaking with the force of its excitement. The stallion bit at the mane and neck of the filly.

Savaric was watching the maid. 'Even though he bites her she wouldn't be anywhere else. You know that, don't you?' His voice was low and seemed to mesmerise her. 'She would rather feel the passion of a real stallion than the pathetic desires of the teasers . . . We both know that.'

Matilda trembled with a turmoil of emotions that threatened to swamp her. She hated him with his arrogant confidence and his naked desire, she hated everything he stood for. And she wanted him too. Her dark eyes glowered at him as she followed her mistress out of the stable. Behind her the mercenary stretched and flexed the muscles of his powerful arms.

'The manor here at Cowley is one of the oldest held by the Order in England.' The Provincial Master rubbed his hands slowly together as he talked. 'Stephen's Queen – Matilda – granted it to the Order. At about the same time as Stephen gave us Cressing and Witham in Essex.'

'It is a fine manor too,' Richard added. 'There can be few better in this part of Oxfordshire. The fields seems heavy with grain.'

'God has been gracious to us. It is a fine holding and the more its revenues grow, the more we can send to the east. Yes,' he smiled, 'I know how dear Jerusalem is to your heart . . .'

He had read the letters, sealed with the sign of the horse and two riders by the Grand Master in the Kingdom of Jerusalem, and was fully aware of de Lacey's mission. It was with some curiosity that he had summoned the confrère knight to the Provincial Chapter meeting. The letter outlined the mission, but that was a mere shadow compared to meeting the man.

Before them in the hall the knights of the Order were seated at table. To the rear were the sergeants; only the native auxiliary troops were missing at the back of the hall. But for that and it could have been the Holy Land. Even the sun was streaming through the open shutters of the windows on to the rush- and sweet-herb-strewn floor.

Richard had arrived the previous evening in time for the

traditional water and wine. As it had been 23 June and the eve of St John the Baptist's Day, the customary fast had dictated no light evening meal. There was no such prohibition today, though, and they had eaten well. Richard had risen with the brother knights even before the early dawn and celebrated the divine office of prayer and meditation. Between the regular times of worship the assembled knights had met to discuss the affairs of the Order.

As an honoured guest – though not yet a brother knight – Richard had been allowed to attend the deliberations. There had been much talk of the revenues due to be sent to the east, and of the affairs of Outremer and the recapture of the Holy City. One of the brothers had now begun to read from the scriptures and the rest of the noontime meal was eaten in silence, accompanied only by his slowly rolling tones.

After the meal and before the mid-afternoon service of nones the Provincial Master invited Richard to walk in the herb garden, formally laid out in geometric beds of lettuce, parsley, mint and sage. On their stroll they were accompanied by a handful of other senior Knights Templar.

'Tell us about your mission.' The Master stood in the shade of an apple tree. 'How does it go?'

Richard shielded his eyes from the sun. 'I have ten destrier mares that I brought from Acre. They are now at Temple Buckland where I have made my base. Already I have purchased the use of stallions from around the manor.'

He raised his hand to demonstrate height. 'Only the greatest stallions will do; selected for their strength and for their courage. It does not come cheap but the Order has backed me and I have also dedicated my own resources to the task.'

There were nods of approval at this display of commitment. 'The King has fine horses. Have you spoken with him regarding your quest?' The questioner was one of the senior knights; balding and sallow-skinned.

'I have, my lord, and with the men of the Bishop of Salisbury too. These negotiations are still under way.' The knights exchanged glances.

For some reason he did not want to tell them of the existence of Soloriens. It was as if the possibility was too precious to talk about, as if the mere mention of his hopes would cause the plans to dissolve. Dismissing his doubts he did briefly describe the mount of Hugh de Lusignan which was held hostage by the King. Several of the Templars exchanged glances which were hard to read.

'And you have manors in France also, where horses are being prepared.' It was the sallow-skinned knight again. 'How do they fare – what with the state of the war?' He leaned and picked a sprig of mint; rubbing it between his palms he breathed in the cool, crisp fragrance. 'It is not an easy time to hold manors in England and France.'

As Richard had learned at the chapter meeting, things were indeed very different in France. The French had opened their campaigning season with the capture of the castle of Vaudreuil and with the fortress of Alençon given up by a traitor; John was under pressure.

'I have no part in the fighting. For my manors in Normandy and Poitou I have sworn fealty to John and through him to his overlord the King of France. But I am a knight of the cross, I have not entered into this conflict. My loyalty is to Jerusalem and its liberation.'

'Quite so, quite so . . .' The Provincial Master spoke soothingly, as if to a passionate child.

'It is not of France that I despair,' Richard said quickly, 'but of the east. Can it be true that the crusade has fallen so far short of its holy aims? Can those who have taken the cross have truly sold themselves to the Venetians in their hatred for the emperor in Constantinople?'

The listening knights did not seem unduly perturbed; they glanced at one another. The knight who had earlier spoken grunted and said: ''Tis common knowledge that the emperor has obstructed more than one crusade. We should not shed tears for him. Our Catholic brothers may yet force the Orthodox heretics to return to the True Faith.'

Richard swallowed hard. 'Do not mistake me, my lord; I wish

as much as you that those who are in error should return, but will this do it? Will swords against fellow Christians do it? I feel that only the heathen will gain from the sight of us divided against each other . . .'

'Believe me, young man, you know little of the treachery of the Byzantines. Leave the conduct of such affairs to those who have more experience . . .'

'I have fought for the cross too, my lord.' Richard's voice contained both annoyance and disappointment. 'And I know that the affairs of men are but a drop in a bucket compared to the salvation of the Holy City . . .'

The yellowed face frowned. 'Do not confuse passion with strategy. Those who know *more* often know *better* too. You get us the great horses and we will use them. Have no fear that we will betray the cause.'

There was a hint of mockery in the words and the others looked faintly bored at Richard's passion. The Provincial Master looked slightly embarrassed. For one painful moment Richard felt utterly alone, even here amidst those who had taken the cross. The feeling came as an utter shock and as a bitter disappointment; surely here of all places he could have expected to be understood. His forehead creased in a frown.

From beyond the enclosing wall he could hear the voice of Mark de Dinan calling for the Saracen groom. For a moment Richard felt as much an outsider as Umar, or the Jew in Dorchester. Then the absurdity of the suggestion made him shake his head, but the feeling remained.

The Provincial Master raised an eyebrow in the direction of his knights. He was relieved that the bell was sounding for nones. He remembered the words of the Grand Master; perhaps he had been right to distance himself from this passionate enterprise. Now was the time for treading softly, and he doubted whether this knight with a mission would be capable of that. Perhaps the Grand Master had been right after all . . .

Matilda did not know what was happening to her. Ever since Savaric had come to the manor her world had begun to fall apart.

She seemed quite incapable of preventing it; indeed she felt at times that she was accelerating it; rushing blindly towards destruction.

That first time he had held her she had been lost in the brutal handsome face. Never before had she thought it possible to fear a man and desire him at the same time. Then she had gone to the woods that evening when the cat-faced man had brought her the message. She had truly thought that the sender of the message had been Stephen Pierson, but there had been the thrill of forbidden excitement, as well as fear, when Savaric had surprised her. When she had broken free of his arms and mouth she had burnt with shame and with contempt for herself, for she had felt the conflicting emotions about her like a whirlpool as the man kissed her.

It had been easy for a while for Savaric had been away so much; Joanna had been right about that. But now he had returned, now she saw him every day. She remembered his words at the coupling of the horses and she hated him for his insolence, and yet her belly melted as she realised that he desired her.

Tilly stood at the edge of the yard and watched Stephen Pierson leading in one of the horses. He glanced away from her and she realised he was but a boy; Savaric was a man. He would not have let her run like a fool, alone, into the woods. The embarrassment still pained her. She avoided Stephen and he seemed to be avoiding her.

Stephen seemed to have lost his noise and resilience. Now he spent more time polishing the harness brasses and oiling the leather. He and the other grooms seemed tucked away in odd corners, while Savaric's men dominated the hall and stables. When Joanna had summoned Stephen and Piers to explain why she had not been warned about Savaric's actions regarding the coverings, both protested that they had known nothing. Matilda felt that it was more complex. Their regulated lives were in turmoil and they did not see what was happening because they could not bear to watch their secure world disintegrate. It was their escape to refuse to see it as it happened about them.

She turned and slowly walked across the meadow. There were

more horses there than ever. She hated de Breaute for what he was doing to the manor, yet still she walked. Each step took her closer to the woods. For days she had fought the temptation, then she had succumbed and gone there again. She had gone and returned alone and relieved. But the next evening she had gone once more, once more to return alone. After that time she had vowed never to go again.

So why was she here now? It was to gather flowers for Joanna. Yes – that was it. She paled at the lie. It was the very first lie she had told to her mistress, the first lie that had ever passed between them. She had expected Joanna to throw it back in her face, to accuse her of being a cheap whore. But instead she had smiled and looked tired and returned to her sewing, her mind on other things. And now Matilda stepped slowly through the grass and with every step she told herself that she was going for flowers. All the while, her belly knotted with terror and excitement, and her mouth was dry.

The familiar wall of the downs was dark green with the evening shadows; only the topmost curve of the ridge was still bright with sunlight. She walked the familiar track into the trees at the foot of the chalk slope. Amidst the ranker grass and hogweed of the woodland clearings, foxgloves rose in tall purple towers. Tilly knelt before the swaying, tapering mass of flowers.

She reached out one small, white hand and touched the base of the tower, the petals cool against her skin. She ran her hand from the swelling base to the tip, and a thrill of pleasure shot through her.

'Oh God,' she murmured, for she knew that every part of the plant was deadly poisonous, yet still she stroked it. 'Oh God . . .' The words slipped between her lips like honey.

She turned with a jump, for he had entered the clearing silently. Only the rustle of the grass betrayed his presence. She stood up, the foxglove in her hand. He seized her and kissed her. She struggled but his mouth fused with hers and his tongue forced the gates of her lips. Against her will she responded. Or was it what she wished to happen? She did not know. She was drowning in a sea of anguished wanting.

One hand ran hard fingers through her loosened hair. The other held her small buttocks, pressing her still-struggling body against him.

'No . . . No . . .'

She twisted her head, breaking off the kiss. But he would not stop now, not now that he had started. Though she struck small fists against his chest, he grappled her to the floor. She writhed and kicked but it only seemed to excite him the more. He was thrusting against her, like the stallion in the stable.

He sat on her, laughing, and pulled her skirt up around her waist. He tore at her kirtle and then snarled at the expanse of naked white thigh revealed by the tearing linen. He stood up and pulled at his own hose and tunic. She could have rolled away – kicked, screamed and run. But she did not, and in that moment knew that he was *not* raping her. She wanted him to possess her.

But he *was* raping her, she pleaded to herself, denying the witness of her senses. It was not her fault or doing, it was his fault and his doing. She screamed it silently inside herself as he pushed open her thighs and as her virginity collapsed before him. He grunted and panted as his weight rose and fell on her in a rhythm which slowly invaded her, as he had. At first she cried out at his violence and then – as the throbbing pleasure began to rise within her and swamp her – with desperate shame and pleasure.

She had never known a man before, and his animal desire terrified and excited her. All the while a voice cried, 'He hungers for me, for me, for me.' It rose with her climax as exploding waves of ecstasy drove aside fear and shame and even the pain of his first determined penetration.

Then she lost control, no longer aware of where she was. Only the shattering pleasure was real; the bursting intensity of physical joy. She heard her voice cry out as if it came from someone else.

'Yes . . . yess . . . yeeessssss . . .' and then, 'Oh, don't stop . . . don't stop . . . Oh, don't stop . . .'

Then all sense was lost in a gasping, panting climax in which she could no longer tell which was his and which was her voice.

★ ★ ★

The Templar manor at Cowley was about one hundred miles from Temple Buckland, yet it was a journey that Richard de Lacey was keen to face. This came as some surprise to him, as he had been looking forward to the chapter meeting of the Order on which he had focused his life. Yet now he was happy to leave; indeed he had taken the first polite opportunity to do so. As he watched his horses being prepared for the journey he told himself that it was simply because he was not yet a brother knight. As such he was bound to feel on the edge of things. All the other soldier-monks were united by their vows and the strange mixture of monastic discipline and military practice.

He told himself that things would be different after he had taken his vows, which he was determined to do as soon as the matter of the great horses had been set in motion – perhaps a summer from now. Despite these considerations he still felt strangely uneasy. He could not forget the altercation in the herbarium, or his sense of isolation. It was a bitter cup to drink and all the more so for it being in these circumstances where he should have felt more at home than anywhere. Here at least his dreams should have been understood. He felt a little betrayed, and very disappointed.

'Come on, Mark,' he muttered with determined cheerfulness, 'we've a long ride ahead of us.'

'Aye, my lord, but a fine day for it and better to come tomorrow, I would wager.' The squire yawned and tried to disguise it as a smile.

Richard looked at the pale-blue vault of cloudless sky. He had not even noticed that the sun was shining. The daylight was still young and the psalms of matins and lauds were still resonating in his head; the night offices which closed at daybreak. Still, early as it was, it was apparent that the day would be clear; the haze of dawn was already breaking before the strengthening midsummer sunlight. They had already taken a breakfast of bread soaked in wine and were ready to go.

The way home lay across the claylands of the Vale of White Horse, where sleepy villeins were already out working the dawn fields. Then a steep climb to the chalk downs and the Ridgeway track which would carry them back to Dorset. Larks were calling – rising and falling – and the bleating of sheep carried on the still air. Apart from this the only sound that could be heard was the beat of their horses' hooves on the rutted, dusty track and the jingle of the bells on their harness. The breeze stirred restlessly across the undulating plateau and the going was cool but pleasant.

For the most part they rode in silence – Richard and Mark in front and Umar behind, leading a pack animal. The way was without significant settlement and their only company was provided by the occasional shepherd and slow-moving pedlars laden down with their wares. It took three days of steady riding to reach Temple Buckland. By the time they dropped down the widening combe to the manor they were ready to be home. The isolated inns and farmsteads where they had purchased a night's lodging had been squalid and dirty. Each morning's ride up to the high track had come as something of a relief, after a flea-bitten few hours in the greasy communal bed with straw pricking through the blanket which passed as a mattress.

They arrived late – it was nearly ten o'clock – and the brothers, monastic and lay, were already asleep in their little dormitories. Early next morning, Mark rose to prepare breakfast with the dawn. Secretly he had hoped that Richard might rest after the journey, but his knight seemed more driven than ever. Yawning and rubbing sleep from his eyes, Mark laid out the bread and watered wine in their shared chamber. There was one concession he was grateful for – Richard had not plunged them immediately back into the monastic routine of the convent; that at least had allowed them a night's unbroken sleep.

After they had eaten breakfast, Richard announced the plans for the day. 'I intend to ride over to Horsingham. If Aaron is right the horse of the Lusignans has been there for a short while. And I want to see it.'

He dipped another sop of wheat bread in his wine. 'It's an easy ride from here. We should be there by just after six of the clock.' He glanced at the slowly burning hour candle. 'And perhaps we shall be invited to eat there. If not it is no great matter, as we can be back here by noon and dinner.'

There was a briskness about him which made Mark tired just watching him. However he nodded vigorously as if the enthusiastic motion could hide his exhaustion.

'Umar saw the horse and I want him to be there when we find it.' Richard chewed on the wet bread. 'After it nearly killed him, he should at least be there to see it again.'

Mark saw no such logic in the decision, feeling such a fair-minded attitude was wasted on a heathen, but wisely he kept his mouth shut. He went out to summon the groom who – to his chagrin – was already prepared and ready. As they rode away from the Templar manor, Richard called Umar up to ride alongside them. 'Tell me again about the high horse that you saw at Caen . . .'

Umar recounted once again his encounter with the mighty destrier, and as he spoke, Richard felt a curious sense of destiny that he was at last to see it. Since the meeting at Cowley the quest had become more important than ever, it was a thread which still connected him to his dreams. When Umar had finished, Richard suddenly surprised him by asking him about his home and family. No one had ever asked him before, and he answered warily and without giving too much of himself away.

Mark de Dinan frowned. Who cared in which sun-bleached hovel this alien had been spawned, or in whose heathen service he had gained his knowledge of the great warhorses? It was surely enough that he had come with the recommendation of the Templars who had hired his services for silver. That to Mark was the measure of the man. Who needed to know anything more? Yet Richard seemed quite interested. It was as strange as it was unexpected.

The manor of Horsingham was situated in lush green meadows and pastures which ran away from the downs. To the east a wooded knoll rose up on the right-hand side of the track from Temple Buckland. Behind the knoll the trees thickened away into Blackmoor Vale. Richard rode his palfrey up to the knoll; it provided an opportunity to see and yet remain unseen. Leaning over his horse's fine neck he studied the compact little group of buildings – hall, church, barns and stables. It was a good-sized manor but there was something about it which troubled him.

'What do you think, Umar?'

The groom was impassive as he turned his attention westward. 'There are too many horses grazing the pastures, my lord. They will eat it away.' He paused as he looked. 'But they are fine horses, there is no doubt of it – sleek and strong, with polished coats . . .'

'Good palfreys?'

'Aye, my lord, there are many noble riding horses there. And the lighter-built ones will give good foals too, though not as strong perhaps.' He shaded his eyes with his hand. 'And some are heavier with the broad backs and feathered legs – the mothers of warhorses . . .'

'The ones we are looking for . . .' Richard spoke as if to himself.

The question was rhetorical, but Umar nodded. 'Yes, my lord. They are worthy mates for the horse that I saw. Queens for a king of stallions to mate with.'

Mark exhaled at the groom's careful eloquence, an exasperated gesture unnoticed by the two men studying the horses. Umar stood in his stirrups, pointing, and for once his calm features were alight with excitement. Even the squire saw it and turned quickly to see what had caught the groom's attention.

'There, my lord,' Umar said in haste. 'See the men leading the horse from the yard into the paddock . . .'

But Richard had already seen it. 'It is Soloriens. My God, he is magnificent. You did not exaggerate when you spoke of him. Mary and all the saints, I have not seen a horse like it.'

'It is the one.' Umar sank back behind his high pommel and into the saddle. 'It is the horse that I saw. The one with hooves of fire and eyes like great coals. It is the one.'

Richard was already urging his horse forward. He jabbed his heels and the horse jumped. 'Then let us see this beast close up.' Then he was out from under the trees and riding down from the knoll towards Horsingham.

Joanna and Matilda were by the edge of the meadow. Joanna was not sure if she was there to count the mares grazing – as part of her complaints against Savaric – or to see the high horse being led forth. If there was any doubt to begin with, it evaporated when the beast was brought out from the stable. Four men surrounded it – like gaolers. It was still heavily bridled and martingaled, like a lunatic held back from acts of savagery. Even so, it tossed its head, fighting to break the leather holding it captive. The soldiers swore and spat but no one took a violent hand to the horse, for more than even the stallion they feared the cold and cruel anger of Savaric de Breaute.

'Let me see him.' Joanna left the fence and advanced towards the stallion. Matilda stood back, more than a little frightened of the destrier.

'God's body, keep your distance,' the leading man-at-arms shouted, then added as an afterthought, 'my lady,' as if it came quite unnaturally to him. It was the soldier who had offered her a drink of sour wine.

'Joanna flashed green eyes at him. 'It's cruelty that makes him the way that he is. You do not know how to treat so royal a stallion.' Her chin was raised at the provocative angle which had become something of a habit over the past few weeks. 'He is worth more than you are. Worth more than all of you put together.'

She approached the horse from the side, slowly and with infinite care, all the time making soothing noises. She raised her hand to touch the dappled neck where the mane fell like blown wood smoke.

'Bloody hell! Watch that bastard!'

The stallion jerked away as if stung. Even Joanna was stunned by its loathing of human touch. It pulled on the ropes, sweeping back its head in rage; a soldier slipped on the grass and let go of the rope, another cried out with alarm. Soloriens gave a wild, high neigh of freedom and began to rise on to its back legs.

'Holy Mother Mary . . .' Joanna murmured, unsure of whether it was a prayer for deliverance, or of thanksgiving at the sight of the stallion unbound before her.

'Get that buggerin' rope, you stupid sod,' the commander of the horse detail shouted to a wavering companion.

'Not on your bleedin' life. I saw what it did last time. You bleedin' well get it . . .' Fear of the horse swept away fear of human wrath. 'You get it yourself . . .'

Joanna was suddenly aware of the sheer size and power of the beast. It was as if it had grown on the new freedom, as if a burden had been lifted from its back. As it broke free she realised that there was nowhere for her to run to. The blood drained from her and she felt heavy as she stepped away; it was as if time was slowing down. She turned to avoid the hooves which slowly rose over her. Voices were calling from a long way off, but all she was aware of was the great dappled mountain of rippling muscle rearing before her and the leaden movements of her own limbs as she strove to turn away from death.

The huge horse was neighing wildly – possessed by an anger she had never experienced before, save in herself. It was as if her own impotent fury was made bone and flesh before her gaze. Soloriens was like a dark rock between her and the summer sun; the light burst about it like a halo around the angel of death . . .

Then the moment's spell was broken. She felt herself seized and turned aside, the speed of the action stunning her. The sun blinded her; actions switched from slow to blurring movement in a twinkling. Another, smaller shadow passed between her and the sun, hands seized the trailing rope and called out in a language she did not understand.

Joanna knew that she must have fainted for a moment, for when things cleared she found herself held firmly against a broad chest, her cheek upon a fine velvet cloth. Shaking the confusion from her head she looked up. The man who held her was a little taller than she was; he seemed familiar and yet she could not place him. The light was on his face and it was tanned, the blond hair was bleached by the sun.

Then she realised who it was – the knight at the abbey. And still his face had the look of being somewhere else. He held her but the blue-grey eyes were focused elsewhere. The intensity of the stare forced her to look herself. A dark-skinned man was standing close to Soloriens. The anger had drained from the stallion; now and then it pawed the ground, but the laid-back ears had risen and the lips had fallen to cover the great ivory teeth. It was as if man and horse were communing in some strange way.

'What is going on here?' The voice was that of Savaric; he was accompanied by Ranulf Dapifer. 'What happened?' The men-at-arms paled before the cold questioning. Matilda came up to her mistress in a defensive gesture of support.

'It got loose. It was her fault . . .'

'Fool.' Savaric's deep voice was contemptuous. 'This is what happens when I give a man's job to children.' He turned and looked at Joanna and the stranger. 'Who are you?' There was no hint of appreciation in his voice, which was as welcoming as a drawn sword.

'I am Richard de Lacey,' the handsome knight replied.

'And what is *that*?' Savaric flicked a look at the dark-skinned man, who was whispering softly into the horse's ear.

Joanna could feel the knight tense beside her. '*He* is my groom. His name is Umar ibn Mamun.'

'What is your business here?'

Joanna was furious; she stood away from the man who held her. 'How dare you speak that way? This man saved my life.' Savaric ignored her and she glanced at the knight, who seemed mesmerised by the great stallion. 'We should be grateful to him for what he has done.'

'May I remind you, my lady de Cantelo, that I have the King's commission to protect you. It was you who put yourself in danger by approaching the beast.' Savaric motioned towards the silent stallion. 'And I answer to the King for all that goes on here.' Joanna flashed her green eyes. 'This manor is in wardship,' he added, as if to remind her of her powerlessness.

'My business,' Richard interrupted him, 'is with regard to the great horse. I too have a commission – from the Knights of the Temple. I have fine Arab mares and seek princes amongst stallions to sire horses greater than any have ever seen.' Richard pointed one jewelled index finger towards Soloriens. 'I have money enough to purchase the covering of my mares. And the King knows of my mission. I spoke with him at Caen where he wore his crown at . . .'

Savaric shrugged. 'I know nothing of this. These are the King's horses. There is nothing here for you. You may ride on.' He waved to his men to take the rope from Umar, who was brushed aside by the nervous soldiers.

Richard stepped forward, away from Joanna and towards the horse, talking softly all the time, the way the Saracen had done, and Soloriens let him touch him. Richard laid one hand upon the dappled face and stared into the blinkered eyes. Joanna was astonished by his power over the horse; mesmerised and intrigued. She moved towards him, admiring the way he touched the horse which everyone else feared, astonished that the stallion had reacted so to his gentle words, and then – on reflection – not surprised at all.

'You will at least take wine with us.' Joanna's voice was level and determined. 'We owe you at least that. And my manor pays its debts to those who aid us.'

She had no wish for him to go; there was something strange about him, and besides she owed him for what he had done. The least she could do was offer to quench his thirst.

'My lady de Cantelo, it is the King's manor, his in lordship.' Savaric inclined his head and raised one eyebrow. 'And so we shall bid good day to our guests.' It was an order.

Before she could rebuke him, Richard de Lacey spoke. 'I think this is not the end. But good day to you for now.'

He did not even look at her; his gaze had turned from the stallion to the mercenary commander. He understood wardship well enough and who held sway here. It was at that moment that Joanna too finally realised the true meaning of her new position. It could no longer be denied and she was forced to face it. She was utterly powerless and a mere woman. Nothing in her upbringing had prepared her for this final recognition of the weakness of her own sex. It was devastating.

She felt suddenly vulnerable and – most sickening of all – ashamed; ashamed of herself, ashamed that she was a woman, ashamed that she was nothing, simply a weaker vessel to be picked up or set aside. And nothing had ever prepared Joanna de Cantelo for such a role as that.

Richard de Lacey retraced his steps towards his horse. Ranulf Dapifer looked contented, and Matilda was watching Savaric with great dark, unblinking eyes, her face taut and her hands clenched to hide their trembling. Joanna gathered up what remained of her dignity and walked back towards the manor house. Tilly stayed for an instant – her eyes torn by storm clouds of emotion – then followed her mistress.

John, King of England, watched his chamberlain refill their wine goblets. De Burgh knew that he was being observed and his heavy cheeks paled a little.

'So I'm sure that you think it is a good idea then . . .'

Hubert looked up quickly – a little too quickly – noticing the way John raised his dark eyebrows just a fraction. The chamberlain pretended to concentrate on the two brimming goblets.

'Of course, my lord.'

He knew that the King was not asking for advice; felt that he was really testing him. The thought made his fingers tighten above the silver stems. He blamed the state of the war and the loss of the previous summer's triumphs, yet he knew that it was more than this which lay behind the unusual stiffness between them. It had been so since de Burgh's return from England, since his reluctance to carry out the orders awaiting him at Falaise: the blinding and castrating of the captured Duke of Brittany. Now the boy was dead anyway, killed at John's express command at Rouen, so Hubert was beginning to wonder if his reluctance had been worth it. Next time . . .

'It always helps to have a man in the bishop's household. And he fought well under my dearly lamented brother . . .' John had moved to the window of the donjon. From the open shutters he idly looked down on the fields of Guibray below the crag on which the castle of Falaise was built.

Hubert carried the goblets to him. 'There is no doubt about it,' he said carefully. 'Though some will . . .' He considered his next words carefully. '. . .will consider the match well below her station – a disparagement.'

John laughed; it was not a very attractive sound. 'She is mine to give to whom I choose. Besides which, by the time my men have finished with the manor, there will be little enough of its former wealth. By then they will be evenly matched.'

Even the cynical Hubert was a little shocked at the monarch's blatant description of the realities of wardship. Wisely, though, he held his peace.

John sipped the white wine. 'No doubt Falkes de Mauleon will consider she is a good enough return for the money that he has offered. And the manor – even well grazed – will be worth the silver he can afford.'

'And he will remember your kindness to him . . .'

John nodded. 'Of course. I am a better strategist than my darling brother and my loving father; both resting on Abraham's bosom as we speak. No doubt even in paradise they are aware of how far my skills surpass their own. Don't you agree?'

Hubert nodded. 'Of course, sire, and everyone will see it – given time. Most of all those traitors who have sold their souls to the French king.' He tried not to remember the fortresses they had lost since the winter, or the French siege which even now was throttling the life out of the frontier castle of Château Gaillard.

'There is one thing more. I have decided to release Hugh de Lusignan from prison. A gesture like this will not be lost on the barons. I want his stallion over as many of my mares as possible this summer. Then I will hand it back to him before Christmas.'

'Another shrewd move, my lord.'

'Thank you, Hubert.' John fingered one of the embroidered wall hangings. 'Now, have we any more news of the almost Templar – the man with a mission?' His thin moustache arched as his lips opened in a mocking smile.

Hubert brightened. 'I am your eyes and ears in England, my liege.' John drank his wine, making no reply. 'It seems he is at one of the Templar manors in north Dorset. He is seeking the horse Soloriens . . .'

'Really?' The King laid down his goblet. The sun caught its

polished surface and the jewelled hand which held it. 'That is . . . interesting.'

Hubert could see that thoughts were flitting over the King's narrow eyes like clouds across the moon. 'He is in the company of his squire and a heathen. All have asked questions concerning the whereabouts of the stallion. It seems that they saw it in Caen last winter.'

'Well, well . . .'

'Would you have me find out more, my lord?'

John paused for some minutes as a plan coalesced in his mind. 'He has money to spend – the Templars always have lots of money to spend.' He smiled slyly. 'I want to know how he is spending it and with whom. And whether he has yet found the stallion.' He was pleased with the strategy that had suddenly occurred to him. 'Find it out for me, Hubert. Send messengers today.'

Chapter 7

Ranulf Dapifer was watching the horses in the pastures beyond the manor buildings. He had had a busy morning, arising at dawn to join the village reeve in reviewing the stock of pike and carp in the fish ponds. Then he had given instructions to have the shallow drainage moat about the manor complex cleared out. It had grown foul and turgid with the summer heat and now the stream which was channelled through it no longer carried off the worst of the rubbish. He had left as a band of sullen villeins waded into the sludge equipped with spades and hooks.

Now he was on his way back to the hall. The lady Joanna would be hearing mass at the manor church and it was his place to be there too. It was just after eight of the clock when he paused to watch the horses. He saw that the mercenary, de Breaute, was supervising them; as usual the commander was doing no work himself.

While he was watching the horses, Dapifer was met by his wife on her way to the church with some other women of the household. She smiled her opaque smile, as she always did when she saw him. He nodded back, more engrossed in his thoughts than in her presence.

'There are more horses than ever,' she said as she looked out over the paddock.

Ranulf glanced up suddenly but saw there was no hint of criticism in her voice, no note of concern. And why should there be? He had told her that all was well. There was no need for her to know more and so he did not tell her more.

'There are, Ellen,' he agreed, 'and there will be more yet.'

She looked at him with mild interest and for a moment he thought that she understood the significance of it. Instead she answered: 'The wax candles are running low; we must order some more from Sherborne.' And he was content that nothing of the reality of the situation had revealed itself to her. But then how could it? She was content that he was her eyes and ears, and he never told her anything of importance.

'We'll get it done after mass,' he said without interest and turned towards the paddock once more. 'Leave it with me.' Ellen nodded and moved towards the church; she always left everything with him. He knew what was best, he had told her enough times, and nothing in her experience gave her cause to disbelieve her husband.

Savaric saw the steward and left the edge of the paddock. He sauntered over with a lazy stride which somehow failed to hide the flow of well-toned muscles beneath his close-belted tunic.

'Good day to you.' Dapifer's voice was formal and the one he reserved for people he regarded as his social inferiors.

Savaric nodded towards the villeins. 'They look happy in their work.' The smooth voice was mocking. 'No doubt they are volunteers all. Shit-shovelling is always popular . . .'

Ranulf would not normally deign to discuss manorial business with someone he considered to be an outsider but he was prepared to make an exception in the case of Savaric. This was despite the fact that he felt that de Breaute treated his responsibilities with little short of contempt. Ranulf had his reasons.

'They have little say in the matter, as they owe the manor two days' unspecified labour service a week in return for their plots of land.'

Savaric looked bored but Ranulf was not put off. 'When my late lord inherited this manor, most of the villeins had been allowed to hold their land at a rent. But we have substituted it for labour service again.

'There is more profit from the wheat grown on the downs now. And we can make more from it by farming it as demesne land, with their free labour. They hate it of course but that is neither here nor there.'

Savaric smiled. 'You must be a much-loved man.' The irony was heavy and obvious.

Ranulf shrugged. 'It is my duty – first to my lord and now to the King. I know the value of loyalty.' He was getting to the point and Savaric no longer looked bored. 'It's hot here. Perhaps you could show me the great stallion it pleased the King to have escorted here.'

Savaric motioned towards the wooden stable block across the dusty yard. When they were in the cool shadows Ranulf showed little interest in the great stallion being groomed in his stall by two nervous manor grooms, escorted by one of Savaric's men. De Breaute took the point and ordered the men out.

'What is it?' He was not a man to mix words.

'It is the lady Joanna.'

'Oh yes?' Savaric turned his hard, square jaw to the steward. 'And what of her?'

'I think she finds it hard on the manor now that her father is dead; this place was always dear to him. It must be hard for her to stay here and . . .' He paused.

'Watch us run the place for her?'

Ranulf could think of better descriptions but declined to suggest them. 'Yes – I am sure that you can understand.'

Savaric looked at him with unblinking, pale-blue eyes. 'I am beginning to, but go on.'

'It might be best,' Ranulf continued slowly, 'if she were to go to the household of one of the King's ministers.'

'Anyone in mind, Ranulf?' Savaric had never used the steward's Christian name before and now it smacked more of insolence than of intimacy.

'There is always the Earl of Essex. John has left him as justiciar of the realm while he himself is in Normandy. Or there again the lady Joanna is well acquainted with the King's chamberlain, Hubert de Burgh. He was a good friend of her father and . . .'

'Is a long way away?' Savaric suggested.

Ranulf ignored the suggestion. 'And he is the one whom it has pleased the lord King to have organise the wardship arrangements. You too know him well. It would seem a wise thing for her to go to his household.'

He tried not to show his thoughts, for Savaric had got it about right. Ranulf wanted Joanna as far away from Horsingham as possible. He knew her too well and realised that he had hoped for too much when he had prayed she might accept the realities of wardship. She seemed to have gone quiet of late; ever since Savaric had sent the knight and his heathen away and cut her short. But it was too good to last, he just knew it. He could not forget the bitter words that had passed between her and the mercenary.

Soon something else would spark a conflict and the girl just would not accept her place. She could make things awkward on the manor and Ranulf needed things to run very smoothly indeed, for everything depended on that. Dapifer could not afford to have a stone thrown into the mill pond – for ripples could go far and wide. He needed to be seen as the steward of a manor which was totally loyal to the King's writ. Nothing less would do.

'I shall mention it to my lord de Burgh. He takes a great interest in this manor and I must give account to him for it. I believe the King too takes a great interest.'

The words were deliberately chosen and Ranulf could not control the sparkle which rose within his own brown eyes. Savaric saw it and understood.

'And how does the lady feel about these . . . plans?'

Ranulf coughed. 'It did not seem right to trouble her with them. I thought I should speak with you only.'

'I understand.'

'Now you must excuse me, or I shall be late for mass.'

Ranulf left the stable hurriedly. He did not like Savaric and was outraged by the familiar tone that the mercenary used with him. Nevertheless there were things which just had to be done.

Joanna left the hall in the middle of the evening. It was a sultry July night and there was a feel of thunder. The darkening air was heavy and overcast with a blanket of yellowish-grey cloud. At this time of night the mercenaries were getting drunk in the hall. It had become a routine with which she was very familiar. The servants were frightened of them but there was nowhere else for them to go. At least one of the teenage kitchen scullions had been raped, but – with Savaric in command – the assault had been passed off as a mere prank by high-spirited men and the tearful girl had been packed off to her village.

The most Joanna could do to alleviate the girl's shame was to send her off with a handful of silver pennies to compensate her family for the loss of her virginity and the subsequent reduction in her marital value – small as it had been to begin with. The more dissolute servants, however, were enjoying the mounting anarchy and it pained Joanna to see the blossoming of the weaker and more disreputable elements amongst the retainers. It was as if they had always waited for such a time as this.

'This cannot go on much longer, Tilly.' Joanna stood in the gloom and listened to the noise.

Matilda was unusually quiet, indeed she had been so for a few weeks now. Her store of gossip seemed to have dried up and she looked strained.

'Are you all right? You don't look well.' Tilly smiled a weak smile but this did not satisfy her mistress. 'You've not been yourself for some time now. What is it? Are you sure that you've not taken a fever?'

'I am well, my lady, just a little tired. I have not been sleeping well.' Tilly's dark eyes stood out large and round in her milk-white face. 'It is nothing to trouble you about, my lady. You have enough on your mind.'

Joanna frowned as she looked more closely at her maid. The girl's small hands were clasped tightly together, and whilst she had always looked petite, now she seemed more vulnerable than small. It was a characteristic which had never occurred to Joanna before. She began to wonder if she had missed this or whether Tilly had changed. The thought troubled her.

'I shall order a little honey and poppy syrup with your wine tonight. That will make you sleep better.' Joanna wondered if her preoccupation with her own problems had blinded her to the needs of her companion. 'Now let us go quickly and then we can return before it is noticed that we are not in the solar.'

It irritated Joanna that she had to creep about the manor like a guilty mouse, but for now it would have to be so. Since the incident with Soloriens and the knight, she had been thinking about her position. It had occurred to her that open confrontation with Savaric was achieving nothing; there had to be a better way.

As yet she had not thought of a plan. The undeniable reality was that she was hemmed in on all sides. She fretted at the powerlessness of her situation but could not see a way out.

She had hoped that her letter to the sheriff might bring some relief, but as yet there had been no reply and he was clearly ignoring her. It was dawning on her that she was alone. Only Tilly stood with her; even the most loyal of the household retainers seemed overawed by the soldiers.

In her present state of frustration and dismay she had developed an undeniable urge to see the horse, Soloriens – to see him without the watchful eyes of Savaric on her. When she had mentioned this to Tilly, the maid had seemed extremely alarmed but Joanna was not to be dissuaded. So it was that they left the solar by a back stairway and crossed the shadowed yard. Joanna stopped before the door of the stable. Soloriens' guard was asleep in a drunken stupor. Savaric would beat him if he knew. The thought made Joanna smile with a very uncharacteristic cruelty. To the powerless and abused even the whiff of retribution can seem like a scented spring breeze. Half ashamed of her hatred, she worked back the well-oiled bolt.

The stable was dark, the last of the sunlight filtered in through the oiled linen sheets nailed over the windows. The great bulk of the stallion shifted in its stall; he had heard her as soon as she pulled on the bolt.

For a moment Joanna was afraid. She stifled the emotion, knowing how it would communicate itself to the horse. Breathing slowly she opened the door of the stall. The wooden gate was scarred with teeth marks. Joanna ran a ringed finger along the marks of equine boredom and frustration. Her cheeks tightened with anger at the imprisonment of this noble horse.

'It is I,' she murmured softly, and when the blinkered stallion snorted and pulled at its martingale, she added, 'I know . . . I understand. We are both prisoners.'

Very slowly she reached out and touched the great dappled muzzle. The horse flinched but she did not stop. Slowly and carefully she ran her fingers up the broad convex face and felt the soft fringe of the fetlock beneath her touch. She repeated the movement, slowly caressing the great beast. The gentleness disarmed the horse's fear and anger, as Umar had done with soft Arabic words of praise and pity.

'It's all right. There is no need to be afraid, for it is only me . . .'

The words were familiar, words her father had spoken to her on dark nights when the wind drove down from the downs and the trees rose and fell like the masts of ships in a gale. Words of reassurance and of comfort.

'It's all right, it is me. Do not be afraid . . .'

She could feel tears on the edges of her eyes, tears which overflowed and ran down her face. She was glad that it was dark and that Tilly could not see the humiliation, shame and sorrow of Gilbert de Cantelo's proud daughter. Soloriens stood quite still beneath her touch, though now and then she could feel a shiver pass through his great neck. Talking softly all the time she moved between the horse and the stable partition. Now was the most dangerous moment of all, for her escape route was blocked by the stallion.

She talked to reassure him and because she knew he would locate the direction of her voice and so not fear the fact that she had passed out of his blinkered vision. Joanna stroked the high arc of his neck from the poll to the withers. Beneath the mane she felt the twisted skin of old wounds; all was revealed to her gentle but firm fingers.

'You are a prince amongst horses and they treat you as a captive. As much a hostage as the knight who rode you. As much a prisoner as me.'

Impulsively she laid her head against Solorien's neck. He blew air through his nose in a wuffle of long-withheld but wary contentment. 'I do not know what to do,' she whispered to him. 'I cannot think of what to do next.' Tears flowed down her ivory cheeks. A tress of red hair escaped her veil and lay against the stallion's hot neck. 'God knows how desperate I feel. I have prayed . . .'

Then the tears blotted out her words and she clung to the great horse's neck. Back in the shadows Matilda was watching, torn with fear and shame. She was in agony to see the intense distress of her beloved mistress. And yet she knew that she could not stop what she had started. She did not know how to; she wanted to and yet did not want to. In fact, she did not know what she truly wanted any more. She thought of Savaric and was torn open by hatred, revulsion and desire.

Richard lay awake in his bed, the heavy, charged air of the room stifling sleep. All day the weight of hot humidity had been building. The horses in the paddocks were restless and the exposed arms and legs of everyone in the convent were crawling with thunder flies like tiny moving commas.

Since his return to the convent he had followed the daily office of the brethren. With them he had risen just after midnight for the night-time services of matins and lauds; slept until dawn and the services of prime, terce and sext – which it was the practice of the Templars to say one after the other; then attended to the horses until the midday dinner which was taken in silence; after, it was time for more work or contemplation until the afternoon services, supper, compline at nine of the clock and then bed.

He had hoped to quieten his thoughts by immersion in the sacred routine which he had resolved to make his own when he took his vows. That he had not found peace had disturbed him. The attitudes expressed at Cowley and the rebuff at Horsingham had knocked his equilibrium which was already strained and fragile from disappointment and tension.

'*Pater noster* . . .' he repeated silently in Latin. For he knew it was wise to repeat the Lord's Prayer in bed, to absolve himself of any sinful thoughts which had entered his mind since the absolution of compline. Quietly he spoke to God. 'Amen,' he muttered at the end of his prayer.

For long, hot moments he stared at the ceiling. His monkish cell – made available by a brother knight's trip to the Holy Land –

was simply furnished with stool, chest and bed. The sheet and blanket lay crumpled on the rush-strewn floor; Richard lay naked on the mattress.

'I must get the use of it . . .' The words sounded feverish even to him but he could not help it. 'They cannot stop me, for I have God's commission.' He thought of the horse Soloriens and clenched his fist. 'It was God's providence that we saw it at Caen. And that providence will not be blocked, or mocked . . .'

In the silence of the night he often talked softly to himself to rehearse his thoughts – that was when there was no Mark de Dinan to bounce them off – but this night he spoke his faith with a vehemence which proclaimed as much his fear that he was about to be thwarted as his belief that he would succeed. He turned restlessly, thinking that even success seemed dangerous now. He remembered Mark's concern about dealing with this particular horse; a horse owned by a Lusignan but held by John, a hostage of great power and danger. Perhaps Mark was right, perhaps this horse would only lead him to destruction.

Richard sat up in bed, his body glazed with perspiration and the muscles of his neck knotted with doubt and frustration. 'The fools,' he muttered bitterly, recalling the Templar words at Cowley. 'The faithless fools . . .'

Then he bowed his head, for his anger had led him further into sin. Once more he prayed, but no matter how he concentrated he could not find peace to soothe his aching body and heart. He had to have the horse, there was no other way. And that too, of course, was sin – the sin of covetousness.

Tired and angry, he began again: '*Pater noster* . . .'

Outside, the first of the rain fell against the roof and thunder rolled about the downland above the manor, as if his anger and his pain had found an incoherent but resounding voice.

Falkes de Mauleon rode into the manor of Horsingham the morning after the storm; he rode in the company of three men-at-arms. It was Tuesday, 15 July – St Swithun's Day. If tradition was proved right it would be wet for forty days. Falkes looked at the clearing sky and was hopeful that it would be proved wrong. He stopped his horse very close to the eminence from where Richard, Mark and Umar had surveyed the manor. Like them he noted the overabundance of horses. Even in the coarser pastures, up against the woods, the grazing chestnut-and-white longhorned cattle shared their grass with horses.

Falkes nodded slowly at the sight. It was predictable but bad; he knew exactly what was going on here. He walked his horse down from the knoll so that he would be seen. Before he had reached the wooden bridge over the shallow moat he was met by two foot soldiers. Roughly challenged, he paused significantly before announcing his business. The pause did not go unnoticed and the soldiers scowled at his refusal to be intimidated.

One of them hurried back into the stockade whilst the other barred the way, and Falkes idly surveyed the drying piles of weed and filth on the bank of the moat. Savaric appeared but Falkes did not dismount. With a slight pressure of his knees he walked his palfrey forward; from it he towered above the mercenary captain.

'You know of my business here?' Falkes' voice was low and cool.

Savaric took in the powerful arms and hands and the axe which hung from the saddle pommel. He had heard of the bishop's marshal and even Savaric knew when to be impressed by a fellow soldier.

'I know about your business here. My lord de Burgh sends me the will of the King.'

Falkes was thoughtful for a moment, wondering just how much Savaric knew. 'So you know I seek the horse. But I have not seen it yet.'

'The King grants you permission to see it and examine it for yourself.'

That satisfied the marshal and he swung down from the saddle, handing the reins up to one of his sergeants. 'Then let's see the beast.'

Savaric led the way across the yard to where Soloriens was held in his pen. 'The beast is a killer. It is only ever exercised by my men and between times it is held here as you see it now.'

Falkes grunted. He was not impressed with the treatment but

was well impressed with the horse. 'And how long is it here for?'

Savaric hesitated for a brief moment. 'I do not yet know.' Falkes saw the lie but made no comment. 'I shall be told in the King's good time. He has other things on his mind at the moment.'

Falkes was well aware of the disaster that seemed to be unfolding across the Channel and he nodded; his narrow grey eyes, though, never left the horse. 'I am authorised to pay you the amount mentioned in my letter to gain the covering of the bishop's mares. It is a good price. Better than the best you will have been offered.' He was thinking of Richard de Lacey's generous bid to the bishop and wondered what the nearly Templar would have offered for the use of the King's stallion.

'I know,' Savaric said in a flat tone. 'I shall let you know if my lord the King agrees with you.'

Falkes looked thoughtful. 'Then you cannot agree it now?' Even he could not hide the fragment of disappointment in his voice.

Savaric smiled. 'I am sorry, but the King takes a great deal of interest in this stallion.' He did not sound sorry at all. 'And besides, there may be others who are interested in such a fine beast.' The last comment was malicious but Falkes refused to be drawn by it.

'So be it then.' He flexed the muscles of his right arm. 'Now I would like to see the lady Joanna.' From the look on Savaric's face it was obvious he knew more in that direction than he was letting on. Falkes was not happy about that. 'Will you escort me, or shall I make my own way?'

'Oh, I would be honoured.' The supercilious tone grated on Falkes. 'It is always a pleasure to see a beautiful woman.'

Joanna was in the solar with Tilly, the windows open to make the most of the air released by the previous night's storm. Both women were sewing and looked up as the men entered. Both wore their hair loose and unfettered by wimple, veil or barbette. It was clear that they were surprised by the visitors. The other women of the household – including Dapifer's wife – rose at the entrance of the menfolk.

Falkes noted once again the radiance of Joanna's hair, the flawless skin like pure parchment and the eyes greener than tree tops in sunshine. He also noted that Savaric did not bother to knock to gain admittance.

'My lady Joanna, I am so happy to see you again. Please excuse my unannounced arrival.'

Unlike Savaric, Falkes spoke with an immediacy which, whilst spartan, was nevertheless wholesome and reassuring. Joanna seemed genuinely pleased to have a visitor. 'You are very welcome,' she said with enthusiasm. 'We have few visitors nowadays and I have not been away from the manor for some time.' She bade him join her on the bench by the window. 'You must take some wine with me. Thank you, Savaric,' she said in a pointed dismissal.

Savaric did not move; instead he settled on a bench near Matilda, who blushed and stared down at her sewing. Joanna glared at him and he smiled back at her. After a minute or two she regained control over her temper and spoke to Falkes. 'As you can see, there have been developments here since you were last with us. The lavish protection offered by the King's Brabançon crossbowmen has become more attentive than ever – and more familiar!'

She spoke about them as if Savaric had not been in the room. 'The kind of cutthroats I once told my maid we would never see in this realm. But then, times change . . .' Joanna nodded to Savaric with a bitter little smile.

Falkes looked thoughtful, then he said quietly, 'I think the lady wishes to speak to me alone.' When Savaric still did not move, Falkes spoke again, and this time there was a flash of steel in his voice. 'I shall thank you for your co-operation in this matter, for I wish to pay her my respects – alone.'

Tilly of course did not count. No woman of Joanna's rank faced a man unchaperoned; the maid was as much part of the furniture as the fine wall hangings on the wood panels. Like them she was sightless, deaf and dumb.

Savaric slowly stretched, then rose from the bench. 'I understand,' he said as if he was privy to a secret. 'You must excuse me.' He went towards the door. 'If you need me, my lady, I am at your command.' The other ladies of the household glanced at each other, gathered up their sewing and followed Savaric from the room.

'Is he always that insolent?' Falkes asked her.

'Oh no,' Joanna replied, looking her visitor straight in the face. 'Sometimes he is really rude.'

The two looked at one another and then they both laughed. It was the first time Joanna had laughed in weeks and Falkes was not given to mirth by nature, but they both laughed as if it cleansed the air. Only Matilda stood outside the circle of their humour. But it was more than etiquette which caused her to be deaf to their conversation as she stared too intently at her pointwork.

'I am grateful to you,' Joanna continued, 'for I am powerless here. Since they arrived I have lost control of the manor and it is being despoiled before my eyes. You knew it before my father died and you can see it is being eaten away by the horses that have been brought here.' The colour rose in her smooth cheeks to match the folds of her long hair.

Falkes sighed. 'I see it, my lady.'

The sigh was enough for Joanna, it spoke volumes about a man who was as outraged as she was at the treatment meted out to her lands. She smiled at him and for the first time noticed how well manicured his hands were for a man so powerful. They were strong hands but not coarse. Her smile suddenly deepened for a reason that she did not understand. To hide her sudden openness she turned to the wine jug to pour him a drink. It was a mark of the passage of the last few months that she acted as she did. The old Joanna had never reflected on her actions or emotions. But lately she had grown careful, self-critical, wary.

Falkes noted it and his almond eyes reflected his thoughts. It pleased him that she smiled, but he saw the wariness too and understood its origins all too well.

'So you have come to rescue us like a knight errant. Tell me that this is so . . .' She had not flirted for a long time and the experience was like mulled wine flowing through her on a cold day – hot and a little heady with spices. 'You will free us from our bondage . . .'

'I fear that my business is all too dull, but in truth I also wanted to see you, for I held your father in high regard.' And when the smiled faded a little from her features he added: 'And all men – myself included – hold *you* in high regard, my lady.'

The flattery was quite unpretentious and without guile. Joanna's smile returned – it had been a long time since a man had spoken to her in this way. Not until this very moment was she aware of how much she had missed it, or how much she welcomed the arrival of this strong and confident man, who was not frightened by Savaric. She looked once more at the narrow grey eyes; at the face too weatherworn to be classically handsome and yet too manly and powerful to be ignored by a woman.

'Well, I shall call you my knight errant,' she concluded, 'for you saw off the dragon like St George, and few maidens have had their prayer for deliverance answered so well.' They both laughed again, but once more Tilly did not join in; she had pricked her finger as she listened to what Joanna was saying and watched as her blood sank into the linen folded on her lap.

The two talked of horses until well into the morning. Then, despite an invitation to stay to dinner, Joanna's guest excused himself. 'I fear I have the bishop's business to attend to and it is a good ride down to Dorchester.' Falkes seemed genuinely reluctant to go.

'You will always find a warm welcome here, be assured of that, for my father's friends are my friends.'

It surprised her how close she felt to a man she had hardly spoken to before. Perhaps it was circumstances which intensified her feelings towards a friendly face. She did not know and was not particularly worried.

As Falkes left the manor he looked once more at the overstocked pasture. His mind focused on the resources of the manor being eaten away and the increased price of siring from the stallion, as well as the plight of Joanna de Cantelo. He had a lot on his mind as he rode away; as he and his escort cantered their horses away from Horsingham and up the track which led towards the downland and the high road to Dorchester.

The summer sunlight filtered through the trees and motes of dust rose like the faint wings of woodland fairies. The woodland glade was silent and no birdsong disturbed the hot breezeless air. Matilda lay amongst the grasses and felt their stems and furry heads tickled her naked legs as she turned slightly. In the shafts of sunlight falling between the arching vault of trees, a brown skipper moth's darting wing beats caught her attention for a moment. She watched the little moth as it moved from sunshine to shadow and then was lost from view.

She was quite naked, her clothes scattered over the crushed and flattened grasses of the secluded glade. She reached out one small white hand and touched the embroidered hem of her long blue gown. The veil which usually so demurely covered the whiteness of her naked throat was twisted in the grass like a snake. She followed its silken coils and thought how appropriate it looked: like a serpent in the Garden of Eden; a serpent of seduction.

'What are you thinking?' Savaric raised himself up on one elbow. 'You weren't so contemplative a minute ago.'

He was so confident and self-assured, and she hated him. She looked across her shoulder and he smiled to see the fire burning in her great dark eyes, flames rising from the coals.

'Worried that they will find out?' The tone was mocking.

Tilly turned her head, rejecting his mockery. If the truth were to be known she knew it was unlikely that she would be discovered; the soldiers were terrified of Savaric, as were the household retainers. They would not dare to whisper about her flower-picking in the woods, or Savaric's absence from the hall at the same time. Ranulf Dapifer was playing his own game of ingratiating himself with Savaric so he would do nothing to disturb the peace. As for Stephen Pierson – she avoided him whenever possible now, for she felt he might read the thoughts in her eyes. And with the soldiers about the stables he seemed to have melted into his own routines, as if the familiar activities could shield him from the madness unfolding around him.

With a sense of betrayal she realised that her secret was safe precisely because of what Savaric had done to the manor. He, who was its destroyer, had now become the shield behind which her guilt could hide unseen.

'You need not worry; no one knows, and if they did they would not dare tell.' It was as if he was reading her thoughts. She blushed and he laughed to see the accuracy of his words hit home. 'You see – I can read you like a book, my little maid . . .'

Tilly looked back at him. 'You *think* that you can.'

Savaric laughed. It only seemed to make him more confident when she spoke against him, as if he enjoyed it and revelled in her hatred as it battled with her desire.

'You are so arrogant. You think that you can have anything you want. I hate you . . .'

She meant it, so why did she lust for him? The contradiction between her sense and sensibility opened like a gulf beneath her feet, like the bottomless pit of guilt and pleasure into which she fell when his experienced hands roamed about her body – caressing, probing, entering her.

'Anyone would think that I was raping you, my dear.' Her eyes flashed again. 'But let's not flatter ourselves, shall we? You want it as much as I do. You might get Joanna to accept that I took you once against your will, but it'll be hard to explain how often you've strayed into the woods since then.' He laughed and leaned forward, a quick hand grasping her right breast.

'You bastard.' Tilly pulled away and grabbed her veil from amongst the grasses. 'You arrogant bastard.' She lifted the blue gown to cover her naked thighs.

'Oh, not yet, Matilda. I want you one more time . . .'

Savaric tore the gown from her grasp. She gave a little cry and her eyes were wide. He looked hungrily at her nakedness: the linen-white firmness of her belly and legs; the snow-pale completeness of her skin broken only by red nipples and the dark triangle between her thighs.

'Very nice, very nice indeed.' His voice was thick with desire. 'Now let's have no more of this crap about who wants it more.'

She struggled to get up but he was far too strong and wrestled her back on to the grass. He tore her hands back from her breasts and spread-eagled her. She gazed at him in silence, excitement rising like a tide to drown her anger and disgust. His mouth was on her breasts, biting and kissing. Tilly writhed but her desire was too strong. Her mind pleaded with her body not to betray her, but it did so as it had done ever since he had held her on the road from the manor.

She screamed at herself with disgust and anger but soon even that cry of remorse was pitching into passion as he worked relentlessly on her. He let go of her hands and she raised them, digging her nails into his back and neck as she arched beneath his experienced lovemaking. Her head hung back and he kissed the arch of her neck with ferocious desire. He had her and she cried out with the ecstasy of their hot union. Lost to all but the rhythm of his pumping body and her own exploding climax.

'That's better. Yes, that's much more civil . . .' Savaric's weight pressed her into the grass; into the folds of her crumpled dress; into the coiled serpent of her veil. 'Much better . . . much, much better . . .'

Away in the woods William Catface could hear but not see the sexual frenzy in the glade. He bit thoughtfully on a piece of grass. Halfway through raising it to his mouth to blow along it, he stopped. It suddenly occurred to him that Savaric would probably not appreciate his climax being musically accompanied by William Catface on the one-note grass stem.

William put it down carefully and a green grasshopper sprang away from his touch. He had been in the wood for what felt like hours, acting as Savaric's lookout. It was funny really how it had happened, and seemed to indicate an upturn in his luck. He had earned several penny clippings for fetching and carrying for the soldiers. Few of them spoke English whilst William – like most of the more enterprising villeins – had a passable vocabulary of Norman-French.

As a result he had made himself useful supplying a translation service into English of such prosaic phrases as: 'This wine stinks of piss', 'How much is that girl for the night?' and 'Of course I love you more than any other woman'.

So far his translation services had earned him as much as his willingness to fetch and carry. At home in a patch of rotten roof thatch he had secreted a greasy leather bag full of silver curlings shaved off the edges of the King's silver pennies. He had earned more in return for little services done for Savaric himself. Little errands and messages carried; little jobs like keeping a watch while the mercenary had his way with the lady de Cantelo's maid.

William was frightened of Savaric. Largely, he surmised, because he knew a thorough and consistent bastard when he saw one. Whatever a lady of quality like Matilda saw in him was lost on William. Her father was only a minor knight but even as that he occupied a plane so loftily above Catface that he seemed to brush the stars. Nevertheless it was clear that she was mad about Savaric.

'From what I've seen she's as mad as a March 'are when 'e's about,' he muttered to himself as he considered the conundrum. 'An 'er grandfather a knight with ol' Richard 'iself . . .'

He mused on the strangeness of women. 'Them's as fickle as . . .' He paused to consider a poetic phrase worthy of a lady of quality. 'As a bitch on heat . . .'

Still, William was not going to judge her. After all, the unexpected infatuation had improved his fortune well enough. He was always doing little jobs for Savaric these days. Soon he would have enough to buy a new milk cow. One of his richer neighbours had such an animal for sale – a scrawny brindled beast with misshapen long horns, but William had loved the animal at first sight.

Just a few more jobs and he would have the thirty-six silver pennies which was the asking price – or more precisely the equivalent in illegal clippings, but it was the same difference to his neighbour. It was a fair price given the milk yield promised by the seller. As the sounds of sexual excitement rose to their climax behind him, William sighed with rare contentment at the thought of three whole shillings hidden in his house, and even more so at the thought of his new cow. Things had definitely looked up since Savaric and his men had arrived at the manor.

★ ★ ★

Richard de Lacey was not a man to take no for an answer. Especially when the no in question involved the stallion Soloriens. After a few sleepless nights he resolved to return to the manor at Horsingham and try again.

'From what we saw last time, I don't think they will be pleased to see us.' Mark de Dinan frowned as he spoke.

'Don't worry, Mark. I daresay the sweet-natured fellow with the honeyed tongue was only shy that we had not introduced ourselves formally. You know what tender plants these crossbowmen are.'

De Dinan laughed at the description of the smooth-voiced captain. 'I fear that one has the manners of a wolf . . .'

'You'd put him that high, would you?' Richard turned in the saddle. 'It seemed to me he had all the grasp of chivalry of a pig with a splinter up its rump . . .'

'Indeed,' Mark interjected, 'he spoke most eloquently considering that most of it was out of his backside!'

Knight and squire laughed together, enjoying the solidarity which came from their mutual class loathing of crossbowmen. Mark was particularly satisfied by the conversation as, by the same token, it excluded Umar too. The Saracen observed the two thoughtfully; he had seen the havoc wrought by crossbowmen on knights and recognised the hatred behind the display of confident humour.

He also knew how laughter could stiffen a man's resolve before battle, and he had seen the look on Richard's face when their first visit to Horsingham had been rebuffed. Umar had no doubt that Malik Rik had resolved to do battle for this horse by whatever means were necessary.

Joanna was returning from praying in the church when she saw the knight. She stopped and watched as he reined in his palfrey. She had been right in her memory of him – he was very handsome. She knew that etiquette frowned on her approaching him directly but ignored it; a spark of her old self had rekindled since the visit of Falkes.

'Good day, sir.' She was bold in her tone. 'So you have come back. Was it the warmth of your welcome from my protector which drew you here again?'

Richard was not used to such directness in a woman. 'I am sorry, madam. Your protector . . .'

'Oh, the King's man who guards me and this manor. He is renowned for his wit and charm.'

Mark grinned but Richard frowned. Wardship was a serious matter and he had no intention of offending the King with regard to its administration. The horse was too important for that; too much was being carried on its broad back. De Lacey dismounted and Mark and Umar did likewise. He introduced them to the young woman, who seemed genuinely interested in their names and mission.

'So you have been in the Holy Land.' Joanna was pleased that the knight was as intriguing as he was handsome. 'My father fought there with King Richard – God bless them both.' She did not allow Richard to commiserate with her but continued: 'And now you have come seeking horses to help free Jerusalem itself. That is a very noble task, but will it be enough?'

Like the woman the question was very forward. 'By God's grace it will be, my lady.'

'Assisted no doubt by your courage and strong arm, I dare say.'

At that a shadow passed over Richard's face, and when he spoke again it was quick-paced and to the point. Joanna noticed the change but could not fathom it. He intrigued her and she wanted to know what lay behind the shadow that covered this man.

'I would be in your debt if you would allow me to see the stallion.' Richard did not need to indicate which one he meant. 'He is . . . magnificent.'

'Of course.'

It pleased Joanna to be able to take the initiative after so much had been lost, first to the sheriff and then to Savaric. It was a little blow struck for herself, even if hardly likely to change her circumstances. What was more, she was convinced that Savaric would be angry, yet his absence meant that she could claim quite rightly that no one in authority over her was present at the manor when she made the decision. Her circumstances were honing her anger and indignation and making them more considered and clever, less impulsive and headstrong.

She led the way along the path which ran from the church to the manor house. It ran beside the little stream which fed the fish ponds and the moat; the stream which separated the complex of buildings from the untidy huts and stockpens of the manor's villein tenants.

As she crossed the wooden bridge into the stockaded manor compound, Joanna noticed with relief that Savaric was nowhere to be seen; even his men seemed to have shrunk away from the hot summer sun and were noticeable by their absence. Soloriens was being groomed in his stable; Joanna saw that the worker was Stephen, under the supervision of one of the crossbowmen. He looked up in alarm to see her.

Joanna was stung by the realisation that he feared for her, because it indicated that Savaric had made it clear she should not go near the horse. She was glad to be defying him – and with the handsome knight who had also gained the mercenary's disapproval.

Richard leaned against the well-chewed crib. 'A Lombard . . . he is a Lombard stallion, is he not?'

Joanna nodded. 'Yes, and perhaps the first to be seen in this realm. I heard Savaric boasting of it to my grooms. He was trying to make them feel small, he wanted to belittle all the breeding they had done when compared to this horse.'

'They can never have seen such a beast. I have never seen one mightier.' Richard's agreement with Savaric's assessment was so matter-of-fact and without malice that it did not offend her. 'There is Arab in him, I would swear it, from the hotness of his blood and the nobility of his carriage, but there is the strength of the northern heavy cold-bloods too.' He pointed to the beast. 'See the strength in that back and in those feathered legs; there is stamina to back up the ferocity of his temper. And someone has trained him to kill. My groom saw how he attacked a man in Normandy; there was singleness of purpose in that attack. He is a prince amongst horses, but a warrior also.'

It overjoyed Joanna to hear someone who loved horses as much as she did. And someone who did not see Soloriens merely as a beast to hold hostage but as a source of admiration. 'They keep him here like a serf . . .' Joanna said bitterly. 'But he has a nobler spirit than any of them.' There was a pitch of passion in her voice which made Richard suddenly look at her, as if seeing her for the first time. 'Can you not see how greatly we are wronged?' She suddenly realised that she had said 'we', and began to correct herself, but blushed to silence instead to see how intently the knight was looking at her.

'I can see that.' Richard ran his hand along the teeth marks on the wood of the stall, breaking the sudden, intense moment. 'He is bored, lonely and frustrated.'

He stared closely at the wood as if the broken, ragged edges were all that mattered, but there was a passion in his voice to match that in Joanna's. It was as if both were speaking of more than the horse of Hugh de Lusignan. She longed to ask him, but knew it was too forward, and anyway, the knight was now gazing at the horse, as if there was nothing else in the world which could so seize and hold his admiration. Joanna felt a quick twist of resentment.

'The King is very jealous of this one.' Both Richard and Joanna jumped at Savaric's voice. 'I am sorry that I was not here to meet you in person, but I see that the lady Joanna has acted as your escort.'

Joanna flushed but was aware that Savaric did not seem unduly angry. It was as if he had expected something like this to happen. The thought puzzled her and disappointed her. It was as if, once more, the Brabançon was ahead of her. She watched him carefully, distrusting him.

'I would like to sire from this horse,' Richard said simply and without a hint of fear. 'What are your terms?'

Even Savaric seemed struck by the directness of the question. 'This horse is the King's.'

'It is actually that of Hugh de Lusignan, and I doubt that the King took it hostage in order to make no profit from it. You must have your orders.'

Savaric was nonplussed; no one spoke to him this way. Well, no one since Falkes de Mauleon. It gave Joanna great pleasure to see him discomfited twice in such a short space of time. And by two male visitors to *her* manor.

'The King is breeding from the beast himself . . .'

'What is the selling price of this horse – thirty pounds? I would think at least that. Well, I am prepared to pay ten pounds just for the successful covering of two of my mares.' There was iron in Richard's voice. 'And with that the King could buy two fair hunting coursers, or five rouncies to carry mounted men-at-arms. It's a price few others will match.'

Savaric seemed to have recovered somewhat. When he answered it was clear that he felt on much firmer ground. 'You must not think that you are the only one to have an interest in this horse, or that the King is unmindful of the beast's worth.'

'I will match that which is offered by any other breeder.'

Joanna saw the sly glint in Savaric's cold eyes and knew he had regained the initiative somehow. It infuriated her and she was not sure at what point it had occurred.

'The negotiations are still in progress so it would not be proper to discuss them yet. But once a price has been established I would be pleased to discuss your response and inform the King of it.'

Richard looked a little disappointed. 'Who else is bidding for this horse?' he asked quietly.

'I am not at liberty to say.' Then Savaric paused. 'I suppose it will do no harm. The Bishop of Salisbury has an interest . . .'

'Falkes de Mauleon!'

Richard saw it all now: the discussions over breeding prices whilst Falkes was planning to visit the manor holding Soloriens. He must have been far down this road before the Templar knight had even started. Inwardly Richard cursed the quietly spoken marshal.

'That is his name; do you know him?' Savaric was at his most offensive when imitating sincerity.

Richard nodded sharply. 'When will you know the price he can afford?'

Savaric leaned against the wooden stall gate. 'It should not be too long, but I cannot guess, I fear.'

The imprecise nature of his reply seemed designed to nettle, but de Lacey refused to allow his desire for the horse to force a hasty reply. 'Very well,' he said in a cool voice, 'I will return to discover the price.' Then he nodded to Joanna. 'I am grateful for your assistance, my lady. Good day to you.'

As he was leaving, Joanna realised that, but for the momentary look of curious intensity, he had shown far more interest in the stallion than in her. Far less interest in her than Falkes, his newly discovered rival for the stallion's favours. Perhaps she should have expected it, given the two other times she had met him, but the realisation still came as a disappointment and a challenge.

In the heat of August, the Grand Master of the Knights Templar moved from the fortress of Acre – firstly to the Templar castle of Tortosa in the County of Tripoli, and then south-eastward, to where the fortress of Chastel Rouge lay beneath the mountain of Qurnat-as-Sawda, dominating the road from the sea into the Syrian desert.

Here, in the hour between supper and the bell for compline at nine o'clock, he was joined by the marshal of the Order. Together they sat in a window seat facing the mountains of Syria. A brown-mantled sergeant served them wine and water and then was dismissed, leaving the two senior knights to enjoy the breeze, which had risen with the shadows of evening.

'So what is the latest news of Richard de Lacey, our Malik Rik?' William de Chartres smiled slightly as he pronounced the Arabic words, but there was no malice in his voice, only a sadness.

The marshal gazed out to where the heads of the peaks deepened to purple. 'As you ordered, I spoke with the Grand Commander, fresh from his visitation to the province of England. He has been in counsel with the Provincial Master and will present his full report to you tomorrow after mass . . .'

'But de Lacey,' the Grand Master interrupted him, 'what of him. I wish to discuss him separately.'

The marshal nodded. 'I understand. He is, as expected, at the manor of Temple Buckland where he has gathered the destrier mares that he took with him last summer. The other horses he has put to stud in Poitou and Normandy. Some have since been sold to raise extra money but he still has the regular allowance paid him by the Order in England according to your instructions.'

'And how goes his mission in England?'

'Ahh.' The old marshal sighed and shook his grey tonsured head. 'There he has set his sights on a horse held hostage by John.'

'That could be dangerous. John is jealous of his horses, but one held hostage is even more complex, for it involves both the holder and the owner. Who is the owner?'

'You are not going to be pleased, my lord.'

De Chartres sighed. 'Tell me.'

'It is the horse of Hugh de Lusignan. The one known as . . .'

'. . .Hugh "the brown". I know him all too well; the nephew of Amalric, King of Jerusalem and Cyprus.'

'The very same,' the marshal added, a note of foreboding in his voice.

'I always had a feeling about him,' de Chartres said softly, referring to Richard. 'But thank God we sent him on a loose rein. Though I doubt even that was loose enough if Amalric discovers we have backed a knight who is benefiting from his nephew's embarrassment. And just when we are locking horns with him over the truce he has signed with the Saracens.' The Grand Master frowned. 'This is not a good time for this to happen.'

'What shall we do?'

De Chartres considered the question. 'Have the English Provincial Chapter cut back on the money funding de Lacey's mission. Not too much at first, but increasing . . . Give the reason that the province has been ordered to increase its contributions to Outremer and consequently must reduce expenditure. It has happened before.'

'And if he persists? If he relies on his own money? For he is a determined one. You saw the fire in his eyes.'

The Grand Master lifted his goblet and drank the wine mixed with water. 'If he persists,' he replied, measuring each word, 'then cut him off completely. And if he proves to be an embarrassment, then . . .' He placed his hands together as if in prayer.

'Then we throw him to the wolves?' the marshal suggested softly.

'It is not how I would have chosen to phrase it.'

'There will be little difference if he has overplayed his hand and then cannot follow through with his promises. King John is not a patient man when it comes to money, especially at this time. You know about the temper that possesses him, as bad as his father's when he is roused or thwarted.'

The Grand Master leaned his chin on his hands and nodded imperceptibly. 'You are right, of course, realities must always be faced and he must have known the sensitive nature of his mission. He can be under no illusions.' As if that justified the decision, he concluded: 'So be it then; if he persists in this matter and it looks set to embarrass the Order, then throw him to the wolves . . .'

Chapter 8

Umar ibn Mamun relaxed for the first time in the afternoon. Hidden amidst the tall hogweed and up against a thicket of blackberries he felt relatively safe. The warm summer had brought on the fruit early and Umar tugged a couple of berries and popped them into his mouth. Chewing the fruit he looked ruefully at where a trailing bramble stem had scored a furrow across the dark skin of his forearm.

The wood thinned out immediately before him in a fringe of foxgloves and the bold crimson splashes of bitter vetchling. Beyond that a sloping pasture of rough grass – grazed by lazy cattle – ran down to where the manor of Horsingham lay in a slight heat haze, where the patches of trees gave way to its meadows and fields. Behind him the wood thickened and darkened into silence.

Mark de Dinan had been gone for only a few minutes but already Umar felt a sense of relief; the intensity of the squire's hatred was like a poisonous miasma which infected the very air. From what he had said it was likely that he would be gone for a little while, so Umar stretched and counted the tiny figures on horses which were cantering towards him from the manor. There were four in all and two carried light lances of the type he had seen wielded in the Holy Land. They seemed harmless enough and soon passed below his vantage point and were lost to view. Still, he had better make sure that he told de Dinan when he returned.

For the present, though, Umar was glad to be rid of the bad-tempered Frank for another more fundamental reason than his own comfort. It was nearly midday and time for the second daylight prayer. Of all the prayers prescribed by the Islamic discipline of *salat*, this was the one Umar found most difficult to perform without insulting those around him. The dawn prayer and those timed for sunset and night posed fewer problems, for then it was easier to find a secluded spot. The midday prayer was a different proposition altogether and he often had to miss it, to his shame.

Away from the eyes of de Dinan, he turned eastward and bent, bowed and prayed with a sense of relief. It was as he was finishing the prayer that he noticed the movement on the track below his vantage point. Umar and Mark had positioned themselves to the south of Horsingham, where the land began to rise towards the downs. Behind the wood, wherein he was now hidden, the slope gathered pace, as if preparing for the final exertion, and then rose in a steep wall of scrubby woodland and orchid-studded grass.

It was a good place to observe the manor, as instructed by Richard de Lacey. On the right of Umar's field of vision lay the tree-covered knoll and the road to Temple Buckland; before him and to his left the plateau of the vale spread away, dotted with a jumble of trees, meadow and pasture, whilst here and there, reluctant fields of wheat had been wrested from the heavy clay. It was not this, however, which caught Umar's attention. His devotions had caused him to turn away from the manor and so notice the figure on the track which led straight into the trees and towards the downs.

The figure was behaving very strangely. He had come out of the woods but was not making for the manor. Instead he was cautiously walking along the very fringe of the trees in the deep shadow thrown by the summer sun. All the while he was staring intently into the woodland beside the track. For a moment he stepped into a patch of sunlight and Umar saw the knife in his hand and the whiteness of his hair and beard. As the sun flashed on the blade it came to Umar exactly what – or rather who – the man was looking for.

Savaric de Breaute was strolling up the dusty chalk track when he was passed by the riders from the manor. He recognised them as some of those who had ridden with Falkes de Mauleon, the marshal of the Bishop of Salisbury. It was fortuitous for them that they coincided, since they had been looking for him at the manor. So private was their mission that they had not left their sealed vellum letter with the steward, Ranulf Dapifer, but instead had followed the route taken by Savaric away from the manor, hoping to find him or else to return their letter to the marshal.

Savaric slipped the letter into the leather purse which hung from his waist belt. 'Tell the marshal that I shall have a reply ready for him shortly.'

The riders made no attempt to go and Savaric was getting impatient. One of the village girls was waiting for him in the familiar glade. When it came to lust the Brabançon was a creature of habit. Each girl, or woman, got the same treatment in the same opening amidst the trees. It gratified him to have them in the same place. As he took one, he could think of one of the others and so have pleasure from more than one at once; and for Savaric there always were others – whether they came willingly, or for half a silver penny, or whether he had to master them by force.

'You've got company in the woods.' Savaric flashed an angry look at the rider, a man with a weatherbeaten face and a jagged scar on his cheek. The man-at-arms recoiled with surprise. 'A man,' he said defensively and the mercenary relaxed. 'We saw him at the wood's edge coming away from the manor.

'Not a clear sight, mind you, but he was there all right. On the right-hand side, going back. Just in from the dead oak with the hollow heart.' He pointed back down the track. 'I thought we should tell you.'

'Thank you.' It was dismissive and without a shred of gratitude. 'I'll deal with it.'

Savaric had already lost interest in both the riders and the girl; he was off down the track. Their mission completed, the bishop's riders carried on their way; as far as they were concerned, Savaric was on his own, his animosity had shut off any fellow feeling on their part.

The Brabançon mercenary captain was taking no chances. The commission he held from the King to guard the manor and its precious horse was no light one. Savaric was not going to let anyone get in the way of that, and right now someone was where they had no right to be. He was determined to find out who it was and put a stop to the activity. Without even thinking, he slipped his dagger out of his right boot.

The woodland path was cool, except for where shafts of light burned through the canopy of overhanging trees in a molten stream of refined gold. Savaric slipped from light to shadow with soft footsteps, peering into the trees. He came to a massive oak, long since stricken with age, its hollow interior laid bare by a dark split in the once mighty trunk. It was half in, half out of the light. Savaric paused for a moment then stepped off the track.

In the wood the air was heavy with its own silence; no birdsong echoed amongst the trees and undergrowth. Listening, he crouched where a patch of enchanter's nightshade thrust its spikes of pale-pink petals through the tangle of dead leaves, ferns and ivy. A movement betrayed the location of his quarry. Ahead amongst the trees he could see a man stand up and then disappear. Holding his knife more firmly Savaric stepped forward as agile as a stoat, his prey as unsuspecting as a rabbit in the cool of evening on the edge of the downs.

The way through the nettles and bushes was marked by the progress of his quarry; branches and leaves were pushed aside and pressed down. The canopy above was thinning and here and there stands of hazel signalled the edge of the wood in a mature coppice. Before the wood gave way to the pasture, on the rise above the manor, an old clearing was still grey with wood ash and the invading splash of purple willowherb. Amidst the great clumps of fireweed a young man was kneeling, peering through the tangle of new growth. Beyond and below lay the manor and village.

Savaric ran his thumb along the edge of his knife blade; a translucent curl of skin hung on the razor edge of the weapon. He smiled with deadly intensity as he stepped into the clearing. Unblinking, his blue eyes were riveted on the spot between the intruder's shoulder blades.

Savaric raised his knife, ready to leap and thrust it beneath the startled throat of the intruder; to pull back the head with his other hand and press the razor edge into the windpipe of the stranger; to feel the fear in the enemy's body and know one quick movement would slice life from that body, in a torrent of blood and soundless writhing. Savaric enjoyed bringing fear to others; he was smiling as he stepped between the clumps of grass and willowherb.

The lump of dead wood caught Savaric on the top of his head, and an explosion of bark and woodlice showered down as he fell. The rotten mass was not heavy enough to knock him out, but he was stunned by the surprise of it. By the time he rose to his feet again, the stranger was on his feet and away into the trees like a startled buck. Swearing with uncharacteristic loss of control, Savaric rounded on the place from where the wood had been thrown. As he did so, he saw a figure fleeing away. With murder in his heart he gave chase, the original would-be victim forgotten.

He chased the wrecker of his plans back towards the track, concerned with only one thing – to destroy the human being who had humiliated him. Umar was running for his life – and he knew it. Leaping fallen trees; pushing through coppices whose poles slapped his face; stumbling and running again.

He leapt through the fringe of bushes beside the track and ran right into the horse. It leapt away with a neigh of terror and Umar was thrown backwards by the collision. Seeking to roll under the beast, he was thwarted by the hands which seized his robe and dragged him back. He had run into a band of Savaric's men who kicked and punched him as he struggled.

Then Umar felt a hand grab his wavy black hair and drag back his head. A knife cut into his throat and he froze; blood coursed over the blade as it slipped into his flesh. A cold voice gasped breathlessly: 'You're a dead man, but I'm going to take my time. And I've got a lot of time . . .'

Richard was watching his mares grazing in the pastures at Temple Buckland. The noontime dinner would soon be taking place and already brothers and sergeants were making their way towards the refectory. He was unmoved by the bright splendour of the day. A Templar brother, fresh home from Acre, had brought the news that the fourth great crusade had degenerated into a war against the Christian emperor of Constantinople, on behalf of the Italian cities who were funding the transportation of the crusaders to the Holy Land and who were trading rivals of the emperor.

As Richard looked out over the grassland and trees he knew in his heart that Jerusalem was lost, and that he was powerless to prevent it. Only the dream remained and now even that seemed threatened by the person of Falkes de Mauleon and his bid for the use of Soloriens. De Lacey was sleeping badly and felt tired and very frustrated. He twisted a grass stem in his hand until it snapped. Looking at his hands he saw blood oozing from where the grass had slashed across his palm.

He was shaken from his dark thoughts by the voice of Mark de Dinan. 'My lord, my lord. They have taken Umar . . .'

The squire was without his horse and was soaked with sweat. Great dark patches stained his tunic which he had kilted about his waist. He had been running a long way in the August sun.

'What happened?' Richard switched from depression to action. 'Who has taken him?'

'The thugs from the manor . . . the crossbowmen. They . . .' He stopped, ashamed of his failure. 'They took me unawares. I would be their prisoner now but for . . .' This was costing Mark very dear. He bit his lip and the words slipped out under protest, squeaking past his teeth. ' . . .but *he* surprised the man who was behind me . . . So I escaped.' The words sounded lame.

Richard was almost relieved by the news. Instead of scolding Mark he grabbed him by the shoulders. 'Get my horse ready. Saddle one of the others for yourself. And get our swords. Do it now.'

Richard looked in the direction of Horsingham; it was strange how events could turn. Now he was the man of action again; the path forward had been revealed again. It had to be God's providence. Richard rejoiced in a chance to do something and escape his impotence. Here was action; who knew where it would lead, but it *was* action. For now, that had to be enough.

Joanna was called on in the privacy of her solar by Stephen

Pierson. He was red-faced and agitated. It was not in character for him to be so upset; in the past he had been the slightly teasing almost elder brother. Now, though, he was looking to her for aid.

'They have taken a prisoner. By God, I think they will kill him, my lady. Father has tried to stop them but I fear he will fail. You must help, my lady . . .'

Joanna threw down her sewing. She was sick of her tedious inactivity. 'Who is doing this?'

'That bastard Savaric,' Stephen cried, forgetting all but his hatred of the man who seemed to embody everything that had disturbed his world. 'And the man they will kill is the heathen. The dark-skinned man who came with the knight . . .'

'Richard de Lacey's groom!' Joanna was on her feet, eyes wide. 'Show me where this is happening.'

Stephen cast a caustic eye towards Tilly, who paled. 'It is where they always are this time of day. Getting drunk by the stables and . . . chasing the girls.' There was bitterness in his voice, and Tilly realised that he knew.

Joanna, though, was halfway to the door of the solar, pursued by her groom and maid. Ranulf Dapifer was in the hall talking to his mousy wife about the state of the food stocks. He saw Joanna and the look on her face. He knew instantly that there was trouble.

'My lady.' He sought to waylay her, turning from his wife, her words forgotten. 'What ails you?' Ranulf was worried that some disaster was about to occur. 'What is it?'

Joanna hardly paused. 'They have seized the Saracen and mean to kill him.'

'Oh God,' Ranulf muttered, but it was not from fear for the Saracen. 'Let me go and see. I think it may be best . . .' Ellen, his wife, touched his arm but he stepped away from her, totally preoccupied with the unfolding drama.

But Joanna was gone; if she had even caught his words, she had ignored them. Ranulf's cheeks were the colour of parchment. She was the old Joanna again; he had seen that look in her eyes as she entered the hall. He swore inwardly; once more she was the girl that the foolish old Gilbert had loved and he had loathed. Now, though, he feared her, for she could ruin everything. And all for a Godforsaken Saracen.

Joanna and Stephen crossed the yard at a run. Chickens scattered before them and servants looked in wonderment. Behind followed a trembling Tilly and a desperate Ranulf. Savaric had Umar in an empty stable, but it was not the groom whose life was in danger at that moment. The life at risk belonged to Piers, the head groom. He was held against a panel and Savaric was advancing on him, knife in hand.

'You upstart yokel. No one lays a hand on me and lives. And after I have finished with you we will find out what this piece of rubbish was doing in the woods.'

The deep voice was abrim with anger, the superciliousness driven out by a blow on the head from a woodlouse-ridden log, and by a grey-haired man who had dared to get between him and vengeance.

'Leave him be.'

Joanna had entered the stable. The time for open opposition had come; though she was not ready for it, she knew it could be avoided no longer. Strangely enough she was not afraid; she was not even wild with anger. Instead she was oddly calm, a fusion of her old and new selves, a woman no longer ready to be treated the way Savaric treated all women.

Ranulf, at her elbow, knew what was happening. He watched the drama unfold and was powerless to direct it. He was horrified; he had laid his plans so well, but Joanna's refusal to be a dutiful woman was about to wreak havoc on them. He clenched his fists to control his desperation.

'Do not dare touch him.'

Savaric, in contrast to Joanna, was lost in his anger. For years he had cultivated the reputation of utter invincibility. Anyone who looked at him wrongly or answered him incorrectly suffered for it, and the sole arbiter of what was wrong, what was incorrect, was Savaric. The King's wars and his own aptitude for killing had given him full scope to play out his egomania. He enjoyed seeing the fear in others, relished their powerless hatred. Now in one morning he had been humiliated twice. He was close to losing control.

'This nobody touched me.' He hissed and pointed towards Piers. 'No one touches me.'

Joanna laughed. 'On the contrary, I had heard that every wench on the manor has touched you. Surely one old man's touch is hard to notice in such a welter of groping.'

Savaric's eyes almost burst from his skull. A vein rose and twitched in his forehead, the knife rose involuntarily. Ranulf Dapifer thought he was going to faint; he could feel the blood rushing in his ears. Instead he stepped forward between the soldier and the lady.

'For the sake of Our Lady, remember that she is a ward of the King.'

The reminder was like a bucket of cold water on the fire of Savaric's anger. He drew back the knife. 'If this old fool is yours then get him away from here,' he muttered with a subdued anger. 'But the heathen is mine. I will find out why he and his friend were spying on us.' Savaric turned to where a bloody and bruised Umar was sprawled in the soiled hay. 'And I will find out in my own way.'

Joanna was already in deep, and threw aside caution. 'I'll not have a man tortured on my manor. No matter what he has done.' She surprised herself, realising that she was saying it as much for Richard as for the battered foreigner.

Savaric was adamant. 'I am charged with the protection of this manor. I shall decide what is necessary and what is not. The man is mine and I shall deal with him.' The old, cold Savaric was returning to replace the stoked-up anger.

'You will not do anything with him, for he is mine.'

No one had seen Richard de Lacey at the doorway. Even the hoof beats on the packed earth and cobbles of the yard had been lost in the confrontation taking place in the stable. Joanna spun around at his voice, almost knocking Ranulf over. The sun broke over Richard's shoulder, dazzling her.

'He was here to alert me concerning the arrival of the bishop's men. He was with my squire – the one whom you attacked.'

Richard accused Savaric in a matter-of-fact tone which made more impact than a display of pique. 'Now I shall take him back with me, if you please.'

Savaric pushed his knife back into his boot and brushed down the rumpled cloth of his knee-length tunic. 'We would not have harmed him,' he said with all the sincerity he could muster. 'But he assaulted me and he should pay for that . . .'

Savaric's change of tone, when Richard appeared, had surprised everyone. Joanna was astonished and knew that there must be a secret motive at work which she could not fathom.

'You were about to attack my squire,' countered Richard. 'And I had charged Umar with guarding him. So if you must confront someone, then it is me.'

Savaric seemed unwilling to do so. 'If I release him into your authority it is your responsibility to discipline him . . .'

'If he has been in error,' Richard interrupted, 'which I do not admit.'

Joanna expected a sharp retort from Savaric but he let it pass with uncharacteristic grace. Ranulf too seemed nonplussed by the turn of events and looked from de Lacey to de Breaute in puzzlement.

'Come here, Umar; help me, Mark.'

De Dinan slipped between Savaric and the silent Piers, and helped Umar to his feet and out of the stable. For the first time Richard really looked at the young woman who had championed his groom.

'I am in your debt, my lady.' He did not need to say why. 'As is my servant. I shall not forget your kindness.'

He stared at her as if concerned at what he saw; as if a thought had struck him and taken him almost completely by surprise. It was not a look that Joanna had seen on the face of this man before – though perhaps there had been a hint of it when they had stood together before in this very stable. But either way, it was akin to looks she had seen before on the faces of other men. She smiled warmly, gratified, and the look seemed to deepen.

'It was my pleasure. But you are not in my debt. If you recall, I am in yours, for you saved me from the stallion.'

Richard smiled slightly. 'I recall it, my lady.' But he appeared to be thinking of it as for the first time. 'Nevertheless, if I can be of service to you . . .'

Joanna was aware of a flicker of flame within herself. It had sparked when he looked at her. What surprised her was the realisation that she had secretly coveted that look. Not merely expected it – as at the door of the church at Sherborne – but actually desired it. That was disconcerting, for she was not used to *relying* on a man for that look. It was a different thing to expect than to desire. The thought made her ponder.

Savaric coughed. 'Before you leave us, perhaps I should show you this.' He handed over the vellum letter, its wax seal broken. 'It is from the bishop's marshal.'

Richard studied the Latin script. As he frowned, the previous look vanished from his face to be replaced by one chiselled out of rock. 'I can meet it and better it. Tell that to my lord the King.'

'It is a lot of money,' Savaric commented, obviously beginning to enjoy himself again. 'And my master the King always expects a debt to be paid.'

Richard raised his head from the letter. 'I know that. And the King knows the importance of my mission. I said I will meet and match this sum, and I will do so.'

Savaric took back the letter. 'Thirty marks – that's twenty pounds in silver,' he said with a shallow smile.

'I know,' Richard replied. 'As I said – I will meet it and more for the breeding use of the stallion.'

Savaric was thinking of the letters he had received from Hubert de Burgh, on behalf of the King. John was going to be very pleased when he heard the news. Very pleased indeed.

'I shall inform the King, but I cannot guarantee when I shall hear his wishes. He is much occupied at present; the French have seized the eastern half of the duchy and he has much on his mind.'

Richard had wanted to have the covering done before the end of August, at the latest, to ensure a foaling in the sweet grass of early summer. However, he reined in his impatience, for there was no choice in the matter. 'I shall await your answer. And next time I shall come in person,' he said, referring to his squire and groom. He took Joanna's hand and kissed it. 'Once more, my lady, I am in your debt.'

As Richard remounted his horse he could no longer be sure of what route providence had taken in the proceedings. To find the price of the use of the stallion so high was a blow. More disturbing still was the face of the young woman. It was as if he had not really noticed her before, or if he had, he had crushed the recognition. Yet now he could not get her face from the front of his thoughts. It was as surprising as it was inappropriate. There was no room for a woman in the life and mission of Richard de Lacey.

As he turned his horse's head he saw her once more, the hair like a robin's breast, a young woman tall and slim, her chin uplifted as if in challenge. Richard found his mouth was dry. He tugged on his reins; the horse – unused to hard handling – snorted with surprise, but Richard was unrepentant and he did not know why.

Tilly did not go to the woods for some time after the affair with the groom of Richard de Lacey. The look from Stephen had frightened her, it had reminded her of what she was doing and of the shame of it. For a week she avoided Savaric; she stuck to Joanna and rarely left the hall on her own. So it was a heart-stopping experience to be met by the cat-faced man as she crossed the courtyard one early evening.

She was not surprised to hear his message but felt all the more ashamed in front of the lowly go-between who shared the secrets of her assignations in the woods. She told him to tell Savaric 'no', then she walked away. Catface, who got his pennies strictly on a payment-by-results basis, was not amused.

That night she lay awake on her pallet next to Joanna. The air was humid again but it was not the threat of an August storm which kept her awake; rather, it was thoughts of Savaric. Part of her was glad that she had rejected his invitation; part of her could not sleep for longing for him. Her body waged a war of attrition with her mind. She tossed and turned and, long before dawn, her body had won. She had to have him but she would change him.

She repeated it to herself – she could and she would. Then she slept uneasily until first light. Beside her, equally awake, was her mistress. Joanna was thinking about Falkes and Richard, and she slept as badly as her maid, though each was unaware of the other's restlessness.

In the morning Tilly took a message from Joanna to Ranulf Dapifer, who was at the stables. On her way there the cat-faced man accosted her again. This time she succumbed, agreeing to meet Savaric after dark in the paddock beyond the stockade. She knew it was madness but she justified it on the grounds that she would only speak with him and that it would go no further.

As she turned away she could have sworn she heard the cat-faced man murmur something to himself as he hurried off. It sounded like 'Three shillings . . . three shillings . . .' but she decided that she must have been mistaken. She felt her mind was being harried to distraction. Returning to the hall she saw there were more visitors to the manor. She recognised Falkes and the riders who had come with a message the previous week and hurried to tell her mistress that they had guests.

Joanna received Falkes in the hall and then escorted him to the solar. Savaric was out somewhere and so she was free of the presence which she found so irksome. Falkes agreed to stay to dinner and enjoy the Wednesday fish dishes concocted from the stock bought from the abbey market at Cerne. He seemed to have more on his mind than fish, however, as he took the wine served by the butler, who was then excused along with the household ladies, leaving him alone with Tilly and Joanna.

'My lady, I must tell you that I have written to the King with regard to your situation.'

Joanna looked surprised but flattered. 'Thank you. I have written to the sheriff but have received no reply. I am indeed grateful for your help, though it comes most unexpectedly. You can see how the manor is being despoiled. If only the King knew, then he would put a stop to it.'

Falkes knew full well that John would do no such thing, but held his peace. When he did speak his subject was not the state of the manor, though it clearly affected it. 'It was concerning you, my lady, rather than the estate, that I wrote to the King, though I believe I may have the answer to both problems.'

'Of me?' Joanna looked surprised, although a look of discernment was growing. 'You wrote concerning my person?'

Falkes was a man to measure his words, not to embroider them. 'I wrote asking for your hand in marriage.' He said it simply, as if he expected no response. 'I knew your father well and I believe that in marriage I could serve both your best interests and those of the manor.'

'You flatter me, sir.' Joanna seemed uncharacteristically flustered. 'I had no knowledge that you were so intended.'

'You must excuse me,' Falkes said, 'for I did not want to mention it until the King had examined the extent of the sum I have offered. Even now he has not committed himself, but neither has he rejected my offer either.

'Therefore I felt I should tell you, out of courtesy. Though it should perhaps be a secret until the formal agreement is made with the King.' The grey eyes watched her every move.

Joanna felt her heart beating faster. She took some wine to steady herself. Until the preamble of Falkes' speech she had had no idea that he was planning anything like this, and so it had taken her by surprise and she was not sure what she felt.

'I am overwhelmed,' she said at last. 'I do not know what to say.'

Since it was not a proposal but a statement that she had received, there was of course no need to say anything, but she felt that she should respond in some way.

'I understand. But I am sure you can see the advantage of it. I will put a stop to the destruction of the manor and will make you a true husband and, I trust, an honourable one.'

'Of course . . . of course,' Joanna replied, her mind whirling.

They took lunch together but Joanna could hardly taste the food. She did not know what she should feel. Falkes was right in that it would be an answer to many of her problems. And he was, as far as she knew, a fair man; strong and admirable. In many ways it would be a good match. Clearly he thought that the King would agree with this assessment and with the money he was prepared to spend to make it a reality.

Falkes was not overtalkative. Having broached the news, he seemed content to eat and did not engage in light conversation. One theme which did interest him, though, was the state of the manor's resources, given the activities of Savaric. Regarding this issue, he seemed very curious indeed.

As he ate, Joanna watched him, this man twenty years her senior. She saw once again the strength in the muscled sword arm and the physical power held within his tight contained body. A body which seemed to promise strength and security; an answer to dilemmas. She saw the careful mouth beneath the sweep of the black moustache, and the eyes – grey and missing nothing. She saw the refined power of the man.

He did not stay long after dinner; he had business in Sherborne and had to leave. Joanna was left with a lot to think about. She went alone to the church where her father was now buried under the finished effigy; a stone dog by his crossed feet, stone-mailed hands clasped across his stone-mailed chest in watchful marbled prayer.

While Tilly knelt beside her, she prayed in silence for the peace to accept the best course of action. However, all the time she prayed for peace, bubbles of doubt rose from the depths of her thoughts. Even in her danger and distress there was part of her which found the obvious answer hard to accept. She was troubled, unsure of why this was so. Was it pride, because she had never been trained to rely on anyone? Her father had always encouraged her to unwomanly independence; that which had so infuriated Dapifer. If so, then pride was a sin.

Or was it something else which troubled her? Something deeper? Something curiously entangled with Richard de Lacey? A knight she hardly knew; had met but three times. She – like him – was troubled now. And like him she did not really know the reason why. She could not deny the attraction that she felt for Falkes, but his mention of a marriage suit had taken her by surprise, for her thoughts had never reached that far. As she tried to piece together what she felt, she realised that it counted for little anyway, for the King was the final master of her situation.

There would be no consideration of her judgement in such a decision; and even that – as familiar a reality as it was – jabbed her like a spur and threw all thoughts and feelings into a whirl of doubt and agitation.

Behind her, Tilly too was praying. Her prayer was that she could divert Savaric from the course of action with which he threatened the manor. She was sure it could be done. Sure that although he hid it beneath layers of ice, he felt something for her. She could not believe that nothing had come from their physical union; from the total surrender of their bodies to each other. She was convinced that she understood him and that somewhere within him there was a spark of appreciation of her.

That night as Joanna slept, Tilly crept from the solar, through the dark, rush-strewn hall, with its snoring servants on their mattresses of straw, then out into the night. She stopped at the foot of the steps, by the undercroft, and looked up at the star-scattered sky. It was vast and immeasurable, and it filled her with awe and terror. She prayed that God would forgive her the fornications that she had committed and give her strength this night to know what to say to her lover.

Savaric was waiting for her beyond the clump of trees by the paddock. As she approached, she heard his low whistle to tell her it was indeed him.

'You have been shy of late,' he said smoothly as he kissed her hungrily. Her mouth was not charged with passion and he stopped, suspicious. 'What's wrong?' he said guardedly.

'Do you love me?' Savaric was staring at her but she could not fully make out his face. 'You have loved me, but do you *love* me?'

Savaric smiled. How many times had he heard that question? 'Of course I love you,' he said and drew her to him.

Tilly felt his mouth and tongue on her throat and his hands on her small waist pressing her into him. Before the sea of desire could rise again in her, she shook herself, and clambered above the tide. 'If you love me, look after Joanna. She loves this manor. Protect it and her.'

Savaric looked at her sharply. 'What are you saying?' He was curious as well as amused.

Tilly trembled. 'Do not destroy the pasture, or speak to her as if she is of no account. I love her and if you love me then do not treat her so. Please, if you love me . . .'

Savaric was well amused by this turn of events. Also, he was aroused and did not want to wait any longer for what he desired. Tonight he did not want to take her by force; the whim varied from time to time. He was prepared to humour her – but not for long.

'Of course, of course,' he muttered thickly. 'Now let me show you how much I love you . . .'

Her resolve melted in the heat of her relief and she cried out: 'Yes, yes, show me how much you love me.'

When he had finished and the last shocks of their mutual climax had subsided into stillness, Tilly lay looking at the stars. Savaric's mind was on other things. 'If you really want me to take care of your mistress, I must know more of what is going on.' He stroked her dark hair in a passable imitation of tenderness, and she sighed. 'Why was Falkes de Mauleon here today? I think it was more than the stallion which drew him.' Fox-like, he smiled. 'Why was he here?'

And because she believed him – had to believe him – she told him.

Three days after Tilly had lain with Savaric in the paddock, Piers went on a short journey to the abbey at Cerne. It was the day after the feast of the Assumption of the Virgin Mary – Saturday, 16 August. The journey was a short one of some ten miles down the winding valley of the river Cerne. He planned to do it after dinner and return home before nightfall.

Gilbert de Cantelo had been on good terms with the Benedictines at both Cerne and Sherborne. He had always been happy to lend the services of his groom to the abbot of either whenever their horses were sick. It was a custom which Joanna had continued and which had survived the onset of wardship. Piers rode in the company of his son, Stephen, who seemed subdued and ill at ease. For much of the way they rode in silence, Piers guessing the reason for his son's mood.

They were halfway to the abbey and had reached the point where the road rose out of the clay on to the first ridge of the chalk, before falling down along the side of the clear little river Cerne. On either hand the slopes curved up away from the river, on to the broad flank of the high downs. Before them the bowl of the valley was wooded and the road twisting.

Piers reined in his horse to rest it a little. 'Out with it, boy. What's ailing you?'

Stephen shook his blond head. 'Nothing,' he lied unconvincingly. 'There's nothing wrong.' Both spoke freely in English as they always did when alone together.

Piers did not look impressed. 'It's the lady Joanna's maid, isn't it? You've carried a torch for her for some time now.' His voice was not unkind, more wary.

Stephen crimsoned, like an orchid on the chalk pastures. 'She means nothing to me.' His protestation was too pained to be true.

'Rest your heart, son. There was no harm in it, but nothing could ever have come from it. You know your place well enough. She is a knight's daughter . . .'

Stephen was embarrassed and shook his head. 'It matters not to me. We were always just friends. There was nothing more.' He motioned down the valley. 'We are going to be late if we just sit here talking.'

Piers made one last attempt to reach his son, as he might to a hurt and angry colt. 'It's the man Savaric, isn't it? It's because you think that . . .'

'It's nothing at all.' Besides which, Stephen did not *think*. He *knew* something was going on between Joanna's maid and de Breaute. It was poison in his belly. 'What she does is her own affair, it's none of my business. She is her own woman. As you said – she is a knight's daughter, she would not lower herself . . .' He said the last bitterly, thinking of Savaric.

Piers, seeing the redness about his son's eyes, let the matter drop. Once more in silence they rode between the trees with the river chattering clearly along its bright bed.

The abbot's own horse had a painful lameness in his front right foot. It took longer than Piers had estimated to find the sharp stone which had worked its way up inside the wall of the hoof. The foot was badly pricked and he and Stephen had a long job cutting away the infected tissue around the tender frog and opening the sole to drain out the pus.

The bell for vespers was ringing when they had finally finished cleaning up the hoof. Even then it would require poulticing for at least a day before the pad was changed. Piers could not afford to stay that long, as a number of the mares were due to drop foal and one had a reputation for breech births. He did not want to be away from the manor for too long. After a brief discussion the two men decided that Stephen would stay at Cerne while his father rode back to Horsingham. The evening shadows were beginning to lengthen about the abbey when Piers left.

It was near the point where he and Stephen had paused in the morning that he met the men. The road was deserted and far from any hamlet or village. Piers recognised them immediately as some of Savaric's Brabançons. Where they had been, he had no idea, but it was none of his business and, like Stephen, he had stayed away from the mercenaries as much as possible. He had kept an even greater distance since the altercation with Savaric over the captured Saracen spy.

The men-at-arms seemed to be waiting for someone. It was only as he approached them that Piers realised that it might be him. By then it was far too late. They were all about his frightened mount, jeering and shouting. He pulled back his horse's head and tried to turn about. Then the screen of soldiers cleared and a crossbow bolt took Piers below his right jaw.

The force of the impact threw him back off his horse. His terrified mount made to gallop away, dragging his body behind, his boots still wedged in the stirrups. The soldiers caught it and prevented its escape.

'Good shot,' one yelled to his mate. 'Almost took the bugger's head off.'

The killer laughed. 'I was aiming at his chest.' All the soldiers roared at this mock humility.

'Now remember what 'is majesty said. Mess up the wound so no one knows it was us . . .' the first speaker reminded his mates.

Mindful of Savaric's instructions, they got to work on the body of the grey-haired old groom, until no one could have identified the weapon which had dispatched him.

'A job well done.' The firer of the bolt surveyed the body. 'Even Savaric 'iself would be pleased.'

King John spent late August 1203 in the vicinity of Rouen, chief city of his duchy. His attempt to relieve the siege on the Château Gaillard had failed and he had been forced to divert himself hunting, while his commanders attempted to contain the worst French and Breton incursions into Normandy. Once more Hubert de Burgh was with him. The talk was of a correspondence that the sheriff of Somerset and Dorset had received from England.

'So,' John said at length, 'it seems there is quite a rivalry growing between Falkes and Richard regarding the horse Soloriens.' He used their Christian names in a way which combined intimacy with power over them. 'What is the latest price offered?'

De Burgh raised the sheet of vellum. 'It seems that our Templar friend has agreed to match and better the sum offered by the bishop's marshal.' He looked again. 'And that was twenty pounds.'

John's close-clipped black beard and moustache trembled with laughter. 'Very good indeed. It's working very well, don't you think?'

'Indeed it is, my liege.' Hubert had to admit that the little strategy of instructing Savaric to pit de Lacey against de Mauleon seemed to be paying dividends; twenty pounds was a lot of money. 'You could buy the swords of fifty mounted men-at-arms, for the best part of a month, with the proceeds of this enterprise.'

'I know,' John said, almond eyes alight. 'It's a stratagem my father would have approved of, don't you think?'

De Burgh nodded but said nothing; always there was this need to gain the posthumous approval of his father; to better his warrior brother. John took one of the hard-boiled eggs from a silver dish in front of him and popped it whole into his mouth. His butler and household knights hovered about him with flagons of wine and bowls of clean water for his hands.

When he had finished chewing he turned his attention once more towards the correspondence from England. 'Tell Savaric that we will accept Richard de Lacey's offer. I doubt that Falkes will go better than that. Besides, he will have the girl and the manor. It will be some consolation.'

'Then you have decided that matter, my lord? Savaric wonders if it might be better for the girl to join the royal household until she is married. But, of course, if you have already decided on Falkes de Mauleon . . .'

'Almost, almost,' John replied, enjoying the delay.

Hubert tapped the sheet of vellum. 'Savaric seems a little disapproving of Falkes. He seems to think the man has already mentioned marriage to the lady Joanna and intends to stop the depasturing of the manor . . .'

John was no longer smiling. 'He is a little forward then, is he not? Falkes should not count his chickens so early.' There was a sudden edge of anger about his voice; the terrible Angevin temper, so easily roused. 'Where has Savaric got this information from?'

'He does not say, but he seems sure about it.' De Burgh attempted to avoid an outburst of John's fury. 'It may be that Savaric merely fears an end to the wardship. It is a better life for him there than fighting here against the French. It may be that which has caused him to accuse Falkes . . .' As soon as he had said it, he knew that it had been an error to remind the King of the state of the war. A black shadow passed over John's features.

'I shall not be abused or anticipated by any man. Neither by a purchaser of an heiress who assumes too quickly, or by a soldier who wishes for feather pillows in England while I am campaigning here.' The anger was banked down but not extinguished. 'Keep me informed about this matter. I hold you responsible for the successful outcome of this wardship sale and the matter of the stallion.' He waved angrily for his wine. 'And I have not yet finally decided in the matter of Falkes de Mauleon and Joanna de Cantelo. I shall make the final decision in my own good time and the marshal can wait . . .'

Hubert nodded; it had never been his idea to accept Falkes' suit, or to pit Templar knight against marshal. Now it was getting sticky, though, he had the distinct feeling that the King would forget that it had been his own idea. The sheriff sighed; royal service was no easy task.

John leaned forward. 'He writes well! Is this his own hand?' He knew that Savaric was no illiterate peasant, but the landless son of a knightly family.

'There is a steward there who served Gilbert and now your servants. He pens the letters for Savaric and advises him . . .'

The King pondered this. 'What does Savaric think of him? You know how valuable a good clerk is. Has he been useful to us?'

'I know the man, my lord. He is of some small use, but I do not think he is of great account.'

Hubert had hardly met Ranulf Dapifer, but he was tiring of this conversation and had other – more important – things to discuss with the King. Besides which, Horsingham was getting to be all too tricky a proposition. De Burgh was happier when the King was not concentrating on it. It was with little thought and no malice that he swept away Ranulf Dapifer's prayers, hopes and dreams.

'A pity,' John murmured. 'But never mind . . .'

Joanna left the manor on her own. She knew it was unheard of but she had to do it. She would face the disapproval of Ranulf and Savaric when she returned. She had tears to shed and she wanted to cry alone. Besides which, she was mistress of the manor, she would do as she wanted. Had she felt confident over this last point she would no doubt have stayed about the hall. But she was less sure than ever since the death of Piers. His killing had seemed to underscore that nothing was permanent and no one was safe.

She had loved the old groom and could not believe he was dead. She knew Savaric was behind it, though she had no evidence at all. When she had confided this to Tilly she had been astonished that her maid had actually pointed out the lack of evidence to her. It was unlike Matilda to take a contrary viewpoint to her own. And to have her defend Savaric was a shock.

It was with some relief that Joanna took her horse up on to the downland. The fresh air could clear her thoughts and give her an opportunity to think. As she rode, she thought about Falkes and his sensible proposition, and of Richard and his passion and shadows, and of her maid who no longer gossiped and seemed unusually quiet, and of an old man murdered on a country road with no one to witness his destruction.

The undulating sweep of green was blissfully quiet and deserted. Below her horse's hooves the sward was a carpet of shimmering quaking grass, strewn with the pink tongues of restharrow and drifts of purple knapweed. To the south a buzzard floated above the woodland which rose from the hollow rounded valleys.

She slowed her horse to a walk, thinking about Piers and Stephen and her father and the good times, and as she thought, she wept. She had not cried since the night in Soloriens' stable; now the tears came as she rode alone. It was a quiet and controlled grief, a sorrow which had grown more determined, a fusion of the old and new Joanna. A more dangerous combination than even Ranulf Dapifer had realised, for the steward had feared flashes of anger and of rebellion. What he had not considered was something as calculated as retribution.

Joanna was thinking of her own answer to her problems, an answer which her father would have approved of, an answer which came from her alone and not from anyone else. As yet she had not found the answer but she was feeling her way towards it.

She rode further than she had intended along the northern rim of the downs. However, the day was hot and the sky was as hazy-blue as the harebells in the grass. It was pleasing to ride and ride. After a while she ceased to think at all, simply becoming one with the rhythm of her mount and the 'peewit' cry of lapwings as they turned above her. She rode for hours, alone with her desire to strike back against the forces ranged so heavily against her.

The sudden fold in the downland took her by surprise. Below her, the slope was steep and the way wooded. She had never seen this place before, it was a long way from Horsingham. She was curious and urged her horse on, despite the voices whispering caution in her ear. Joanna rode down into the valley and through the trees. The way was close but not closed and, by urging her horse forward, she slipped between the trees. From below she could hear a brook, and the smell of clean water drew the horse on.

It was with a twist of alarm that she came upon the cottages, mouldering under sagging thatch and amidst waist-high grass. She reined in her horse. When it became clear that the place was deserted, she walked him forward again. Dismounting, she surveyed the hamlet. A curious pattern drew her attention to the door frame of one building, and she traced the scratch marks on the cob.

'It's a cat,' she said with delight. 'Now I wonder who scratched you there?'

Then she froze, her finger halfway round the whiskered face, for a thought had come to her; the germ of an idea. The kind of idea that would have made Ranulf Dapifer have apoplexy on the spot.

Richard de Lacey faced his squire and groom. His frustration had overcome his caution and he wanted them both to know what was going on. After all, they were in this together.

'They are stopping the money,' he said for the second time, as if repetition would make the news more comprehensible. 'Well, not exactly stopping it; more drying it up, like a stream in summer. Less now, not as much next month . . .'

'But why, my lord?' Mark de Dinan shared the grief of his knight, as he always did.

'I do not know,' Richard replied slowly. 'There is an official reason, of course, but I am not convinced. This must have come from the Grand Master himself.' He paused as he recalled the exhilaration of that meeting in Acre over a year before. 'For some reason he has lost interest in our mission. Or perhaps we have displeased him in some way.' He paused to consider the awful thought that an error on his part might have been to blame for the lack of Templar financial support.

'Do you think it is because of Soloriens? Because it is a Lusignan horse?' Richard shrugged and Mark frowned. 'And now we have offered to pay the King for it. And we don't have the money . . .'

The terrible statement hung over them like an axe blade, and no one spoke for some time. At length it was Richard who broke the silence. 'I can no longer pay you, Umar; you are free to go. To return to your own land, or to take up service with another. I will do all that I can for you by way of recommendation.'

Umar shrugged. 'I have come this far, my lord. I will go all the way.' Mark was staring at him intently.

'You don't understand, I cannot afford to . . .'

'It is you who do not understand, my lord.' The impertinence was startling but Richard only laughed. 'I will serve the man who saved my life. I will serve you, my lord, for you did not desert me. I will not go now, and besides, I fear to leave my fine horses in the hands of grooms who are but Franks!'

Richard looked away. 'Thank you,' he said quietly, 'but God knows what will become of us.'

Mark looked at Umar and at Richard, still stunned by what the groom had said. 'And I am your sworn servant, my lord, in life and in death. It seems now that we both are.' He glanced at Umar, still critical but thawing a little. 'And I would like to say that I am grateful that this man saved my life.'

Richard looked at them both. What a shame, he thought, to have this bond, at last, when we have no future . . .

Chapter 9

William Catface was in love. She was the prettiest thing he had ever seen, and he had desired her since the first meeting. Nothing was going to stand in his way of possessing her. Already he could imagine getting her back home to the warmth of the hay in the damp byre attached to the house.

The cow in question looked at him with the lazy detachment of all her kind, as if bovine contemplations did not stretch as far as comprehending the lofty dreams of men. A scrawny calf pushed at her swollen udder. In the patched pocket of his threadbare tunic William had a greasy leather pouch and in it were the pieces of silver which he had earned from the soldiers. One hand was closed firmly about that pouch, as if at any moment he expected a thief to seize his little hoard of treasure.

'Got it then, Catface? As from what I've 'eard, yer short of the wherewithal . . .'

William's richer villein neighbour – who owned three such beasts, a good plot of land and lived in the luxury of a house possessing a separate bedchamber for himself, his wife and five surviving children – looked with ill-disguised condescension on the planning of his poorer neighbour.

'I've got it.' Catface's reply was a challenge. 'From honest toil too.' William was proud of his achievements and enterprise.

'Well, and I'd 'eard yer'd borrowed the money . . .'

William frowned peevishly, as he had in fact been forced to borrow some money in order to make up the full amount. Even the money earned from Savaric had not been quite enough. Another neighbour had leant him the necessary amount, but the matter was supposed to be private.

William poured the money from his bag on to the packed-earth floor of the chamber. 'Are yer sellin' this beast or not . . .'

His neighbour shrugged and began picking up the scraps of silver and here and there a quarter of the King's head on a divided coin. He did not really care where Catface had got the money; all that mattered was that it came to the right amount, and it did: three shillings in coins and parings. He pocketed the money and handed the beast's tether to William.

'Take 'er. And the rope's in at the price. Gift from me . . .'

Catface looked critically at the frayed leather thong. 'Now you go careful. Yer'll soon be as poor as me, with such kindnesses . . .'

Proud of his new possessions, he led the lazy beast towards the door, the calf trotting dutifully behind its mother. In his own mind, William was already calculating how much soft green cheese and buttermilk he could sell to Savaric's boys. The loan would be paid off in no time, then it would be sheer profit. In addition he could sell the calf, and that would raise some more silver – at least a shilling. He grinned at the thought of the twelve silver pennies in his own hand! It might even raise more, if it looked healthy.

Who knew where it might end? He might even buy a sow to replace the one that they had been forced to kill and eat the previous winter. Things were looking up, he decided, as he ostentatiously paraded his purchase back down the rutted track between the cottages and tiny garden plots.

In the cooler days of autumn Joanna resolved to visit the holy well at Cerne, south of the manor. It was hardly an exhausting pilgrimage to the Silver Well, but she felt that even the small effort might have spiritual benefits, and she was in need of insight. She had planned the journey carefully so that it would coincide with the feast day of the Nativity of the Virgin Mary. This seemed particularly auspicious, given the dedication of the abbey at Cerne to the mother of Jesus. Since this feast fell on Monday, 8 September, her journey needed to take place on the preceding Saturday, so as to give her a day of prayer and meditation prior to the festival.

She watched as Stephen Pierson saddled her horse. 'How are you, Stephen?' she asked with real tenderness.

The groom turned his blond head towards her. 'As well as can be expected, my lady.' His mouth, set between fair moustache and beard, clamped shut for a moment. Then he said quietly: 'Considering that my father is murdered and those responsible for it are living on this very manor.'

There was a slight note of accusation in his voice, as if he half expected Joanna to have done something about it. She leaned forward to remove a wisp of straw from his beard. 'I know, Stephen.' She was not angered at his tone. 'And no one knows it more than I do, but for now we can do nothing . . .'

The young man's eyes, which had once danced with fun and sport, now clouded with shadows of anger and despair. 'Nothing! Can we truly do nothing, my lady?' No longer was he accusing, now he was almost pleading with her.

Across the courtyard, Joanna saw Savaric emerge from the hall. There was the architect of their despair and she watched him carefully. He walked with the self-conscious air of one who felt he commanded the attention of all about him. He stopped to talk to a passing servant and the girl dissolved into stammering blushes. The sight of his paraded sexual confidence made Joanna clench her fists with fury. How could any woman fall for the lecherous attentions of such a man?

She watched the turn of his head and the confident way that he brushed a piece of dirt from his well-formed thigh. At the slight tightening in her stomach, she turned away in horror and disgust at her own interest and her reaction that betrayed her higher thoughts. She shook her head at the maelstrom of confusion and turbulence that Savaric had brought to the manor. It was with renewed determination to thwart him and prove herself a match for him that she turned back to Stephen.

'There is nothing we can do at present.' Before he could interrupt her she silenced him with a raised hand. 'You know as well as I do that there were no witnesses to the crime . . .'

'God's blood, my lady. If there had been, these bastards would have terrified them into silence, or worse, and . . .'

'I know, Stephen, but be that as it may, there were no witnesses.' It pained her to educate him so in the harsh realities of a world that neither of them had been prepared for. 'The coroner knights have summoned juries from the four neighbouring villages about the spot where he was killed, and no one saw anything.'

When Stephen hissed between his teeth, she added: 'It is not in their interests to remain silent if they know anything. As there has been no arrest the freemen of the hundred where he was killed must pay the murder fine to the shire court. No man willingly hands over four mark to the King if he can avoid it; the fine, even when divided out, will hurt them. 'Tis the price of fifty sheep . . .'

Stephen did not seem very sympathetic. 'I do not believe that no one saw a thing,' he observed doggedly. 'And all the while my father was being stuck like a pig.' Tears rose in his eyes as he recalled Piers' mutilated body.

Joanna touched his arm, understanding the grief all too well. 'I loved him too, Stephen. God knows he was kind to me, and he was loyal to my father.' She faltered as she spoke, as if his grief was awakening her own. 'And we will be revenged. Do not mistake my inaction for surrender. You know me better than that, but the time is not yet right. You must be patient.'

Then she stepped away, because Savaric was approaching, and because she did not wish to be pressed regarding the details of her plans, for they did not yet exist. Matilda came from the hall, carrying a bundle of Joanna's belongings carefully wrapped in a riding cloak and ready to be slung across her saddle. She stopped when she saw Savaric with her mistress. Then she took a deep breath and gave the bundle to Stephen. He took it from her without a word and tied it across the pommel of the saddle. For a moment their eyes met, and then he looked away. In that moment, though, she saw all of his pain, mixed with his confusion and anger.

She longed to throw her arms about him and say how sorry she was, but she knew that the time for that was long past. Perhaps it had gone for ever. Tilly felt that she saw something of herself dying in those sad and bitter eyes. But now there was no going back; she was committed and knew of no way out. Desperately she reminded herself of Savaric's promises and of his protestations of innocence regarding the death of Piers.

'What time do you expect him?'

Joanna resented his questioning, but as the King's agent he had a right to know. 'Falkes should be here soon,' was however as far as she was prepared to go by way of conversation.

Her request – for such plans had to go through Savaric – to go to Cerne had only been allowed if a suitable escort could be found. Falkes had volunteered for the task as soon as he had heard of her desire to go. Savaric had not been pleased but had been caught in a cleft stick. Given Falkes' negotiations with the King, he was in a strong position. Besides which, the King's instruction to Savaric to force the marshal and the wounded Templar into competition made it imperative that neither should be offended. Savaric reserved his best behaviour for these two.

Falkes rode into the manor stockade while Savaric was engaged in the one-sided conversation with Joanna. The mercenary was not put off by her resentment at his presence. Like most men he found her very attractive, but it was his way to bully and browbeat women that he really desired. It was a way to bring the attraction under a tight rein, so that he never became emotionally vulnerable. That way, when women eventually fell prey to his desires, they did so on his terms and under his command. If the truth were to be known, he was incapable of acknowledging desire for a woman whom he could not master.

For Savaric, sexual conquest was always just that – a subjugating of the object of his lust. Chivalric service of unattainable fine ladies was suitable for the knights at court and the troubadours. For Savaric, passion was a much earthier affair, akin to warfare. On that score the conquest of Matilda had been hardly a challenge. The physical pleasure of having her was rapidly waning in the face of the lack of satisfaction it brought to him. It had ceased to be a conquest and had turned into a rout. After a while that bored him; he wanted a greater sense of gratification. Like that which would come from the seduction of Joanna de Cantelo.

Quite unaware of the complex undercurrents of Savaric's mind, Joanna had no way of knowing that her disdain for him was actually fuelling his desire. Since she had begun to assert herself, that desire had increased and now Savaric was determined to have her, but he was shrewd enough to realise that this time he was playing a very dangerous game indeed. Seducing Joanna – even if it was possible – would hardly be overlooked by the King, or by Falkes de Mauleon. Her marital value would be destroyed and the deflowerer of the lady in question could expect some severe action in response to damaging so valuable an asset. It was a point for Savaric to ponder on as he and Joanna exchanged barbed conversation.

Falkes insisted on helping Joanna into her saddle personally. He dismissed both Savaric and the hovering Stephen with a glance, and both deferred to him. His strong arms lifted her with ease. Stephen and Tilly mounted when she had done so, as both were to escort her, along with Falkes and his two men-at-arms.

They rode out of the stockade together but, just outside, Joanna reined in her horse. She pointed to the paddock. 'See how heavily they are grazing the land.' Falkes nodded as he looked towards the large number of horses at pasture. Joanna continued: 'My grooms inform me that already more foals are sick with worms than in any other year, the pasture is so soiled. And over there,' she pointed to where the grazing gave way to woodland, 'the earth is already bared by the cropping. Is that not so, Stephen?'

Pierson nodded as he was drawn into the conversation. 'It is, my lady. And what is worse, the weeds that have begun to invade the grass include ragwort.' He looked at the bishop's marshal who comprehended the problem caused by the yellow daisy-like flowers. 'We have had three mares poisoned with it since the end of August,' he said angrily. 'And one of the stallions brought from the King's stud at Gillingham is losing the shine on his coat. 'tis a sure sign of the start of the poison . . .'

'But not the stallion from France?' Falkes' forehead creased with a rare display of emotion. 'The stallion Soloriens is well, I trust . . .'

'He is well, my lord. He does not go to grass with the others. They have reserved a paddock for him alone and he will get the sweetest of the meadow hay this winter too, no doubt. They cosset him as though he were the most precious prisoner on earth.'

Joanna realised why Falkes was concerned. 'Soloriens will come to no harm, though they fear him rather than love him.' She remembered her own tears against his fine grey mane. 'But the rest of the manor is being eaten out of house and home.' Joanna looked at him meaningfully, knowing that he would comprehend the loss in its value and set it to balance his relief that the Lusignan stallion was well. 'It must be stopped.'

Then – before he could reply – she kicked her horse lightly and the well-trained mount sprang forward. It was as if she was challenging him to match her and with it match her outrage at the loss of the manor. Falkes forced his horse forward immediately and went after her at a quick canter. But whether he would or could save the manor it was not possible to read in the veiled grey eyes.

Richard de Lacey stopped his horse at the top of the steep hill, called the Trendle, which overlooked the village of Cerne and the Abbey of SS Mary, Peter and Benedict, with its complex of buildings, fishponds and closes. Below him, on his right, a great figure of a giant was carved in chalk through the thin turf; a vast erection proclaimed its virulent masculinity. It was not this, though, that attracted Richard's attention; as he leaned forward in the saddle, he was looking down into the valley. South of the abbey church stood a grove of lime trees. He nodded as he saw it, for it was his goal.

Behind him Mark and Umar sat on their mounts in private contemplation. The late-afternoon sunshine played over the giant at their feet but already the shadows of the settlement to the south were lengthening.

Richard dismounted. 'From here we go on foot. It's fitting for pilgrims to do so.' He glanced at Umar. 'Even for you,' and the Saracen groom smiled a rare smile. 'Besides which, the hill is too steep for the horses.'

Laughing at his own mixture of practicality and piety, Richard led the way down towards the abbey. In his heart, though, he was not laughing; this was, perhaps, his last hope. As he descended the chalky path he prayed that here he might find the way forward once more, for somewhere, as in a deep dark wood, he had lost his way. It was his manner to laugh at the fears that would not go away, and so he laughed as he walked through the trees, although his belly felt hollow with an aching loneliness.

The abbey guesthouse lay to the south-west of the abbey church and on the western extremity of the monastic precinct. It lay cheek by jowl with the north–south street which linked the abbey to the settlement beyond its walls. The bell for vespers was ringing as Richard and his two companions rode up to the guesthouse. In the precincts beyond, the black-robed monks were making their way to worship in the abbey church. Many townsfolk and benefactors were also gravitating towards the abbey courts as the great festival day drew to a close.

By the time that they had stabled their horses and left Umar grooming them, the bells had stopped and the abbey was silent but for the rising and falling of voices in the nearby church. 'You may rest, Mark,' Richard instructed his squire. And when the young man would have persisted, added: 'I want to pray alone at the holy well. Have you the package?'

Mark nodded and handed the knight a small parcel of linen cloth, then he reluctantly backed away. On his knight's instructions he was to make a gift of ten marks of silver to the abbey treasurer at the close of vespers. It was to coincide with Richard's visit to the holy well. Richard looked intently at the package, then sighed as if something too precious to contemplate lay in his grasp.

The Silver Well of St Catherine was in deep shadow when Richard approached it. Its close guard of tall lime trees made it a place of peculiar quiet and mystery, even though it lay between the church and the closes of the village. All other pilgrims were attending the service in the church and the place was deserted.

Richard descended the path between the trees. A high wall

rose on his left to show where the path fell below ground level, and moss and ferns grew in its cool shade. At the end of the path a pool lay in a basin of hewn rock. The high wall surrounded it on two sides, on the third side the path approached it, on the other the spring ran away down a stone conduit.

Richard knelt beside the pool. Before him an image of St Catherine's wheel had been carved on an upright stone by some unknown hand. Carefully he laid down his package and opened it, gently unfolding the linen to reveal the contents.

'Holy Mary, Mother of Our Lord, intercede for me,' he intoned softly. 'Virgin Catherine – chaste and pure – pray for me.' He turned back the final fold of cloth.

He had chosen this day of all days for his visit with some care, but preferred his devotions to take place in secret solitude, rather than with the crowd at the church; for Richard de Lacey had come on a peculiar pilgrimage. In the dim silence he could hear only his own breathing and the pumping of his heart. He stared at the thing revealed. Now that he had come to it he was fearful of going through with his task. He could not bear the thought of failure.

It had been easy to plan it, but now the testing time had come; the time of trial for his faith. He wished he had put it off until the morrow. He wished that it was yesterday and all this still lay ahead. He wished that it was any time but now.

With trembling hands he lifted out the waxy laurel leaves. With reverence he formed them into a simple cup in the palm of his cradled hands, then he bent and dipped the cup in the cold water. The spring water ran down his wrists as he raised the laurel cup to his lips. He drank greedily, as if urgency alone was enough to secure the answer to his prayers.

The soft footfall behind him caused him to start. Turning sharply, the laurel cup fell apart and the last of the precious liquid ran on to the flag stones. A sudden cry signalled that he was not alone in being surprised. A slim figure, cloaked against the evening chill, stepped backwards. Richard rose and the recognition was simultaneous.

'I did not realise . . .' Joanna had her back to the high wall. 'I came full of my own thoughts . . .'

Richard was on his feet now. 'There is no fault in it.' But his voice was strained with embarrassment. He crumpled up the leaves but it was too late.

'A cup of leaves . . .' Joanna stepped forward away from the wall. 'What were you wishing for?'

'So you understand?' Richard laughed bitterly as his secret was made a secret no more.

'Of course. My father brought me here when I was a little girl.' Joanna stepped past him and as he turned she bent and touched the water. 'They say that the first person to gaze into the pool at daybreak on Easter morning will see the faces of all who will die in the next year.' She grimaced at the macabre thought. 'And it heals those women who cannot have children. My father said he knew of many local women who were so blessed by this place.' Then she stopped as if the memory of her father brought a cold wind on her words. 'And it is also said . . . that anyone who drinks the water from a cup of laurel leaves – and looks south as they pray – will have their wish come true.'

Richard laughed, and it was harsh and unlike him. He saw his desperate thoughts hung out like clothes to dry, for all to see.

Joanna faced him, her back to the well. 'What did you wish for?' She did not know what made her so bold. It clearly surprised Richard too.

He blurted out: 'That I might be a soldier of Our Lord again.' When she looked at him without comprehension, he added: 'I cannot fight. I have an old wound and with it I am useless – a cripple.'

He threw the handful of laurel into the pool. 'Do you know what that means? I am a failure.' He longed to stop himself but he could not; it was as if a dam had burst. He lost control of his words. 'I vowed to free Jerusalem and to defend Christendom, and now I can scarce defend myself. God knows how I have tried, but it will not work.'

He flung his right arm out towards her and felt the familiar throb of the ruptured muscles in his shoulder. His blue eyes were sparking fire and she looked at his passion in astonishment. No man had ever spoken so in her presence before; so unguarded and with such raw, bitter energy. She was awed and amazed.

'All I have are the horses, that is all I have left. There is nothing more.' His breath came fast and hard as if he had run down from the Trendle instead of walked. 'I love them – God knows I love them. And the dream is mine, his providence gave it to me . . .'

'I know,' Joanna said softly, for she too loved the horses. 'I too love them. I know how you feel.'

But Richard was beyond consolation. The gallows humour and surface play had been honed away in an instant by her surprise footfall at his moment of deep vulnerability. He hardly heard her. 'And now I am losing even that, now even that is denied me.' He looked up at the dark canopy of branches. 'Sweet Christ, why is this happening to me?'

Joanna thought she understood. 'It is the matter of Falkes and the use of Soloriens. Is that what it is? Yes, surely . . .'

Richard suddenly clamped his mouth shut. He did not know if he could trust her. In no way could he dare admit that Falkes had beaten him. Not before her, for he hardly knew her.

'Is it the competition with Falkes?' she insisted.

'I have said too much, my lady. You must think me a raving fool.' Despite her shake of the head he said, 'You must forgive me, it is rudeness itself to burden a lady with such as I have done.' He was in control once more. 'I hope you can forgive me.' Then he turned and walked away.

'Sir . . .'

Halfway up the darkened pathway he stopped and turned around, proud lines rising about his mouth. He lifted his chin and she recognised the movement, knew it for the desperate attempt to salvage pride that it was.

'My lady?' His voice was strong but still throbbed with the emotion that had overwhelmed him.

'I have nothing to forgive you for. You have done nothing wrong. You are a brave knight.'

They stared at one another with an intensity that was like fine glass – lambent with a glowing life and clear without blemish. Then he was gone.

Joanna felt suddenly tired and quite weak, and she sat down beside the pool. The cast-down laurel leaves floated on the slow current. She reached out one ivory-pale fingertip and touched the discarded hope.

'You were not facing south and so your wish will not come true.' She said it with as much pain as if it had been her own disappointed hope. 'You were facing east.' She looked at the dark, moss-glistening stones of the wall. 'You were facing towards Jerusalem . . .'

William had decided to call the cow Eleanor. It was a name that he admired and was a good noble one; after all it was good enough for the King's powerful mother and that spoke volumes. Secretly, Catface also chose this particular name because it amused him to have a cow named after the Queen Dowager. It was a mixture of his usual ambition and lack of respect for his betters.

Eleanor, though, was not well. The trouble had started soon after she returned home to William's tumbledown cottage. The calf was just over a week old and so it was time to share the milk between it and Catface's pail. That had been fine for the first three days. At each of the two daily milkings he had allowed the first pailful of creamy milk to go to the calf and the second to himself. It was on the dawn milking of the fourth day that it all started to go wrong. Afterwards he remembered it well because it was the day that the lady Joanna went off to Cerne in the company of the man with the black moustache and the body of a wrestler.

That morning, while the last stars were fading, William had crawled out of his bed of greasy wheat straw, cracked the first flea of the day and groped his way through the wicker divide which separated his family from the cow and her calf. As he padded over the packed-clay floor, he could hear the rats and mice scrabbling about; he cursed a rat as it ran over his foot.

Eleanor was restless as he stuck the bucket under her. She

lowed with pain as he touched her udder, and when he squeezed the teats with his sleepy fingers she shifted away and tried to kick him. The few squirts of milk in the pail were clotted and tasted sour. William dipped a fingertip in and grimaced at the flavour, spitting into the soiled straw. Something was wrong.

In the hope that by leaving her alone she would get better, Catface left off the milking and went outside. He resolved not to tell his wife, as she had been against borrowing the money in the first place. The decision to keep silent was a sure sign of how worried he was.

That evening Eleanor was no better; if anything, she seemed worse. The next morning she would not tolerate any touch of his fingers and the little milk that squirted out was halfway to cheese, and rancid.

''Tis milk fever,' he whispered to his wife. 'See what it smells of . . .' He raised the pail to his wife, who turned away in disgust.

William was desperate. While his wife held the bellowing cow, he rubbed the swollen udder with a little stinking goose grease he had scrounged from a neighbour. It did no good. On his wife's suggestion he plied the cow with a soup of borage leaves, mixed with feathery fronds of dried parsley, but the laxative unblocked the cow everywhere but in the udder. Catface was at his wits' end.

Four days after the trouble started, Eleanor died in rolling-eyed agony. Catface was mopping her long, sad face with water when she died. He was crying when his wife found him. He expected her to scold him and demand how they would repay the loan now that the cow was dead, but all she did was put her arms around him. In many ways that was worse; it was a clear sign that she understood, as well as he did, just how deep a pit of trouble they were in.

'Hush,' she said quietly. 'Don' take on so. Could be worse . . .'

She was quite right, in fact more correct than she realised. Three days later the calf died. This time, though, they were both crying.

Falkes and Matilda searched for Joanna around the abbey guesthouse the night that she went after vespers to the Silver

Well. It was just like her to go off alone, and Tilly was only a little surprised. Falkes, though, was far more concerned; he was not used to a woman like Joanna de Cantelo. At last they found her on her way back up from the softly gurgling spring. By this time it was virtually dark and most of the townsfolk were home to their beds. The abbey porter was fastening the heavy precinct gates and soon the grounds would be plunged into silence.

'Where have you been?' Falkes asked carefully but expecting an answer. 'We have searched all over for you.'

Joanna seemed rather surprised. 'I went to pray at the holy well,' she replied a little too guardedly.

Falkes had run into Richard de Lacey in his search for Joanna. The shock had been mutual and – in the light of their competition for Soloriens – a little embarrassing. In Falkes' negotiations with Savaric he had at last learned of Richard's discovery of the whereabouts of the stallion. Now a curious look caught about the mouth below the drooping moustache, as the marshal looked at Joanna.

'Did you see our mutual friend the Templar?' The question was less inquisitive than inquisitorial.

Joanna was never one to answer questions readily. 'Why? Have you met him?'

The question, turned about, caught Falkes by surprise. He was not used to having his enquiries met in such a way. For a moment he frowned and paused. 'I did meet him – briefly – this evening. He seemed somewhat distracted.' Then he returned to his theme. 'Did you meet him, my lady?' The tone was quite polite but it was clear he expected an answer.

'Yes, I did. I fear that I interrupted his devotions at the spring. But he was most courteous and forgave my abrupt intrusion.' She lifted her chin in the familiar way. 'Why do you ask?' The question was innocently phrased but her green eyes twinkled mischievously.

If she hoped to see a little jealousy in the eyes of her suitor, she was disappointed. Falkes dropped a veil over his thoughts and the grey eyes told her nothing. 'He is a man who has a great interest in your manor, my lady. I wonder if he spoke of it with you? You will understand that I too now have a great interest in its welfare. And your own.'

Joanna sighed. She would have been happier if the latter point had sounded a little less like an afterthought. 'I fear that he said very little, and nothing about the manor. I think that he had other things on his mind. Such a knight sworn to free the Holy Places is not as other men.'

She was punishing Falkes for his lack of jealousy, but her compliment to Richard failed to produce any reaction, so she gave up. Matilda smiled – she knew exactly what was going on in Joanna's mind. She was less sure of what was going on in the mind of the bishop's marshal.

That night as Joanna and Tilly slipped into their shared bed, Joanna asked her maid a question which caused Tilly to think carefully before replying.

'What do you think of Falkes de Mauleon?'

Tilly sat up and leaned her chin on her naked white knees. 'He is a courteous knight and they say that he is a brave one too.' She flicked a look at her lady, who nodded. 'And he is a strong man and not unhandsome . . .'

'That is a curious way of putting it, Tilly . . .'

Matilda laughed. It was an echo of her old self again. 'Well,' she said thoughtfully, 'he is strong and not bad-looking. Though he is not the most handsome of men.'

She grinned at her own impertinence. 'Though I daresay he knows how to take care of a woman in bed.' She was lost in her analysis and did not notice the look of interest which had grown on her lady's face.

'Go on . . .' Joanna encouraged.

'He is an experienced man, isn't he?' Joanna nodded. 'No doubt he can please a woman.' The maid's look was a little distant, as if she was remembering something.

Joanna was curious. It was a curiosity which trailed off into a mild alarm, for Matilda seemed very convincing for a virgin. Even given Tilly's once fabled nose for gossip, Joanna had never heard her speak this way before. It was as if the young innocence had faded away. Joanna wondered when it had happened.

Perhaps she had been too locked into her own affairs to notice it. Joanna was as concerned as she was intrigued.

'I pity a woman,' Tilly continued, 'whose husband cannot quicken her desire.'

'But he is no passionate youth . . .'

'No,' Tilly admitted with disappointment. 'And he does seem more interested in the King's stallion than in . . .' She stifled her words with one pale hand. 'I beg your pardon, my lady, I was not meaning . . .'

Joanna laughed. '"Tis all right, Tilly, I know what you mean, and besides, I did ask you for your opinion.' She sighed. 'Falkes is no doubt as much moved by the manor as by me. Perhaps more so. I suppose it is naive to think otherwise.'

'But he would make a fine husband, my lady.'

'True enough,' Joanna conceded. 'He would do that all right. And no doubt he would honour me and protect me, and the manor would be preserved.' It was not an unattractive thought and yet it failed to fully satisfy her even as she put it into words.

'There then, my lady. He is a fine match. Although . . .'

'Go on . . .'

Tilly was unsure of herself. 'Some might say that you are worth a higher suitor than the bishop's marshal. Though no doubt the King is well pleased with him . . .' She trailed off and looked at her mistress nervously.

'No doubt my father would have desired a marriage with a knight of minor baronial rank. There is no gainsaying it and I have not forgotten it. Or one perhaps more colourful and eye-catching . . . But Falkes is a fine man and a marriage to him would rid me of that brute Savaric and his foul crew.'

Joanna was talking to herself as she leaned forward and blew out the candle. It perturbed her slightly that she had come to view her own future in such dispassionate terms, even given the attraction of a marriage to the bishop's marshal. Consequently she could not see the crosscurrents of emotion which marked her maid's face.

In the darkness, Joanna got to thinking again, about the strong and honourable knight who would preserve the manor and make her a good husband. A match which was sure to go ahead now, with a man who held her in high regard, but without apparent passion for her. A strong man, but one tight-laced and controlled. Perhaps it was for the best; it would be security at the price of her wilful independence . . . Ranulf Dapifer would no doubt think so, but it was hard for Joanna to convince herself.

Was Falkes the man she desired? Try as she might she could not forget the bitter passion of Richard de Lacey. It was more than pity that he stirred; she had never met a man who made her so curious. What was going on inside him; with his fanatical commitment to his mission and his turbulent desperation?

She wanted to talk with him again and ask him questions. That too disquieted her, for no other man before had given rise to such feelings. Prior to de Lacey, men had pursued her, not she them. The very thought was unseemly and perplexing; it threatened her independence as much as the cool strength of Falkes.

There seemed no easy answer, and besides which, no one was interested in her opinion so the whole matter was out of her hands anyway. Despite this – or perhaps because of it – she was awake long into the night. She heard the bell ring for matins and lauds from the cavernous dark outside, and still she did not sleep.

Richard de Lacey arose early in the morning, while Joanna was still racked by her thoughts. He summoned a startled Umar and Mark and all three left as soon as the porter opened the abbey gatehouse doors. The pain in his back seemed worse than ever, despite a linament of lanolin and fragrant pine resin rubbed into his shoulder by Umar.

Richard feared meeting the young and disturbing woman who had surprised him at the spring. The woman before whom he had lowered the shield which covered his desperation. The woman who travelled with his rival and who had no part in the plan for his life, save that a strange providence had twisted horse and she and he together, in disconcerting knots too hard to fathom or untie. A woman whose blazing hair and deep-green eyes had invaded his thoughts the whole night long.

By full light, Richard and his yawning companions were high on the downs, amidst the breeze-stirred grass and the trackside verges – a glowing flower border of golden autumn hawkbit. The bleating of sheep carried beneath the haunting pipe of curlews drifting southwards to the sea.

Ranulf was determined to get Joanna to the King in France or at least to the household of Hubert de Burgh. Since her return from the pilgrimage to Cerne she had been decidedly moody. The steward decided that there was too much danger of a confrontation with Savaric, and that would upset the applecart of his plans.

From Savaric, Ranulf had garnered the information that Joanna would soon be betrothed to Falkes de Mauleon. He also gained the impression that Savaric was none too pleased at this end to his soft posting. All in all, the situation was too dangerous. Ranulf had pestered Savaric to write again to de Burgh in France regarding the best place for Joanna to spend the winter.

Savaric now seemed a little reluctant to get rid of Joanna, and this troubled Dapifer somewhat; nevertheless, the steward insisted that this was the price to be paid for his careful penning of Savaric's reports detailing the forwardness of Falkes with regard to the lady Joanna.

Ranulf laid down his pen and carefully sealed the vellum with a blob of scarlet wax. He scattered sand across it to dry the molten seal. Upstairs in the hall the Michaelmas goose would soon be clapped to the top table, and he would be expected to be there. For once the main meal of the day was to be in the evening, as opposed to the noontime dinner. Before he went, though, he leaned against his desk, thinking of his situation.

He had insisted that Savaric include a reference to his own faithful service, as it was essential that the King, or the sheriff, recognised the loyal part that he had played in the wardship. After all, if Thomas Becket could rise through the royal household, so could he. It was being done all the time; it would happen again. It must happen to him; it was his only hope and dream.

In the morning, one of Savaric's crossbowmen would take the report to de Burgh at Falaise. Perhaps the King himself would be reading it before the end of the week. The thought of John reading his handwriting gave Dapifer a rare thrill of excitement. It also made him frightened, for what if he failed to excite the attention of the King? Then he would be trapped at Horsingham for the rest of his life; the steward of Joanna and Falkes. Lacking any more exalted patron to recommend him, he would go no further. It would be the end of the dreams which Gilbert de Cantelo's tragic accident had brought to birth.

'No – it will not be so.' Ranulf stared intently at the grains of fine sand adhering to the drying blob of sealing wax. 'The King will recognise my work. He will!' The intensity of his stare made his mind ache, it was as if by willpower alone he could influence the King in his favour.

Then he thought of Savaric and the girl Matilda, and he shook his head in revulsion. He could never understand those whose lives were ruled by their passions. They were little better than the beasts rutting in the woods. For a moment he imagined Savaric rutting with the maid. The thought was curiously appealing and he entertained it longer than he had intended. Then he caught himself and dismissed it in disgust. Nevertheless the image lingered as he attended to his ink and vellum.

'She has got to go . . .' he muttered to himself. 'And as quickly as possible.'

Ranulf was worried about the scandal if the affair between the mercenary and Joanna's maid become public knowledge. It was in no way his responsibility but he feared all disquieting disturbances, for who knew where the mud would stick once it was being thrown about?

Ranulf rubbed his clean-shaven chin with a slightly agitated hand. More than ever it was necessary to get Joanna away from the manor, for both maid and lady would go together. Then the danger would be averted. Ranulf stared at the letter once more; he wanted both of them as far away as possible.

Ellen, his wife, peered into the cold accounting room, entering as she caught sight of him. 'Are you well, husband?' she asked with a look at his pale cheeks. 'You seem tired.'

Ranulf had never mentioned any of his plans to his wife and was nettled by her concern, which indicated that his worries were open to scrutiny. 'Of course I am well. I would have told you if I was ill, wouldn't I?'

Ellen nodded in agreement, for he was right of course; if it had been of importance for her to know, then she would have been informed. 'It is just that you seem a little tired . . .'

Ranulf stepped away from his desk with its sealed letter. 'We will be late for the meal,' he said brusquely. He offered her his arm so that they could enter the hall decorously, and she took it as bidden. 'Come now, there is nothing more of importance to be said.' Together they left the room, arm in arm and each quite alone.

While Ranulf was contemplating his future, Joanna had called for Tilly. None of the servants had seen her and said so, but as they spoke, they glanced at one another, and Joanna caught the looks. Dismissing them, she retired alone to the solar. Sitting by the shuttered window, she warmed her hands by the flames of a small brazier. The late-September air was damp and the evening a little chill.

Only now did Joanna realise that Tilly was often out of the hall in the early evening. It had not really caught her attention in the summer, as there were flowers to pick and arrange, although it suddenly occurred to her that she could not recall which servants had gone with Tilly on her evening walks. Then there were the looks cast between the servants, and the way Tilly had talked in the guestroom at Cerne.

Joanna toyed with her goblet of wine. Was it Stephen? Perhaps that was why the two of them had been so stilted with each other of late. Perhaps that was why Matilda so rarely spoke of the groom these days. Joanna shook her head; surely Tilly had sense enough not to allow a harmless flirtation with the groom to turn into an affair. It had never occurred to her that encouragement of innocent affection might lead to actual foolishness. For, despite Dapifer's doubts, Joanna de Cantelo knew her station and that of her maid.

'Well, well . . .' she said to herself. 'I shall confront her with this, the secretive little minx.' Joanna was less angry than surprised.

While Joanna mused, Tilly was *not* with Stephen Pierson. She was with someone who had succeeded in exciting much more interest than the inexperienced boy. She was not happy, though, as she fastened the veil about her head and neck.

'So, what does she think of him then?' Savaric lay back on the straw as he questioned her. 'Does she want him for her husband?'

Tilly was reluctant to reply. Answering Savaric's interrogation was straying close to making her feel like a spy. 'I do not really know. She has never talked about him,' she lied.

Savaric stared at her with a cold look. 'Don't give me that. I know how women talk. I bet she knows all about us . . .'

'Of course she doesn't. I would never dare tell her about this. She would . . .' Her words trailed away.

'Yes?' His voice was smooth, but mocking.

Tilly hesitated. 'She would be furious. She hates you.'

'No?'

'Yes – she hates you and loathes you for what you have done to the manor.'

Savaric leaned up on one elbow. 'The way you talk, anyone would think that you felt the same way.'

Matilda gave a broken half-laugh and turned away. Savaric grinned behind her back and lifted a piece of straw and began to chew on it.

'She never talks of Falkes.' Tilly persisted in her lie.

'Well I don't believe you. You are going to have to listen more carefully in future.' The girl shot him a furious glance of hatred.

For the first time in weeks, Savaric felt a thrill of pleasure regarding the maid. It was more than the plain physical gratification he gained from intercourse; it was the satisfaction of knowing she hated him but could not resist him.

He laughed at the thought. 'I want to know exactly what is going on before you leave . . .' Then he realised what he had said and his mouth shut like a portcullis.

Tilly narrowed her eyes. 'What do you mean? Where are you sending us?'

Savaric cursed his words but refused to be questioned further.

'It's nothing that concerns you. Just get back to the hall before you're missed.'

He pulled on his boots and walked over to the ladder of the hayloft. With any luck she would forget it; anyway, he thought, what could she do to stop him? Still, he must watch his words in future. He was getting too confident, and that would never do.

Joanna asked Tilly her question and the maid went red and denied it. As a result Joanna was convinced that there was something between the maid and Stephen. The next morning she summoned Stephen, who denied the suggestion with a vehemence which made Joanna wince. But if not Stephen, then who? A casual interest was becoming a strong desire to know.

One tense evening, a few days later, maid and mistress were sewing in the solar, alone. Matilda was restless and seemed to be constantly looking at the door. At last she broke her silence.

'They are going to send you away.' She was pale and her lips were thin and clamped tight together. Her hands lay clasped on her lap.

'What do you mean?'

'Savaric is trying to get rid of you. I don't know how but he is determined to get you off the manor.'

'Off the manor? Away from here?' Joanna rose to her feet. Her embroidery fell to the planks and rushes. Before the death of her father she had frequently moved with him from manor to manor, but now she felt that the survival of Horsingham depended on her physical presence. The words of her maid dismayed and shocked her. 'How do you know this? How can you possibly know this?'

Tilly ground her hands together until blood trickled from where a nail dug into her palm. She opened her mouth but no words came out; they cowered deep within the fortress which Savaric had mastered so easily and made his own.

Joanna stood over her maid. 'How do you know?' she insisted. 'How?' She was relentless, for a terrible and obscene realisation was unfolding within her like a cankered bud.

Tilly stared at her with wide dark eyes, and Joanna knew. 'Savaric . . .' The word was enough and Matilda began to cry.

Joanna seized her by the shoulders. 'This cannot be true. By Our Lady, tell me this is not true and I am a fool.'

At no point had Joanna stated her knowledge, but both of them knew. There was no hiding it now, yet still the words would not pass between Tilly's teeth.

'In God's name, what is there between you two?' Joanna felt sick as she hurled the question at her friend. 'Tell me – I command you to tell me!'

'We have been lovers,' Tilly said at last, and then broke into sobs which racked her body.

Joanna let go of her and stepped away, her mind reeling. That thing had possessed her maid; her friend. She felt unclean and profaned.

'He raped you . . .'

Tilly mustered her honour and blurted out, 'He did not rape me. I went to him willingly.'

'Sweet Mother of God . . .' Joanna was appalled. 'Why?' Then another thought hit her. 'You are sure he means to send me away?'

'Us . . .' Matilda said the word as if desperate to re-establish some link with her mistress. 'He intends to send *us* away. Both of us.'

Joanna's mind was racing from thought to thought. She would not leave the manor; not to a man like Savaric. A thought that had bobbed about her head for weeks now resurfaced. She considered it, she looked at it from this way and that. It was madness, simply madness, but then her whole world had gone mad, so what was one more act of insanity, one grand gesture of lunacy to cap all the others? She was decided and, while she was still reeling at the news, part of her mind wildly flew forward to the moment of decision and destiny.

'We will talk of this again.' Her voice was uncharacteristically hard and she spoke as to a stranger, so deep was her sense of betrayal. 'But now there are things to be done. Get Stephen Pierson.' When Tilly looked confused and afraid, Joanna added with more authority, 'Get him now, bring him here.'

Within ten minutes the groom was standing breathless before

her; his Saxon beard and hair uncombed, a smell of ale on his breath. Joanna's eyes were afire with a strangely animated and dangerously bright light.

'You want revenge?'

'My lady?'

'You want revenge on those who murdered your father? On those who killed him and walked away from it?' She hated herself for putting it that way.

'By God's body, you know I do.' Stephen cast a bitter smile towards Matilda, who closed her eyes.

'I know all about *that*, Stephen.' The groom was astonished and made as if to speak. 'Not now, for now I want you to listen. Will you do whatever I ask you?'

'I will.'

She marvelled at his trust – or was it his hunger for vengeance? – for he had no idea of what she was going to ask him to do. 'There is a deserted hamlet below the northern lip of the downs, I found it quite by accident. We are all going there.' When Stephen made to protest, Joanna silenced him. 'Yes, Tilly is coming too. The three of us are going there and, what is more, we are taking the stallion, Soloriens . . .'

'Bloody hell . . .' Stephen's eyes were wide.

'That, I imagine, will be the least that Savaric will say when he discovers the horse is gone. Then they will listen to us. Then we will put a stop to this madness. This is something that even the dullest will be wakened by – from Savaric to the King himself.'

She clenched her fist and held it before Stephen's nose. 'Not much of a blow from this little hand, eh, Stephen? But by the time we have finished, they will think twice before destroying the Cantelo manor . . . It will be a blow to bloody a few noses.'

Stephen Pierson nodded vehemently; he did not care about the consequences. Tilly was silent, for she could scarcely begin to imagine them. And Joanna was steadfast and defiant, which was all the more striking because she alone knew what the consequences might really be.

Chapter 10

Stephen Pierson held the heavy flagon carefully in both hands, concealed beneath the cloak draped about his shoulders. The night was damp, though not cold, and the October mist had risen from the stream to fill the slight hollow in which the manor of Horsingham lay.

There was no reason for anyone to notice his movement away from the hall. It was late – almost ten o'clock – but that was no great matter; he usually did a round of the stables about this time of night – it was a routine established by his father. There was no need to think anything strange about the son carrying on in the old man's footsteps. Already he had taken food and drink to the man who guarded the gate of the manor stockade; now he was on his way to the stables. It was as any night.

Despite this, Stephen felt conspicuous, as if everyone he met secretly understood the nature of his task. Savaric had seemed to eye him strangely in the hall; the servants glanced at him suspiciously as if they did not know him. He told himself that it was all in his mind, but it troubled him nevertheless. At the stables, the guards were camped in a great pile of the precious wheat straw thrown up by the doorway. Out in the yard a fire was burning, but Savaric had forbidden a brazier to be set up in the building itself; he cared more about the safety of his horses than the comfort of his men. So far the cooler air of autumn was kept at bay by the wine which warmed their bellies.

The two Brabançons were dicing and a small pile of silver on the stable cobbles betrayed the winner, whose companion seemed especially keen to welcome the diversion offered by the approaching groom.

'What's it tonight, boy?' he said, almost jovially.

Stephen shrugged back the enveloping wool cloak to display the flagon. 'Cider,' he said nonchalantly, using the beverage's English name. 'It's a new drink hereabouts; the monks at Forde Abbey brew it. My father got the recipe from a monk at Cerne who owed him a favour. It's made from apples . . .'

The men-at-arms looked interested. Anything different was worth a look, and even the winner seemed content to leave off the game for a moment or two. Stephen uncorked the flagon and the jar was seized from his hands. He made no protest as first one, then the other man, downed great gulps of the raw scrumpy.

'I'll just see to the horse,' Stephen murmured, hoping his words would drown out the thud of his heart within his chest. Moving away into the stable he could hear behind him Savaric's men comparing the flavour with the stinking sour wine they were used to. They seemed content.

Stephen smiled and there was a rare element of maliciousness in the tilt of his mouth. He thought of the concentrated poppy syrup and distilled primrose and cowslip leaves that Joanna herself had added to the flagon – all the ingredients of sleep. That was if they were not already drunk out of their minds by the time they had drained the heavy container.

Deep in the shadows, Soloriens gave a low whicker at the familiar approach of the groom. Stephen came slowly to the beast, respecting both teeth and hooves. He was one of the few people whom Savaric allowed near the precious animal, but even so he still felt nervous in the same stall as the stallion. There was something terribly powerful and explosive in that great dappled body and Stephen knew enough to respect the feelings the horse aroused, and treated Soloriens with greater care than any other horse he had ever been responsible for. Nevertheless he made sure that he was always firm but decisive with the beast, for the mere scent of fear, or a hint of fumbling, could provoke it.

'Easy, easy . . .' he whispered as he ran his hand along the high neck, 'just be easy . . .' Was it his fantasy or was the animal tense? Did it understand what was about to happen, or did it merely mirror his own tension?

Such contemplations did not sit easily in Stephen's mind; it made him restless to face such uncertainties. He did not like the unknown and his once apparent ready confidence came from the easy familiarity of the commonplace and the routine. He hated Savaric for destroying that as much as for killing his father; for he had no doubts as to who lay behind the death of the grey-haired head groom. And now was a time for revenge; he grinned as he pictured Savaric's face when he discovered what they had done. Then the familiar would return – when Savaric was defeated and finally brought to heel.

He was not sure how it would happen, and he did not care either; the lady Joanna knew what she was doing. The most important thing was to be striking back, that was enough. Stephen gave the stallion a thorough strapping – the rigorous grooming that picked out hooves, dandy-brushed away the dried mud and sweat of the day's exercise and then brushed and polished the proud back with body-brush and rubber.

The cider was being quaffed with abandon and the dice game was forgotten. Stephen sneaked a look at the men and was content that all was going to plan. He picked up a mass of straw and used it to rub the tightly bunched muscles of the horse's loins and croup. He was lost in the rhythmic pressure, following the direction of the hair, when the voice cut him out of his dreaming. The accented Norman-French was unmistakable.

'It's late for this . . .'

Savaric was in the stable. The men-at-arms were silent and the flagon had been thrust away, under a cloak, at the first footfall of their leader.

Stephen was sweating with fear. 'It seemed a good idea to get him cleaned up, what with the Templar and the bishop's marshal coming to see him,' he suggested, as if ashamed of his own care and concern.

Savaric did not reply, leaning instead on the edge of the chewed door frame and eyeing the horse. 'Yes . . .' he said at last, as if only marginally convinced. 'But you've never done it before. Not this late . . .'

Stephen knew that was true and that his real reason was to see that the cider was drunk deeply. He cursed himself for breaking his own habits; he should have known not to have strayed from the usual on this of all nights. Behind him the stallion grunted as it stretched its freshly massaged muscles. Savaric looked at Stephen with those marbles of clear ice.

'He took a good exercise at the lunging today,' Stephen suggested, trying to throw off the burden of the cold stare. 'And he worked up quite a sweat and the ground was soft too. There was mud on his coat from running on the rein . . .' He gestured to where the lunge rein hung from a nearby beam, as if it supported his alibi.

Savaric glanced at the leather. 'But you groomed him off afterwards . . .'

'Ah yes,' Stephen said with a boldness sired by desperation, 'but I did not finish the job, meaning to return before bed.'

Savaric yawned; his curiosity was drowning in the boredom caused by the groom's horse-centred talk. Even the fear that his enquiries had caused was no longer giving him the same pleasure as when he had entered the stable. Besides which, he had another appointment and it was more appealing than frightening the son of the man he had caused to be murdered. After all, he could do that in the morning.

'Get him rugged and bank up the straw,' Savaric ordered sharply, 'then leave him be.'

'Yes, sir,' Stephen said and reached for the four-pronged wooden stable-fork. 'I'll do it right away.'

But Savaric had lost interest and was already gone. When Stephen looked up from his work all he could see was the shimmering grey mist beyond the firelight. And beyond that only darkness.

In their chamber, Joanna and Tilly were busy packing. Two leather satchels were stuffed with carefully folded clothes, and another with hard white cheese and flat cakes of bread. A fourth and fifth – containing Stephen's horse linaments, brushes, knives and potions – was secreted in a copse beyond the manor paddocks.

The two women worked in a tense silence. The yearly routine

of travel from manor to manor made Joanna no stranger to having her life carried in panniers on pack animals. But to reduce her needs to a leather scrip and to pack it herself was a departure from both her routine and her station. Yet novelty made it almost exciting and, like Stephen, she was driven by the desire to strike back at last.

Tilly folded a blanket and pushed it between two long wool tunics and a linen kirtle, all crisply folded by her own hands. She worked as if half asleep, moving by habit as if not fully aware of what she was doing. At all times she avoided the eyes of her mistress and when they could not be avoided, suffered their look as if they were living coals laid upon her flesh.

'What time did you tell him?'

Without looking up, Matilda answered, 'At about eleven of the clock, my lady.'

Joanna was thoughtful. 'And in the far hay barn beyond the meadow, as usual?'

The words ate into Matilda like acid and she writhed under their burning fire. 'Aye, my lady.' Her voice was very small and broken. 'As usual . . .'

'Good. Then we must soon be going. I suppose he will not wait long when you do not appear. I do not expect that he is a man used to being kept waiting . . .'

'No, my lady . . .'

Matilda's voice was so utterly wretched that Joanna involuntarily relented a little. 'Have you all you need?' she enquired with a little less stiffness in her voice, and when Tilly cast her a look overflowing with gratitude, Joanna felt sick that so small a morsel of pity could produce such a result.

She turned from her maid and closed the scrip, finding it hard to speak to the girl. A gulf of great darkness had opened between them, made all the more terrible by Joanna's inability to accept that Matilda had given herself willingly to Savaric. When she thought of the two lying together it made her sick with confusion. The thought of the mercenary possessing her trusted maid fuelled her fury, and yet Tilly had confessed it had not been rape. That made it harder to understand, because then the focus of Joanna's anger fell on Tilly, as well as on Savaric. She hated him the more for that.

And then she hated Tilly for making her even imagine the thrusting coupling of the two in the dark hiding place of glade or barn. She hated her because the thought stirred a curious concoction of emotions within her; as contradictory a mixture of loathing and arousal as that which the fantasy had stirred in Dapifer. It was a fractured and warped emotion which sucked in too much of her own loneliness and conflicting thoughts about Falkes and the bitter knight, Richard de Lacey. But to have them and herself bound up with Savaric, within the same dark sack of emotions, was intolerable. And for the guilt and confusion of that she hated both Savaric and Matilda.

In the heat of her confusion she found herself remembering Richard de Lacey in his impassioned outburst at the Silver Well. Try as she might, she could not fully understand why. Biting her lip, she pulled savagely at the straps securing the satchel.

There was a tap at the door which led from the solar into the chamber. Joanna had shooed the servants who normally bedded down in the solar into the great hall. It was a step away from routine, but a necessary one, and one which she hoped would not be noticed until it was too late. Joanna lifted the latch to reveal Stephen Pierson. After a few low words she came back into the chamber and the three of them shouldered the full scrips. Joanna bent under the unaccustomed physical weight. By the guttering light of the tallow candles the three looked like the conspirators that indeed they were.

One by one they tiptoed out through the darkened solar and to the side stair which was usually used by servants bringing food and drink from the detached kitchen. The moon and stars were covered and, as agreed, Joanna and Tilly made their way to the gate, which was unlocked, its guard lying to one side in a drunken stupor.

Outside the compound the only sound came from the stream feeding the moat and fishstews and from a barn owl which floated in silent luminescent flight across the open pasture of the paddock. For what felt like a thousand years of continuous torture they waited in agony, then at last came the muffled sound of hooves. Joanna clenched her fists with the expectancy of one prepared at any moment for the driving impact of an arrow shaft, but there was no cry of alarm.

Out of the mist loomed the great grey bulk of Soloriens; a more solid figure amidst a wavering world of shadows. Stephen led it by the tethering rope and the horse wore the binding harness first put on by some terrified groom in Normandy. There would be time enough to reconsider that decision. The sharpened hooves were bound as securely as those of the lame horse at Cerne. The result was the most muffled of steps despite its bulk. As it passed out of the compound it gave an unexpected whicker at the scent of Joanna. Humbled and intensely touched, she moved forward and allowed the horse to push against her shoulder. She whispered to it softly; words too quiet for anyone else to hear.

Stephen looked anxiously over his shoulder to where Savaric's men lay in their drunken sleep. Without a further word the three cloaked figures and the horse moved away and were swallowed up in the enveloping night. From the woods beyond the paddock came the piercing shriek of an owl.

Savaric waited longer than usual in the barn. He was tired and sat down on the fragrant hay. Leaning back, he waited for Tilly to come. As he rested, he pondered the matter of getting Joanna off the manor. It was a task which he faced with mixed feelings. On the one hand he was loath to release her, arousing as she did the hot, hard desire within him; on the other hand he knew that keeping her apart from Falkes de Mauleon was his best bet of lengthening his own stay at Horsingham. That and the letters he regularly sent to John, sniping at the bishop's marshal.

The thought of the letters caused Savaric to consider Ranulf Dapifer. The steward seemed desperate to get Joanna de Cantelo away and Savaric had decided that it was worth it to secure the active co-operation of Dapifer in his stratagems. Still, he had very mixed feelings about the matter and fantasised about how he could have the lady before she was packed away.

He lay back and dreamed of the pleasure of the moment, and

so, before his waiting could turn to puzzled irritation, he had drifted off to sleep. Only the rats scurried and scuffled amongst the bales of hay.

He woke in the cold hours before dawn and was chilled and stiff. The realisation grew within him that he had been made a fool of. Angrily, he strode back towards the manor through the eddying mist. He found the gate unlocked and the guard asleep. When he failed to arouse the man he grew suddenly suspicious. He had spent too much of his life deceiving others not to sense deception himself.

He remembered the behaviour of the groom in the stable with the stallion of Hugh de Lusignan. A germ of concern took root in his mind, and he hurried towards the stable. As he did so he thought of the failed rendezvous with Matilda. Soon he was running. Inside the stable door he found his sentries lost to the world. Then he knew. He knew before he saw the stall empty and the stallion gone; he knew, and his anger rose like a wild, high sea in a winter storm. It was a furious tide, foam-headed with humiliation that *she* could have dared to do this to *him*. Then, amongst the storm-driven waves bobbed the flotsam of fear, when he thought of what Hubert de Burgh would say; when he thought of what the King would do . . .

William Catface heard about the missing horse early the next morning. The whole hamlet was roused from sleep just after dawn by Savaric's soldiery. For once the soldiers seemed as frightened as they were brutal. It gave William a curious pleasure to see them so alarmed.

'There's money in fear,' he muttered to his wife as he pulled on his tunic over his flea-bitten nakedness. 'An' I've never seen men so frightened . . .'

'Go careful, for yer a 'eadstrong fool,' his wife counselled.

Catface was unrepentant. 'From what I've seen, yon missin' 'orse has got they so frightened, they'll pay a man like me to find it . . .' Already he was imagining the reward money to pay off his debt.

In the manor courtyard soldiers were milling about as if unsure of what to do next. Clearly they had gained little from the interrogation of the manor so far. At the foot of the steps – by the undercroft – Savaric and Ranulf Dapifer were engaged in a far from calm conversation. The usually taciturn steward was babbling as if he would burst and Savaric looked anything but his usual supercilious self. Indeed, both looked as if they would be felled by a stroke at any moment. The poacher could pick out fear and panic from the babble of Norman-French issuing from Dapifer.

Catface was right in what he had said to his wife – a reward had been offered for any information regarding the missing horse. No one was using the word 'stolen', as if the avoidance of the accusation somehow cushioned the full force of the blow. Nevertheless the implication was clear.

What was clearer to William, however, was the size of the reward – Savaric was offering four pounds. Such a princely sum had the whole manor talking. Catface slipped away and began to lay his plans.

Ranulf Dapifer wanted to slip away too. In fact he wanted to crawl away and die. He had been roused from sleep by Savaric and the nightmare had begun where sleep had ended. 'I still cannot believe it,' he said to the pale Savaric. 'Even her head-strong will should have balked at this.' He quite forgot he was speaking about his mistress. 'What in God's name will the sheriff say? What will the King do?' It was a question he kept on repeating as if it formed part of some out-of-key litany.

'You mean before, or after, he hangs the both of us?' Though Savaric mocked the look of horror on Ranulf's face, he was only just in control of himself.

'He won't hang me!' Ranulf was horrified. 'It was your soldiers who were asleep, the horse was your responsibility.' He saw his hopes slip away between his fingers; he could not begin to consider his life going the same way. 'It was their fault. He won't hang me.'

Savaric looked at him angrily. 'And why, pray, did he starve the noble prisoners held at Corfe?' He lowered his voice. 'And have you heard the rumours about his nephew . . .?'

'For God's sake!' Ranulf looked about him in alarm.

'So if he did that to them, what do you think he will do to a halfpenny clerk who stewarded the manor whence the most valuable horse in Christendom has been stolen?' Savaric shook his head. 'But it won't come to that, you old woman, because I am going to get the horse back. And if I have to flog every filthy villein between here and Southampton to do it, then so be it.'

His returning iron will nerved Ranulf. 'You will find it?'

Savaric nodded. 'Of course I'll find it, you buffoon. Who has taken it?' He gave a contemptuous shrug. 'A fool of a groom whose father couldn't stay alive going from here to Cerne . . .'

He laughed at Dapifer's look of disapproval. 'And two *women* . . .' He said the word as if describing some lower form of animal life. 'One of them a high and mighty lady who has never got her hands dirty before, and the other a pathetic nobody of a maid who wasn't even much fun on her back.'

The openness of Savaric's crude hatred was clear and it shocked Dapifer. It was only then that he realised that, for all of his bravado, Savaric was afraid. He turned away in a daze to see his wife approaching him. She made as if to lay a hand on his arm.

'I pray that the lady Joanna will be safe . . .'

Ranulf looked at her for a moment without comprehension. Then he suddenly understood what she had said – she was worried about the girl! All his pent-up fury spilled out at this woman who knew nothing of his plans and the realities of his situation. He shook off her hand with a bitter glance which slapped away her open look of concern.

'Don't be a fool . . .'

She was astonished, never having seen passion of any kind in his eyes before. 'I do not understand. I am sorry . . .' She faltered in her apology, sure that in some way she had erred and yet unable to trace the track of her sin. 'I do not understand . . .'

'Quite,' he said, mastering his anger. 'You do not understand.' Then he turned his back on her and walked away.

Unaware of the domestic incident between the steward and his docile wife, Savaric was instructing his men to begin a search of the surrounding woods. In his heart he nurtured the belief that the horse was being hidden within a mile or two of the manor.

Such a fit of pique was fitting for a woman and he would soon crush it. He rattled off his instructions to the men and saw that half were mounted to explore the slopes of the downs, whilst the others searched through the woods that spread over the south of the vale.

'I want the horse and the girls,' he told his men, 'and you can rape the maid but leave the lady alone. Do you understand me?' Then he had a moment of doubt; he did not want any more embarrassment. 'On second thoughts,' he pondered with a brittle, icy calm, 'keep off both of them.' Then he laughed viciously. 'But you can have your sport with the boy. I don't want to see that bastard alive again . . .'

His men sighed; this was not like the war in France. Still, orders were orders and they concluded that Savaric must have reasons for his restraint. Obediently they jogged off to search as bidden.

William Catface watched them go. As he stood pondering the scene he noticed a group of riders approaching the manor. Even at a distance he recognised the Templar from Buckland and his squire and the dark-skinned man. It gave Catface some consolation to think of Savaric trying to explain to these visitors what had happened to his prize horse. To William it was some small comfort to reflect that life was not out to get only him. Now he had company he felt more like his old self again and, what was more, he was sure that he could turn the situation to his own advantage.

Joanna, Tilly and Stephen were well out on the downs by first light. They stopped briefly to rest the horse and breakfast on the hard cheeses and a mouthful of bread washed down with a sip of wine from a leather bag carried by the groom. The day was misty long into the morning and while Joanna and Matilda went on a little ahead, Stephen led the horse. At all costs they had to avoid meeting anyone and they went warily, in total silence.

From noon to sunset they sheltered in a copse rank with weeds and grass. The wind was blowing away the damp mist and by late afternoon a pale sun shone from a hazy but clearing sky. Joanna had brought a handful of apples and beans in her scrip. She fed them to the stallion which Stephen had tied to a twisted tree trunk.

'We'll get this martingale off as soon as we get there.'

Stephen watched the horse as it gleefully crunched on the green and red apple. 'But watch his teeth, my lady. You have charmed him – no doubt about it – but he is still a beast of moods. We should be wary of him a little.'

Joanna touched the fine mane. 'We shall see,' was all she said, but inside she felt excited as if a whole new world was opening up before her.

The clear air of the downs and the escape from the manor had somehow cast away all of her concerns and doubts regarding the venture. She felt as if at last she was in control of her life, as if she had shaken off the heavy hand of Savaric and Ranulf, as if she had burst back into that past life that she thought had died with her father.

'He would have understood,' she said to herself.

'My lady?'

Joanna smiled to realise that she had spoken her thoughts out loud. 'Nothing, Stephen.' But in her heart she was sure Gilbert would have approved. It meant a lot to her to believe that.

Across the clearing Tilly sat on a mossy stump. She was separated from the other two by only some ten feet but she might as well have been in another country. Isolated and alone, she looked back to the manor where she could no longer return and then at the friends who were now like strangers to her. And despite it all, part of her longed to be back in the barn with Savaric.

With the coming of dark they set off once more. The stars were out, in contrast to the night before, and both Joanna and Stephen knew the way. In the days since Joanna had announced the plan to him, he had ridden along the edge of the downs when official journeys had taken him away from the manor. On each excursion, he had prepared for the flight and panniers of flour and beans, freshly salted bacon and hard cheese had been carried to the lonely hamlet, amongst the goods that Joanna had ordered him to take, or collect, from the market at Cerne. The provisions would not last long but they would give them a start.

It was long after midnight on the next day, that they came to the break in the wall of the chalk. The little valley lay below them, lost in the dark. Even the most adventurous moonbeams would not venture there. As they stopped and looked into the black trees, Joanna felt the first fear since the flight from Horsingham, for down there in the dark lay her destiny. She glanced at Stephen but he was too busy adjusting a pannier slung over the stallion's back. She looked across at Tilly too, but even by moonlight saw only bleak devastation and took no comfort there.

Joanna adjusted the unfamiliar weight of the scrip on her shoulders. It had already rubbed the ivory skin raw to accompany the blister on one of her small feet. Then she plunged down into the trees, for there was no going back now.

Richard de Lacey leaned back in his saddle and stretched; he had been riding since dawn and the day was far spent. He was hungry and tired and, what was worse, it was starting to rain a mild drizzle. Below him the chalk scarp fell away steeply and darkened into the Blackmoor forest. Little columns of smoke betrayed the hamlets far off in the vale.

Mark looked at him expectantly and he nodded. 'Time to head back.' They wheeled their horses and rode back to where Umar stood by his mount in the shelter of a clump of once pollarded beech trees.

'Nothing, my lord?' The groom looked disappointed too.

'No one moving at all,' Richard replied. 'And no surprise with this weather closing in.'

Together they had searched the woods and combes to the south and west of Horsingham. No one they met had seen anything, and though they looked in every sheltered clump where a horse might be hidden they had seen nothing, not even a great hoof print to reward their pains. It had been disheartening.

'Where shall we try tomorrow, my lord?' Mark's assumption that they would continue the search was encouraging.

Richard wiped the moisture from his beard. 'We shall sweep

away into the high country itself. This search along the edge is getting us nowhere. Savaric is having no more luck than we are.'

'Though his methods are more . . . demanding!' Mark raised an eyebrow as he spoke.

Richard recalled the black eyes of a shepherd they had met only that morning. 'They are getting frightened now. They thought she would turn up within a day or two. Now it has been . . .' He stopped to think.

'We heard it on the Tuesday after the fast day,' Mark said helpfully.

Richard nodded. 'Right enough, and tomorrow is Martinmas so that makes it a fortnight tonight that they left the manor . . . It would have been October the twenty-seventh. Yes . . .' he sighed, 'the day before the feast of SS Peter and Jude.' He remembered the fast that they had undertaken at the Templar convent on that momentous Monday, quite ignorant of what was about to befall.

'I never thought they could last so long.' Mark was puzzled.

'It has been well planned . . .' Umar was usually quiet during these conversations between Richard and Mark, but the nature of their search was drawing them all closer together. 'To hide the three and a horse . . .' He paused to consider it. 'They must have help.'

'Go on,' Richard said encouragingly.

Umar thought again. 'Winter is coming on.' He glanced at the scudding grey clouds. 'And though the winters are not hard here, they will need food and shelter for themselves as well as for the horse.' Mark nodded and Umar noted the gesture and smiled slightly. 'They have planned more than just a camp in the woods. Someone is helping them . . .'

Richard mulled over the groom's words. He had been coming to much the same conclusion. 'You speak a lot of sense. I must admit that when this started I was as shocked as anyone. I thought we would find them living in some sheltered hollow or copse, and as anxious to be discovered as we would be to discover them.

'But they are worthier than I thought. To have escaped so long without detection suggests a much greater degree of thought than I had credited them with. And perhaps they have been aided. But by whom?'

'There are those who hate the sheriff and the King,' Mark ventured cautiously. 'Some of the barons of southern Somerset have been forced to loan great sums of money to the Crown, so I hear. Perhaps they have aided the lady Joanna . . .'

'A very dangerous business,' Richard interrupted him. He picked up a fallen twig from the turf and brushed mud from his mount's hock. The horse stamped its feet at the surprise grooming. 'It would be a very dangerous business indeed . . .'

'But the King is away in Normandy and the war is going badly.' Mark took heart from the fact that Richard had argued against but not dismissed his idea. 'They may feel free to act while he is gone. While the cat's away . . .'

' . . .the mice will play.' Richard laughed as he completed the proverb. 'You may be right, it may be part of a larger scheme. If so, then the lady Joanna may be taking a greater risk than she thinks.'

Umar looked confused. 'My lord, I do not understand this matter of vermin . . .'

'I'll explain later.' Richard gestured to the gathering clouds. 'The wind is bringing in the rain again. We had better return to Buckland while there is still light.'

He was reluctant to return. Since the drying-up of the money, the atmosphere had become tense at the convent. It was as if the Templars were now embarrassed at the presence of their guests. Both Richard and Mark had sensed it. How long they would be welcome at all was open to question. For Richard it was the last in the catalogue of bitter blows which seemed to have pushed his life off course. It was as if he had fallen in the path of a wind so strong that he could not go against it or change course.

'Do you think that the King knows yet?' Mark asked as they were mounting.

Richard stopped, one foot in the stirrup. 'I doubt it. If I were Savaric I would do all I could to get the stallion and the ward back before the King learned anything about it. It is always better to report a problem after you have solved it.'

Mark grinned. 'So it is our secret then?'

'But one that will become more open with every passing day.' The thought of John had prompted another idea, however. 'But mark my words – if we can recapture the stallion, then the King may look with a little mercy on our inability to pay the sum we have offered.'

'And no doubt he will be keen to have the girl back safe,' Mark suggested innocently.

Richard, in the saddle, seemed lost in thought. What really mattered was getting the horse; it was the last fraying thread which connected him to the dream that had started in Acre. That was all that mattered, so why was he worried about the girl? A girl who had witnessed his humiliation and who had no place in the plan for his life.

'My lord.' Umar leaned across the horse's neck. 'Are you well? Does something ail you?' Mark too looked concerned.

Richard shook his head and faked a quick smile. 'No, I was just thinking of what to do tomorrow,' he lied. 'Perhaps Mark is right after all. We will ride north into Somerset and see if anyone has clapped eyes on the horse.'

'And the girl,' Mark added, as if he was the embodiment of the echoes within de Lacey's mind. 'Someone will surely recall her.'

'Yes,' Richard concurred with a rare note of irritation. 'And that girl . . .'

'It's getting colder.' Joanna observed the same moving clouds as Richard de Lacey but many miles to the east of where he was sheltering. 'We'll need more firewood.' She and her groom were standing by the rick in the rough yard; the rick with the green thatch and sagging sides.

Stephen nodded. 'Though I do not suppose it will get much colder than this. There has not been snow on the downs since my grandfather's day. But still the nights will be chilly and there will be grey, cheerless days, no doubt.'

Joanna frowned, for life in the hamlet was proving more testing than she had imagined. For the first week or so the very air had smelled of freedom and excitement. She was free at last from the judgemental eyes of Dapifer and the cold glance of Savaric and she had revelled in her rebellion.

Then the rain had come. The shortening days had turned the ground to mud and the thatch leaked badly, an experience of dampness unknown in the snug chamber at the manor. Her dress had torn and Tilly could not mend it – the thread being at Horsingham and forgotten in their escape. Then she had worn a blister on her hand helping cut firewood – a task she had never done before in her life. Freedom was beginning to be as tiresome as servitude and certainly less comfortable. The realisation had come as something of a shock, and she was disturbed by it.

'We should have brought a hammer.' When Stephen looked surprised, she added, 'To break up the cheeses. Tilly has soaked them in water but they are still solid.'

The mention of the maid brought a shadow across Stephen's face. 'Yes, my lady,' he said, trying to hide the reaction. 'I shall try to get one. In a day or two I shall go down into Sturminster. We need more flour and beans and I shall attend to all these matters together . . .'

'We are going to have to come to terms with it, you know.'

'It will be no problem. I'll get a hammer . . .'

Joanna sighed. 'I was not talking of the cheese. I meant Matilda.'

It seemed strange to talk so openly, even with Stephen. For all their linked upbringing she had never spoken so plainly about the feelings between groom and maid.

Stephen reddened. 'What is there to say, my lady? She betrayed you.'

'Don't you mean *us*?'

Stephen bit his lip. 'With respect, my lady, she is your maid and I am but a groom.'

'For God's sake, Stephen, do not speak to me as if I was a fool. I know that you are fond of her. Perhaps you even loved her a little . . .'

'I must go and see to the horse, if you will excuse me. He seemed over-sweated this morning. I fear that . . .'

'Not yet.' Even her beloved horse could not be used to throw her off the scent. 'I know that she loved you and you her. I also know that it was incorrect and nothing could ever come of it, but do not deny its reality.'

Stephen trembled with emotions of shame and rage. 'And what if I did, my lady? She showed us all that *she* loved another. To her that beast was more acceptable than I. She whored with the man who killed my father . . .'

'Stephen! Enough!'

'Is it not true? Everyone knows it.'

'There is no doubt that she lay with Savaric and God knows I do not understand it, but she is bitterly sorry. You cannot begin to understand how sorry she is. And as to your father's death – she knew nothing about it, she had fallen completely under Savaric's evil magic. You must believe this as I do.' The doubt was present in her voice but she persevered, not sure if her hurt would allow her to continue with the thin defence of her maid and friend.

Stephen's face was cast in bronze. 'I am sure that you are right, my lady.'

I cannot reach him, Joanna thought. I cannot get near him on this. And little wonder.

'Will you excuse me? I really should examine the stallion.'

'Of course,' she said, conceding defeat, 'and let me know what you think about him.'

As he left her, Matilda returned from the nearby trees with an armful of dead wood. Her tunic was soiled; her veil had been pulled from her head by the undergrowth and she carried it in entangled with the firewood.

'Well done, Tilly, you've found a large amount.'

In the first week of their hermit-like existence Joanna had volunteered to feed the fire which burned continuously on the central hearth in the larger of the thatched cottages. The resulting smoke from the green wood had almost choked them all and Matilda had volunteered to collect wood in future. It took her out away from the eyes of her lady and the groom. It was a self-imposed exile.

Joanna's praise caused Tilly to look up. 'It was an easy enough task. There is plenty in the woods.'

'Let me help you.' Despite Tilly's protests, Joanna took some of the wood. 'It is too heavy for one to carry.'

They went in silence through the low door and entered the cob-walled room with the smoke hanging below the rafters. Laying down the pile, Tilly began to build up the fire.

'I spoke with Stephen this morning.' Joanna said it quietly, aware that the stable was under the same roof.

Tilly froze, a piece of wood halfway between pile and fire. 'What did he say?' She did not even enquire as to the topic of conversation.

Joanna ignored the question for the present. 'I told him that you were sorry.' Tilly looked up, a smudge of charcoal on her button nose. 'I said that I did not understand, but that we must put it behind us.'

'Thank you, my lady.'

'I cannot claim to comprehend it, though. You know that. It would have been easier if . . .'

'If he had raped me,' Tilly almost whispered.

Joanna looked away. 'It is harder because you desired him. Harder to understand. Can you comprehend that?' Matilda nodded. 'And that makes it harder for Stephen too. For he loved you.'

Tilly shook her head. 'I do not understand it myself,' she began. 'I was a fool, but . . .'

'But?'

'I do not know what drew me to him. But he is a savagely good-looking man. You must have seen that?'

Joanna shook her head, denying the physical attraction she had felt move within her.

'Well, I fear that I thought he was more than handsome,' Matilda continued, low-voiced. 'And it blinded me to all else. I saw but I did not see. I really did not mean to betray you. I thought I could change him. I thought . . . I hoped that he loved me. I thought that was why . . .'

'Why he lay with you.'

The maid bit her lip and nodded. What she did not say was how her body had craved him since the first time he had gripped her. And how – for all her shame and grief – she still longed for him to possess her again, to blot out all worry and doubt in the consuming fire of the physical ecstasy that he had awoken in her.

'I cannot understand,' Joanna said, touching the maid's arm and burying her own ambiguity towards Savaric beneath her words, 'but I know that it is over. I told Stephen that. And we will speak of it no more. It is behind us and it must be this way if we are to survive. That is all that matters now; nothing else is of consequence,' Joanna lied, and looked away before the revulsion that her words concealed could be seen.

Matilda touched Joanna's hand in gratitude. Her lady steeled herself and did not pull away, as part of her demanded. 'What did Stephen say?' Tilly asked, staring at her own hand.

At that moment the young groom entered the room from the stables. 'It is as I feared, my lady. The stallion has a fever.'

Joanna was on her feet, the contact with Matilda broken. 'God knows, this is the last thing we need. Is it bad?'

'It is bad enough and may get worse . . .'

'I'll see him myself.' She walked away from the fireside.

Stephen dropped his eyes to where Matilda was kneeling by the baked clay of the hearth. Their eyes met and Tilly had no need to ask Joanna what Stephen Pierson thought of her.

'Hit him again.'

A leather-gloved fist slammed into the belly of the middle-aged villein. If the man had not been held by two of Savaric's men he would have fallen backwards into his own pigsty. As it was he screamed and then retched. Savaric was beginning to think the man really did know nothing but, he decided, it would be foolish to relax the pressure now. Others in the village were watching.

'Into the sty with him.' The gasping man was flung over the cob wall of the pigpen to land in a flurry of filth and squealing piglets. Savaric turned to where the other men and women were cowering against the trees at the edge of the combe. 'Just remember – anyone who conceals the truth from me will be killed . . .' The cat-faced man from Horsingham translated the threat into English for the benefit of the cowering villeins. A woman started to cry, and a child whimpered.

'Shall we burn down his hovel?' The soldier smirked as he asked.

Savaric looked coldly at the cottage with its mildewed walls and scrawny hens. 'Why not? It's been chilly standing here.'

The soldiers went into the dilapidated cottage to kick the embers of the fire about the place, and soon smoke was billowing through the doorway and seeping like a black tide through the holes in the thatch. The mercenary leader clicked his fingers and his men retired from the hamlet, leaving the terrified inhabitants to put out the fire.

It was only then that Savaric realised that he was being watched. Falkes de Mauleon was mounted with four armed companions and all were cloaked against the autumn air.

'I assume by your questioning of the villagers that you have not yet got her back?'

Savaric found the marshal's cool attitude very hard to counter, especially at this moment. 'No, I have not yet found her,' he admitted reluctantly.

Falkes did not look surprised. 'I thought she might have taken the horse towards Dorchester, but we have ridden the country that way and there is no sign of any of them.' The tone of his voice revealed concern, but whether for Joanna or the horse it was hard to tell. 'Two of my men rode as far as Corfe but there was no news there either.'

If his disclosure was designed to elicit more information from Savaric it failed to do so. Falkes seemed to take the obvious animosity of the Brabançon easily enough and was not provoked by the shunning of his news.

'Have you told the King yet?'

Savaric scowled. 'I'll worry about that.' He resented Falkes' participation in the search but his own failure did not make it easy to reject offers of help.

'I'm sure that you will.' Falkes seemed more prepared than usual to goad the man. 'And no doubt so will he when he hears.

Then you'll worry even more. What does de Burgh think?'

'He does not know yet . . .' Savaric bit his tongue.

'Ahh, so you've not told either of them. Since I assume that you go through the sheriff to the King. Well, no doubt you will inform both in due course.'

'I can't stand here gossiping like an old woman.'

Falkes shifted his weight in the saddle. 'No doubt of that. Not when there are other old women to beat up. Best of luck and may the best man find them all.' He pushed his heels into his horse's flanks and rode on.

Falkes had decided that Savaric was finished the moment he had heard the news of Joanna's escape with Soloriens. From that moment he had decided he must recapture the horse. It was also only proper that he should secure Joanna's safety. He was very concerned about the safety of the red-headed beauty but the recapture of the horse was also in his mind. Only that could upstage the Templar, with his inexhaustible money, and make a lasting impression on the King.

Savaric watched the marshal ride away and could hardly contain the fury which engulfed him in a cold fire. *She* had humiliated him; a *woman* had made him look a fool, and it was more than he could bear. He felt that everyone was laughing at him. Someone was going to pay for this, someone was going to die.

William Catface had set about finding the horse with the eagerness of one deeply in debt who has decided that heaven has dropped an escape route into his lap. However, unlike the other searchers, he had to spend time performing labour service for the manor and carry out those tasks which he had already agreed to do for his richer villein neighbours. It being November, most of the work had been slaughtering the beasts which could not be overwintered on the precious hay stocks. During long mornings singeing off the coarse bristles from dead pigs he had thought about where the horse might be hidden.

Between that and his feudal service – of unpaid hedging and ditching for the manor – he had begun to roam the woods of the vale. When that turned up nothing, he had switched his attention to the wilder downland sheep grazings, beyond the open wheat fields that lay closer to the northern scarp.

It was on one such foray in the late afternoon that he ran into Ranulf Dapifer. The meeting was something of a surprise for both of them. Dapifer did not venture out on to the downs and was a rare sight outside the manor compound or the surrounding hamlet. Catface was astonished at the sight.

Ranulf was mounted on one of the manor's better palfreys, while William was on foot. The latter saw the former first but with little cover was soon overtaken by the mounted man.

'Catface, isn't it?' Ranulf asked disdainfully, in the English he usually reserved for the manorial court.

William touched his forelock in the practised manner which pleased his betters and made them go away quickly. ''Tis I, sir.'

'What are you doing out this far from the manor?'

Catface considered the question carefully. 'Oh, 'tis not so far, sir, when yer be used to it.' He thanked God that he had returned his dogs to their secret home amidst the tangled undergrowth.

Dapifer sighed. It was always difficult communicating with the more obtuse of the villagers. But Catface was a funny one and Ranulf was not entirely sure that he was as obligingly docile as he made out.

'It's almost ten miles, you fool. What are you doing here? Out with it.'

William decided that open-hearted sincerity was probably his best defence. 'I've been worried about 'er ladyship. From what I've 'eard, summit 'ave befallen 'er.'

Ranulf guessed as much. 'No doubt your deep concern has been assisted by the sizeable reward offered for her safe return.'

'A reward, sir! Is there one like?'

'As well you know, you ruffian. Now have you seen, or heard, a thing?'

'I ain't seen nothin', sir.'

Ranulf, not yet convinced, decided on another tack. 'We are all as worried as you are. I know how much you love the lady Joanna. Now have you seen a thing that might help us?'

'No,' Catface lied. 'I've seen nought, sir . . .'

Ranulf frowned. 'Then you had best be heading back to the manor before night falls and you are accused of poaching the King's deer.'

'God's sake, sir. They 'ud never accuse I of that, would 'em?' William's horror was etched in deep lines across his small face, and the snub nose twitched in consternation.

'They might well do,' Ranulf replied icily, unmoved by the innocence on the man's face. 'So be off with you.'

Catface obediently jogged off. Ranulf watched him go, as convinced that the man was an unrepentant poacher as he was that if Joanna and the horse were not quickly taken, a disaster would fall on them all.

Catface, on the other hand, had the distinct impression that the steward's heart was not bleeding too profusely on behalf of Joanna, but was in fact moved by some other motive which would only be understood by those who never needed to poach in order to eat fresh meat.

More importantly, William had lied to the steward. He was in fact in possession of information, in return for which Ranulf would have danced naked around the manor. But Catface was keeping it to himself, for he had spotted it and was not about to share it with anyone, least of all the steward.

It was sufficient to make him whistle as he trotted home. It was a truly dreadful, tuneless sound and a sure indication that William Catface had stumbled on something big.

On Friday, 5 December 1203, King John sailed from Normandy for England. It was a bad crossing and he landed in Kent in a foul mood late the next day. The eventual journey to Canterbury did little to improve his humour. On his arrival he was met by messengers from Normandy with more bad news concerning losses in the east of the duchy and raids from Breton lords, who seemed far from cowed by John's autumnal raid into Brittany and the vanishing of their duke into the King of England's hands.

Worse was to follow after the noon dinner. A letter-bearer arrived from one of the King's manors in the West Country. As

John read the letter his face shaded red to scarlet and then to a darkness the colour of a winter storm. His hands trembled as he gripped the vellum and the more experienced royal retainers drifted off to a safe distance.

'God's body,' he swore, 'the fools have lost it. By God, I will see the last one of them hanged if it's not found safely.'

He flung out a hand and sent silver goblets and platters of salted meat and eels flying on to the rushes. Dogs rose and leapt upon the unexpected feast. Again and again he drove his fist on to the table, blood trickling from broken flesh, and howled with wolf-like fury. The servants and chamber knights kept their distance as the monarch descended into a wild rage which left him chewing the stem of a silver goblet which alone had escaped his flailing fist.

Chapter 11

The stallion was clearly ill and Joanna could no longer deny it. As she leaned against the wattle panel she could see that even the half-light could not hide the lack of gloss on Soloriens' sweeping back. The hay in the wooden bin before him was hardly touched and the fire in his eyes seemed to have been banked down to glowing embers.

Stephen was trying to tempt the horse with a handful of the hay he had brought in from the thatched rick in the yard; though old, it was good quality. Despite this, the horse seemed quite unmoved and, hissing peevishly, the groom stepped back and his eyes shifted from the stallion to his mistress.

'He's not shaking it off,' he concluded with an irritation which betrayed his concern. 'The fever is well rooted now.' He ran a hand over the hot withers and the horse barely noticed the firm touch. 'And his spirit is down. He is as gentle as a gelding now, for the fight is going out of him.'

Joanna pondered what the groom had just said. 'He needs more green food,' she concluded at last. 'I've sent Tilly out to pull up as much grass as she can carry. Thank God there has been no frost and it's still fairly lush beside the stream.' She stepped forward and adjusted the blanket which had been carefully draped over the stallion's back. 'If this beast should die . . .'

Stephen looked up sharply as she spoke the words he had dared not frame. 'He will not die, my lady.' His tone gave little support to his optimism but the empty words alone shamed Joanna.

'You're right,' she replied, still unable to remove her gaze from the horse. 'It is just that I had never really imagined just what it would be like here.' Then she bit her lip before any more regrets could well to the surface.

The weather had been mild but damp, and little in Joanna's experience had prepared her for the dirt and inconvenience of camping in the deserted settlement. Now the horse's ailments further sapped her resolve and it was with an enormous effort of will that she maintained her determination. She had never felt so tired and the initial excitement of the theft of the stallion was beginning to succumb to the realities of life in the hidden valley. More than that, she was no longer sure that she could see the way out of what she had done. That they were all committed beyond retreat was undeniable; however, she was beginning to wonder how easy it would be to triumph. If the horse died, they were all lost – it did not bear thinking about.

'There is an old cure that my father used sometimes.' Stephen's voice broke the dim, depressed silence. 'He said it often worked when a horse was fevered.' The mention of the murdered Piers seemed to detract from this news, which would otherwise have been heartening.

'What was it then?' Joanna regretted her moment of weakness. She had led Stephen and Tilly into this trouble and she would lead them out. Her fear she would keep to herself as best she could; what they needed was leadership and only she could provide it. 'Tell me what this cure was, for we'll try anything to keep this horse well. The King won't be persuaded to review the wardship if we kill the beast.'

The joke was a mistake and both Joanna and the groom knew it. Stephen shook his head but answered her question. 'He would take a knife . . .' He scrabbled in one corner of the stable where he had hung his bag of tools from a rusted nail. 'He always said it should have a horn handle and three brass nails in it – one for each of the Blessed Trinity,' he added by way of explanation.

Stephen found the knife and laid it on the back of the horse, and Soloriens stamped his feet at the cold touch of the blade. 'Then we have to scratch on the handle. Have you a pin, my lady?'

'I think so.' Joanna pulled off one of the brooches which secured her cloak to her long gown. 'Will this do?' When Stephen nodded, she handed it to him.

He took the brooch and the knife and, followed by Joanna, went out of the stable to where the thin light ventured along the passageway which separated byre from living room. Kneeling, he began to scratch on the handle, while a fascinated Joanna crouched beside him to watch. Crude and spindly letters began to appear on the cream bone. When at last he had finished, he handed it to his mistress.

Joanna read the words aloud. '*Benedicite omnia opera domini dominum.*' She glanced at the groom, whose face bore the solemnity of one who did not fully understand what he had written. 'And what do we do now?'

'We place it on the back of the beast once more and then hide it in a crevice in the wall. It will draw off the fever.' He paused, then added, 'It is better if you do it. My father says it has greater power when applied by a virgin – begging your pardon, my lady.' Then he realised the tense that he had used and a bitter shadow crossed his bearded features, eclipsing the smile which had risen in his clear blue eyes. 'I mean that my father *used* to say it.' The hatred was rising in his voice. 'And it is a good thing that you are here, my lady, as it would clearly not have worked if I had had to rely on Matilda doing it, for my father insisted it should be a virgin and not a . . .'

'Enough, Stephen.' Joanna's voice was final. 'It will do no good now, you can see that, can't you? We must work together now, or we are lost.'

'Yes, my lady.' His eyes were as lifeless as his voice now. 'You are right, of course.' There was no conviction in his words.

Sighing, Joanna took the knife and did as she had been told, then forced it into a crevice in the wattle wall. Withdrawing her hand she surveyed the dirt clinging to her long slim fingers and once polished nails. She sighed again, but before she could speak, Tilly had arrived.

'I've got the grass you spoke of, my lady.' Arms full of it, she looked at Stephen but he made no attempt to help her.

'Put it in the feed bin,' he said as if talking to no one in particular. His tone was not rude, just totally devoid of any warmth. Then he looked at Joanna. 'There is still some of the bran left; if you will excuse me, my lady, I shall boil it up with the linseed to make a mash. I think that the supply of linseed oil will not outlast this use, so I had better go down into Sturminster market tomorrow, or the day after.' He paused and looked straight at Tilly for the first time. 'Along with the charm, my late father swore by it as a cure for fever.'

Matilda paled at the intensity of feeling which had suddenly flooded his voice. Noticing this, and alarmed at the tension in the air, Joanna nodded. 'Go and do it, Stephen, it is a good idea and no doubt it will help.' Then she said to Tilly: 'Bring the grass here and then help me bandage up his legs to keep him warm.' She motioned to where Soloriens stood in the piled straw.

Without thinking, she touched her maid's hand in an automatic gesture of conciliation. The look of gratitude which flooded the girl's face stabbed Joanna with the realisation of the desperate loneliness of the maid now cast adrift from her friends. But Joanna looked away, unable to follow on from the touch, for, though the pain of her maid was raw, so was that of Stephen Pierson. And Joanna could not forget the man who stood at the pivot of both those pains. The thought of Savaric made her stomach turn in churning sickness, for she could not clear her mind of Tilly's betrayal.

Seeking to drive contemplation away by action, she gestured to the horse. 'Try to feed him by hand.' Her voice cancelled out the softness of her touch and Matilda's eyes filled with tears. 'He will not harm you,' she added briskly and turned away, ashamed of her own lack of forgiveness and yet unable to master it.

William Catface was out early that December morning, but it was not the King's deer that he was poaching; he had his eyes on something rarer and altogether more valuable. Crouching low amongst the trees, he kept a good distance from his quarry and was sure that he had not been seen.

He had first noticed Stephen Pierson the day before the meeting with Dapifer on the downs. The sighting had not come entirely by chance, for Catface had put a lot of thought into the matter. When the weeks had rolled by since the theft of the horse, it had become clear that Joanna and her fellow conspirators were intent on more than an impetuous flight into the wilds. The more he thought about this, the more Catface began to realise that such an expedition could not sustain itself for long without provisions. As a result he had kept an eye on the marketplaces north and south of the high land.

It had been a slow business, as he had to squeeze it in between his villein duties on the manor and the work on his tiny plot of land. Every hour spent away from the manor risked disciplining at the manor court, or at least the loss of the pittance he gained by the hire of his labour. Nevertheless, the possibility of the four pounds' reward had always been before his eyes – as had his debts.

It was while wandering along the vale on the northern edge of the downs that he had first caught sight of someone he had recognised. Catface had glimpsed the solitary figure with a sack slung over one shoulder, but had lost him again in the woods that overshadowed the encroaching assarts. Since then he had spent every spare minute amongst the farmsteads and forest south of Sturminster, for he was sure that Stephen Pierson would appear again. Now his patience had been rewarded and he had seen the young man once more, and from the determined stride it was clear that he was making for Sturminster again.

'That's it, my lover,' Catface muttered to himself as he trailed the unsuspecting youth. 'Yer just keep on goin' that way.' His heart was beating fast and he could almost feel Savaric's silver in his hand. 'An' don't yer worry about a thing, for yer Uncle William is keepin' an eye on yer.' He grinned until he struck his head on a low branch, but even that only reduced his humour for a few seconds, for in his mind he was already counting the silver pennies.

Catface followed Stephen until he crossed the river Stour and then the poacher made off west as fast as he could. He had seen some of Savaric's men that morning and had a fair idea of where they were. It was vital that he locate them again and get them back to Sturminster. As he jogged, he whistled. It came in a tuneless stream between the puffing of his breath but he was – at last – a happy man.

Richard de Lacey's excursion into south Somerset had achieved nothing. There had been no word of a girl with blazing hair, or of a horse that was worth a king's ransom. Since it was unlikely that either could have passed unnoticed he had been forced to conclude that they had not gone north from the manor. The realisation had refocused his attention on the hills to the south. Since Savaric's men had found nothing, he and his two attendants pushed further east along the crest of the downs. They became a familiar sight to the more hardy shepherds – three closely cloaked figures on mud-splashed horses.

Christmas was only two weeks away when the three riders pulled up their horses by an isolated farmstead – one of the granges of Glastonbury Abbey. The smoke curling from the thatch indicated the presence of at least one of the abbey's lay brothers. Mark de Dinan dismounted and his knocks brought forth a surprised and curious face, which threw a hostile and fearful glance towards Umar.

'We are from the Templar manor at Buckland,' Mark said quickly, before the startled face could withdraw. 'We seek a meal and will pay for it.' He flashed one of Richard's dwindling stock of Templar silver pennies. The money wrought a transformation in the suspicious look and the three riders were eagerly welcomed into the smoky house. Even the presence of the strangely tanned groom seemed acceptable now that money had changed hands.

While they ate the coarse bread and vegetable soup purchased by the penny, Richard considered the state of their search so far. 'So she did not go north,' he said as he raised a stained wooden tankard of unhopped ale. 'And that implies that she may still be somewhere here about the downs, though God alone knows how they have survived this long out in the open.' He sipped the thick liquid of the heavily spiced drink and felt he had come a long way from the wine and optimism of the Holy Land.

'Is it always this cold?' Umar was swaddled in his cloak despite the fire that filled the hut with smoke. 'I can never get warm.'

Mark laughed, but the cruelty had gone out of it and a sense of desperate camaraderie had embraced even the Saracen. 'This is not cold!' When Umar looked unconvinced he added: 'Sometimes it snows, though thank God rarely enough. And sometimes there's a frost, but like the snow it's no regular thing. But when it comes you will find it colder yet.' Umar recalled with sorrow the passing of the hot, golden summer days that were so recent and yet seemed so far away.

'We can be grateful,' Richard interjected, 'that the weather is as fine as it has been these past few weeks and the wet days have been mild. If it really had been cold, our mission would have been more tedious than it has been.'

'There you are.' Mark nodded towards Umar. 'I told you it has been a mild winter.' The Saracen looked unimpressed.

Richard put down his tankard. 'What is more worrying is that we have more to say about the weather than about the girl . . .'

'And the horse . . .' Mark added, and as he did so was struck by the fact that Richard had mentioned only the girl.

De Lacey cast him a look of rare public irritation. 'Of course I meant the horse! That's what we're after, isn't it?' Mark de Dinan nodded emphatically, not daring to add that it was not his but Richard's change in emphasis that he had absent-mindedly corrected.

Richard felt angry but did not truly know why. It was as if more than the loss of Soloriens and the drying-up of the Templar funds was troubling him – as if these were not enough on their own to drive him to distraction! There was something else that was goading him, some invisible spur which kept jabbing him. He was puzzled by it, and by his inability to hide his frustration under the usual display of crafted good humour. He could only conclude that it was the fruitless search that was so disturbing him and yet – though that was enough to explain it – he was curiously unconvinced.

Mark felt responsible for the gloom which had suddenly enveloped his master. He was not sure what he had done to cause it but felt he should do something to end it. He called to the lay brother stirring the fire to bring over the cauldron of soup –

Richard's bowl lay empty. When it arrived, de Dinan took the wooden ladle from the man and served his knight, as was only proper.

'Where might a person find shelter between here and Gillingham?' he said, in English, to the man holding the cauldron. He had meant for themselves, but the man's answer was not what he had expected.

Richard was woken from his contemplations too. 'Say that again.' The man looked surprised. 'Tell me again what you just said to my squire.'

The lay brother frowned, taken aback at the reaction to his innocently given information. 'There is a hamlet,' he said slowly, fearful of making an error in the presence of his social superiors. 'An assart on the edge of the downs.' He looked from Richard to Mark. 'The white fever was there a few years ago, my lord. And it has lain idle since. I have never been there, for it has a bad name . . .'

'What is it called? Where is it and how far from here?'

The multiple questions confused the man and he paused to consider his reply. 'They call it Woolcombe and it lies north-east of here, my lord.' Calmed by the look of encouragement the knight gave him, he added: 'It is about an hour's ride from here, my lord.'

Richard was on his feet. 'This is it.' He turned to Umar and repeated the lay brother's news – this time in Norman-French for the benefit of the Arab groom. 'There is enough light left and if we ride hard we will be there before dark. This must be the place.' Turning back to the man with the pot he cast him another silver penny. The man dropped the soup and grabbed the coin, unable to believe his luck.

Stephen Pierson lay in the stall which had once held Soloriens. Ropes bound his ankles and his hands were tied behind his back; the twisted fibres cut into his skin and the flesh was raw. He cursed himself for being caught and his mind hovered over the moment, the previous day in Sturminster market, when he had been seized. Up against the stable wall his sack still contained the cheese and bread that he had purchased, along with apples for the horse and a sealed jar of linseed oil to add to the stallion's feed. Now all his efforts had been wasted and he had spent a night and a day as a prisoner, awaiting the return of Savaric and Dapifer from Sherborne. As he thought of that, his anger and frustration turned to fear.

It was after dark when Savaric and Ranulf returned to the manor to be greeted with the news of the capture of the runaway groom. At once they hurried to the stables where two of the mercenaries were standing guard and the cat-faced villein was hovering like a gadfly.

'You'll get the money – so clear off,' Savaric said with excitement in his voice. William frowned at Savaric and hesitated. 'Are you going deaf?' Savaric was impatient. 'Now get lost, or I'll change my mind.' William reluctantly took the hint. 'Now, Dapifer, we have work to do . . .'

The mercenary and the steward entered the stable preceded by a soldier carrying a burning torch. Stephen blinked at the sudden light and Savaric laughed. 'It's him all right, well done, lads. Now stand him up.' Two of the mercenaries pulled Stephen to his feet. He stumbled on numb legs.

'I'll tell you nothing,' he spat at Savaric.

One of the soldiers whispered in the ear of de Breauté, who grinned. 'So, as well as getting provisions you were paying someone to take a message to the royal lodge at Gillingham, were you?' Stephen made no reply and Savaric continued: 'A nice little message telling the King that all was well with the horse but he was a hostage until His Majesty reconsidered the state of the de Cantelo wardship.' Savaric grinned at Dapifer before returning his attention to Stephen. 'But of course you neglected to tell the man where the horse was being kept, which was very forgetful of you. So where is it and who is sheltering you?'

When Stephen shook his head, Savaric motioned to one of the mercenaries. 'Hit him.' The soldier turned and punched Stephen in the stomach, and as he fell, a knee caught him in the face. 'Do it again.' The order was obeyed, and Stephen was spitting blood where once he had spat defiance.

Ranulf Dapifer grimaced at the violence but he did not stop it; the boy had to tell them where the horse was, everything depended on that. All his hopes hung on recapturing Soloriens; without the stallion he was finished. Besides which, he had no authority over Savaric – so he told himself as Pierson was struck again.

'Where are they?' Savaric's question was unambiguous; he cared for nothing else. 'Tell us and this will stop.' Stephen shook his head and the soldiers looked at their leader, who nodded. 'I know that one of the King's enemies is sheltering you, but which one? Which petty little baron, or knight, is doing this service for Joanna de Cantelo? Out with it.'

'Don't be a fool, boy, tell us!' Ranulf felt a trembling anger at this damned boy who stood between them and the capture of the hostage stallion and Joanna. 'Tell us.'

Savaric grinned at Ranulf's excited anger. He himself was suddenly calm once more. He knew he could make the boy talk and there was no need to get excited.

'I'll tell you nothing, you bastard.' Stephen turned his swollen face to Savaric. 'Nothing . . . nothing . . .'

'Again . . .' Savaric waved his hand and the beating continued with a systematic brutality born of experience. 'He'll tell us . . .'

'Tell us, Pierson, you stupid fool, tell us . . .' Ranulf wanted to hit him himself. He wanted to beat the boy until he poured out his information. He wanted to kick and punch him until he talked. He had never felt such anger. 'Tell us, damn you, tell us . . .' Dapifer could see all his hopes snared by this boy and his pathetic loyalty to the headstrong young woman who had ruined everything. 'Damn you – you will tell us. You will, you will . . .'

The soldiers continued to drive their fists – and, when he fell, their nail-studded boots – into Stephen. Kicks and blows landed with sickening regularity on his body and on the bleeding hands clasped about his broken head.

Ranulf Dapifer clenched his fists with fury at the dumb stupidity of the groom. He wanted them to kick the truth out of him, to smash it from him until everything was revealed. There was no other way. Pierson's stubbornness stood between them and escape from the crisis which gripped them, and if he would not yield, then he would be kicked aside. A mist of passion, quite alien to Dapifer, floated before his eyes.

Suddenly Savaric pushed aside his men. 'You stupid bastards,' he yelled, his voice suddenly as excited as Dapifer's. 'You bloody useless sons of whores.'

'What is it?' Ranulf had suddenly realised that the mercenary captain was not shouting at Pierson. Instead he was cupping his hands into a nearby bucket of water and splashing it on to the groom's bloodied face. 'What's wrong?' The steward's voice was shrill with alarm.

'The sod's dead.' Savaric's face was dancing with a furious twitching now. 'He's dead. The useless little git's dead.'

Ranulf felt the blood rush from his face. And yet at that moment he could not tell what was the greater blow: that they had killed Stephen Pierson, or that the groom had died without telling them what they so desperately needed to know.

Joanna and Tilly had bidden Stephen goodbye as soon as the December night sky had paled into dawn, then they had turned to making the most of the short day before Stephen returned. Joanna had spent much of the morning with Soloriens. It seemed that either Stephen's charm, the powerful touch of a virgin or the combination of fresh green food and bran mashes were having some effect on the fever. The stallion seemed cooler and his appetite was returning – much to Joanna's intense relief.

'That's better,' she murmured softly as she fed him one of the apples that Stephen had brought back from his last foray to Sturminster market. 'You're getting back to your old self again.' The dapple-grey seized the fruit between its great teeth and snatched it from her hand. 'As devoid of table manners as ever you were.' She stroked the smoky mane, content at the return of the stallion's independent spirit.

In one corner of the stable an iron-hooped bucket contained a steaming mess of bran. Joanna left the horse munching on its apples and began to ladle linseed into the thick porridge. Drops of the oil fell on her dress and she wiped them with a clutch of straw. It was the green dress with the knotted trailing sleeves that she had worn to Melcombe. As she rubbed at the oil she could not help but see how battered it now was, how grimy and frayed.

Joanna stirred in the last of the linseed, then sat down in the straw. All was quiet except for the chewing of the great horse and the scuttering of rats in the thatch. The quiet gave her a moment to think, a moment alone to consider the state of things. Perhaps the message she had instructed Stephen to have carried to the King's men would provide a way out. She was beginning to doubt it, though, for what if it only provoked the King to anger? That appeared all too likely now that she considered matters, but there seemed no other way out. If the truth were to be known, she had not fully planned the end of the adventure when she had stolen the horse. Her mind had been concentrated more on the doing of the deed and on triumphing over Savaric. Now she was having to think of the future, for the present situation could not go on indefinitely.

'What would you do, Father?' she murmured softly, then refocused her thoughts. 'Dear God, grant that the King will see this theft of the horse for what it is – a cry for justice . . .' As she pondered on her prayer she finally realised the enormity of the miracle for which she was asking. 'I am sorry that I have not confessed my sins for so long,' she continued, 'or attended mass, but it has been impossible here.' She faltered, thinking that God must know this anyway. Nevertheless it would do no harm to confess it, as she could not afford any sin to stand between her and the answer to her prayers. 'And I forgive Matilda . . .'

She let out her breath in a sigh, for she did not forgive Tilly her betrayal of manor and mistress. Try as she might the thought still horrified her. She put her head back against the cold wall of the stable. Thinking of Tilly brought Savaric into the room, and an animal passion into the quiet of her prayers. Joanna shuddered but did not cast out the apparition which haunted her thoughts. She remembered Savaric and faintly felt a crosscurrent of both revulsion and desire. Was that what the maid had felt? The sudden empathy appalled her.

She bit on a clenched fist, for the thought of desire for a man like Savaric was too dreadful to consider. But as she turned from it she ran into visions of Falkes and Richard. Each was so different yet neither fully comforted her, for Falkes offered security with passion disciplined, and Richard offered passion – even danger – without security.

Suddenly she laughed. 'You're a little forward, Joanna,' she chided herself. 'That knight cares only for the horses. And there is a destroying fire burning within him. What is he to you?' The truth was that he was nothing to her, whereas Falkes was reliable and offered a way out. 'Perhaps I should go to him,' she said quietly. 'He would help me; he is a fine man, if less than my father might have hoped for.'

Joanna shook her head at her own thoughts. There would have been a time when such matters would have been alien to her. Now, though, safety and security no longer seemed quite such foolish and uninspiring compromises as once they had done. A winter in the wilds, with Savaric hunting her, had begun to reveal the limitations to freedom and independence. Of late it had dawned on her that the freedom of the days before her father's death had only existed because of the security and protection he offered; she had not been free or independent at all, merely protected. The thought was painful, for it forced her to reassess herself and what she truly desired. Much of what she had once valued now seemed an illusion.

'My lady.' Matilda was at the door; with the pale winter light behind her she looked like a ghost. 'I have finished washing your clothes in the stream; will you eat now? I have a little salted bacon and the vegetables left from . . .'

'Come here and sit down.' The command was firmly given. 'I want to talk to you.' Matilda did as she was bidden and only then did Joanna realise how frightened she looked. 'We have not talked for a long time, have we?'

'Not since . . .' The maid's voice trailed away.

'Not since you told me about what happened with Savaric.' When Tilly paled and looked away, Joanna shook her head. 'No, Tilly, I have no desire to chide you. I want to talk to you. I need to . . .' She faltered. 'I need to understand.'

For what felt like a very long time the two young women sat in silence, as neither knew where to begin. Then at last Joanna ventured a question. 'Do you still desire him?'

'I hate him.'

'That is not what I asked,' Joanna reminded her gently. 'Do you still desire him?'

Matilda bit her lip. 'Yes,' she said at last. 'Yes, I do.'

'Because he desired you?'

'Yes, because he made me feel like a woman. Because he . . .' She struggled to find the words. 'Because he shook me out of childhood and made me important. Because he knew how to awaken desire in a woman . . .'

'And because it was the wildest thing that you had ever done?'

Matilda considered the suggestion carefully. 'It was the most foolish thing I have done in my life and yet I could not stop it. I really could not.' She looked imploringly at her mistress. 'I felt carried away. It was so bad and so exciting. It was the most terrible thing I had ever done. I cannot explain why I did it . . .'

Joanna sighed. 'It is all right, Tilly. You have explained it well enough, for I understand.' It was true, for she could now reflect on her own impetuous desire to assert herself and to dare and triumph without thought of the end of the action. 'I have been half in love myself with danger for its own sake; with passion over common sense.' But whether she was talking of horses, or of men, it was hard to tell. She was not sure herself.

Falkes de Mauleon was hunting for Joanna and the horse as determinedly as Richard and Savaric. Unlike them he had begun on the eastern reaches of the high country beyond the river Stour and on the joint borders of Dorset, Hampshire and Wiltshire. He had reasoned that this was as far as the fugitives might have reached without being seen. Now he was moving slowly westward. As November had turned to December he had crossed the Stour at Blandford and begun to scour the country south of the Blackmoor Vale.

The land was high and wild and still thinly inhabited. It was a dry land above the shallow streams which chuckled over their clear gravel beds far below in the valleys cutting south from the chalk hills.

Falkes turned in his high-pommelled saddle and surveyed the mist rising from the vale. Already the sun was well down in the west as the afternoon sank through imperceptibly deepening shades of palest pink to dove-wing grey. In the twilight the furthest hills were hardly of greater substance than distant shadows.

He had ridden all day and was tired; his men were restless and cold and soon it would be time to turn for the shelter of one of the inns at Blandford or Sturminster. 'We'll ride across the head of that valley,' he said, pointing towards the north, 'and up on to the high land beyond, before heading back.'

Without waiting for them to respond, he jigged his heels into his horse's flanks and led the way down through the wooded slopes of the valley. As he rode he planned the next day's search, with the characteristic thoroughness he had always applied to every task, and was sure his cool calculations would eventually flush out his quarry.

Falkes had heard that the King was back in England. The bishop had been summoned to the Christmas crown-wearing at Oxford and Falkes hoped to have found Joanna by then. It would be quite a triumph to ride to meet the King with both Joanna and the stallion. Falkes knew that John appreciated a bold gesture and there would be none more striking than the sight of the bishop's marshal returning both the runaways. No doubt it would prompt the King into confirming de Mauleon's possession of the de Cantelo estates through marriage to Joanna. And no doubt it would make it more likely than ever that the stallion would cover the bishop's mares, in preference to those of the restless Templar knight. The bishop would be very grateful to Falkes for that.

The whole matter sounded well ordered and meticulously planned. It was very much how Falkes conducted his life, and he was determined to turn the plans into reality. Now all that remained to be done was to find the horse and Joanna. It was this which was on his mind as his horse splashed through the stream in the shadows of the valley bottom.

A movement on his left alerted him. There was a flash of colour amidst the trees. It was there and then it was gone. One of his experienced men-at-arms – a big man with a scarred leather face – had seen it too. 'Over there, my lord. Someone ran into the woods.'

'I saw it,' Falkes replied and was already turning his horse. Water rose in a fine spray as the hooves churned up the gravel bed. 'After them. I want to know who they are.'

The horsemen mounted the slippery bank and made for the trees but already the movement was hard to distinguish between the dark trunks. Ducking on to their horses' necks, they made into the woods. A branch struck the head of one of de Mauleon's men and he fell from the saddle. Undeterred, the others pressed on but the trees were thickening and the path through the woods was narrowing.

'It's no good, my lord,' the man who had seen the movement called out. 'We'll not find whoever it was now.'

Falkes pulled up his panting mount. 'You're right,' he conceded, disappointed but ever practical. 'Did you see if it was a man or a woman? And was it just the one?'

'I could not tell. They were too far off.'

'Neither could I,' Falkes said, almost consolingly. 'And it could have been anyone, frightened of strangers in the hour before dark. A pity, though – I would have liked to have confirmed who it was.' He peered into the gloom as if half considering whether to press on. 'But no matter,' he conceded at last. 'We'll turn back before we lose our way. We'll come back this way tomorrow.'

Slowly the horsemen retired from the wood. The one who had fallen remounted accompanied by the jeers of his mates and they recrossed the stream, winding their way up through the trees on the opposite side of the valley until they were gone.

Richard de Lacey and his two companions watched Falkes until he vanished from sight. They had come up on the brow of the very hill that Falkes had recently descended, while the bishop's marshal was crossing the stream in the valley. Like him they had seen the movement far below in the woods and had watched as the mounted searchers made their foray into the trees.

'Did you see who it was?' Richard asked, searching the wood with his eyes.

'No, my lord,' Mark replied, 'but I don't think they did either.'

'They're turning back,' Richard commented as he watched Falkes and his men come out of the trees and recross the stream. 'They have given up, and who could blame them?'

Umar was standing in his saddle and looking away from the retreating riders. 'My lord, I see the person again . . .'

'Where?' Both de Lacey and de Dinan spoke at once.

'Down there, where the trees thin out.' Umar pointed up the valley to where the woodland gave way to an area of coppice. 'See there . . .'

'Yes.' Richard's voice was raised with excitement, for even in the twilight it was clear that the fugitive was a woman. 'She has stopped and is looking back into the trees.'

Mark de Dinan pulled up his reins. 'If we ride along the ridge we can cut her off.'

'I agree,' Richard replied smartly. 'Umar, drop down through the trees, cut off her retreat into the woods. Then ride towards her and force her on. Mark, you and I will ride forward and descend beyond the coppice. We'll tie up our horses and wait for her just there.' He pointed with his riding crop to where a fresh patch of trees rose beyond the coppice in which the young woman stood. 'Now let's be sharp, or we shall lose her in the dark.'

While Umar dropped out of sight, guiding his horse down into the shadows, Richard and Mark rode along the ridge which was still cloaked in the last sunlight. At the head of the hill they turned their mounts and dropped down into the trees. Halfway down the hillside they dismounted and tied up their horses. Proceeding on foot, they slipped and slithered in the dark.

At last they were down on the valley floor. They could hear Umar's horse pushing its way into the yielding hazel rods of the coppice. Then lighter feet could be heard running between the coppice stools and into their wood. A woman – head covered – ran between the trees.

'Get her, Mark.' De Dinan was closest and leapt from his place of concealment. There was a scream, followed by a string of oaths. 'Damn – she's bitten me.'

'Have you got her?' Richard stumbled through the brambles to join his squire. 'Well done,' he said as he saw that Mark had not lost his grip on the captive. 'Now let's see who we've caught.' De Dinan manhandled his kicking and struggling prisoner, pulling down her hood as he did so. Little white hands clutched at the falling cloth and Richard caught a glimpse of big dark eyes and a pretty button nose.

'Who is it?' Mark was struggling to get a look himself.

'Well, well, well.' Richard's voice was a mix of excitement and satisfaction. 'It's the maid of Joanna de Cantelo.'

Joanna was very worried. Stephen had not returned that evening, nor had he appeared the next day. By this time both she and Matilda feared that the worst had happened. With the realisation that he had probably been captured, a great fear gripped them. Now they suddenly felt utterly vulnerable in the tiny settlement. As another dark afternoon settled into twilight they stared at the shadows creeping about the hamlet and waited for the enemy to pounce.

They heaped wood on to the hearth that night as if the light which kept the darkness at bay might do the same to their enemies. Neither of them slept well. The only consolation was that they were more united than before as a result of the frank talk in the stable. That at least was a morsel of comfort as they began to face up to the worst thing that had happened to them since the flight from the manor.

On the morning of the third day since Stephen had left they did not venture far from the little collection of buildings. By afternoon, though, their supply of firewood was running low and Tilly offered to collect some more. Soloriens needed exercise and so the two women parted company for the first time in two days. The separation was almost physically painful.

Joanna led the horse to the clear stream for him to drink. He still wore the blanket and leg bandages to keep him warm but the worst of the illness seemed to have passed. Then, reluctant to return to the gloomy little stable, Joanna hobbled the stallion and let him graze on the last of the grass in the mild shelter of the valley. She was glad to let the horse out for a long spell. Too much confinement in the stable at Horsingham and here had made him restless and constipated. A good afternoon in the fresh air would be only beneficial.

Sorely missing Stephen's assistance, Joanna mucked out the stable using a long-handled rake that they had discovered. It took her over an hour to remove the soiled bedding and replace it from the rapidly diminishing stock of wheat straw that the former owner of the farmstead had built up. Then she brought the stallion back inside to groom him.

The day was far spent when she had finished. Tilly had not yet returned and Joanna was beginning to feel uneasy. She built up the fire with the last of the wood and began to prepare a soup from the remaining dried beans and fat bacon, a far cry from the feasts on the manor. From the stable across the passageway the stallion snorted. Joanna put down her knife and listened; what had the beast heard? Rising to her feet, she went out into the yard. It was nearly dark and the surrounding trees were like a great black wall about the settlement.

Joanna heard a movement to her left. She started to step forward, then remembered the knife in the stable. She turned back to get it and a horse snorted – it came from the darkness outside and was answered by a neigh from Soloriens. Joanna began to run but at that moment a figure stepped from around the corner of the hut. Joanna made to duck through the doorway but she was not quick enough and an arm caught her neatly around the waist, lifting her from her feet.

It was late at night when William Catface was summoned from his bed by a group of crossbowmen carrying rush torches. They pushed into the hut, breaking the door latch. While his wife and children watched in terror, Catface was hauled away into the night. William could not fathom out why he was about to be killed, but it seemed fairly certain that that was what was going to happen. The men were grim and meant business and the most terrifying thing was that not a word was spoken as they dragged him through the night.

'Easy now, me lads,' he murmured in an attempt to ingratiate himself. 'Yer 'ave no cause to fear I'll run away. See, I'm comin' quietly. I ain't done nothing wrong . . .' The fearsome summoners made no reply.

Savaric was waiting for them by the open door of the stables. As William tripped over the cobbles he saw that Ranulf Dapifer was standing at the edge of the pool of light cast by the torches. Bewildered, the villein looked from steward to mercenary captain.

'I want a word with you and it won't wait until morning.' Savaric seemed uncharacteristically agitated, but William was too frightened to consider why this might be. 'I want you to forget something . . .'

'Well, sir,' Catface stammered, 'I've forgot it already. Can't recall a thing, yer . . .'

'Shut up, you fool.' Savaric was growing impatient. 'I'll tell you what you are going to forget, you bumbling idiot.' He brought his handsome face very close to that of William. 'You will forget absolutely that you told me about the boy Pierson. You will forget absolutely that he was brought back here . . .'

'Certainly, sir . . .'

'Because if you don't . . .' Savaric stared hard into Catface's eyes and bored cold tunnels into the frightened man's thoughts. 'Because if you should remember at any time, I will cut pieces off your body until you'll be grateful to me for killing you. And as for your disgusting little family . . .'

'I understand, yer honour. I never saw Pierson and I never told yer about 'im. I never said a word – not a word. I 'ave forgot completely – honest I 'ave.'

'Very good – but to show that I am a man of my word.' Savaric clicked his fingers and one of the soldiers brought forward a leather bag. 'Here is a little something for your trouble. And there will always be more for a man who can keep his mouth shut.'

William reached out his hand and took the money, feeling the reassuring weight of the coins within the bag. Relief flooded over him at the realisation that he was not about to die. More than that, he could hardly believe his luck, that a night-time terror had turned into the longed-for reward.

'Now get out of here.'

Catface needed no further prompting. He turned and squeezed between the men who he had thought were going to be his executioners. Halfway across the yard – before the gateway – he stopped. The cat-curiosity was too much and he just had to see. All about him was the cold night but the flicker of torchlight still illuminated a patch of ground by the door of the stable. As William watched, the soldiers went into the stable, to return a few moments later carrying something heavy in a horse blanket. It was hard to make out anything clearly but as the soldiers moved off into the darkness William saw a booted foot hanging limply from the blanket. He had a fair idea of what was concealed therein, and clutching his money he ran home, as if pursued by his own sins.

Richard de Lacey stood in the stable watching Soloriens. Mark de Dinan held a rush torch which cast grotesque shadows up and along the mud-daubed walls of the room. Umar was examining the stallion, while Joanna and Matilda watched silently from the shadows.

Richard could hardly contain his exhilaration. After all the weeks of searching, the stallion was his. It had been a simple enough matter to follow the pathway that Matilda had pushed through the wood on her outward journey from the hamlet of Woolcombe. It had been almost dark when they had reached the place, but at first glimpse Richard knew that he had found what he was looking for. And yet something gnawed at the edges of his triumph.

He approached the beast slowly and stroked the broad dappled back. As he did so he glanced at the young woman nearest to him. Her green dress was torn and crumpled and her hair fell in chaotic folds of fireside red about her shoulders, but the proud green eyes watched him openly and uncowed. They questioned him and their interrogation made his mouth dry.

He turned away from her, angry at his doubts, for there was no room for wavering now. At last he had found what he was looking for, and he would not be diverted from his purpose. At the first opportunity he would return horse and heiress to the manor at Horsingham. Then the King would look more kindly on his inability to pay the sum that he had promised for the covering of the mares. And after that – if he kept his wits about him – he might secure that breeding which had been his quest since he left the sun-bleached walls of Acre, so many months before. It would be a triumph despite the Templars and all obstacles thrown in his path. The route forward was clear enough and there was no denying it, so why was he so unsure? He simply did not know.

'The horse is a little out of condition but it will recover quickly enough.' Umar smiled, for he too could share in this triumph.

'What shall we do now?' Mark asked without intending the question to be particularly profound.

Richard frowned and looked once more into the young woman's clear green eyes. 'I do not know,' he replied, with a voice dropping low through tones of turbulent passion.

Mark and Umar looked surprised. 'My lord?' Mark queried, quick to notice the surprising tone in his knight's reply.

'I do not know,' Richard repeated more loudly. 'God help me but I do not know.' Then he turned and left the stable, with its flickering light and the horse that he had set his heart on gaining.

Ranulf Dapifer sat alone on the edge of his bed, the room cold and dark. He could not sleep and had at last given in to his restlessness. The world had gone mad and he could no longer trace a path through the insanity. As he ground his brows together he could not deny that he had contributed in some measure to the madness. The feeling of guilt battled with his anger at Joanna and Stephen for causing all his plans to go awry in the first place. He clenched his fists as his thoughts and feelings whirlpooled about him.

He stepped away from the box bed and groped for a jar of wine which stood on the only other furniture in the room – a low wooden chest. In the dark he poured a little of the wine into a pewter goblet, liquid running over the brim. As he raised the drink to his lips he realised that his hand was trembling.

'What is it, Ranulf?' his wife's timid voice whispered from the bed.

He started at the sound. 'Nothing, go to sleep . . .' He could almost feel her shrink away at his harsh tone.

Part of him wanted to tell someone – even her – about what was happening; to confide and seek consolation, even advice, for his dreams were in ruins and a boy was dead. Ranulf gulped at his wine and his throat worked convulsively as he struggled to swallow the liquor and his panic.

For the first time in his life he wanted to share himself but he had no idea how to. He had spent a lifetime building relationships that he would never need to rely on, and only now did he grieve for the total absence of companionship in his life. But now it was too late to do anything about it. He took another gulp of the wine and stared bleakly into the cold and unforgiving dark.

Chapter 12

It was shortly before dawn, at about seven of the clock, and the little hour candle which Joanna had brought with her from Horsingham had burned down to its lowest red ring. The room was cold, despite the blankets that covered her, and the piled up wheat straw. But it was not the temperature alone which was to blame for her restlessness, and she knew it. She had been awake for hours; awake even before the fire in the hearth had collapsed in on its own pyre of glowing ashes.

There was too much to think about to let her mind slip into sleep and even when she tried to relax, she found she could not stop from wandering remorselessly over the events of the past few days. And on each one of her mental wanderings she always passed the same milestones: Stephen's disappearance, the hours of anxious waiting, Tilly's foray for firewood, and then – the last milestone of all on this nocturnal journey – the previous night's arrival of Richard de Lacey. But for the end of a journey this last event seemed without conclusion, for she did not truly know where she had arrived at, or what would now be her fate. It was a journey's end which seemed to have more in common with a journey's beginning, but a journey into the unknown and the uncharted.

Richard de Lacey and his two companions lay wrapped in their riding blankets across the room from the two women, with only the dying fire between them. It was as the hour candle sank into its last ring that Richard stirred and threw aside his covering. He was – against all custom – as fully dressed as the rest were, against the cool of December. Joanna watched from the corner of her eye as he sat up and stretched, then stood up, wrapped his cloak about himself and went out into the pre-dawn dark.

Joanna waited a few moments and then threw aside her own blanket. While the others still slept she picked up her cloak and wrapped it around herself. Outside the longhouse the mist filled the valley with a thin sea of silver grey, but already there was a faint lightening in the darkness. Water dripped from the overhanging thatch as Joanna looked out of the doorway. Richard was nowhere to be seen but Joanna was undeterred – she had guessed that he had not gone outside.

Retracing her steps she felt her way down the passageway, already aware of the fresh glow of a candle from the stable containing Soloriens. As if further evidence was required regarding the whereabouts of de Lacey, she heard the low whicker of the stallion. A little stir of surprise rose in her that he could have won the trust of the horse so quickly, but then she remembered how he had approached the stallion back at the manor and she knew there was no reason for amazement.

Richard had lit a small candle and stuck it in its own wax on top of a broken wattle partition. He stood beside the horse's neck and was caressing the beast as it pushed its nose against him, wuffling contentedly as if to deny the killing power which was coiled within its massive frame. For a minute or two, Joanna stood watching the knight as he whispered to the horse and the horse nuzzled him, then she spoke.

'He does not fear you because he knows that you are not afraid of him . . .'

Richard did not turn. Instead he replied as if he had been half expecting her to be there. 'So you know that it is fear as well as strength that lies behind the urge to kill . . .'

Joanna moved into the stable and her shadow swayed across the dark recesses of the thatched ceiling. 'He is used to people being afraid of him and it prompts fear and anger in him. He kills because he knows that those who fear him would kill him . . .'

'Very deep, maiden,' Richard said a little teasingly. 'You should have been a philosopher in the east. There are few there as beautiful . . .' He stopped, suddenly unsure at the moment of familiarity between them and surprised at the looseness of his tongue.

Joanna had not noticed the significance of the silence. She laughed – quite unoffended – for it was in the same way that her father had both encouraged her comments and jested with her. 'But it is true, is it not? Fear breeds violence.' Without waiting for his answer she continued: 'But we are not afraid of him and so he does not fear us either.'

Richard continued to stroke the smoky mane but his eyes were fixed on Joanna's shadow on the wall as it shifted with the movement of the candle flame. The shadow of a girl so graceful and yet unafraid of the beast which could have snuffed her out with one surge of its great body. Richard could not help but admire such skill with horses. It spoke to his own experience and what was dear to him too. Yet for a few moments, as he watched her slim shadow, he found that he was not thinking of Soloriens at all. He wrestled with his straying thoughts and, with difficulty, brought them under control. He shook his head in despair at the complexity of the confused thinking which had replaced his once clear and simple determination.

'How long did you think that you could have stayed here?'

The question put an end to the informality of the moment and dismissed his own inner turmoil. Joanna frowned at the words. 'As long as it was necessary.'

'Necessary for what?'

It was the very question that Joanna had asked herself without being able to frame a persuasive reply. Formed by the lips of somebody else the question sounded even more disturbing, and nettled her. 'Until the King discovered how my manor was being destroyed and the way in which Savaric was treating us. Only by taking the horse could we make him look this way again. It was our only hope – there was no other way.'

'So you intended to blackmail the King . . .'

'I did not!' Joanna was indignant. 'I made no demands – only that he should stop Savaric from despoiling what is mine.'

'And that is not a demand?' The question was not put unkindly but it made Joanna stumble.

'I . . .' She hesitated. 'I did not demand it from the King.' The words did not sound very convincing now that they were out for public scrutiny. 'It was Savaric who was in the wrong and my demand was against him.'

Richard stopped his stroking of the horse and turned to face her fully for the first time. 'Your enemy was not Savaric, my lady de Cantelo, it was and is the King.'

'What do you mean, sir?'

Richard looked at her and for the first time realised how young she was, for all her woman's turn of the head and flash of the eyes. 'Savaric would not have acted as he did without the permission of John.' He raised his hand to halt the immediate response. 'Do not take my words wrongly; I am not implying that every insolence and every act of violence was ordered by the King, or the sheriff. What I am referring to is the generality of what has happened. John knew that your manor was being despoiled because it was his will that it should be so.'

He felt disturbed at the cold tone of his own words. It was as if he had to clear his mind of the lithe and alluring shadow and only a return to reality could do it. Yet he felt reluctant to do so; there seemed to be something in him that he could not put words to – something disturbingly out of place in his plans but something that had been growing over the few months since he had first really noticed Joanna de Cantelo. Something that had grown, whilst everything else had begun to collapse in upon itself.

'How can you know that the King would will these things?' Joanna's voice was slight and suddenly a little vulnerable.

Richard regretted the loss of intimacy that his words had caused, but he was committed now and concerned at his own regrets. 'Because it is the way that the King deals with wards.' Then, because he felt the expression sounded too hard, he added, softly, by way of explanation, 'He exhausts the resources of their properties then gives them in marriage to whoever is in his favour, or whoever pays him enough.' When he saw the pain in her eyes he added, 'But surely you knew this, my lady? Has he not yet sent word about your own future?'

Joanna stared through him as if fully occupied with events that were only now falling into place. 'I understand what you are saying,' she answered cryptically, avoiding the directness of his question. 'I suppose that I always did, only . . .'

'Only?'

'Only to accept that it is *all* as the King wills leaves no way out, no escape, no hope . . .'

'My lady, I am no stranger to that,' he said bitterly. 'For my hopes have been dashed again and again. I sought to serve the holy crusade and found it but a pack of curs and whoresons. I know what it is to live without hope . . .' The words made his hand stiffen on the back of the horse, and Soloriens shifted, sensing the tension in voice and touch.

'I will not accept it,' Joanna said defiantly. 'You may be satisfied with such a situation, but I am not. *I* cannot wallow in my own despair . . .'

'Good God, girl – you make it sound as if I am enjoying it.' Richard was suddenly angry.

'You talk of it so much that I doubt you would have conversation if you found yourself happy . . .' Her distress had made her careless and she suddenly realised what she had said; the enormity of her presumption. 'I am sorry, I should not have said that. I do not know what came over me.' The green eyes were wide.

Richard turned and began rhythmically to rub the horse. He felt twisted up with fury but did not know where to direct it. All his despair and confusion welled up within him. And yet now it was different, for he had been forced to face the turmoil more frankly than ever before. And what was more, in the company of one who had disturbed his peace of mind.

Joanna stepped beside him. 'I had no right to say what I did. It is just that I too have been under pressure and . . .'

'Perhaps it is time that I faced up to things,' Richard said very quietly, at long last. 'And perhaps you are right. Perhaps I have become drunk on my own pain and despair.' He did not look at her but his eyes watched her shadow once more as it moved on the wall. This time, though, he found he could not turn away from it, no matter how hard he tried.

'There must always be hope,' Joanna suggested, approaching him as carefully as a skater putting a foot on to groaning ice. 'Must there not?'

Richard felt a sudden emotion welling within him as she spoke, and was caught quite unawares. 'There *is* always hope, I know that you are right,' he agreed, though without any evidence to back up his consolation. 'There is always hope . . . It is lack of faith that has made me stumble.' Joanna stared at him and he felt something within himself crumble before the great green eyes. 'I shall not do anything to worsen your situation – trust me,' he added quickly and was surprised to hear the words, for what had she got to do with him? 'Trust me,' he repeated a little less convincingly, and she nodded, warily.

'What are you going to do with us?' Joanna was very careful now but still she had to know.

'I have not yet decided . . .'

Joanna took a deep breath. 'Surely the choices are quite clear: you can return us to Horsingham and to Savaric, or take us to the King and let him deal with us as he wills. What other option do you have?'

Once more he was thrown back on his own defences. 'You have a way with words, Joanna de Cantelo,' he replied, forcing himself to laugh. 'But I have not yet decided.' His answer sounded as inadequate as her reliance on the King's justice; indeed it sounded even less convincing.

Falkes de Mauleon arrived at the inn in Blandford when it was dark. It had been a hard ride from the downland valley with its shadowy wood; a ride in which he had considered the next phase in his careful search of the high country for the missing ward and the precious horse. Night caught them before they crossed the gravel ford of the Stour and it was with relief that they stabled the horses and made to retire to their room and a light supper.

'We will rest tomorrow,' Falkes said quietly to his men, 'and then the day after we will leave and stay in the high country.' He saw the look of disappointment that they would have to miss several days of the twelve-day Christmas festivities in the bishop's household while they searched the combes and spent nights bivouacked in the shelter of trees. 'So sleep well tonight and make the most of it,' he added, as if this concession was enough to make up for their deprivations. 'And when we have found the horse . . .' he smiled, 'and the lady de Cantelo, safe and sound, there will be celebrations enough to make up for the loss of this festive season.'

The men-at-arms nodded, aware that it did not matter what they thought but appreciating the comradely turn of de Mauleon's mind which made him give the impression that it did. However, when Falkes returned to his lodging, he found two tired and slightly irritated messengers waiting for him with a sealed letter. Falkes recognised the seal at once and did not need the words of the carriers to identify where the message had come from. He broke the seal and bent beside the roaring fire to illuminate the words. He read the letter twice before he straightened up.

'I will return with you in the morning,' he said to the travel-stained riders. 'And I shall see that you are fed and bedded well tonight.' Then he turned to the most senior of his men-at-arms who was cleaning mud from his master's boots. 'We will ride at dawn, so see to it that the horses are well watered and rested tonight. They will have a hard day's ride tomorrow.'

'Yes, my lord.' The man, with a face like creased leather, was disappointed at the news but hid the look as best he could. 'I shall see to it at once.' He knew he had no say in the matter.

Falkes reached for a jug of hot, spiced red wine. 'I fear they have no white, but this will lift the cold from your bones.' He pushed out a steaming goblet and the air was rich with the mingled scent of cinnamon and cloves. 'Let us drink to the good health of the King and to the defeat of his enemies.' He lifted his drink and his companions did likewise. 'And to a good journey to see him – God's blessing on us all.'

'To the King,' they replied and all three drank deeply.

Falkes' narrow grey eyes betrayed little of what was passing behind them and he made no attempt to press his visitors for more information as to why King John had summoned Falkes de Mauleon to the crown-wearing at Oxford. Perhaps, though, he had hopes, for there was a rare light in the grey depths which signalled a clear pleasure at the royal summons. And as he sipped the hot drink, he thought of Joanna de Cantelo. The thought was indeed a pleasurable one, for she was a beautiful young woman and stirred Falkes. And then he thought of Soloriens and of the fine manor at Horsingham, and the pleasure deepened.

Richard de Lacey could feel the sheer power of the horse rippling beneath him. He had wanted to ride Soloriens ever since he had first set eyes on the beast, and the experience was no disappointment. Carefully – mindful of its value – he picked his way up the track which led out of the combe and on to the higher ground above the deserted hamlet. Clearing the last of the trees, the more open country unfolded before him, quite deserted. He pushed his heels into the dappled flanks and let the horse have its head; it galloped across the downland turf, hurling up great clods of earth in its wake, the ground throbbing beneath the insistent hoof beats.

After about half a mile he gently drew back on the reins, lifting the proud head, no longer constrained by the imprisoning martingale with which it had been bound when he had first seen the stallion at Horsingham. They had ridden far enough for exercise and Richard was wary of straying too far into the downs. 'Easy, my prince,' he called as the careering progress was brought to a halt, the stallion snorting with irritation at the end of its wild run. 'I doubt that you have run this far and fast for some time.' He leaned forward and patted the high-crested neck. Then he stared out over the deserted countryside, eyes alert to any movement but there was none.

Behind him, Joanna de Cantelo, mounted on Richard's own horse, and Mark de Dinan and Umar finally caught up with him. The horses milled together, snorting and neighing with excitement, the air about them a mist of visible breath. Mark stood up in his stirrups and – like his master – surveyed their surroundings for any sign of life.

'He is magnificent!' Richard said, with feeling.

'You speak as if you doubted it . . .'

Richard laughed at her chiding. 'Never!' he said as he caught his breath. 'But no stretch of the imagination could reach as far as actually riding him. He is amazing, with such grace and yet such power . . .'

'Worth a king's ransom, my lord.' Mark eyed the stallion with admiration. 'And before we saw him we would have thought our own palfreys were fine mounts and our Arab destriers the best in the world. But now . . .' He looked at his knight as words failed him. 'Hugh de Lusignan is a lucky man . . .'

Richard frowned at the reminder of the true owner of the horse. 'Yes, Mark,' he said reluctantly, 'that he is.' He sat back in the saddle and was thoughtful. 'Watch out for strangers,' he said, gesturing into the empty expanse of rolling grass and trees. 'Be twice as alert by day as you have been by night.' Their eyes shared a mutual concern. 'We will ride on, to that knoll.' He pointed with his crop towards where a swelling rise of green was topped by a knot of beeches. 'I pray that you will ride with me, my lady de Cantelo.' His calm voice concealed his alert and tense mood of wariness.

'Have I a choice, sir knight?' Her tone was guarded and it was hard to know if she was being provocative or genuine.

Richard glanced at the knoll and then back at her. 'Of course you do . . .' Then he jabbed in his knees and Soloriens sprang forward, snorting through suddenly flared nostrils.

Umar glanced at his companion, as the other two rode away. 'I think that my lord de Lacey loves the lady de Cantelo.' It was rare for Umar to speak so openly but the weeks of searching had softened the edges between him and de Dinan.

Mark was incredulous. 'I think not!' It nettled him to have such a thought articulated by someone else, for he knew there was no place for a woman in their plans. It also disturbed him because he was not convinced by his own denial. 'Richard de Lacey has a mission. You know it as well as I do. You have ridden the same roads as he and I and you know how he feels about the horses and about the east!'

Umar wondered if he had been a little too open in his thoughts. 'Perhaps you are right,' he said enigmatically. 'But . . .'

'But what?' A little of the old edge had returned to Mark's voice, for he felt that whatever had changed between them, the

Saracen groom was straying on to forbidden ground. 'But what?'

Umar leaned forward and patted his horse. 'I had thought that my lord de Lacey looked at her very caringly.' The fire rose in de Dinan's eyes. 'Though no doubt I am wrong.' Umar fell silent, deciding that he had indeed gone too far.

'Yes,' Mark agreed, but with no warmth in his voice. 'You are no doubt wrong.'

He frowned, for it was hard to hear such thoughts put into words by the groom. Whatever the debt that Mark owed the man and whatever the companionship that had grown between them, it still did not allow an alien – even an accepted one – to say such things about Mark's knight. To say things that Mark thought himself but could not admit to be true. A little of the old gulf opened between them as the two sat in a sudden and tense silence. Neither looked at the other; instead they followed the galloping progress of the two objects of their thoughts.

Richard did not glance back until he reached the knoll, though he could hear the sound of the hooves of Joanna's mount behind him. Ducking, he cantered through the fringe of trees, avoiding the outspilled earth of a badgers' sett which hollowed out the roots of the greatest of the beeches. The centre of the knoll was open to the sky and it was as if the trees provided a tightly spaced amphitheatre for their conversation. He let Soloriens rest as Joanna came up beside him, her eyes never leaving his face, her unbound red hair rolling free over her cloaked shoulders.

'Richard,' she asked, her voice serious, 'will you do something for me?'

'If I can.'

'Find out what has happened to Stephen.' The great green eyes were full of concern. 'I must know that he is all right. He is always before my thoughts. Will you find out that he is safe?'

Richard admired her concern for a loyal servant. 'I will do what I can, though I must go carefully, for Savaric has a nose like a fox and will sniff his way back to here if I am not careful.' Then he glanced away from her, before she could discern the concern which his prudence concealed.

'Thank you, for he loved me and the horses more than anyone except my father and Tilly.'

Richard patted Soloriens. 'Well, you and he have taken good care of this horse since . . .'

'Since we stole him?'

'As I said before, my lady de Cantelo, you have a way with words. But since you framed it so well, I cannot deny it. You have looked after him very well since *you* stole him.' Richard leaned back in the saddle. 'I know how much you love him . . .'

'I love all of the horses,' she said frankly.

'I know you do. The way he responds to you shows the depth of your love and your skill. You love the horses as I do.'

'I know, and I too have seen your skill with him. They,' she disparagingly referred to Savaric's men, 'handled him with the skill of a pig sewing a tapestry. You handle him as one who understands the magnificence of what he sees.'

They stared at one another, appreciating the genuineness of their mutual praise. At last, Richard broke the silence. 'I have staked all on returning this horse to the King.'

Joanna nodded. 'I remember the conversation that we had at the Silver Well; Jerusalem calls you . . .'

Richard sighed and looked away. 'A lot has happened since then,' he replied ruefully.

'Can you tell me?'

'I can . . .'

'But *will* you tell me?' she added with a raise of her fine eyebrows and the familiar lift of the firm, precise chin. '*Will* you tell me, Richard de Lacey?'

'Why not, Joanna de Cantelo,' he said after a moment's consideration. 'For I seem to have blurted out enough to you already. And I did not know you at all then.'

'Whereas now?' She was studying him closely, although there was a tremble in her fingers on the reins.

He ignored her probing question. 'The King has promised me the right to breed from this horse, in return for a very large sum of money that I have promised him.' He laughed and suddenly the trees were ringing with his mirth. 'Only I do not have the money to pay him . . .'

Joanna shook her head. 'You are joking?' Then she laughed too, caught up in his foolishness. 'You're not, are you? Holy Mary, you really have not got the money!'

'That's about the long and the short of it. I have not got the money. My Templar allies have clearly decided that, for matters of politics too complex for a simple knight to understand, they will no longer fund me. I am about as welcome at Temple Buckland these days as a begger with the itch.'

'So that is why you have not simply returned there with me. It's been three days now since you discovered us. I was beginning to imagine that the simple life appealed to you and that you intended to live out your days in my humble cottage.'

'Well, a deserted hermitage might have its appeal, you know. In fact, anywhere where I might stay out of John's clutches, for I think that he will be sore stretched to see the funny side of my predicament.'

He tried to make a joke of the situation but the humour was strained, for he had more than his financial problems weighing on his mind. Now he was responsible for the safety of Joanna de Cantelo and for three days the worry about their predicament had lain beneath his masquerade of firm confidence.

The brutal reality was that there was not a more secure place for them to hide while he decided what to do. To make matters worse, it was risky to stray too far from the hamlet for fear of being seen. Richard felt uneasy at the lack of room for manoeuvre. In an attempt to reassure himself he had posted Mark and Umar at the head of the combe each night to keep watch for intruders. The undisturbed solitude had finally persuaded him that Falkes had not recognised the fleeing figure of Tilly in the dark woods. Or else why had he not reappeared? The thought brought some consolation and a greater sense of security.

More worrying still was the disappearance of Stephen. Unknown to Joanna, Richard had already dispatched Mark to Horsingham but there had been no sign of the groom and the squire had reported that the soldiers on the manor were unfriendly but seemed frustrated. The realisation was slowly dawning on Richard that, whatever the fate of Pierson, he had somehow contrived not to give away the place where his mistress was hiding. That thought brought some comfort and hope for them, though offered no encouragement regarding the groom's safety.

'I did not imagine that you would take to such a simple life.' Joanna would not let him escape into his own worries or their consolation.

Richard shook the concerns from his head. 'It has its compensations when compared to the anger of the King.' As he replied, he considered how – if their hiding place was discovered – he could claim to have found her first, intending to bring her in; that way something of the initiative would remain with them. There seemed no other way out. 'My options are limited,' he said as he gave Joanna his full attention again, relaxing in the certainty that he was doing the right thing in staying at the hamlet.

'You could always return the horse to John and throw yourself on his mercy,' she suggested, very serious now. 'For in such circumstances he might overlook your financial problems.' Richard nodded. 'So why, pray, have you not done so?'

'It would mean returning you to Savaric.'

'What is that to you? You would still have the use of the horse and your dreams would still be intact. So what does it matter to you if I am returned to the manor?'

Richard coughed. 'That is a very good question.' He raised his head to see the naked branches stir in the lifting breeze. 'I am not unimpressed with your courage,' he began softly, 'and it would seem a poor reward to be thrown back to the tender mercies of Savaric and his boys . . .'

'Falkes de Mauleon would no doubt look after me, so you need not fear for my safety.' At the mention of the bishop's marshal, Richard looked at her very sharply. It was an action which pleased her. 'I did not tell you before, but John intends that we should be married.'

At the mention of his rival's name, Richard sat up as if stung by a wasp. Soloriens started at the sudden movement of his rider.

'You never mentioned this before?'

'I hardly knew you, so it did not seem relevant. Besides,' she added casually, 'I hardly know you now. But it seemed only fair to put your mind at rest.' Joanna smiled with a fair degree of satisfaction, for, from the look on the young knight's face, the unexpected news brought nothing approaching peace of mind.

'I had no idea that you were affianced.' Richard glanced through the trees at his distant squire and groom and was suddenly aware of the closeness of his female companion. 'If I had known that you were contracted . . .'

She did not let him finish. 'I am not contracted to him – yet. It is just that he has told me that he is confident he knows the King's mind in this matter. But I am not yet affianced.'

'He is a very confident man, is Falkes de Mauleon,' Richard commented with a curiously jagged edge to his voice. 'A very confident man indeed.' Then it was as if he had finally resolved some difficult matter in his own mind, for he pulled up his reins and nodded as he looked at Joanna. 'It is time we were getting back,' he said and drew his horse away.

Together they rode out of the knoll and down to where de Dinan was waiting for them. 'Do you wish to ride back to the hamlet, my lord?' Mark enquired.

'I do.' There was a note of finality in the voice which made the squire knit his brows. 'We will be staying here for some weeks – at least until after Twelfth Night.' When Mark looked surprised, Richard added: 'We will need more supplies and more hay for the horses.' Turning to Umar he said curtly: 'Tomorrow you will need to ride to Sturminster to purchase them.' Umar nodded and tried not to look at Mark de Dinan.

'You have made up your mind then,' Joanna said quietly. 'But what good will come of staying here like this? And what of the King and your promise?'

Richard did not answer her question. Instead, he reached out and laid one gloved hand on her arm. 'Do you love him?' When Joanna reddened at the forwardness – and indeed the irrelevance of such a question preceding a noble marriage – but did not reply, he nodded. 'I understand.' Then he moved away from her and they rode back towards the hamlet which was hidden in the fold of the downs.

Ranulf Dapifer's mind was not on the preparations for the Christmas festivities. As he checked through the accounts of the butler and pantler his mind was wandering and he found he could no longer concentrate his thoughts. Despairing of the attempt, he dismissed the other servants and went outside.

A weak December sun was shining and the weather was mild, although it was St Thomas' day and only four days before the great winter feast. He was intensely restless but knew it went deeper than the results of the previous day's fast. It was more than a hunger for food that disturbed Dapifer – it was a hunger for peace.

As he crossed the yard he ran into Savaric. 'The King has sent a summons,' the mercenary commander said stiffly.

Ranulf went whiter than a bank of hoarfrost. 'He has not . . . he cannot have . . . You hid the body too well . . .'

Savaric shook his head and sneered. 'Do not be a fool. He knows nothing about Pierson and would care less if he did so. But I have no doubt that he wishes to hear of our progress in the search for that bitch . . .' There was no disguising the frustration and anger in the mercenary's voice; it was as obvious as Dapifer's fear.

Ranulf made no attempt to rebuke the soldier. 'You will tell him that it was not our fault, won't you? Mention that I did all that I could to ensure her obedience.'

'Of course I'll tell him that it was not our fault.' Savaric did not sound overly confident. 'Though he is not renowned as an understanding man. But as to your glorious part in all this, I doubt if he has the tiniest interest.'

'But . . .' Dapifer wanted to beg Savaric to speak up for him; how else would he ever be noticed? 'But you know I have done all that I could to help you.' The mercenary just laughed and walked away.

Ranulf was left standing in the yard with a pulse twitching in his cheek. He wished that he had never set eyes on Savaric de

Breaute. He wished that Joanna had kept to her place. He wished and wished . . . Unable to face the business of the day, he wandered off towards the fish ponds. As he walked, he ran through all of the ways in which he had been of service to the Crown. Then a horrendous thought struck him – what if Savaric told the King that the steward had not prevented the escape of the girl and the horse? The thought ferreted away at his overstretched and desperate mind. What if Savaric passed the buck and ruined everything for him?

Ranulf sat on a damp tree stump, feeling sick as he considered the ruin of all of his plans. Then another thought struck him – what if he was to reach the King first? What if he was able to tell the King about all the terrible things that *Savaric* had done, and how he, Dapifer, had done his best to safeguard the manor? Surely the King would listen to such an appeal? And surely if he, Ranulf Dapifer, was to accuse Savaric of the killing of Pierson, then he would be excused of blame? The questions and the desperate answer went round his mind like a weasel after a rabbit. When he rose from his perch he was resolved to do it; it would have to be done quickly, though, for Savaric intended to set out for Oxford the very next day.

Falkes was pleased that the King had summoned him to Oxford, but was disappointed to discover that he had to wait several days before he was brought into the royal presence. Being a man of spartan habits, he was ill suited to whiling away his time with the whores and pedlars who hung about Woodstock Palace like bees about a comb of honey, whenever the court was in residence. It was not that Falkes was overawed by the grandeur of the place and the occasion. After all, as marshal of the Bishop of Salisbury he was used to hordes of John's servants and household descending on Old Sarum whenever John came hunting at the nearby palace of Clarendon. No, Falkes was not overawed; rather he was bored waiting, and eager to return to his hunt for Joanna de Cantelo.

One morning after mass he decided to walk about the pools and garden that John's father, King Henry II, had built around the complex of buildings at Everswell. Here amidst the date palms and the orangery he could spend some time anticipating what John would say. He had scarcely started his walk when he was accosted by an armed man who announced himself as one of the marshals of the royal courtyard and responsible for escorting Falkes to the King. Far from being disappointed to have his stroll interrupted, Falkes was delighted that he was finally to be admitted to the royal presence.

They found John in his private chamber dictating to a bevy of scribes. Hubert de Burgh sat in a window seat eating a sweetmeat. John waved the clerks away as Falkes was brought in. 'I have wanted to see you for some time.'

Falkes noticed that he was not being offered any wine and wondered if his pleasure at the summons might have been misplaced. 'It is my honour to be here, my liege.'

'I know that,' John said a little slyly. 'I want to talk about a girl and a stallion.'

'The lady de Cantelo . . .'

'Is there another who would steal my horse and humiliate me before my enemies?' Falkes said nothing. 'I take your silence for agreement.' John narrowed his dark eyes. 'I want that damned horse, de Mauleon, and I do not care how I get it. Do you understand me?'

'I do, my liege.'

'I wonder if you truly do. Explain it to him fully, Hubert.'

The royal chamberlain put down his unfinished sweetmeat. 'The situation in Normandy requires the safe conduct of that horse. It is important to keep the Lusignans loyal, and the King will brook no embarrassment in this matter.' De Burgh shook his heavy jowls. 'Furthermore, the King is surprised that you have anticipated his royal pleasure with regard to the lady de Cantelo . . .'

Falkes swallowed. 'My lord?' He tried hard to sound very calm, knowing that they would scent weakness. 'I do not understand.'

'Do not treat me like a fool.' John cut in on his chamberlain, his anger rising like a dark sea. 'I will not be made a fool of . . .'

'By God's body, I would die before I did such a thing,' Falkes said firmly. He noticed that de Burgh was smiling a wolfish smile as if enjoying the sight of someone else experiencing disfavour. 'I would never do such a thing.'

John laughed, and the sound was bitter. 'I know that you have spoken to Joanna de Cantelo. I take that as presumptuous.'

'I meant no such thing.' Falkes felt that he was on quicksand, the ground shifting beneath his feet. 'I meant only to . . .'

'It does not matter what you *meant*,' John said sharply. 'The fact is that you presumed on my decision.' He clapped his hands, and spiced wine was brought to de Burgh and himself. Pointedly, none was provided for Falkes. 'Never do that again. If you want to regain my pleasure you will bring me the girl and the horse, assuming that you still want the girl. If not . . .' The sentence ended ominously short of a specific threat.

'The King is busy,' de Burgh said before Falkes could reply. 'You will go now . . .'

'I shall have the stallion by Candlemas,' Falkes said quickly. 'Have no fear of it, my liege.'

'Oh,' John smiled a thin smile. '*I* have no fears whatsoever.'

Falkes bowed and left. When he had gone, John laughed again. 'And what news of the Templar?'

De Burgh frowned. 'Nothing since we accepted his offer, my lord.'

'What?' The anger was back.

'I will see that the matter is pursued . . .'

'By St Peter's chains, you will. I will not be messed with, de Burgh. Let them all know that. I will not be made a fool of, or there will be blood. Do you hear me, de Burgh, there will be blood.'

Umar ibn Mamun led the great horse from the broken-down stable and into the bright winter sunshine. Once outside, he groomed the horse carefully as he had been ordered to do. As he did so he thought of the wild scene that he had witnessed on the quay in Normandy, on the first occasion that he had seen the stallion. It felt like a lifetime ago.

'We understand each other, you and I,' he whispered in Arabic as he brushed straw from the fine mane. 'You are a prince amongst horses and you would never do harm to one who gives you as much homage as I do.' He smiled as the stallion turned its head and pushed against his shoulder. 'Easy with your caresses, or you will push me over.'

'You have it bewitched.' Mark de Dinan had come out into the yard and had been watching the Saracen groom for some moments. He found that he felt a little jealous of the way that the groom could charm the horse. He was more aware of the feeling since the Saracen had dared comment on Richard de Lacey's motives, as if the fracturing of the truce between them had allowed still-unresolved springs of resentment to seep to the surface. Mark wished that he was not in the man's debt but did not allow the thought to colour the tone of his voice. 'You have him in the palm of your hand,' he commented, and then, as if to put the praise in its proper perspective, he added, 'A skill nearly as impressive as that of my lord de Lacey . . .'

' . . .or the lady de Cantelo?' Umar volunteered.

'Quite so,' Mark agreed, resentful again, for the groom's mention of Joanna only served to remind de Dinan of the tense conversation they had shared while waiting near the wooded knoll. 'She is quite an astonishing woman,' he added, as if to disguise his thoughts. Umar nodded. 'Is he nearly ready?'

'Just a little longer,' Umar advised, 'and we shall be at your service.'

Umar sighed; for a while now there had been an easier atmosphere between Mark and himself. The charge of thunderstorm static had seemed to have died away. Something more resilient had taken its place; something less threatening. It had happened in the weeks following Umar's saving of Mark's life and the grudging gratitude of the squire. A growing respect had seemed to replace the hatred Mark had shown openly before. Umar had known it would never be close friendship but it had been better than the burning animosity that had once gripped de Dinan. Now, though, the squire seemed on edge again and Umar regretted his own openness about Richard.

While Umar groomed Soloriens, Richard and Joanna appeared

from amongst the trees, chaperoned by Matilda, who walked a dozen paces behind them. She was smiling as she followed her mistress and the knight. She felt more at ease now in Joanna's presence and away from the judging eyes of the groom, whose safety she feared for and yet whose presence had become a constant reminder of her failure. What was more, Richard knew nothing of her disgrace and treated her with genial disinterest. It was an anonymity that she welcomed after the bitter notoriety that had clung to her. She continued to smile to see her mistress and the knight talking low as they strolled. Matilda, like Umar, had seen the way that Richard looked at Joanna.

When de Lacey saw the horse, he nodded in approval to his two men and they nodded back. Joanna looked puzzled but before she could speak, Richard anticipated her words. 'Mark and Umar are going to exercise him today . . .'

'Again?' she queried. 'They take him out for such long periods. Do you think it is wise, for what if he is seen?'

'It is good for him to get used to others than just us two. And Umar leads him on a rein, so I am not pushing the relationship too far; not that I am doubting his ability to handle the beast.' Richard treated her anxious question as if he had not even heard it.

'We are ready to go, my lord.' Mark led out both his and Umar's palfreys.

The two men mounted the fine riding horses and waited for Richard's command. He patted Soloriens and then waved them away. With Mark de Dinan in the lead they slowly walked their horses up the narrow trackway that led on to the downs, watched from the hamlet by Richard, Joanna and Matilda.

'When I have my manor back I shall breed many like him,' Joanna said as the trees closed behind Soloriens.

'You will do it, I have no doubt,' Richard said with approval.

'Somehow,' she confided. 'But what about you? What will you do?'

She found herself no longer wanting to hear what he was planning. Suddenly it did not matter any more because for all her talk of the future she was enjoying the present too much. He was warm, and funny when he wanted to be, yet passionate about what mattered to him. She had come to enjoy his company even in the unlikely setting of the deserted valley. Now was enough and she did not want to talk of when they would have to leave the hamlet. There was only one thing which blighted the moment, and she was determined to speak of it with de Lacey again, but in a moment or two, not now.

'What will you do?' she said again, not caring if he answered her question.

'I no longer know,' he said, brushing mud from his boot. 'I once built a lifetime on my dreams of glory, and then a Saracen crossbow bolt put an end to that.' He sighed and shook his head. 'But I know better than to beg sympathy from as hard-hearted a woman as yourself.' She laughed and he continued: 'And then I built my life again around the Templars and this crusade and now that too seems to have fallen apart.' He grinned a lopsided grin. 'No doubt you are amazed by my ability to construct such enduring plans.'

She laid a hand on his arm. 'You are too hard on yourself, Richard,' she said.

'You think so?' He spoke to her openly as he had done at the Silver Well, although there was less of the fragile and bitter disappointment in his voice. Its absence surprised him. 'I feel sometimes that I have not been hard enough. How else can I explain the failures that have followed me?'

Together they walked down beside the stream that gurgled through the narrow combe. At last they reached a sheltered spot where stumps of trees stood back from the path and the winter sunshine warmed the glade.

'It was hardly your fault that a Saracen shot you, was it? And hardly your idea that the crusaders should abandon their high calling and sell their swords to the Italian cities against the emperor. Even you cannot be so vain as to think they did it just to spite you!'

The well-aimed jibe made Richard laugh. 'A fair point, but it is sometimes easier for another to say it than for oneself to see it.'

'Oh, I know,' she agreed. 'My father always told me that my

genius lay in giving good advice to others and ignoring it when it came to myself.'

'I think I would have liked your father.'

Joanna looked down to where the sun played upon the mist lower down the combe. 'You would have loved him as I did. Everybody loved him.' She looked up at the knight and was smiling. 'I have not talked about him this way to anyone since he died. I have not thought of him with joy, only with sorrow that God took him from me.'

Richard nodded. 'And I have not talked of my disappointments before. It is a strange providence that has thrown us together like this.'

She nodded. 'It seems to me that life is not always what you plan it to be . . .' She stopped to consider her next sentence. 'None of this is how I thought it would be,' she said with a laugh. 'I never thought, nor wished, to be secreted away in some verminous hamlet stealing a horse from the King. Things do not turn out as we plan. But it is up to us and our faith in God either to be destroyed by them, or to take another path . . .'

She wanted to add: 'And if it had been as I had hoped and expected, then I would never have met you,' but she fell short of the shocking and disrespectful impertinence. She blushed at the mere thought of the words and looked away. It was a reticence quite new to Joanna de Cantelo and it surprised her.

'Your father was right, you know. You give good advice.'

He wanted to say something else but did not, because he did not know what it was. The absurdity of the situation puzzled him, for he felt the force of thoughts, as water behind a dam, but could not frame the words to release the pressure. It was because the words expressed a feeling that was so alien to him as to be almost sacrilegious. As he faced up to the enormity of his disappointment, he now found he was beginning to cope with it. And this despite the enormity of his hopes now in jeopardy and the depth of his alienation from the Order in which he had resolved to sink his pain and his life. As yet he could not express how such a situation was possible but the more he considered the conundrum, the more he knew it was intimately bound up with the red-haired girl opposite him.

'I must ride down to Dorchester tomorrow, for I have some business there which will not be put off much longer.' He glanced at her but she did not press him for more information, and he smiled. 'I fear we have not had much of a Christmas feast this year but I promise that I will find a way to make up for it.'

'Salt bacon in pease pottage was not the usual seasonal fare at Horsingham,' she teased him, 'but I have survived it well enough.' Then she added, a little more seriously, 'Not that I intend to make a habit of it.' It was funny how even the squalor and sparsity of the place did not seem quite so galling to her any more.

'Well, it will not go on much longer.'

Joanna was thoughtful for a moment. 'I am *very* worried about Stephen Pierson. Please find out what you can about him. I have no doubt that he has been held on the manor by Savaric. Even that brute would not dare openly to harm him, for he knows that would be going too far, but I must know . . .'

'I will do my best,' Richard said consolingly. 'There are those in Dorchester who know everything, believe me. If anyone knows, then they will know. And if not – I shall send Mark to the manor.'

Richard did not add that he had already done so but that de Dinan's visit had turned up no sign of the groom. He did not want to distress her if there was a less sinister explanation than the one which lingered on the edge of his thoughts.

'I have lost track of the days since Christmas,' Joanna said, watching a magpie flaunt itself in the naked trees.

'It's Thursday, January the seventh, the day after Epiphany,' he said cheekily.

'I know it's the day after Epiphany,' she scolded him. 'I feel like a Queen of Misrule living in this world turned upside down, so it's not likely I should forget Twelfth Night. It's the days of the week that have blurred.'

'I know. Time has flowed so fast since we found you, and yet I feel as if I have been here for months.' Then, unsure of where the sentence was leading, he drew her back to the subject in hand. 'I'll ride down tomorrow. Friday will be a good day to see the man I have business with. He will be less willing to see me come Saturday,' he added cryptically. 'And I shall take Mark with me and let Umar exercise the stallion while I am away.'

'When will you return?'

'I shall be back, God willing, on Saturday night.' The look on her face pleased him and he added, 'I shall hardly be away any time at all.'

'Good,' Joanna said, almost inaudibly, but he heard it and smiled.

William Catface was not a happy man. When he had counted out his money he had discovered that Savaric had cheated him. There was far less than half the silver pennies that he had been promised for the capture of Stephen Pierson. Not that he had complained, for he had decided that being cheated by de Breaute was an occupational hazard. Nevertheless it rankled, and though it met his debts his Christmas was not spent in the high living that he had promised himself. Furthermore, he felt bad about what had happened to the groom. It had never occurred to him that the soldiers would kill the lad; from the way that they had acted it seemed that they had been taken unawares by their own handiwork too.

On the Friday after Twelfth Night, Catface decided to go poaching. He was feeling restless and the weather was mild so the darkness beckoned to him again. As well as that, he had picked up a nasty rat bite on his rump and it made sleeping difficult. While his wife and children slept, he tugged his gnarled old bow and a handful of arrows out of the thatch and slipped out into the night.

Up in the sheltered dell where he kept his unlawed dogs, he found the two hounds as hungry as ever within their ramshackle kennel. Fondling their lopsided ears, he untied them. One was the dog that had killed Gilbert de Cantelo, and William could not help but recall that distant morning when the dog had turned the life of the manor upside down. Tucked away under the brambles of the dell was an old leather scrip in which Catface kept more of his illegal gear. He slung it over his shoulder and padded off, followed by his dogs.

Together, William and his dogs wandered for most of the night, enjoying the cool air and the hooting of the owls in the woodland below the more open brow of the downs. As he walked, the sky began to clear and a thin crescent moon appeared amidst the ragged clouds. He pulled his threadbare cloak about himself, for it was turning colder.

Despite the change in the weather, he determined to be out for a day and a night away from the fetid hovel that he called home. As it was, it seemed that his determination was justified. For just after dawn he brought down a deer far to the east of Horsingham; in a place that he would never have reached if he had turned back to the manor at the usual time.

It was a four-year-old fallow buck with a good head of antlers. In his scrip he kept a little wood-saw which he had purchased off a man in the hamlet years before. The poor-quality blade was pitted with rust but there was still sufficient bite on the serrated edge. Methodically he set to work on the antlers, sawing off the proud horns. It took him a while to complete the task, but it was time well spent; he could not afford to have them catching on every branch and bush that he passed. With a sigh he took the two detached trophies and tossed them far over the lip of the slope. They fell amongst the trees like fallen boughs.

'Now, me boys,' he muttered to his dogs, 'let's be 'avin' yer, for we've a pace or two before we gets to where we're 'eaded.'

He checked that the coast was clear before he followed the edge of the woodland eastward. To the south the rolling hills and clumps of trees were already beginning to emerge from the pale lilac-grey of the freezing morning mist. He had decided to take his quarry to the hamlet in the combe, where he could hide it away from prying eyes and deal with it at his leisure. It seemed wiser than hauling the deer back towards Horsingham now that it was getting light.

Joanna and Tilly stayed around the longhouse after the men had left. Umar had taken the great horse away onto the downs for exercise. It had turned unusually cold in the night and they sat close to the fire on the hearth.

'Do you like him, my lady?' Tilly hardly looked up from the fire as she asked the question.

'Who?'

The maid glanced up at the obvious attempt to appear innocent. 'I think that he likes you. He is always looking at you, my lady.' Something of the Tilly who always had an eye for gossip was returning.

'You still have not identified the object of our conversation,' Joanna said, making no attempt to assist the probing curiosity of her companion.

'Why, Richard de Lacey, my lady. You must have seen how he gazes at you! He is a fine-looking man and there's no doubt about it!'

'The fire is burning low. If we do not put more wood on it we will freeze tonight.' Joanna stood up and brushed down the creased folds of her battered gown. 'Put on a little of the pottage and I will get the wood.'

'Yes, my lady.' Tilly grinned as she did so, for Joanna had rarely volunteered to get the wood before. The fact that she had chosen this very moment to do so gave Matilda all the answer that she needed. The maid hummed softly to herself as she stirred a handful of beans into the pottage.

Outside, the mist had not risen even though it was well after dawn. Icy cobwebs hung in silver swags from the stiff silver eves of the frozen thatch. The stones were sheened with ice and Joanna trod carefully, feeling the grass crackle underfoot. The store of firewood lay in one of the smaller cottages and, wrapping her cloak tightly about her body, Joanna went to get some. It was while she was on her way back that she heard the noise in the woods.

She stood quite still and listened to the clear, crystal silence. There it was again – the unmistakable sound of movement higher up the combe. A dog barked and there was no doubt about it any more. The firewood clutched to her breast, she ran back to the longhouse. She fell in the icy yard but struggled to her feet again, ducking her head as she ran into the dark passageway.

'For God's sake, Tilly, someone has found us.'

Matilda was on her feet, the pottage knocked over and spreading into the straw and rushes on the beaten-earth floor. 'Who is it, my lady?'

'I do not know, but we must get out of here.'

Together they ran into the passageway but Tilly collided with her mistress who had stopped at the doorway. 'They're in the clearing, I saw one coming out of the trees. Quick – back inside and hide.' But there was nowhere to hide and they cowered in the darkest corner of the room after having dashed a jug of icy water on to the glowing fire.

William Catface entered the house warily. He had heard movement and knew that someone was there. 'Who is it?' he called out, half afraid and half annoyed to have found his hideaway discovered. 'Who the bloody 'ell is it? Out with yer, I'm armed, yer bastards. Out with yer . . .' In the ill-lit room it took a while for his eyes to adjust, and it was some minutes before he saw the women in the corner. 'Get up and show yerself. An' who the 'ell are yer?'

Joanna stood up, defiance replacing her fear. 'I am Joanna de Cantelo. Who are you?'

'Bloody 'ell.' Catface almost dropped the deer which hung over his shoulders. 'It's yer ladyship . . .'

Outside, the dogs were barking and he turned to shout at them, but the words were stopped in his mouth, for he heard male voices and knew that he had been followed. The voices were unafraid and loud, in accented Norman-French.

'Get down, you cur . . .' one of the voices outside shouted, and a yelp of pain signalled a blow dealt to one of Catface's dogs.

Another voice shouted: 'We've got the whoreson, whoever he is. Led us right to it – stupid sod . . .'

'It's Savaric's men,' Catface whispered to Joanna in his best French. 'They've been an' followed me . . .'

'Well done,' Joanna replied bitterly. 'No doubt there will be a substantial reward for you.'

A curious look passed over Catface's small features and his snub nose twitched. He turned away, then twisted back towards Joanna. He stared at her intently, as if trying to resolve some terrible dilemma which threatened to tear him apart. Then he was off and out, like a hare startled by a dog.

Outside, the soldiers leapt forward to grab him. 'It's just me, lads. I'm comin' quietly,' he yelled as they grabbed him, dragging the deer from his shoulders.

'It's a bleedin' poacher, the little git from the manor,' one of the soldiers yelled, cuffing him. 'Caught yer this time, you little bastard. This'll teach yer to sell us sour wine.'

'Never on purpose, yer honour,' Catface pleaded, warding off a kick but failing to intercept another one. 'Have pity, boys . . . An' yer'll recall I fixed yer up with some fine girls . . .' It was to no avail.

'And I thought we'd caught that stuck-up bitch and Savaric's whore,' the soldier muttered bitterly. He gave William another savage kick to vent his feelings. 'That'll teach yer to nick the King's deer . . .' The poacher doubled up with pain and was kicked again. 'Get the bastard on his feet, there's no point in hanging about this bleedin' dump. There's no one about here, or this little runt would be trading information for his poxy life . . . Get the little sod on his feet . . .'

'I thought I might 'ave seen a sight of 'em aways back, yer honour,' Catface pleaded. 'An' I could show yer . . .'

'You must think we are as stupid as you are. Yer'd have told us long ago if yer'd seen anything. The likes of you would sell yer mother for a handful of pennies.'

Catface stood up unsteadily and glared into the face of the taunting soldier. Out of the corner of his eye he saw one of the other soldiers idly peering into the doorway from which the little poacher had emerged. In a moment of inspiration, Catface spat full in the face of his tormentor. The ruse worked, for after that the soldiers had only one thing on their minds and that was kicking William Catface into a bloody mess and then dragging him away into the freezing, dark woods.

★ ★ ★

Ranulf Dapifer had set out from his overnight stop at a manor just off the Wiltshire Ridgeway, and had followed the high track north-eastward into Berkshire. He estimated that it would be another two days' ride to Oxford. He was desperate to get there and pour out his story to the King; it was, he had decided, his only hope.

But now he was afraid, for he knew that he was being followed. Far behind him two riders kept pace with him. As the track rose he would glance back and see them; as it fell again they would be lost to view, but he knew that they were always there. He took his lunch in the saddle and did not rest his horse. By late afternoon, as the twilight gathered, he was very frightened, for they seemed to be closer.

It was on a stretch of the track which was badly rutted that his horse fell. He had been pushing it too hard and it lost its footing and hurled him to the ground. For a few minutes he lay senseless, until the seeping cold brought him round. He could see at a glance that the horse had broken its leg, and in panic he began to run, stumbling and plunging into ice-rimmed puddles.

Stopping to catch his breath, he looked back down the track. The riders were nearer now and were catching up with him. Ranulf gasped as he recognised them. 'Oh God,' he cried. Then he was off the track and into the woodland, running for his life.

Back on the track, Savaric and his companion pulled up their horses. 'It's him all right,' Savaric murmured. 'Go out wide on that side,' he motioned with one gauntleted hand, 'and I'll follow in from the left.' The two riders pushed their horses into the bushes.

The track was deserted and no one passed as night shadows crept amidst the trees. The day was almost spent when the two soldiers returned, this time together.

'I can come back and bury him if you want,' the soldier offered casually.

'Don't bother,' Savaric said contemptuously. 'He's not worth the effort. He was nothing . . . Let the wolves have him.' He bent and wiped his knife blade on his horse's blanket. 'Just a little man with big ideas who couldn't take the pace when it came to it. And now he is a dead little man.'

The other soldier laughed. 'You can say that again. Funny thing, though, he was so frightened I think he was almost relieved when we finally caught him.'

Savaric nodded. 'Ever watched a rabbit with a stoat? It just freezes and watches the stoat come for it.' He laughed. 'It's so gut-scared it can't wait to get it over with.' Then he laughed again. 'Well, he was just a rabbit . . . And now he's a dead rabbit.'

Behind them, in the dark woodland, Ranulf Dapifer, steward of the de Cantelo manors, lay twisted up in the ice-sheened bracken. One hand still clutched at the tear in his cloak where the knife had passed through. His eyes stared at the canopy of trees, to where a single star blinked coldly through the black filigree of branches.

Chapter 13

William Catface was beginning to regret his moment of self-sacrifice, and the regret increased as he and his captors drew ever closer to the royal hunting lodge at Gillingham. He stumbled along between two of his tormentors, who seemed to delight in his discomfort and pain.

'Get a move on, yer bastard, or we'll beat you up again,' one of the soldiers remarked menacingly, then laughed as William did his best to increase the pace of his movements.

'I'm goin' as fast as I can, yer honour,' the poacher muttered in a desperate attempt to sound willing and to ward off another thrashing. 'I'm doin' as yer told me . . .' he pleaded in his best Norman-French, of the type he normally reserved for his social superiors, when they deigned to notice his humble existence. He recalled bitterly that it was for these very men that he had procured girls and wine and run little errands. 'I'm goin' as fast as I can, sir . . .'

'Well, it's not fast enough!' The soldier turned like an adder and struck William a glancing blow. The poacher tumbled into a ditch, white with hoarfrost, to the delighted whoops of the mercenaries. 'Clumsy oaf,' his tormentor scolded him. 'Yer ran into me, stupid pig.'

'I'm sorry, sir,' Catface whispered as the wet earth and bracken soaked through his thin woollen tunic. 'I am a clumsy pig all right . . .' Then he staggered back into the ditch as a booted foot caught him in the ribs.

The leader of the party of Savaric's men watched the brutality with detachment, until at last it looked as if the diversion was going to slow them down too much. 'That's enough,' he finally intervened. 'We've got to dump this rubbish on the King's foresters and then it's back to the manor. Savaric'll be back soon and he won't appreciate time spent having a bit of sport while that bloody girl and stallion are still on the loose.'

The mention of Savaric concentrated minds with amazing speed. The soldiers stopped their games and the participant in their sport crawled – bloody and battered – out of the cold ditch.

Prompted by the reminder of Savaric, the party speeded up their progress and reached Gillingham just after noon. The mist had lifted and the stockaded lodge was hung with dripping silver cobwebs. It stood on a slight knoll cradled in the outstretched arms of the Fern and Lodden brooks, with the flat land of the vale stretching about it. Catface collapsed, panting, while the leading soldier smartened himself up.

'Is the King here?' one of his men asked.

'Don't be an idiot,' his superior replied. 'If Savaric has gone to Oxford, how can the King be here, ferret brain?' He surveyed the soldier with contempt. 'The King keeps four huntsmen here and a housekeeper the year round.' He turned his attention to Catface for the first time since the incident at the ditch. 'Ever been here before?' he asked maliciously.

'No, sir,' Catface said very quietly.

'Well, yer'll be here for a while, so I hope that it takes yer fancy. I've heard that it can take a year or two before the forest justices get around to trying miserable little poachers like you.' Catface made no reply. 'But I doubt yer'll be able to pay the fine that they fix on, so yer might be here even longer. I hope the place is to yer liking.' Then, shifting his attention, he barked an order. 'Get him on his feet, we've got work to do.'

A reluctant and slow-footed William was hauled to his feet and dragged over the timber bridge across the Fern Brook, the stockade of the lodge seeming to rise before him, set behind a double bank and ditch. An armed guard was leaning from the brattice suspended over the gateway. The leader of Savaric's men called up to the man in the covered gallery, but Catface could not hear the words. Instead, he was desperately twisting round to look away from the royal lodge. A couple of miles to his left a clear, abrupt ridge rose, on the edge of which the towers and walls of Shaftesbury teetered, as if about to cascade into the vale. Catface stared at it desperately, his eyes clinging on to the world outside the threatening stockade with its gates opening like a monster's mouth. Yet, despite his fear, he did not cry out that he knew where the girl and the stallion were hidden, and so it was in silence that he vanished into the mouth of the monster.

Richard de Lacey did not return on the Saturday night as he had promised. Instead, it was late on the Sunday afternoon that he and Mark de Dinan rode north across the rolling downs. The sudden cold snap of the previous Friday had passed and the milder weather had returned. It was the evening of Plough Monday and as they passed the isolated hamlets they could see the ploughs being prepared for the next day's ploughing-in of the corn dollies. But Richard had other things on his mind as he rode towards his destination.

The sun was low in the west as they dropped over the lip of the hill and ducked beneath the trees that shielded the deserted hamlet from prying eyes. As they broke through the screen of trees and heard once more the chatter of the brook, the first thing that struck Richard was the silence of the place. He swung down from his horse and was astonished to see Umar appear, like a shadow, from the trees across the brook.

'What is this game?' he asked in a curious tone. 'Twelfth Night is past now and we've no more licence for foolish . . .' He stopped mid-sentence as he saw that Joanna and Tilly were emerging from the trees behind the groom and that Joanna was leading Soloriens. 'What game is this, Umar?' The humour had gone from his voice, for he knew that something was very wrong.

Joanna slipped the leading rein to Umar and ran to meet Richard, her hair flowing about her shoulders. He took her in his arms, delighted, shocked and surprised. 'What is it?' he asked as she embraced him.

Suddenly aware of how forward she had been, Joanna drew away from his embrace. 'Thank God you are back.' Despite the recovery of her decorum, her relief at his return was clear.

'What has happened? This is more than a hearty welcome after

I have been later than I promised! What has happened?'

Joanna drew a long breath. '*They* came here . . .'

'Savaric! In God's name, what happened?' Richard held her wrist in an automatic action, as if to stop her being taken away. 'By Our Lady, how is it that you have not been seized?' The very thought turned his stomach. 'Thank God for it, but how did you escape?'

Joanna felt the strength of his grip on her wrist but made no attempt to draw away this time, for he was as forward as she had been and she no longer felt foolish. 'Come inside by the fire, for it is quite a tale. Come,' she said softly when he seemed reluctant to let go of her. 'For I am safe now – you are back.' The look on his face was ample enough reward for this unguarded revelation of her feelings.

'You are right,' he conceded, 'we should go inside, for it's getting dark.'

Inside the longhouse, the fire was a heap of wet ashes and it took a while before they could restart it with fresh kindling. 'We put it out when we heard your approach,' Joanna explained as Umar and Matilda attended to the task. 'Umar was keeping watch in the woods and gave a call that riders were coming.'

'Tell me,' Richard said firmly, and Joanna retold how they had been surprised first by the cat-faced villein from Horsingham and then by the rude arrival of some of Savaric's men.

'So you see,' she concluded, 'we were within their grasp and they failed to catch us.'

'And all because the poacher refused to betray you. That is astonishing, because Savaric has put out a high reward for your capture and no doubt it will be even higher now that he has been summoned to the King.'

'What is this?' Joanna was intrigued.

'It seems that our friend has gone to see the King at Oxford, though I do not suppose that it is a social call. No doubt John will have made it clear to him that he wants the horse back in double-quick time. The King is not a man who looks kindly on the failure of others, so I should imagine Savaric will come back with a hornet behind him. But enough of this . . .' Richard turned to Umar. 'So you returned to find all this had happened?'

'Yes, my lord,' the Saracen answered from where he was breathing life into a flickering and fragile flame. 'I brought the stallion back just before sunset, though by that time all had come and gone and I could offer little protection.'

'But you took precautions thereafter,' Richard noted with approval.

'I did as I thought you would have wanted, my lord. We kept the fire low and I kept watch in the woods. We feared that the men might return again. Perhaps they might have remembered something and come back.' It was rare for the groom to speak so much and he seemed surprised at his own fluency.

'He did well, did he not, Mark?' Richard looked over at his squire, who seemed to be looking at Joanna in a concentrated way.

'It was well done,' Mark said quietly, shaken from his private thoughts. 'We did not know that they were watching in the woods and they kept the stallion quiet.' It was praise well deserved but, coming from Mark – and following the disagreement over Joanna – it was precious. Umar nodded his thanks and Richard put an approving hand on his squire's shoulder. That at last brought a smile to Mark's otherwise serious features.

'Yes, Umar,' Richard concurred, 'you did well.'

'It was the lady Joanna who worked wonders with the horse.' Umar was not one to hog undeserved praise. 'She has the way with him and he is like tallow in her hands, to be moulded as she wills.'

'I know.' Richard smiled at Joanna, who blushed only a little paler than her hair.

Seeking to escape from the unusual state of embarrassment, Joanna asked Tilly: 'Have we pottage ready for all of us?'

Tilly grinned. 'It will take only a little time to warm through, my lady. And I have some of the salt bacon that we were saving. We can have a feast to celebrate our escape.'

'There,' Joanna said laughingly to Richard, 'we have salt bacon and two-day-old pease pottage. Who could ask for more?'

'I can think of nowhere else I would rather be, my lady,'

Richard replied, 'neither in palace, nor hall.' Despite the damp in the thatch and the poor fare, his voice carried conviction. For it was more than the food that was stilling the ache which had churned in his belly for months and years.

Falkes de Mauleon returned to the West Country on the eve of Plough Monday, 10 January 1204. For a man usually well composed he felt decidedly rattled. He gathered his companions at the bishop's palace at Old Sarum, in Wiltshire, and the next day rode westward into Dorset. He had gained the bishop's permission for a three-week leave of absence and was determined not to squander the time. He had promised that he would have the girl and the horse by Candlemas, which left him only just over three weeks to fulfil his promise.

He and his men took a drink at their usual pothouse in Blandford and Falkes briefed them regarding the nature of their quest. 'We are going to ride for every hour of daylight, so as to maximise the time available to us. That means we will be up and out before dawn every day until we find the horse. The King wants it back and I have promised it to him.'

The men-at-arms glanced at each other and Falkes noticed the look. 'Quite!' he said, summing up their response. 'John is not a man who takes pleasure in empty words and the situation in Normandy has done little to lighten his mood. As a result we are going to find them ahead of anyone else and deliver them to the King at Gillingham for Candlemas. Now what have we heard in my absence?'

One of his men coughed. It was the man who had alerted Savaric to the watcher in the woods at Horsingham; the winter wind had weathered his face and a scar ran from one eye to his mouth. 'It seems Savaric seized the boy who went with the lady Joanna.'

'Really?' Falkes could not hide the disappointment in his voice that the capture of Stephen Pierson had not fallen to him. 'When was that?'

'I do not rightly know, my lord. We heard the rumour from a shepherd coming east along the Stour. He said that a lad looking like the groom had been picked up by some of Savaric's men. There was nothing else and we thought it futile to enquire at Horsingham.'

'Quite right, Savaric would have told you nothing. A pity, though . . .' Falkes mused. 'If only we had taken the lad . . . But it is no matter, for we are going to find the horse.'

He took his cup of wine and poured a little of it on to the wooden boards of the table. With a crust of bread he drew a wavy line through the puddle. 'And this is how we are going to do it. This is the line of the downs . . .' He tapped the line he had made. 'We are going to work in pairs: one pair riding to the north of the slope and two pairs riding south of it, in the high country itself. We will ride as far as Cerne and then reverse it. I know that they are in there somewhere and we are going to go backwards and forwards until we flush them out.'

'The lad that Savaric took was going to Sturminster.' One of Falkes' men offered the observation.

'Really?' Falkes replied. 'Which implies that they are somewhere between here and Horsingham, as I had imagined. And not too far either side of the edge of the high ground. They must be within half a day's walk of Sturminster . . .' He looked at his own crude map and imagined the open countryside in winter, the dark woods and the hamlets and farmsteads with smoke drifting through the thatch. 'And we have another advantage – it seems that Savaric has also been summoned to Oxford. He must have arrived as I was leaving, though I did not see him, so we can get to work before he returns.'

'We could break the boy out of Horsingham,' offered the scarred retainer who had volunteered the earlier information.

Falkes considered the option. 'If need be, we will do it. But I'll not rush into breaking into a manor in wardship. The last thing we need is an open war with Savaric.' He paused as he recalled John's words at Woodstock and realised that Savaric would do all that he could to obstruct his plans and betray him to the King. But he would not succeed, for Falkes was utterly determined to get the stallion and of course the lady Joanna de Cantelo, and no one was going to prevent it.

Falkes thought of Joanna and her green eyes and red hair. It was a thought to quicken the desire in any man and Falkes was no exception. But *he* was a man who had his desires under control, and as he thought of Joanna, he also thought of the manor and the horses; of his own plans. The memory of Horsingham reminded him of something else, and he frowned slightly. 'Any news of the Templar; has he been searching too? Have we heard where he is and what he is about?' He mopped up the wine with his bread as he asked the question of his men.

'Nothing, my lord.'

'Nothing?'

'He seems to have vanished. We have not seen anything of him since you left.'

All for the best, Falkes said to himself; but he was not convinced that he had seen the last of Richard de Lacey, or his outrageous offers for the use of the stallion which had been stolen. One thing he was sure about, though, was that he, Falkes de Mauleon, was going to regain Soloriens and take Joanna de Cantelo as his own. And as well as winning Joanna, he would soon be lord of the de Cantelo manors.

It was sunrise on the day after he had arrived back from Dorchester, and Richard took the stallion out above the hidden valley. He did not ride alone; Joanna was beside him and Umar an escort at a discreet distance. As the light spread across a sky scattered with mackerel clouds, they came once more to the little wooded knoll. At a signal from Richard, the Saracen groom stood off and let his horse graze at the tufts of grass.

'I must speak with you.' Richard and Joanna were in the centre of the copse. 'And what I want to discuss with you is for us alone to consider. I do not want to talk of it yet in the hearing of the others.'

Joanna urged her mount a little nearer. 'Has it come from your visit to Dorchester?'

'It has, though it has more to do with us than I led you to believe. And that was not because I wished to cover my plans, but because I needed to establish something.'

'To do with *us*?' Joanna said the words very quietly but the emphasis was not lost on Richard.

'I have found a buyer for eight of my Arab destrier mares. Aaron of Dorchester will purchase them and will pay a fair price.'

'What?' Joanna was stunned and confused. 'Why are you selling the mares? And what has this to do with us?'

Richard paused before answering her question, replying at last, 'I can raise seventy pounds in cash against the sale of the mares . . .'

'But why? Why are you doing this?' Then a look of understanding dawned on her and her high, fine cheeks coloured, though she was well out of the cold wind. 'Oh, Richard . . .'

'All my life I have chased after something and yet never found peace. Since I was wounded, I have found that the things I have searched for and built my life on have fallen apart in my hands.' He paused to look at her. 'I thought I had nothing else left to live for. I thought that God had deserted me and I was desolate; my heart withered within me and the fire which drove me on had begun to consume me.

'Then hunting for the high horse brought me to you. It was a stranger turn of providence than I had ever experienced before and at first I did not know it.' He laughed incredulously. 'As God is my judge, I fear that at first I did not even see you – all I could see was the horse and my dreams collapsing . . .'

'I had noticed that.' Joanna smiled at him as she spoke. 'Do you remember how at Sherborne Abbey you almost ran me down and then looked right through me?'

'Pardon me for being a fool, Joanna . . .'

'You are pardoned and you were not a fool. To tell you the truth, I noticed you because you ignored me, so there's a strange twist, isn't it?'

Richard nodded. 'As you once said, we may end up where we did not intend to go. But I swear to God I would not have gone any other way, because if I had I would never have met you.'

The two fell silent, for neither had yet stated why the horses were being sold and yet both knew exactly why: one because he had planned it and the other because it was as she had finally come to hope it would be. Richard dismounted and reached for Joanna, drawing her down from her horse. Without a word they tied the animals to the branches of one of the encircling trees.

At last Richard broke the silence. 'It was as if I was half awake and so walking in two worlds at once. In one my plans to which I was clinging were melting away, and all the time I was moving into another world – seeing you, noticing you as if for the first time. And for a while I was in both worlds – half awake and half asleep. But now my eyes are fully open and I know what reality is. I love you, Joanna, I realised that when I finally found you – and this horse – for I discovered I could not hand you back to Savaric, or the King, in order to gain what I had desperately striven for. It was then I woke up, then that I finally recognised what had been happening to me over the weeks and months before that point. I love you, Joanna de Cantelo.'

'And you are prepared to sacrifice all that you have worked for in order to buy me from the King.' It was less of a question than a statement and Joanna's green eyes were shining with a joy that Richard had never seen there before. 'You truly are a knight without equal. The kind of passionate fool that my father would have loved . . .'

'And what about you?'

Joanna shook her head. 'You know as well as I do that that is of no consequence. The King will not consult me before he gives me in marriage. Did Falkes de Mauleon ask me if I loved him – though he is, no doubt, a desirable man? It is of no . . .'

'Do not jest with me, Joanna.' Richard cut her short. 'I am not King John and I am not the bishop's marshal. And it *does* matter to me if you love me. God knows, everyone else will laugh at me for it, for what has love got to do with marriage? But it matters to me, Joanna, though the good ladies and knights of the court will tell you that the highest and purest courtly love can only be had from afar, by craving the unobtainable – like another man's wife!'

He could not take his eyes from her as he spoke. 'But I am not that way. I am no Lancelot desperate for another man's Guinevere; I desire to love my wife and be loved . . .'

'Richard de Lacey,' Joanna scolded him, 'you do not know

when to stop once you get started. Of course I love you! I was intrigued by you, then amazed by your skill with the horse, but my love for you is more than this. You are a handsome and a brave and a passionate knight and I could not wish for a more noble husband than you.'

'Thank God for that,' Richard exclaimed, 'for I could not live without you.'

'But will the King accept your offer, and what about Falkes de Mauleon?'

At the second mention of the bishop's marshal, Richard frowned. 'I do not know what John will accept but I have taken good advice from Aaron the Jew, of Dorchester.'

'Ah, the money-lender. I have heard of him.'

'He has eyes and ears everywhere,' Richard confided, 'and he says that Normandy is lost.' Joanna gasped. 'Believe me, if he says it then it is true, though it sounds impossible to believe. The French and Bretons have broken all John's defences. It seems that he has come to England to collect money to buy more swords; he will press more pennies from the barons and the Jews, and then return to Normandy this summer.'

'But you said that the duchy is lost . . .'

'Aaron believes that the King's efforts are in vain. Already it seems that the greatest lords who hold land in both Normandy and England are coming to terms with the reality and are preparing to swear fealty to the King of France in return for their French lands. John's efforts are his last attempt to put off the inevitable, and one that seems sure to fail; but the point is – he needs ready cash.'

'Your seventy pounds . . .'

'Exactly! It is hardly a king's ransom but it will buy swords for this summer's campaign. It is said,' and at this point he lowered his voice, although they were alone, 'that the King is desperate for men. It is rumoured that he has offered knights two shillings a day to fight for him in France. But he is equally desperate for the money to pay them . . .'

'My father said – though he loved him much – that the King's brother Richard and their father Henry left little enough in the royal exchequer for John to be king on.'

Richard smiled. 'He was a shrewd one, your father, for there's truth in what he said. John has always lacked money, the way that he lacked his brother's looks and his luck, though few will blame the dearly departed and would prefer to make John the guilty party. Anyway, the point is that he needs money like a drowning man needs air, and I doubt that Falkes de Mauleon can match what I will offer the King for you.'

Joanna could hardly believe the pace at which events were moving. She felt her mind racing. 'When will Aaron the Jew have the money?'

'He has said that I should return before Candlemas and it will be available. Then we will take the horse and the money and ride direct to the King. Aaron says that the court is travelling to Gillingham to hunt before John returns to Normandy, and that will be our chance.'

'Will it be enough to persuade the King and to cover up his anger at me?' Joanna was beginning to count the possible cost of her flight in the face of the King.

'I think it will be enough to cover the entry fine for your coming into your inheritance, and to pay the fine for the taking of the horse and your marriage to me. I think it will be enough. If not, then I shall have to find more.'

'More?' She looked amazed and excited at the generosity and abandon of his feelings for her.

'I will find more if I have to, but we shall not cross that bridge until we come to it.'

Joanna stepped towards him. 'I would go through it all again if it was the price of finding you . . .'

Richard took her in his arms and kissed her, their mouths merging and melting together as he folded her body against his own. The wind brushed the tops of the trees and the horses nudged their riders, but nothing could stir Richard and Joanna from the passion of their first kiss.

At last Richard raised his head and she laid her cheek against his chest. 'I dread to break the beauty of this moment,' he said gently, 'but you must hear of this.' She looked up at him, realising that his tone had changed. 'I think that Stephen Pierson is dead.'

'At the hands of Savaric? No, I cannot believe it. He would hold him prisoner but he would never dare to . . .'

'I cannot be sure, but I think it was an accident . . .'

'An accident? In the name of God, how can they have killed him by accident?' Joanna's grief and outrage was the more intense for the moment of tenderness that had been shattered by the unexpected news.

'I went with Mark to the manor on our way back from Dorchester; that was why I was late. Savaric was not there and neither was the steward . . .'

'Ranulf Dapifer.' Joanna pronounced the name with a rare note of bitterness. 'He goes where Savaric goes, for they are close allies and as thick as thieves.'

'Well, this Dapifer was not there, but neither was Pierson. We were given a very cold welcome by Savaric's men and I began to wonder what it was they were so carefully hiding. Well, as you can imagine, no one would talk to us, but we had the luck to run into a ploughman working that heavy soil that passes for earth at your manor and, for a silver piece, he admitted to knowing Stephen, which did not surprise us.

'What did surprise us, though, was the terror that the mention of his name produced. For another silver piece we got a garbled bit of gossip about something terrible that had happened the night following Stephen's return to the manor.' Richard paused to let his words sink in. 'But there was nothing more, and even our pennies could not open his mouth. I am sure that they killed the lad, probably trying to discover where you were hidden . . .'

Joanna wept. 'If what you say is true, then he has paid a heavy price for my gesture of defiance. Oh, God forgive me for what I have caused.'

'It was not your doing. Savaric must be punished for his own evil and, believe me, I will see that he pays every last crumb of what he owes.'

Joanna nodded through her tears. 'But that will not bring Stephen Pierson back.'

'No,' Richard agreed solemnly, 'it will not bring him back. But still, Savaric will pay, believe me – he will pay.

William Catface sat in the tiny wooden-walled cell and watched a rat scurry into a corner. It was damp and cold in the room and the only light came from a high, narrow barred window. The room contained no furniture of any kind, and the packed-clay floor was poorly covered with straw, some of which Catface had scraped together into one corner to pass as a bed.

On the ground before him a wooden bowl contained a thin cabbage soup which tasted of grease and sweat. With one patched boot he pushed it away in disgust. As he contemplated the room, he once more decided that keeping silent about the lady de Cantelo had been an act of utter foolishness and one which seemed to grow more terrible with each passing hour.

'I should never 'ave spit in 'is face,' he mused bitterly. 'They'd 'ave just done a bit of kickin' if I'd not done that. They brought me 'ere 'cos I done that,' he sobbed to himself. But then, he reminded himself, if he had not caught their attention, they would have looked in the cottage and found the girls. 'An' what had that to bleedin' do with me, bloody fool as I was?' he cursed himself, knowing that it was that moment of self-sacrifice that had brought him to the gaol in the hunting lodge.

'Well now, Will me lad, at least they won't cut bits off of yer.' The thought gave him some consolation as it was common knowledge that in his great-grandfather's day *they* most definitely would have cut bits off him. Nowadays it was money they were after. William sighed, for he had little enough of that; far too little to pay the huge fine which would be levied on him and his squalid little home.

At the thought of this he began to wonder if his wife and children had heard yet what had happened to him. He had no means of contacting them, nor they of reaching him. He felt wretched and deeply depressed and longed to face the rats and mice in his little house, where at least the soiled straw was his own and his wife and children were nearby. A little tear ran down his cheek, for the downturn that had started with the death of the cow had turned into a bottomless trough of darkness.

'I should never 'ave turned 'im in, not to they bastards.' Catface could not get the memory of Pierson's body out of his mind, nor the guilt, which was strange, for he considered himself free from sentiment. 'God knows I never meant 'im no 'arm. All I wanted was the price of that bleedin' cow . . .' Now his sins had caught up with him and he was convinced that he would die in this rotten, stinking hole.

Richard, Umar and Mark de Dinan rode to Dorchester two weeks after Richard and Joanna spoke at the wooded knoll. They left at dawn, though Richard had been out in the damp woods at prayers since midnight, in support of the task he was about to perform. The three rode in silence, contemplating the enormity of the gamble they were going to take. Richard was rehearsing the words that he would say to the King, while his squire was engrossed in thoughts of his own. The task was one that Mark found very unattractive for it involved a visit to Aaron the Jew. Mark had made an exception in the case of Umar, due to circumstances of particular courage and loyalty, but it was not a gesture of magnanimity that he was prepared to extend to all aliens. And even that gesture was wearing thin the more Mark contemplated the debt of honour that he owed the Saracen.

He was of course honoured that Richard had chosen him to ride on a mission that was of great importance, though that mission gave him qualms. He knew by now what Richard was planning and had been astonished at the news. The realisation that Richard was about to saddle himself with debts in order to marry the girl was difficult to accept. Mark was prepared to admit that she was a beauty, for no one could deny that, but was not convinced that any woman was worth what Richard was about to do. As he rode he decided that he would never fathom the mind of Richard de Lacey, but that was as nothing compared to his utter loyalty to his knight. He did not need to understand, he told himself – only to obey. But still, he was very troubled by the overturning of all their plans.

Umar was thinking of the horses, the fine, hot-blooded horses that they had brought from the east and that were now going to be sold. He was silent because he would miss the horses and because, like Mark de Dinan, he could not fully understand why a man like the knight would gamble all for a woman. Try as he might, Umar could not puzzle it out. And yet he was not entirely surprised, for, unlike de Dinan, he had always been able to recognise the spark of impetuous passion in the knight whom he now served for nothing.

At the remembrance of that, he could not help but grin at his own folly. He was careful, though, to turn his head away as he did so, for he did not want Mark to see him smiling at such a serious juncture. Umar was no fool and knew that the young man was beginning to chafe under a debt owed to an outsider – even one who had been allowed, by the strangest circumstances, into the hallowed ground of comradeship that the squire shared with his knight.

So it was, with each in his private reflections, that the three companions rode the high, wild track. On Richard's instructions they rode first to Temple Buckland, dropping down on to the manor before mid-morning, while the convent Templars were returning from mass to their duties about the manor. The reception offered to the returning knights was frosty, and Richard stopped only long enough to leave a message for the commander of the convent that he would soon be returning to remove eight of the destrier mares currently stabled at Buckland and that, within the month, he would be leaving the convent for good with the remaining two Arab horses. The relief on the face of the brother knight who took the message was sufficient to remind de Lacey that he was now on his own.

As Richard left his message, Mark collected their gear from their quarters and strapped it on to two hairy little cob horses. Then they left, and from Temple Buckland the three riders took the steep road which wound up on to the high ridge which divided the valley of the rivers Piddle and Cerne. The sun had broken through the clouds and warmed the ride a little. The journey south was broken at the abbey of Cerne, where Richard and his companions took dinner in the guesthouse and made a significant gift of money to the Benedictine house from their dwindling stock of silver pennies.

It was early afternoon when Richard once more knelt beside the Silver Well; this time he was alone. For a few moments he recalled the last time that he had knelt there, and all the memories of bitter confusion and violent emotions rose within him at the recollection. Yet this time the turbulence spent itself and he found himself quiet and calm, with a peace that he had not known for years.

'Joanna,' he said quietly to himself, 'I am so glad that I found you.' He recalled all the terrible desperation and disappointments which had driven them together; which neither of them would have wished for and which now neither of them would have changed. 'I have not come to where I intended, but that path was shut off to me . . .' He thought about the quest that others had closed to him and how once the disappointment had been like wormwood in his mouth. 'But finding you has made it bearable and – more than that – it has given me another reason to live, a purpose . . .'

'My lord . . .' The voice was that of Umar, who was keeping watch on the path whilst Mark de Dinan made the offering at the altar. 'There is someone coming.'

Richard smiled at his own habit of rehearsing his thoughts aloud, and reflected how he would soon have to change it when another shared his bed and life. 'Thank you, Father,' he whispered in prayer, as he flexed his chilled knees, 'for bringing us together and teaching me to trust you to transform the chaos of my life into order.' He cupped one hand and sipped the clear, cold water, which shocked his throat. 'Now guard us, I pray, for we are entering a battle more difficult to predict than any other that I have ever fought and with adversaries who are experienced and strong.'

He pondered the faces of John and Falkes in his mind. 'And I still pray for the liberation of Jerusalem . . .' His stubborn refusal to let go of the last thread of the dream made him smile where once it would have made him despair. That was the difference that meeting her had made.

'My lord . . .' Umar's voice was becoming urgent and the noise of an approaching group of pilgrims more noticeable.

Richard made the sign of the cross with the water and rose to his feet. 'I am coming, for we have work to do, my true friend.' He clapped Umar on the back as if it was the Arab who had been keeping *him* waiting. The Saracen smiled his elusive smile at the mystery of westerners and their strange ways.

The midday meal over, the riders followed the valley of the Cerne south and reached Dorchester at dusk on Monday, January 25, the feast of the Conversion of St Paul. The gates were closing and they only just gained admittance as the curfew was about to begin with the approach of dark.

As before, they made for the stone-built house in the shadow of the royal castle. The thump of Mark de Dinan's gauntleted fist brought the familiar hiss of bolts and a nod of welcome from the servants of Aaron of Dorchester.

A great fire warmed the hall and Aaron himself came to greet Richard as he entered. 'You are expected, my friend,' the old Jew said with a warmth he rarely felt for Gentiles. 'And all is ready.' Then he smiled, for he knew all about Richard's mission. 'But are *you* ready, my young friend?'

Richard pulled back his scarlet riding cloak to reveal the long sword which hung at his side. 'I am ready.' He motioned to Mark and Umar who likewise displayed their weapons. 'We are all ready . . .'

'Good, good,' Aaron said at the sight of the two swords and the curved blade of the turbaned Arab. 'For you will be carrying enough silver to turn the heads of a thousand thieves.' He smiled as the long cloaks fell back over the weapons. 'Now I have wine and meat for all of you, for you will be tired from your journey. And my serving maids will bathe you before you retire for the night.'

After they had eaten, Aaron leaned close to Richard. 'I must speak with you alone, before you take to your bed.' Richard nodded and the two went in silence to Aaron's counting house.

The room was well protected by a metal-studded and many-locked door. Aaron worked at the lock with his keys and then led the way inside. A servant brought hot spiced wine and Aaron bade Richard take a seat on a richly carved wooden bench. 'It is from Sicily,' he remarked casually, as if to remind his guest of the wealth and influence of his host.

A sheet of linen covered a dark wooden table. Aaron lifted the sheet to reveal piles of silver coins beneath. 'Seventy pounds is a lot of pennies, my friend.' He picked up one of the coins stamped with its distinctive little cross. 'And John will check the amount very carefully.'

'I have no doubt that he will count them,' Richard said drily. 'He is not a man to take something on trust.'

'Quite so,' Aaron agreed. 'The loss of Normandy will have taught him that, if he did not know it before. But I mean much more than that he will simply count the coins.' The old Jew held out a penny to Richard. 'They are not as good as they were in his father's reign. The stamping dies are shoddy nowadays and the silver content variable, not to mention the clipping . . .' He raised his hands at the thought of falling standards.

Richard turned the coin over in his hand. 'John will not thank me for lecturing him on the state of his coinage.'

'He knows all about it, believe me, and as a result he will not take your word that these coins amount to what you say.'

Richard frowned. 'What do you mean? I dare not risk arousing his ire. God knows it will be enough of a job to make him sweet as it is.'

Aaron took back the coin. 'It is the standard custom to melt down a sample of all coins paid to the Crown and charge you for any shortfall revealed by this blanching . . .'

'I have not got sufficient cash available to make up a shortfall, if such is revealed by the firing.' Richard pursed his lips. 'This is not good news at all.'

Aaron raised one hand. 'There is another practice, however. If the coins are not fired, the servants of the King's treasurer will charge you a flat rate of one shilling in the pound extra . . .'

'Seventy shillings!' Richard was appalled. 'This is costing me as much as I can quickly raise as it is! Where am I going to find another three or four pounds in ready silver at this late stage?'

'I have it.'

'I do not understand.'

'You saved my life, Richard de Lacey,' Aaron reminded him, 'and now I shall repay the debt. You will find that in addition to the seventy pounds on this table there are also eight hundred and forty of my own coins, which I give you as a gift.'

'Holy Mother of God, Aaron, you cannot mean this. I do not know what to say.'

'Then it is best to say nothing,' the money-lender advised. 'Personally I think that it is a small price to pay for my life; I know others of my people who have had to pay a lot more for theirs . . .'

'That was not why I saved you,' Richard replied indignantly.

'I know that,' Aaron said softly. 'You saved me because you are a good man.'

The two sat in silence for a while and then, while Richard watched him, Aaron raised the cloth to cover the coins once more. 'I will not forget this, Aaron of Dorchester,' the knight said with feeling.

'I should hope not,' the Jew replied with a rare grin. 'After all, I expect you to deliver eight hot-blooded mares to my servants within a fortnight. I am counting on you not to forget, Richard de Lacey.'

The knight raised his goblet of wine. 'Then here is to remembrance!' Aaron lifted his own wine and the silver vessels touched with a light 'clink'.

'For God's sake, be careful when you go to John,' Aaron advised, with humour forgotten. 'He is a dangerous man, so never underestimate him. Others have done so and are now dead.'

Richard raised his eyes from his wine. 'Believe me, Aaron, I know. And more than my life hangs on this. I shall be careful; very, very careful.

The night after Richard, Mark and Umar left the hidden valley, Joanna curled up in the straw next to Tilly. The fire was still bright on the packed clay and stones of the hearth and the dark room was heavily scented with the smell of wood smoke. From the byre across the passageway came the sound of Soloriens shifting his great weight.

'Richard is going to the Jew of Dorchester,' Joanna began to explain to her maid, who lay beside her in the dark. 'He has arranged to sell eight of his mares . . .'

Tilly turned to her mistress. 'He means to marry you?'

Joanna did not seem surprised that Matilda had guessed. In the old days they had always known what the other was up to. There was a difference now, though, for Tilly seemed older. Joanna knew why that was and tried not to think about it on this of all nights.

'Yes,' she replied and the one word seemed charged with emotion. 'He means to marry me and I am more than happy with the news; indeed I pray God that nothing will come in the way of it. I am sure that nothing can do so.' She fell silent at the thought of what she had said and crossed herself in the dark.

Tilly noticed the gesture and understood the fear of failure which lay beneath the apparent confidence. The past few months had changed both of them. 'You love him?'

'Yes, I do. I truly do and there is no doubt in my mind.' Joanna paused. 'There was a time when I did not care for security but only for independence. Though I know now that that was because my father shielded me from the realities of the world and my independence was a flower protected from the winter wind by his strong wall. Then,' she thought of the disasters following Gilbert's death, 'there was a time when I would have traded all for security . . .'

'You are thinking of Falkes de Mauleon, my lady,' Tilly said a little teasingly.

'He is a good-looking man,' Joanna said defensively. 'And he offered much. God knows he would have driven out that brute . . .' The atmosphere was chilled by the allusion to Savaric. Joanna sighed and mastered her sudden surge of anger. 'He would have saved the manor, but . . .'

'He did not stir the woman within you.' Tilly's assertion seemed as much a defence against the veiled condemnation of the previous moment as a description of the relationship between Joanna and the bishop's marshal.

'That is true – he did not stir me. Though, God knows, Hubert de Burgh had made it clear to me that it was of no consequence what I desired about any matter! I thought myself lucky to have been found by a man as honourable as Falkes. And when we came here, and the dirt and cold replaced the excitement, I began to hope that he would find me, regardless of how I felt for him!' She pressed her hands together at the thought of how much her seemingly independent world had collapsed with the death of her father. 'Though in the old days I would never have imagined I could *ever* have come to think that way . . .' She did not need to mention the death of Gilbert de Cantelo, for both women understood the inference.

'But now Richard de Lacey loves you and you love him.' Tilly sounded envious.

'Yes, and the strange thing is that though he is the man I desire, he can only offer me risk and the chance of losing everything . . .' She mused on this latest development in her journey of emotions. 'And yet, now that we have found each other, it is a risk I am prepared to take.' She glanced at the silhouetted face of her maid. 'I have come a long way from the girl who had everything and never knew anything about danger, don't you think?' Tilly did not reply and Joanna did not press her for an answer, for the assertion had been as much to herself as to her maid.

'When will he return?'

Joanna rejoiced at the thought. 'He has promised to be here before nightfall tomorrow, and this time he will not be late!' The memory of why the previous return had been delayed sobered her. It made her realise that she could no longer hold back the feared news about Stephen from the girl who had once loved him. 'Tilly,' she said very gently, 'Richard thinks that Stephen is dead.' There was no reply and Joanna wondered if her maid had heard her. 'I said that we fear that they have killed him . . .'

'No . . .' Matilda's voice was brittle. 'No, I cannot believe it. *He* would not have done such a thing.'

Joanna heard the way Matilda spoke of Savaric but found her

previous surge of anger had fallen back. 'We do not know for sure, but there seems to be no news of him . . .'

'Then he might be alive,' Tilly interrupted as if the guilt for the harm done to Stephen lay on her. 'If we do not know, then he might be well.' It was as if she had to deny that such a thing could have happened, despite the fact that the terrible possibility had haunted both women since Stephen had failed to return.

Joanna was firmer now. 'Richard is sure of it. He has picked up scraps of rumours and is convinced that something terrible has happened.'

The fire was just a red glow, but even by the fading light Joanna could see the tears flowing down Tilly's face. 'Why don't you say it, my lady?' the young maid said in a wretched small voice of misery.

'Say what?' But Joanna knew.

'Say that it was me who killed him, that it was me who destroyed him.'

'Oh God, Tilly, it was not you. No matter what you did, it was not you.' Joanna put her arms around her broken friend and now both of them were crying. 'It was me who took us away and it was me they were searching for – me and Soloriens. It was my fault that he was seized and not yours.' Both were sobbing and folded against each other. 'If anyone is to blame, then it is me . . .'

'He went to his death hating me . . . that was all my doing.'

Joanna held Matilda tightly. 'No! I am sure that he had forgiven you. You must not say such things.'

Tilly fought back her sobs and raised her little face. The glow from the fire shone on the wet, white cheeks. 'No, my lady, I am not that much of a fool. I know that he hated me, and that that was how he went to his death. And it was a hate that I richly deserved, though God knows I would now purge myself of it if I could.'

For the first time since the passion for Savaric had first risen within her, she confronted the chaos of her life; the physical ecstasy that had come from the same man who had snuffed out the life of Stephen Pierson. Tilly groaned and the sound came from the very core of her. 'He hated me and he had every right to. God help me, he had every right to . . .'

Savaric had returned to Horsingham from Woodstock in a dangerous mood. The men-at-arms were frightened, for they had seen the look before; it was Savaric at his most brutal.

He called the soldiers together in the hall. 'Right, you whoresons, just listen to me.' There was little left of the suave arrogance now; all that remained was the menace that had lurked beneath. 'I want the girl and the horse and if I don't get her then people are going to start dying around here.' The threat was just sufficiently vague, and the soldiers glanced at each other.

'We've done our best . . .' one volunteered.

A gloved fist sent him sprawling into the rushes of the hall. There were angry murmurs from his mates, instantly stilled by a step forward by Savaric. 'Well, it's not good enough, is it?' The fallen man wiped blood from his mouth. 'Is it, you useless cur?' The man shook his head. 'That's better,' Savaric said, having regained control of himself. 'I am back now and things are going to be different from now on. I've had enough of treating the scum around here with compassion. I'm going to get her and we are going to be out before dawn tomorrow to get started. We are going to wreck every house within miles of here until someone tells us something; until we get some idea of where she might be hiding. We are going to find her and that horse . . .'

Richard, Mark and Umar left Dorchester in the late morning. The boxes containing the money were strapped to the backs of the packhorses in place of the packs of chain mail which had hung there the previous day. Now each rider wore the mail beneath his riding cloak and flowing surcoat. They rode in silence, eyes alert, for they knew the value of what was strapped to the horses; the last and greatest gamble had begun. As they rode north and the track began to climb away from the wide valley of the Frome, each was locked into his own thoughts.

No one was deeper in thought than Richard de Lacey. He had no need of anyone to remind him of the risk he was taking in throwing in his lot with Joanna de Cantelo, or of the volatile nature of the King that he would have to deal with. As he thought about the way ahead, he could not help but reflect that he had come a long way since the day in the palace at Acre. He had come a very long way, along roads unexpected and strange, to a destination he could never have anticipated.

As he rode, his hand dropped occasionally to the hilt of his sword but his mind was far away with the girl with the flash of vixen hair and the eyes as green and challenging as the rising waves of the sea.

Joanna and Tilly rose after dawn and went about the usual routine of the day. As the sun marked the passage of the hours, Joanna grew more excited at the thought of Richard's return. It amused her to experience this at the thought of a man; amused her, and pleased her.

After a simple midday meal the two women walked Soloriens and led him to drink at the spring. Then they stabled and groomed him as once Stephen Pierson had done. The light was dim in the stable when Joanna heard the sound of the returning horsemen.

'You finish,' she said to Tilly, dropping her brush. 'It's Richard . . .'

She lifted the hem of her once rich gown and ran out to meet the knight. He had dismounted in the yard just beyond the doorway and was adjusting the horse's harness. The light had almost gone from the valley.

'Richard, it is so good to see you . . .' she called out in the passageway. Then she froze and raised one slim hand to her mouth in shock, for the rider had turned. The face was well known to her, but it was not the face of Richard de Lacey.

Chapter 14

The long shadows lay like a heavy hand on the folds between the downs when Richard, Mark and Umar finally returned to the secret hamlet. The sinking January afternoon had drained the light from the day in the little valley, though the last few drops of sunshine were still scattered across the high hills. The evening dropped from twilight to darkness as the three horsemen rode down the winding track into the familiar woods, on that Tuesday afternoon.

'Nearly there,' Richard remarked to Mark in a casual way, but the pleasure at returning was clear in his voice. 'And I am ready for more of Matilda's soup . . .'

Mark smiled, a little wearily, for unlike his knight, his share of the monotonous food in the hideaway was not spiced with the heady flavour of newly discovered love. All he was glad of was the approaching opportunity of getting out of the saddle. He glanced at the Saracen to see how he had responded to de Lacey's good cheer, but the Arab groom seemed engrossed in the task of walking his nervous mount down the slope.

At last they broke through the wall of screening trees and the dark shapes of the familiar buildings rose from the shadows. There was a homely smell of wood smoke on the air and it was obvious that supper was cooking on the fire.

'It certainly smells like soup again,' Mark commented, but Richard had already dismounted and was not listening.

'Joanna,' the knight called as he fiddled with the ties of his riding cloak, 'we are back and I have something to show you.' He waved to a dismounting Umar, who immediately began to tug at the leather straps holding the boxes of cash on to the packhorses.

Joanna did not appear and so Richard went into the longhouse.

He returned immediately, almost running down Mark, who was entering the doorway. 'They are gone.' Richard's voice was low and pitched with an edge of shock.

'I'm sorry, my lord . . .'

'They are gone!' Richard's voice was no longer subdued, as if the blow had finally sunk into him, drawing blood. 'They are both gone . . .' He pushed past his squire and stood in the yard, staring down the combe into the darkness. 'Joanna . . . Joanna . . .' His great bellow echoed from the curve of trees as if ghost voices had been raised by his aching and anguished call. 'Joanna . . .'

'My lord, my lord . . .' Umar was bending in the darkness, waving a brand which he had seized from the hearth within the house. 'Horses were here, see.' He pointed to where the damp earth was marked with the jumbled prints of hooves. 'Horses have been here – the ground is covered with their prints.'

'Sweet Holy Mary,' Richard exclaimed as he saw the tracks. He grabbed the torch from the Saracen and – waving it ahead of his face – followed the route of the riders down the valley. 'They went this way.'

Mark was stunned; he could not believe what was happening, any more than his knight could. But the sight of his master racing headlong into danger spurred him into movement. He drew his sword and shouted to the Saracen: 'Tie up the horses – they'll be little use to us in the dark. And stay here with them.' Then he was after Richard without thought to what dangers might threaten from the gathering night.

Umar tied up the horses, then drew his sword, in defiance of the squire's command, and followed the two shadows vanishing into the blackness.

Joanna sat frozen upon the high saddle. She was overwhelmed with shock and rode the horse stiffly, prey to every jolt and jar that she would normally have flowed over. Behind her, Matilda was just a small shape on the bulk of the beast which carried her. Both horses were guided by men-at-arms in heavy leather gambesons and riding cloaks. Ahead, Joanna could make out the head of her surprise visitor, who was leading his own horse.

'Where are you taking us?' Joanna could not hide the dismay in her voice. 'You must tell me where it is that you are taking us.'

The head twisted about and, even in the darkness, she could recognise the familiar shape of the face. But the face did not speak; instead it turned and they continued on their way.

'You must tell me,' Joanna almost shouted. 'I demand that you tell me. You have no right . . . I may be a ward of the King but I am an heiress to Gilbert de Cantelo. You may not treat us this way . . .' The words were as desperate and angry as they were futile.

Ahead of her the great stallion Soloriens lifted his mighty head at the sound of her raised voice and called to her with a wild, high neigh. But her captor gave her no like comfort, or recognition, as the soldiers led their prisoners slowly and carefully through the dark.

It was first light and the grey mist was settled in the tiny valley like a land-locked pool of translucent cold paleness. Already, though, the horses were out in the yard and saddled. Their breath rose like thin smoke as they nuzzled one another and waited.

Richard, Mark and Umar crouched beside the last of the fire which was burning on the hearth; the very fire by which Joanna and Matilda had warmed themselves the day before. Umar had heated a little porridge and they ate it with bread and strips of salted bacon that they had brought back from Dorchester. It was a meal taken hurriedly, without ceremony and without joy.

'Whoever took them was here not long before we returned . . .' Mark suggested.

Richard nodded. 'The fire needed more wood and it could not have burned long in that condition. No doubt they were taken just before they would have built it up for the night.' He paused and stared into the glowing ashes as he recalled Tilly's nightly ritual of tending the fire. As he did so he could almost hear Joanna's voice in the dark room. His jaw tightened and he clenched his fist. 'They must have been only a little way ahead of us . . .' His voice was charged with the tension born of anger and frustration.

'We could never have followed them, my lord,' Mark said in a sympathetic voice. 'It would have been folly in the dark. No man could have done it, not in the wild and in the dark.'

Richard took little comfort from the squire's words, but rose to his feet. 'Whatever the truth of that now, they are no more than an hour ahead of us, for the dark that frustrated us will have made them blind too.' The thought energised him and he put his despair behind himself. 'So if we ride hard and fast we might yet overtake them.' The knight glanced at Umar. 'Have you hidden the money boxes well?'

The Saracen nodded. 'The thatch is rotten but thick and I have lodged them above the crossbeams in the stable, my lord. No one shall find them there.'

'Good, well done.' Richard pointed to his sheathed sword and Mark rose at once and lifted it from its place on Richard's discarded bedding. 'Arm me, Mark, for this may be a day for fighting rather than talking.'

'I fear they will not give her up easily,' Mark agreed as he armed his lord. 'Our swords may be the only persuasion that we have to offer them.'

As de Lacey raised his arms the squire attached the weapon to the leather baldrick which was fastened about his waist, drawing in the folds of his knee-length surcoat with its rampant snarling lion emblazoned across the chest. Both Richard and Mark were wearing their long coats of mail and the squire could feel the links cold beneath the cloth as he finished the belting. He looked at his knight to gauge his mood but was not prepared for the words when they came.

'They will find that we are ready to kill them as they are us.' Richard spoke without hesitation. 'Be sure that we are of one mind, for we are few and they will be many . . .'

'I am ready,' Mark replied. 'I shall follow you to the death.'

'And I shall follow too, Malik Rik.'

At the sound of the familiar Arabic, Mark turned, unsure of whether to censure the groom for his impertinence, despite their comradeship, or to praise him for his unpaid loyalty. Such were the conflicting emotions which Umar could still stir. But it was Richard de Lacey who replied.

'I know that you will. I know that I can rely on both of you – to the death . . .'

The doused the fire and left the house. Mounting their horses in silence they filed at a walk down beside the little stream which gurgled away into the vale. It was not difficult, in daylight, to follow the tracks of the previous day, or the bushes pressed back by the passage of a number of horses. After about half a mile the ground levelled out into mature woodland that had not been coppiced, or cut, for some generations. But still the widening track led on through the naked trees. After a while Umar pointed and the three men paused.

'They camped here last night,' the groom noted at the sight of the flattened grass and the scattered wood ash of a couple of large fires. 'I think that there are not that many of them . . .'

'I agree,' Richard commented as he surveyed the deserted campsite. 'Probably no more than six of them, and *our* women.' He said the word in a defiant manner, as if by mere assertion he could regain what he had lost.

'They moved off this way.' Mark had guided his horse to one side of the camp. 'They rode off the track there, where the trees thin out . . .'

'Going west,' Richard observed as he shifted the weight of the shield which was slung across his back.

'Towards Horsingham?' Mark questioned.

'Aye,' Richard replied, his mouth drawn tight at the mere thought of the mercenary Savaric de Breaute. 'They rode towards Horsingham.' Then he kicked his heels into his horse's flanks, and the hunt was on.

William Catface mournfully faced the man who brought in his breakfast of sour lard spread on green-speckled stale bread. The food was thrown on to the floor in front of him.

'That's the best yer'll be gettin', so make the most of it. As it's Wednesday, an' a fast day, we couldn't run to the usual rich fare.'

He chortled at his own wit. 'But we managed to get a fish course.' He tossed a handful of rotten fish heads next to the bread.

Catface summoned up his courage. 'How long . . .' He coughed and cleared his throat. 'How long before . . .'

'Before the justices try yer case?' The man was quite unfeeling and obviously impatient at being delayed.

'Yes, yer honour . . .' Catface moved a step towards his gaoler. 'How long would yer think, sir?'

The man laughed. 'Don't hold breath until they come! There are more important things on our minds than you.' At the sight of the poacher's fallen face he relented a little. 'The King is coming – coming here to hunt, and in a few days too; for Candlemas. So yer'll have to wait.'

'How long?' William stared with large eyes at his informant.

'By the Virgin, I do not know. Probably until after Easter. Now just eat yer bread and shut up.' He turned as he reached the door. 'An' don't waste the fish . . .'

As the heavy door closed and the thin daylight was snuffed out, William Catface bent and picked up the crust of stale bread. With one grimy finger he rubbed the surface and then licked the lard. It was rancid and yet he took a bite, for if he was going to be here until Easter, he was going to have to eat. He hunkered down, holding the bread with trembling hands. And as he ate, he cried.

Richard reached Horsingham after the noon meal. He was challenged by a couple of Savaric's crossbowmen as he rode over the bridge into the familiar stockade; he ignored their command and almost rode them down. They unslung their crossbows but thought better of it and ran after the intruders.

Richard rode up to the stables and dismounted. There were a couple of soldiers at the door but Richard drew his sword and they stood away, unsure of the status of the uninvited visitor. One sidled off and then ran towards the manor house for all he was worth.

'Gone to get Savaric,' Mark observed.

'No doubt of it,' Richard replied. Then he turned to the soldier who had finally decided to block his path. 'Out of my way.' The command was imperious and the man stepped aside, all the time looking towards the manor complex and rescue by the only one who would give him authority to strike at such a high-born knight.

Inside the stable, Richard sheathed his sword and almost ran to the familiar stall. A welcome whicker of recognition greeted him as he pushed open the chewed gate. 'Soloriens!' he called at the sight of the mighty stallion.

'Then they have her too,' Mark said as he watched his knight running his fingers through the mane of the horse, which had turned its great proud face to welcome a friend. 'They must have all of them.'

'By God, I shall not stand idly by and see them made prisoner again.' Richard touched the martingale which the Lusignan stallion was once more wearing and began to remove it. 'I shall have an accounting for this from that dog Savaric . . .' His mail coif was down and the horse – free of the martingale – struggled to turn and nuzzle his blond hair.

'Well, well, well, the knight who cannot pay what he promises . . . And one who trespasses on a manor of the King.' Savaric de Breaute stood at the doorway, flanked and backed by a knot of his men. 'And I thought that you had run away for good. At least that is what our mutual friend Falkes de Mauleon assured me, but I see that he was wrong and that, in your absence from here, you still have not managed to learn that the King does not like his property soiled. So get your hands off that horse!'

Richard took a step towards the mercenary. 'Where is she?' he demanded, with a menace to match that of Savaric.

The mercenary commander laughed at the obvious concern of the knight. 'Who would that be?' he said with a leering grin at his watching men.

Richard reddened and Mark's hand dropped to his sword hilt. 'By God, I will not play your foul game, for I have killed better men than you, though they were heathen . . .'

'Damn you.' Savaric snarled at the insult and drew his sword. 'No one speaks to me like that and lives . . .'

Richard ignored the words and pressed again – this time with a voice trembling with passion. 'If you have hurt her . . .'

Mark stepped forward beside his lord; the squire had drawn his weapon as Savaric had unsheathed his own. 'Give the word and I shall put down this cur, my lord.'

The atmosphere in the stable was charged with emotional intensity. Umar pushed back his riding cloak and began to unsheath his own curving blade. For Savaric it was the last straw. He held up the point of his sword towards Richard's face and called to his men who hovered on the edge of the stable.

'Bring him down, bring the arrogant dog down.' When his men made no move, he looked at them with an astonishment which crumbled into searing rage. 'Frightened of them, are you? Frightened to raise a hand against men of quality?' His tone was contemptuous and his men muttered at the venom in his voice. Savaric heard them and snarled, 'I'll deal with you later, but first I will kill this bastard . . .'

He turned to Richard and his eyes were cold like a December sky. 'You invaded the manor, you laid hands on the horse, so you are mine for the taking. And have no thought that the King will pine at your death. I know full well that you have reneged on your debts. The court is full of it.' He laughed at the look on Richard's face. 'You have no secrets from me. And it is obvious that you love the girl . . .'

'You will die for what you have done to her.' As Mark moved towards Savaric, Richard commanded him firmly: 'This is my job, my loyal friend, a job that I shall delight in doing. Step back, for this brute is mine.'

The two men began to circle in the straw while the Brabançon mercenaries and Richard's two companions watched; the former with obvious enjoyment and the latter with concern. Mark did not sheath his sword but kept his eyes fixed on the slowly gyrating blade of de Breaute.

'And you've lost her as well as the horse,' Savaric taunted. 'The King will give her to Falkes de Mauleon now, for sure. You have lost the horse and the girl.' The union of Joanna and Falkes – which once the mercenary had done his best to sabotage – now gave him savage pleasure. For the return of the horse had saved him from the wrath of the King and was a goad with which to taunt the knight. 'She is lost to you, you have failed . . .'

Richard jerked his sword forward. 'When you are dead I shall take her away from here . . .'

Savaric sidestepped, with a laugh. 'It was Falkes who found her, you fool – not I! And he is taking her to the King at this very moment. She is not here because he has got her. And no doubt he is looking forward to possessing her, once the King has heard of the stallion's recapture.' His face was full of cold pleasure at the veil of pain which fell over de Lacey's eyes. 'She will be a good mare to mount, I should think. And Falkes is a lucky sod to have the mounting of her . . .'

'You bastard . . .' Clutching the sword hilt with both hands, Richard brought the blade down towards Savaric's head in a swinging silver arc.

Anticipating the fury of the action, Savaric hurled his shoulders back and his own sword rose in defiant defence to meet de Lacey's blade in a teeth-jarring crash of steel. Richard hacked again and once more Savaric held the blow. Then they were back and forth across the stable, the noise of their combat crushing the air with the weight of its violence. Soloriens snorted at the bloodied sound of fighting and his ears were laid back as he stamped and tugged on the restraining rope.

Mark and Umar stepped back hurriedly as the two combatants crashed about the stable. Chips flew from the wooden walls as Savaric's blade narrowly missed Richard's head and sliced against the wooden roof supports.

Mark seized Umar's arm and whispered in horror, 'His wound will not take much more of this.' His desperation cast out any resentment he still felt for the Saracen, for the situation was critical. 'And then he will be finished . . .'

Richard did not hear the words of his squire, for his thoughts sagged under the burden of the pain which broke his shoulder open and which numbed his hands at every clash of swords. He knew that it could not go on much longer. Soon his shoulder would give up completely and he would be unable to raise the blade at all. The dreadful thought drove him on to strike while he yet could. And as he tensed his screaming muscles for the last desperate blow, his mind was full of the face of Joanna, and his nerves were stiffened by the appeal of their mutual love.

The great sword rose above his head and he brought it down to cleave Savaric from crown to breast bone. Both his hands gripped the hilt as he threw the whole of his weight behind the killing sweep.

The rounded tip of the blade hammered into the wooden cruck beam of the roof. The instant and terrible halt to the downward descent threw Richard backwards. His hands were wrenched from their grip and the great sword of war hung from the wood into which its razor-sharp edge had sunk. Richard was hurled on to his back, his head hammered into the packed earth and cobbles, and a wave of agony pitched him into darkness.

Savaric gave a little, low laugh of surprise and leapt forward to finish the fight, but the movement of Mark de Dinan on his right checked him in mid-movement. He turned his sword to stop the blade which drove at him and, as Mark stumbled, swung his sword in a tight circle. The flat of the blade struck Mark's face with a singing smack and the squire sprawled headlong.

At that moment, Soloriens threw the whole of his massive bulk backwards. The staples that held the tethering ring to the stall surround sprang out and the dapple-grey head turned with a squeal of anger.

Eager to finish the battle, Savaric swung at the dizzy Mark but his sword did not connect with the young squire. Instead, it drove down on to the shoulder of Umar ibn Mamun, who had flung himself between the mercenary and de Dinan. Even as his body broke under the violent blow, the Saracen jerked his own sword upwards, slashing Savaric's face and causing him to fall.

As he rose, Savaric suddenly heard the warning cries of his own men. Wiping blood from his eyes he turned as the stallion's great teeth clamped on the back of his neck and raised him, shrieking, from his feet. He fell heavily, and then the stallion reared and plunged, the iron-shod hooves smashing Savaric's upraised arms. Again and again the hooves rose and fell until the mercenary commander was driven into the cobbles and his last screams were lost in the snorting and squealing triumph of Hugh de Lusignan's stallion.

Joanna jerked her bridle and jigged her heels into the flanks of the palfrey that she was riding. The horse jolted forward and ahead of the soldiers who rode on either side of her. In a moment she was up beside the turning head of Falkes de Mauleon.

'I will not ride in silence while you decide my fate alone, sir.' Joanna's green eyes flashed like sun-struck emeralds. 'I will know what you mean to do with us. In God's name, sir, you owe me that much for the regard in which you once held me.'

Falkes waved back the men-at-arms who had ridden up to retrieve their wayward charge. 'You imply that I no longer hold you in regard, Joanna, and there is no truth in that.' His grey eyes took in the lift of her chin and narrowed. He had known, from the moment that he had discovered her the day before, that he was not welcome in her heart. 'I have all proper regard for you – now as I always did.'

'Proper regard? You seized us and took us back to Horsingham. You left Soloriens with that thug, Savaric – who has treated him abominably – and now you ride on with us, and at no time have you thought to tell me your plans.' Joanna was openly dismayed. 'I do not call that proper regard, sir . . .'

Falkes turned a little in the saddle, and the hand holding his reins dropped to the high pommel. 'There is no reason why you should not know where we are riding,' he said quietly, unruffled by her denunciation of his actions. 'I am taking you to the King.'

Joanna nodded. 'As I thought – you are betraying me to John!'

Falkes looked a little irritated at last. 'I am not betraying you to anyone, Joanna. I am returning you to the safe wardship of your liege lord, the King; to a wardship that you broke when you stole the horse and ran off into the hills.'

'How dare you speak . . .'

'Enough,' he said firmly, for he had no intention of enduring such assertive behaviour from the woman destined to be his wife. 'You cannot run from the King with impunity. It is only by my returning you in some suitable state of contrition that the King will look upon your folly with kindness.' He snorted, in a rare show of emotion. 'And, by Our Lady, after what you have done, it will take all your pleas and my careful words to ward off his anger . . .'

'And gain for you my father's manors.' Joanna interrupted the bishop's marshal with the sudden accusation as she realised the placing of priorities in his cool and careful mind. 'I have no doubt that you are returning me like a runaway villein in order to gain the favour of the King.' She raised one slim finger. 'Richard de Lacey would never have done this to me. He was prepared to sacrifice all for me, so great was his love – a knight's love.'

Falkes pulled back the bridle and brought his horse up with a start. 'De Lacey is a fool; he has promised the King what he cannot pay, for he is a headstrong fool. His heart is where his brain should be. I will not be lectured on behalf of him; I who care only for your safety.' He looked genuinely outraged and offended now and Joanna paled at the anger in his narrow eyes.

'All I know is that he was prepared to lose all for me. He would not have handed me over to John's mercy.' She refused to be cowed by the look on her captor's face. 'That is the kind of man that you call a headstrong fool. How can you ever say that *you* love me . . .' And then she stopped, suddenly aware of what she had lost, for, of course, Falkes de Mauleon had never told her that he loved her.

Mark de Dinan rose shakily from where Savaric's swinging blow had thrown him. As his mind cleared and the singing in his ears diminished, he became aware of the horror before him. His mind clambered through the agony of his aching face and back into reality. Soloriens was stamping and squealing in his stable, Richard de Lacey lay groaning on the ground, and Umar was sprawled in a heap on the bloodied straw. Mark pulled himself to his feet – aware of the pale and silent faces of Savaric's men – and looked for the mercenary. It was some moments before he saw the boots protruding from the edge of the stallion's stall and realised what had happened.

The squire crossed himself in the presence of death and looked from his master to the Saracen groom. He crouched down beside Richard and muttered: 'My lord, Umar is badly injured and Savaric is dead.'

Richard shook the confusion from his head. 'Then attend to him,' he muttered thickly; when Mark was slow to move, he repeated his command: 'Help Umar, I am all right.'

The squire turned to the groom, who was lying like a broken doll, his breath coming in shallow gasps of pain. 'Easy,' he muttered to him, 'lie still.'

Umar turned dark eyes on him. 'It is mortal.' It was a statement, not a question, and Mark nodded.

Now Richard was at his side too. 'Savaric did this?'

'Aye, my lord,' de Dinan replied quietly. 'Umar threw himself between us, that much I recollect. He threw himself between Savaric and me . . .'

'Oh my God, I never thought it would come to this.' Richard stared at his dying companion. 'If anyone was to die, then it should have been me.'

Umar heard him and smiled weakly. 'I was eager to go before you, my lord, for I must put in a word for you with Allah . . .'

Richard glanced at Mark, who looked away. 'My God will find room for one as faithful as you, Umar ibn Mamun.'

'Ahh . . .' the groom sighed, but did not make a reply.

Mark bent low over the Saracen. 'Now I am in your debt twice.' His eyes did not shift from the Arab's face. 'And now I cannot pay back either of the debts. My honour is heavy with you but you will not live for me to lighten it.'

Umar clutched Mark's surcoat with bloody hands. 'Repay the debt to my brother. Look kindly on him and the debt is repaid, Mark de Dinan . . .'

The squire looked helplessly at Richard and then said, 'I do not know who he is. How shall I know who he is? What is he like?'

Umar's hands tightened their grip on the white linen. 'He looks like me . . . He believes as I do . . .' He coughed horribly. 'You will meet him . . . You will meet them . . . somewhere.' The coughing racked him for several minutes. 'The debt you owe me you owe him . . . You owe them . . .' Then a spasm ran through his broken body and he died.

Mark and Richard watched in silence; a silence disturbed only by the stamping of Soloriens, now standing calmly in his pen. At last Richard spoke: 'The debt continues, my friend. It is a debt of honour now . . .'

Mark slowly unfastened Umar's hands. 'A debt that will never end . . .' His voice was choked and he did not dare raise his eyes from the still face of the dead groom.

Falkes rode in silence and no longer looked back at Joanna. The fiery temperament which had at first been so striking was beginning to unsettle him, as was her refusal to accept the fact that there was only one course of action open to him. He decided that they must get to Gillingham as quickly as possible. At least there, he would find no one to question the rightness of his actions. It faintly irritated him that he was even thinking these thoughts; they were far removed from his usual confident and quiet planning.

At last he did turn in the saddle. The green eyes were latched on to him. For a moment he considered how beautiful she was and then he turned back, aware of the challenge in her look more than the beauty in her face.

He urged his horse forward at a faster pace. It was time that the whole matter was decided; time that the de Cantelo estates were settled on him, with marriage to Joanna. There was no doubt in his mind about one thing – that his steady hand was what the spirited girl needed.

None of Savaric's men touched Richard, or Mark, as they left the stable. It was as if the death of Savaric had left them without a role and, more so than before, they were loath to lay hands on knights who might yet be in the favour of the King. With difficulty – for they were bruised and tired – the two companions wrapped Umar's body in his riding cloak and laid him across the back of his horse.

Richard pulled himself painfully up into his high saddle. He leaned back on the tall cantle to watch as his squire mounted too. 'Look to the safety of the horse,' he commanded the silent watching soldiery. 'He is worth more than all of you put together, and the King will deal most harshly with any man who lays a cruel hand upon him.' Such concern for the beast which had just hurled their leader from their presence to the judgement seat of God caused the mercenaries to mutter, but none dared contradict the order.

'Are we riding to Gillingham?' Mark was sure of the answer.

Richard gritted his teeth at the agony in his back. 'Yes, we shall ride to snatch her from the hands of Falkes. And if needs must, we shall seize her from the hands of the King himself. But first we shall take Umar to the Templar convent at Buckland. Unpopular as we are, they will just have to live with us, for we must stay there tonight. Then we shall go on to the King's hunting lodge tomorrow.'

Richard paused and looked towards the eastern winter sky. 'She will be safe until then, God keep her. And we are in no fit state to rescue her this afternoon. And besides,' he explained, 'we shall do no good trying to gain admittance after dark. There will be enough time to offend the King's majesty tomorrow when we ride to free Joanna . . .'

Mark sighed, for that seemed more than a likely ending. 'I am with you, my lord. I shall ride where you ride.' It all seemed a far cry from the heady days of hope in the light-painted palace at Acre. 'I shall not desert you now.'

'I know that,' Richard replied. 'You will not desert me, any more than he did.' He glanced to where Umar's body lay across his mount. 'And I shall return to bury him . . .' Strangely enough, he too was thinking of where it had all started, in the fortress of the Grand Master of the Templars. But how it now would end, he dared not say. More than ever he realised that he was in the hands of God.

The household servants of King John had arrived at Gillingham while their monarch was still wearing his crown for the twelve days of Christmas and dealing with Falkes de Mauleon and

Savaric de Breaute at Woodstock. Even as he was making the bishop's marshal and the mercenary commander painfully aware of his displeasure, the royal bakers were buying corn across north Dorset and south Somerset to feed the small army of the mobile household which was soon to descend like locusts on Gillingham.

On Thursday, 28 January, John rode down from the royal residence at Ludgershall, in Wiltshire, where he had broken his journey, and reached the north Dorset hunting lodge in the late afternoon. It was in the grand style that his household knights rode up to the opening gates, with the cry that sent servants and soldiers scurrying: '*Reaus*! Royal knights, King's men, King's men . . . *Reaus*!' Even William Catface – deep in his dark cell – turned from his thin grey soup at the sudden cries from the world outside.

John was met by the men of his royal chamber who had preceded him. They ran to greet him, ignoring the mud that splashed their silken hose and fine belted gowns. All about the chaos of the royal arrival milled the bearers of the King's cup and bed and ewer; the constables and marshals of the courtyard; and the innumerable keepers of the King's staghounds, the King's wolfhounds, the King's cathounds – each at the centre of his own constellation of barking and leaping dogs.

The object of the devoted attention of the royal household seemed scarcely to notice their attentive presence until one of his constables of the courtyard whispered something in his ear. At the whispered message the King gave a thin but widening smile. 'How long have they been here? Since last night?' The constable nodded and the King seemed very pleased. 'Have them brought to me after supper. I would speak with them both together – but especially with the girl who dared steal my horse.'

As he turned to enter the lodge he did not know that he was being watched from one of the unshuttered windows of the building; watched by a young woman with red hair and green eyes.

Joanna de Cantelo stepped back from the wooden window seat. 'He has arrived,' she said finally.

Matilda did not need any confirmation of what was taking place outside, but nodded just the same. 'What will you say to him, my lady?'

Joanna was thoughtful for a moment, for she had not fully made up her own mind. 'I shall tell him why I did it!'

'I think that Falkes would prefer it if you threw yourself on the King's mercy. Indeed I am sure that he is counting on it, my lady.'

'No doubt of that, Tilly.' Joanna sat down at the window seat. 'Falkes has wagered all on the King accepting his recapture of me as the final payment in his bid to marry me.' She laughed. 'Though it is my lands that he desires more than me.'

'But you will not throw yourself on the King's pity?'

'Matilda, it is me that you are talking to! Of course I will not do such a thing. Do you think that I should?'

Matilda looked at the floor for a moment. 'No, my lady, I do not think that you should.' The maid was thinking of when she herself had put the desires of her heart before all sanity and common sense. She could not ignore the disaster that had ensued, but still she clung defiantly to her mistress and her decision as if, in some way, it vindicated a little of her own madness. 'No, my lady, you should not give in. Follow the leading of your heart, just follow the leading of your heart.'

Joanna looked out at the low grey sky. 'Amen, I shall do that, by the Grace of God. I shall follow my heart once more.' But as she said it, she was not thinking of either John, King of England, or Falkes, marshal of the Bishop of Salisbury.

Richard rose early on the Thursday morning, having no desire to breakfast with his one-time allies at Temple Buckland. He prayed for some time in the room where Umar's body was laid out. Soon he would attend to the burial of the faithful groom, but before that there were momentous tasks to face.

As Richard de Lacey rose from his knees and clasped the arm of his squire, he felt as if he was going into battle again at last. 'Remember, Mark,' he said quietly, 'no surrender.' Then, with a sense of irony, he added, 'A Templar never surrenders! And neither does an almost Templar either.' He tried to smile at his friend, but both knew that there was little to smile about.

★ ★ ★

John took a light supper on the Thursday evening that he arrived at Gillingham; a simple repast of roasted swan, salted herrings, pies and pâtés, dried fruits, fritters, jellies and gingerbread. As the servants cleared away the bread trenchers, heavy with gravy and garlic sauce, he popped another hard-boiled egg into his mouth and raised one ruby-ringed hand. Immediately, the royal steward was at his side, while the ever-present butler and cup-bearers backed away.

'My lord?'

John chewed on the egg and reached for another one from the pile heaped in the silver bowl. 'I want to see de Mauleon and the lady Joanna de Cantelo.'

At once the steward stepped back to convey the instruction down the line of high-table attendants. John took no more notice until, a few minutes later, the door at the end of the hall opened and a slim young woman with red hair was escorted in, accompanied by the bishop's marshal and a maid. The two chief newcomers were led by one of the constables to the steward, who brought them to where the King was sitting. The talk at the table stilled at their approach. A minstrel, halfway through a lilting recitation of a poem beloved at the court of John's mother, faltered in his rendition. John snapped his fingers and the song stopped.

'Well done, Falkes, and it is still five days to Candlemas.' Falkes bowed and did not reply. John's dark and mocking eyes flickered. 'And where is the horse?'

Falkes glanced at Joanna. 'The stallion is safe with your soldiers at Horsingham, my liege. I returned it there and brought the lady Joanna straight here. We arrived last night . . .'

'I know.' John enjoyed cutting in on his visitors; it made the point who was in control of the conversation. 'And this is the lady who stole my horse. Come closer, girl.' Joanna stepped forward. 'Come, come . . .' he said coldly. Soon only the table lay between them. 'How should I deal with you?' His voice was stern and he looked for the rising of fear in her eyes. 'How should I punish one who affronts my royal dignity and pours scorn upon all courtesy and obedience?' He stopped to take in the patched and ragged dress that hung about the curves of her figure; he watched the beautiful young face. 'How should I punish you, girl?' He waited for the tears and supplications and reached for another hard-boiled egg.

'My lord – I think that you should stop the despoiling of my manor and call off the men who do your bidding there.'

John dropped the egg. It rolled off the table to be pounced on by one of the prowling wolfhounds. 'What?' He dismissed the servant who offered him another egg. 'By God's body, what did you just say, girl?'

Joanna's hands were clasped behind her back and only Tilly saw the whiteness of the tightened knuckles as her mistress replied. 'The men who came to my father's manor treated me like dirt, though I was the daughter of your most loyal tenant-in-chief. They set out to ruin my manor and,' she paused to give effect to her next statement, 'they treated the great horse like a slave, with cruelty and violence . . .'

John's face – which had coloured even darker than his usual swarthy complexion – twitched at her accusation of cruelty to the horse. 'What is this that you are telling me, girl?' He noticed the movement of her bosom, like linnets fluttering in a cage, and suddenly found an undercurrent of pleasure amidst the swirling flotsam of his anger.

'They treated the horse cruelly, so I took him from them.' It was a slightly disingenuous answer but not wholly a lie, and it clearly had the desired effect on the King, who felt as if his fury had lost its clear focus. Before John could reply, Joanna continued: 'I knew of no other way to appeal to you, my liege. I took the horse to cause you to notice the injustice of my plight. I stole him to save myself, my manor and the horse that you cherished so highly.'

Joanna glanced at the pale features of Falkes before she added: 'I would do it again tomorrow, if it was the only way. I know you will understand, for no one loves justice more than you, or values more highly honour held truly and honestly. I will not and cannot lie to you, to gain the favour that others creep to obtain and then repay with treachery . . .'

'I am sorry,' Falkes said quickly and shut off Joanna's speech.

'She does not understand the words that she is saying. She is but a child, my liege. A beautiful child in need of the strong guidance of the husband of your choosing.'

'Who is no doubt yourself,' John remarked drily, without taking his eyes off the girl with the disconcerting green eyes and the uplifted chin. 'Which is no doubt the reason why you brought her straight to me.'

Falkes was nonplussed, which was a rarity. 'My liege, it was as we agreed. I merely sought to display my loyalty to yourself and to . . .'

'And to persuade me that you were the only candidate for her hand. Do not dissemble with me, sir, for I can see through a man's motives. God knows I have seen through enough this past year. I want the truth, and that is that from the word go you anticipated my decision in this matter.' John smiled at the discomfort on the face of the usually imperturbable marshal.

Falkes looked swiftly at Joanna. He could not understand it, but knew that he had aroused the King's distrust. He could not grasp how, but knew it was in some way related to the outrageous way that Joanna had spoken to the King. And, far from plunging John into a rage, it seemed to have appealed to him. Falkes narrowed his eyes as he desperately considered a way out of the hole that he found himself in.

John watched with interest the drama that he had helped create. The girl was very beautiful and rich; he could see why Falkes wanted her and why he had overstretched himself. John felt the familiar stir of desire. The girl before him offered something that the gaggle of whores who were even now warming his bed could not hope to offer: a proud spirit and a noble soul. In a year in Normandy he had found few enough of those.

The thought turned the edge of his anger, for this girl intrigued and amused him. The unspoken friction between her and the marshal made it clear that she considered his delivery of her to Gillingham as a betrayal. The nerve of the girl appealed to him, and yet he knew he could not turn a blind eye to her actions.

It was a dilemma, but one that interested him and took his mind off the disasters that had obsessed his thoughts for months;

a diversion that he had not expected at the end of a long day's ride. It was better than the minstrels and poets who had been laid on for his entertainment. It was the kind of human tangle that John loved to manipulate, and it offered a welcome break from events elsewhere which were fast running out of his control.

'What will you do with me, my liege?' Once before, Joanna de Cantelo had asked that question and was surprised to find that, as with the first time, the question produced more than she had expected.

'Pick up that jug, girl, and give me some wine. I am thinking, and you will not rush my thoughts with as much speed as you stole my horse . . .'

John drank the wine, aware that all eyes in the hall were on him; it gave him a great sense of wellbeing. He looked at the proud yet tense face of Joanna and the narrow eyes of Falkes, who seemed unsure of whether to look at the woman he had bid for, or the King. Content that his pause had wound the dramatic tension a notch higher, the King at last spoke.

'It is clear that you want her, Falkes. What man would not want so beautiful a bride? And no doubt your loyalty to the King who agreed to your request would be immense . . .'

Falkes stepped forward. 'You know that it would be so, my liege.'

'She is yours, if . . .'

Richard de Lacey had ridden into Gillingham from the west just after sunset. During his ride across the Blackmoor Vale from Temple Buckland, his horse had thrown a shoe. It had been after they had collected the money boxes from their hiding place. He and Mark had been forced to take shelter in a hamlet half hidden in an assart in the woods, whilst a blacksmith had repaired the damage. When the two companions were once again mounted and ready, no amount of urging could make their horses win the race against the sinking winter sun.

John was at table and the entertainment in full swing when they arrived, and so Richard had been forced to wait in the corridor outside the hall. It was from this position that he had caught a glimpse of Joanna and Falkes as they were led in. He had risen to his feet but she had not seen him in the crowd.

Desperate to gain admittance, de Lacey twice gave information concerning his name and status, but it was evident that the King was fully occupied with events that were not to be disturbed. At last Richard could contain his feelings no longer.

'We are going in, Mark.'

His squire paled at the thought of an unbidden entrance, but nodded, his discipline subduing his fear. 'As you wish, my lord.' His back was bowed with the weight of the money boxes he was hugging.

Richard touched him on the shoulder. 'No, not as I wish – how it must be.'

At that moment a group of servants came with platters from the kitchen. Richard and Mark mingled with them, despite the mutters of surprise, and, before anybody could act, knight and squire had walked into the room.

Ahead of them the raised dais seemed higher than they could have imagined. It was then that Richard saw Joanna standing before the King. His heart pounded to see her like a prisoner before her judge. Without a thought he stepped forward into the light of the flaring torches, and as he did so he heard the pronouncement of the King.

'She is yours, if . . .'

'No, my liege, do not say it.' All eyes, which had been hooked on Joanna, flashed about. Richard saw from the corner of his own eye the movement of the household knights and servants. 'Do not say it, my lord, for she is worth a higher price.'

John remained seated, unsure of whether to order the arrest of the intruder, or bid him approach. At last his curiosity got the better of him; he had heard words that seemed to promise a veritable auction. 'Come forward,' he commanded, 'and explain why you failed to keep your promise to your King. Explain before I have you taken and chained!'

Richard gave one look at Joanna before replying. 'I shall pay you all that my honour promised.' He signalled to Mark, who dropped the two money boxes. Richard wrenched off the lid of one and poured the shining cascade of silver on to the rushes. 'Here is twice what I promised you . . .' He broke open the second box and added its contents to the shining pile. 'And here is more than twice again.' A great murmur ran about the hall like a rising wind.

John put down his wine. 'What is this game, Richard de Lacey? I know for sure that the Templars have cut you off, so whose money is this?'

'It is mine. I have sold my horses.'

The King leaned forward, visibly surprised. Falkes opened his mouth and then shut it again. John pursed his lips. 'I thought you were a man with a mission?'

'And I still am, my lord. If your grace wills it, my mission is to pay the fine for the entry of Joanna de Cantelo into her inheritance and pay amercement for her taking of the horse.'

John looked hard at the money on the floor. 'You offer a high price, Richard de Lacey.' He was clearly impressed and moved.

'It is all I have – I will give all I have for her, if the King will grant me her hand.' Before John could reply, Richard made his final move. 'And here and now I renounce all fealty I might owe the King of France for my manors in the lands that he has taken from you by treachery. I renounce all fealty to him, for you are my only overlord and sovereign . . .'

John sneered. '*If* I give you what you want?'

Richard laid his hand on his heart. 'I renounce it anyway, my King – regardless of what you may decide!' The wind of voices became a gale. 'But the money I offer for her – for the lady de Cantelo.'

Falkes was pale. 'This cannot be, my liege, for you promised . . .' Then he regained his old composure and stepped backwards, away from the glance of the King.

John stood up and the voices fell silent. He looked about the room, sensing the surprise, but also the approval for the impetuous knight in their midst. And he himself was amused by the display of reckless love; it touched that mercurial side of his nature that could leap from black anger to generosity and as quickly plunge back again. More than that, it was a display of the kind of loyalty that he craved, even if it owed more to Joanna de Cantelo than to himself.

The King looked at his barons sat about him at table and wondered how many of them would soon be seeking accommodation with the French King who had dispossessed him of his royal lands. Then he looked at the silver on the floor and decided that the time had come to seize winnings that he had never expected and win praise at the same time. In that moment the matter was decided by his sudden impulse; Falkes and the schemes of last year were forgotten.

'She is yours, Richard de Lacey, and I hope that she is worth the price that you have paid. God's body, but a month from now and every troubadour and minstrel at my mother's court will be singing of this night's dealing of the heart . . .' The hall was full of abrupt, approving noise and he was content that he had made the right decision. He basked in the praise of the assembled host as if the gesture of self-sacrificing love had been his own.

Joanna ran from the dais and threw herself into the arms of the knight who had so wildly paid all he had for her. He held her tightly and her red hair flowed about him like cascading coals; like the suffused sky on the day that they had ridden with their stallion to the wooded knoll at sunrise.

In mid-June 1204, King John returned once more to Gillingham to feast his nobles and loyal servants on St Alban's Day. But of all those present none drew more attention than the lady Joanna de Lacey and her husband, Richard, who had paid so high a price for her.

Joanna wore the robe that Richard had bought especially for this day; a long scarlet gown inset with embroidery of golden thread. Her hair was caught up within a flowing linen veil, and the creamy bands of the barbette about her throat seemed to raise the fine tilt of her chin as she acknowledged the bows of her fellow guests.

The sun was shining brightly as the King entered the hall. Ignoring the others, he commanded Joanna and Richard to stand beside him as guests of honour. 'Marriage suits you, my lady de

Lacey,' he said as he raised the slim white hand to his lips. 'And you look as if you are thriving, Richard.'

Richard nodded. 'It is the result of your kindness, my lord, that I am honoured with so fine a friend and wife.'

John shook his head. 'You are a strange one, de Lacey. For anyone would think that your wife was also your lover!' The narrow dark eyes glittered at the blush that swept across Joanna's face. 'But then, you are a unique man, for who else has ever paid so much for a bride?'

Richard glanced at his lover, who was also his wife. 'It was a small price. When all my plans were in ruins I found the wisdom that teaches that only our despair is to be feared. Faith opens doors to worlds that we had never imagined were there, if we will but let it. I have paid a small price to enter that door and find real joy. And what is more, to find peace in loving and being loved. It is worth double what I have paid.' Then he grinned. 'But it is too late to up the price now, my lord – for the deed is done!'

John laughed. 'I may have ways of making you pay with service, Richard, for I have few who I can trust. Can I trust you, Richard de Lacey?'

'I am your man, my lord. You know that.'

The King nodded. 'I think I can judge a man as noble as he is foolishly passionate, and I like you. You are a man after my own heart. When today is over you must come and talk with me, for I have plans for you. I may even hope that your love for me will yet rival the love that you have for your wife! After all, you gave up the horses for her! And what greater price could a man with a mission pay?' He smiled enigmatically and moved away.

'You seem to have fallen on your feet,' Joanna remarked impertinently. 'Does he know that your remaining mares are carrying foal?'

Richard glanced sideways at his wife. 'I shouldn't think so. And he had better not find out!'

'The trouble is,' she continued, 'I was so busy falling in love with you that it never occurred to me at the time why you were taking Soloriens out for such excessive exercise. Where did he cover the mares then?'

Richard smiled a conspiratorial smile. 'We found a sheltered spot, halfway between the hamlet and Temple Buckland!'

'I think you had better keep very quiet when your Arabs give birth to dapple-grey champions, Richard de Lacey – favoured knight of the King!'

'They will always be a reminder to us . . .'

'We don't need reminders,' she said, smiling. 'We've got here and now.' Richard took her hand and kissed it. 'People are looking, you know,' she said teasingly, but she did not care.

William Catface returned to his cottage the afternoon after his fine was paid. From the sudden care that his gaolers paid to him, he knew that whoever it was who had come as a liberating angel was someone with power. His surprise was second only to his exhilaration.

At the cottage door he was overwhelmed by his wife and two children. He felt quite the returning hero; even the neighbours cheered. The moment was interrupted by one of the grooms from the manor, who appeared carrying a heavy basket and a leather bag.

'You the one everyone calls "Catface"?'

''Tis I,' William said suspiciously. 'Who's askin'?'

The groom pulled a face. 'You had better mind your manners, for you seem to have made friends well above your station. Before long you'll be dining on the top table.' He laid down the basket and the purse.

William picked up the purse and weighed it in his hand. Then he tipped it open and the silver pennies cascaded on to the ground.

'There is a message,' the groom concluded, as William fiddled with the catch on the basket. 'The lady de Lacey says that she never forgets a loyal man . . . or his name, once she has discovered it.'

William was no longer listening. Instead, he was grinning from ear to ear, for out of the basket he had lifted the most magnificent ginger tomcat that he had ever seen in his life.